"I WAS WONDERING IF WE COULD GET TOGETHER AGAIN."

I knew I at least owed him an honest answer. "Mr. Brown, I think you're a nice, friendly person and this is all very flattering, but I'm attracted to African-American men."

"Well, you see, I'm only seeking a certain kind of woman. She's got to be strong. Secure. Positive. And a woman of God. I, too, have discriminating tastes."

I walked toward the door. "Mr. Brown, this isn't going anywhere."

"LaShondra"—I almost jumped when he said my first name—"can you give a *brother* a *chance*?"

I laughed at him, sitting there in his khakis and Polo shirt looking like a regular Tom Cruise wanna-be. "You are not a brother!"

"If I'm not mistaken, I *am* your brother—in Christ. Doesn't that count for something?"

▣ ▣ ▣

"Not since the hit movie *Guess Who's Coming to Dinner* has the racial dating issue been this well addressed. Stimpson's humor and voice carry through loud and clear. Her strong opinions state what others only hint at: there's prejudice in the church pews. Read BOAZ BROWN, and examine your own viewpoints in light of God's word. I highly recommend this fun romance story with a deep, timely message."

—DancingWord.com

"A book of God's forgiveness and healing power. This dynamic book should be a must-read for Christians of whatever color."

—Come.To/Bookreviews

BOAZ BROWN

Michelle Stimpson

Walk Worthy Press
West Bloomfield, Michigan

WARNER BOOKS

NEW YORK BOSTON

Published by Warner Books with Walk Worthy Press™

Warner Books

Time Warner Book Group
1271 Avenue of the Americas, New York, NY 10020

Walk Worthy Press
33290 West Fourteen Mile Road, #482, West Bloomfield, MI 48322

Visit our Web sites at www.twbookmark.com and www.walkworthypress.net.

Printed in the United States of America
Originally published in hardcover by Warner Books
First Trade Edition: October 2005
10 9 8 7 6 5 4 3 2 1

The Library of Congress has cataloged the hardcover edition as follows:

Stimpson, Michelle.
Boaz Brown / Michelle Stimpson.
p. cm.
ISBN 0-446-53247-9
1. African American women—Fiction. 2. Dating (Social customs)—Fiction. 3. Interracial dating—Fiction. 4. Christian women—Fiction. 5. White men—Fiction. 6. Racism—Fiction. I. Title PS3619.T56B63 2004 813'.6—dc22
2003023751

ISBN: 0-446-69641-2 (pbk.)

Book design by Giorgetta Bell McRee

This book is dedicated to my immediate family—
Stevie, Steven, and Kalen—who so graciously loaned me out
to this novel. Your love and unfailing support
mean so much to me. Thank you.

Acknowledgments

Of all the pages I have written, perhaps these are the most crucial. The word "thanks" does not begin to do justice in expressing my gratitude and appreciation, but I will try. I thank my closest and dearest friend, my Lord and Savior Jesus Christ, for the freedom that comes with resting in Him. I thank God for His sovereignty and His ever-present Spirit in my life. You're always pushing me—and I always need it. I feel as though God looked out and said, "I choose you, Michelle, to write for me." Thank You for choosing me.

To my husband and children for taking on many of "Mommy's" tasks, allowing me the time I needed to complete this novel. The love and peace in our home is priceless. Thanks, Steven, for always believing and hoping the best for me. Thanks, Kalen, for literally pulling me from the computer when I got too busy. And thanks, babe, for being you.

I owe thanks to my parents, Michael and Wilma Music, for giving me everything that I ever needed, including much love and a great education. It's a blessing to be able to look back upon my childhood and pull up any number of fond memories. I think the world is ready for your book, too, Mom! To my brother Michael Music Jr. and his family for ideas, prayers, and support. And to Tony—I didn't forget about you, little brother.

To my aunts, uncles, and cousins who laid the foundation of worship and service unto the Lord in so many ministries. Thank you for being a family that thinks it "strange" *not* to serve God actively: Missionary Dorcas Ruth Smith (grandma), the late Reverend Wiley D. Williams (grandpa), Aunt Tonie and the Reverend Brent Butler (uncle), Aunt Carolyn and Uncle Tucson Johnson, Aunt LaTriece Williams, the Reverend Wiley Williams Jr. (uncle) and Aunt Stella Williams, Pastors Charles (uncle) and Tammy (aunt) Williams, Uncle Kenneth and Aunt Dollie Williams, and Uncle Fred and Aunt Denise Williams. I have too many cousins to name individually, but I must thank Stephanie Johnson for her continued support and encouragement. I can't think of a time that I ran something by you and you shot it down. Ever. That means a lot. To my paternal side, the Music family of Grand Prairie, Texas. And to the entire Smith, Williams, and Lenear families.

For the Stimpson family, who baby-sat for me when I needed time alone to think and write. Your encouragement and support in words *and* action made all the difference—especially during crunch time. Thanks Jurlene, Demetria and Darren, Verdell and Jackie, and Nadjala. Also, to Tina and Shannon for encouragement.

Now on to my prayer partners, who prayed for this novel from its conception to its completion: Jeanne Muldrew and Opal Robertson. Cross this off the prayer list! It is so wonderful to be hooked up with you two in Spirit and in truth. Thanks for fasting and praying with me and for standing for the completion of this novel when I was in no emotional shape to do so. What a blessing to have spiritual sisters who will pray me through and speak positive words into my life. It's so great to have the two of you on either side of me as we fight the enemy and claim victory in every area of our lives. Let's keep fighting—this is only the beginning!

Thanks to Karen Bradford, my big sister in Christ. Girl, sometimes I don't even want to call you, because I know you are always willing and ready to lay down the law for me—and pull out the Scriptures to back it up! I appreciate and respect your spiritual perspective. Thanks for *not* going easy on me, even when I whine.

To the first person ever to read one of my novellas—a former student of mine named Jhalilah Avery. Your enthusiasm for my writing did more for me than you know. Thanks to the students at Nichols Junior High in Arlington, Texas, at Sunset High School in Dallas, and at Joe Wilson Intermediate School and Waterford Oaks Elementary School in Cedar Hill, Texas. Thanks for being guinea pigs and reading/discussing my shorter, earlier writings. You taught the teacher.

To Vicki Ozuna, the looniest friend I have. Thanks for all your encouragement and for listening to every detail, from the beginning to the end. You guys (Crystal, Paige, Jonell, Roberta) were so great to me during the initial drafts. Thanks, Ms. Betty Murray, for reading the second draft in its entirety.

A special thanks to Denise Stinson, my publisher, for bringing me into the Walk Worthy Press family. After all the rejection letters, it was a blessing to get "the call." Thanks for seeing the message and honing it to professional quality. Thanks, Monica Harris Mindolovich, for your editorial insight. You saw some stuff that went "whoop" over my head! It is great working with you.

Thanks to my professors and classmates at the University of Texas at Arlington's English literature program for your brutal critiques of my writing. You were hard on me, and I thank you.

To my church families at Lighthouse Church of God in

Christ (my old stomping ground), Abundant Life COGIC, and my new family at Oak Cliff Bible Fellowship—thanks for your prayers.

Throughout the years, there have been so many people who have watered the writing seed that God placed in my heart. From my sixth-grade teacher (Mrs. Carlon) to my colleagues and students at Joe Wilson and at Region 10 Education Service Center—I have had, literally, hundreds of cheerleaders. For everyone who said a kind word or sent a blessing my way, I thank you for lifting me up in prayer and encouragement.

To the editors and staff at Warner Books, thank you for your patience and expertise.

Finally, to all the writers who know that they are called to write for the King. This is no time to sit on our talents. Rather, we must do the work that we have been called to do. What an awesome endowment it is to write for the King.

Michelle Stimpson
September 1, 2003

And hath made of one blood all nations of men for to dwell on all the face of the earth, and hath determined the times before appointed, and the bounds of their habitation.

Acts 17:26

BOAZ
BROWN

CHAPTER 1

When I was growing up, Sunday mornings always found me out of bed by eight. The scent and sizzle of bacon and eggs frying on the stove wafted through the house, gently waking my senses first. I would lie there with my eyes closed, absorbing everything that meant Sunday morning to me: warm sheets beneath me, a blanket that I had pulled up to my neck in the middle of the night, Jonathan's favorite cartoon characters singing along with the white ball as it bounced over the words, and Daddy humming an incomprehensible tune while shaving in the hallway bathroom (though I never could understand why somebody who rarely saw the church's interior would get up so early on a Sunday). Still, Daddy's scrambling right along with us was a part of the routine. If nothing else, he would help Jonathan get his tie on right.

"Shondra!" Momma called from the kitchen, "Get a move on!"

I poked my head out from under the covers and answered, "Yes, ma'am," in that high-pitched "I'm up" tone. Just one more minute. Then I began to think about my new white socks and my dress or the way Momma had rolled my hair the night before. I reasoned with myself, willing my feet to swing out and meet the cool rush of air on the other side of that bedspread.

I made my first stop at the mirror, unfastened one of the pink hair rollers, and watched my bangs spring out of the foam. A smile spread across my face at the sight of that spiral curl. I pulled it down until it met my nose. My hair still smelled like Royal Crown grease and the smoke that embedded itself in each shaft during the pressing process. If I'd held my head perfectly still the night before, I wouldn't have any burns behind my ears or at my temples. If I'd jumped at the sound of the hot comb frying what Momma claimed was "only grease," I might have the marks to show for it.

Momma took a break from cooking breakfast to come in and check on me. She wore a brown fleece robe with pink house shoes, but I had lived the routine enough to know that she already had on her girdle and white stockings underneath. She'd brushed her hair back, but there was no bun at the nape. Only a few bobby pins to hold the mass down. She would be wearing a hat that covered her entire head this morning. Probably the white one with sequins and feathers all over it.

"Turn 'round here. I'm gonna let your slip down a little more. I believe that hem on your white dress is pretty low." She stood behind me and adjusted the straps on my slip such that it fell another inch or two. "There you go. Let me see you."

I turned to face her, all smiles. The bags puffed up beneath her eyes as she pushed her cheeks toward a wide smile of her own. "Look at my baby. You're the prettiest little girl in the whole wide world."

"Really, Momma?" I asked.

"No doubt about it. God blessed me with a pretty, smart, wonderful little girl." She planted a soft kiss on my forehead and stood at arm's length to look at me again. "Won't be long before those little boys at church start takin' a liking to you, you know."

"I don't like boys." I wrinkled my nose and bared my teeth. I didn't like it when she teased me about boys. Especially not since I'd started getting that tickly, peculiar sensation in my stomach every time I saw people kiss on television.

She gave me a glance that said, "you-just-wait-and-see."

Then she left my room, half singing and half moaning one of her favorite congregational hymns: "Servin' the Lord Will Pay Off After While." I wished that she would come back and do something—anything—in my room. I wanted to smell her powder, hear her sing, and feel the warmth in her notes surround me like a tattered family quilt passed down through generations. Worn to threads in some spots, but worth its original weight in gold.

▣ ▣ ▣

"Now may the grace and mercy of our Lord and Savior Jesus Christ rest, rule, and abide in us all until we meet again. Let the church sing, Aaaa-men." Pastor Simmons dismissed the congregation of True Way Church of God in Christ, and a bustle of conversation began. Sisters and Mothers, clad in a colorful array of tailored suits with fancy hats and sparkling jewelry, hugged each other and planted soft, saintly kisses on each other's cheeks. Mother Frances hugged me and told me what a wonderful job I was doing with the children, as she always did when I saw her. "You keep up the good work, baby. God's got a blessing for you."

I kissed her soft, wrinkled cheek and replied, "Thank you, Mother Frances."

"How's your mother?" she asked. Mother Frances was part of the underground reporting agency my mother used to keep tabs on me at True Way—I was sure of it.

"Oh, she's doing fine."

"Tell her I said hi."

"Yes, ma'am."

The men, what few there were, exchanged handshakes and visual inspections on their way to the vestibule. Younger children, who rarely got the chance to beat on the drums, ran to the drummer's empty seat to beat out a few loud clashes before the organist shooed them away. The cheerful hum of church folk idly socializing filled the sanctuary but quickly succumbed to Deacon Bradbury's it's-time-to-go signal of dimming the lights.

I grabbed my tote bag filled with pencils, pens, and paper, and rushed over to talk with Sister Charles. I found her just past the swinging doors of the sanctuary at the water fountain. She was bent over, Bible in left hand and the bag from our denomination's annual women's convention slung over her right shoulder.

"Hello, Sister Charles." I tapped her as she swallowed her last gulp.

"Hi, Sister Smith." She wiped the stray drops from her lips and then pulled me into a hearty hug. "How did Alvin do in tutoring tonight?"

"That's what I came over to tell you—he worked so hard! I have never seen anyone put so much effort into learning fractions in all of my life," I laughed. Alvin, who was standing at her side, put his head down and smiled. Sister Charles's face lit up, her oily, smooth complexion catching every bit of light that bounced off it. I got the feeling that this was the first piece of good news Sister Charles had heard about her Alvin in a long time.

"Did he really?"

I placed my left hand on Alvin's shoulder, animating my words with my right hand. "Alvin, you can do anything you put your mind to. But you cannot give up when things get hard."

"I'm so glad you all started this Wednesday night tutoring before service here at the church. I can't afford any of those fancy tutoring centers right now." Sister Charles shook her head and smacked her lips. "Besides, you all are doing a better job here than anybody who's ever worked with Alvin. I didn't see Brother Jenkins tonight. Isn't he the one who usually tutors Alvin?"

"Yes, but Brother and Sister Jenkins just had a new baby,

so Brother Jenkins has taken some overtime at his job. Looks like it's going to be just me for now," I admitted. I curled my lips in and let out a heavy sigh. At the rate the tutoring program at our church was growing, I knew that I would soon be overwhelmed with struggling students.

"Well, I'll see you next time, Alvin. Keep me in your prayers."

"And you do the same." Sister Charles smiled back. "Have a blessed evening."

I walked out of the church and into the blanket of night interrupted only by the two street lamps recently added to our church's parking lot. Those things cost an arm and a leg, I'd heard, but came with the price of progress. True Way was growing each week as people sought out what older saints called "the *old* way."

I knew that sanctified path well. I understood the dos and don'ts: do raise your index finger if you need to walk in church; don't sit with your legs crossed knee over knee—cross at the ankle. The traditions and idiosyncrasies of the Church of God in Christ, whether founded or flippant, had been instilled in me from childhood. As I walked to my car with my black skirt brushing my ankles, I was ever thankful to have been raised in *somebody's* church; with faith, and love and a quick pinch from an usher for passing notes during the sermon.

I noticed Brother Paul Pruitt's red BMW parked next to my Honda in the lot. I hurried to unarm my car, hoping to get inside, buckle up, and drive off so that he and I wouldn't have to cross paths. I didn't have anything against Brother Pruitt. He was the "okay" kind. He had a lot going for him—he was active in the church, mentored young boys, had a good job, had a good attitude, held the door open for women, and so on. But he just didn't make my heart go do any flips. Not at all. And although True

Way COGIC was filled with single black women, nobody was knocking on his door so far as I knew.

Mother Moore, however, believed that Brother Pruitt was "sweet" on me. She'd pulled me aside a few Sundays ago after church and whispered into my ear with her rickety voice, "I think he's got his eye on you." That was all I needed to know. I figured I'd just steer clear of him until whatever it was that Mother Moore saw brewing in him faded away. I didn't want any ill feelings between us. And I didn't want him wasting any time pursuing me, missing out on his Miss Right.

His headlights blinked on and off. *Now I've got to speak.* I casually looked back over my shoulder and said good night to Paul as we both opened our car doors. We spoke our last words over the roof of his car.

"How did the tutoring go tonight?" he asked.

"It went very well." I put my foot inside my car.

"That's great! Keep up the good work!" Then he nodded, got into his car, closed the door, and started his engine.

Mental note: Mother Moore is not the authority on sweets.

Coming home that night, I kicked off my low-heeled shoes at the doorstep and dropped my bags on the leopard-print chaise—the finishing touch that made my living room look like something straight out of Africa. Miniature giraffes, elephants, and cheetahs lined the mantel, adding to the overall safari motif in my formal living room. Candles filled the room with strawberries, despite the label's warnings that I shouldn't burn them in my absence.

In the kitchen, I emptied the dishwasher and loaded in my breakfast dishes: a bowl, a cup, and a spoon. It would be a while before the dishwasher filled up again.

There was a peaceful silence about my home—except for the swish of my pantyhose as I walked through, picking up things that were haphazardly misplaced during my morning rush out of the house. Everything was just as it was when I left: toiletries strewn across my bathroom counter, the ironing board standing in the hallway, and the windbreaker that I'd quickly traded for a leather coat upon opening my front door at six a.m. and meeting Jack Frost face to face. It was still early November, but it's hard to tell the season by a calendar in Texas.

I rotated the gold-toned faucets clockwise and felt my tensions ease at the sound of rushing water. I'd looked forward to this bath all day long. The midweek tutoring followed by regular service was wearing me out, especially on the nights when I had to work late because of some sporting event at the local middle school, where I served as vice principal. But it was well worth the sacrifice. The church kids' grades were up, their parents were optimistic, church attendance was higher, and more children heard the gospel. Well, some of them didn't have any other choice because they'd hitched a ride with someone who stayed through service, but that was all right. They were there, and I'd done my part to bring them to the Word.

I inched into the tub, controlling my reaction to the splendid heat that soothed me while stinging me simultaneously. Resting my head on the bathtub pillow, I closed my eyes and began thinking. My birthday was just around the corner. My soul could only look back in wonder at the years that had gone by. So many blessings and so much favor that I couldn't even begin to explain. My mind began drifting down the path that only opens up in complete inner and outer silence. I was in my right mind. My soul was free. But I was alone.

Thirty had come and almost gone without so much as a little poof. Thirty-one wasn't far away, which would make me officially *in* my thirties. Being *in* my thirties, I'd reasoned, was different from being thirty. Thirty said that I was still a little wet behind the ears, just getting over the twenties. But *in* my thirties was different. Somebody *in* the thirties could be anybody from a newlywed to a grandmother. On the upside of youth or the underside of senior citizenry. Either way, it was time to reevaluate some things; carefully consider how to expend my time and energy. I was too young to be worried about getting married, yet too old to take for granted that my body would cooperate fully with pregnancy. But me pregnant at my biological peak would have been a nightmare. At my biological childbearing peak, I'd been running myself ragged, doing everything from "people pleasing" to conducting my very own search-and-rescue missions, looking for love in the most desperate dead-end relationships, abusing my body and my faith in the process.

Now, *in* my thirties and with roots that had grown deeper in the knowledge and wisdom of God, there was a part of me that had begun longing for companionship again. I'd been blessed with many accomplishments educationally and professionally, but I was quickly falling out of ladder-climbing mode. Rather, I wanted to enjoy the rung I was on—to live the thirties without chasing the forties. I wanted to rest in the fact that God was the head of my life, my constant source.

Stepping out of the tub and onto the cream-colored bathroom rug, I caught my reflection in the mirror and took a long look at my body. *Is this what* in *the thirties looks like? Not bad.* My light brown skin was still evenly toned and taut in most places. Breasts and behind still holding up strong. Stomach a little pudgy—nothing serious. Time had done a number on my hips, but the curves were a welcome change, adding femininity to the body once referred to as a "beanpole."

Next I examined my face. I was truly blessed with clear, healthy skin. I didn't wear makeup in high school or college, but after taking a professional job I decided to start wearing foundation, mascara, and lipstick. Every once in a while I did something with my eyes, but it never amounted to much behind the lenses of my glasses.

I got closer to the mirror, running my hands along my cheeks. That thirty-something face belonged to a single, African-American Christian woman. My eyebrows were perfectly arched, and all other facial hair had been removed. My thick lips took on a life of their own with their natural outline and plump staging. I studied the outline of my face: high cheekbones, dimples, clearly defined chin, and slightly widened nose. It all played together pretty well, if I may say so myself.

After getting into my nightclothes, I walked down the center hall of my home to the guest bedroom, better known as my prayer closet. Though the small room was furnished only with a desk, a mauve halogen lamp, a painting of a richly brown woman braiding a young girl's hair, and a daybed, it was completely filled with the soft reign of peace. Peace that settled on my mind like several feet of snow, insulating me from the noise of life. I reserved this space, kept it free of clutter, for simple reasons. There, as I knelt down by the side of the daybed and folded my hands in prayer, I could feel His presence, as though He had been anticipating this time alone as much as I had. We had both been awaiting the time to sit down and talk, commune about the day. A time to receive instruction, chastening, share a word or a laugh.

Father, I honor You for who You are. For being the sovereign Lord of my life. I ask your forgiveness for being impatient today with a few students and colleagues. I thank You for covering me when I'm wrong and extending Your grace and mercy in every area of my life. And I thank You for leaving Your Spirit as a constant friend. Now, Father, I pray that You would help me to rest in where I am right now. Humph, I'm in my thirties, Father, help me to trust in You all the more. My time on earth seems even more precious now. I thank and praise You for being at the center of my life. Now, as I prepare to study Your Word, show me what You want me to know. Speak to my heart and help me to be not only a hearer but also a doer of Your Word. In Jesus' name, amen.

Through divine planning, in the midst of my simmering anticipation, I could only laugh at where God placed me in my week's devotional study on that night, right at Matthew 6:34: *Therefore do not worry about tomorrow, for tomorrow will worry about itself. Each day has enough trouble of its own.*

Thank You, Father. You always know.

I finished up my devotional time with a journal entry, making note of this special verse that seemed to have been written just for me tonight. As I placed my journal into the old cedar desk and twisted the gold, ribbed knob to extinguish the lamp, my thoughts reconciled themselves, lined up with the Word, lulled me into a drowsiness that I knew would bring about a good night's rest.

CHAPTER 2

I smoothed out my skirt, which I'd managed to get all wrinkled up in a game of hide-and-seek with the Sunshine Band kids, who'd just been released from their choir practice in the sanctuary. I'd jumped in, claiming to help my little brother, Jonathan, find a good hiding place. But I really had enjoyed the game even more than Jonathan and the rest of the kids. Being twelve had its complexities: periods, perms, training bras. One minute I was laughing out loud at cartoons; the next, sadly, I was stuffing my bra. Every once in a while, however, I managed to squeeze in one of the last ounces of childhood. Now, as Sister Lacefield motioned for the Purity Class members to come into the building and the older youth began arriving, the smell of firewood burning made me want to go back home and cuddle up in my bed. But I was Puritan now. Our practice lasted late on Saturdays. I rearranged my headband, dusted the leaves off my sweater, put my preteen aura back on. Jonathan joined my mother in the car, and I was off to the fellowship hall for my turn to meet and practice for the Youth-in-Action Sunday morning program.

Dry leaves crunched beneath my feet as I walked toward the back porch of the church. The two steps leading to the back door were crooked and cracked, and a stream of ants was busy using the inadvertent shortcut to prepare for the winter. Inside the building, the smell of new carpet reminded me to go back out again and check my feet for mud. Mother Bohanan had said that we were to be grateful and respect the house of the Lord, especially now that the church had new carpet. And she'd already told us that she would pop anybody she saw chewing gum.

I reentered the building and walked past the water fountain and the makeshift window we used to order plates on Sunday afternoons. The poster board displaying the prices of chicken dinners, pies, and other fund-raising eats was cleverly displayed near the entrance of the room with clear stipulations: NO CREDIT. NO CHECKS.

Sister Lacefield called the Purity Class to order in the back room of the church, which functioned as both the cafeteria and large group meeting room. The walls were partially lined with imitation wood, and the faded wallpaper was peeling near the ceiling. But there was a realness about the room, an intangible authenticity that sanctified this space of fellowship. We gathered in the usual circle—older kids on one side, us on the other, everyone holding hands—and waited for Sister Lacefield to appoint someone to offer the prayer.

"Let's have Kelvin open us up in prayer," she said.

Jovanna, also new to the Purity Class, squeezed my hand and looked up at me, smiling. It took everything in me to keep from smiling at Kelvin Nash. All the younger girls in the Purity Class thought he was to die for. He had a long, silky Jheri curl cut into a perfect shag, skin as smooth as butter, and a voice that carried the entire tenor section. One glance from him made me feel as though someone had cinched a belt all the way around my torso and pulled it to the very first hole. Problem was, Kelvin was nearing eighteen, and my little crew had just turned twelve. In the words of the elders, "He wudn't studyin' me."

Purity Class was the one place we could be real with a man or woman of God besides our parents. We talked about the issues that faced us as young adults, teens, and preteens, and how we should use our lives to be of service to God. It was there and in Young People Willing Workers (YPWW) that we focused on the everyday life that God intends for us: from the way we act at school to how we talk to our parents, to the rewards God has in store for those who love Him. One of those rewards was a fulfilling relationship with the mate God intended for us. Jovanna and I laughed through much of it, but the seed was planted. It would take years of watering and tending to blossom.

◻ ◻ ◻

Saturday night I invited my best friend, Peaches, over for a girls' night of fun and relaxation. Peaches brought along Deniessa, one of her acquaintances from work, who was down and out over a man. I only knew Deniessa casually, but I figured, the more the merrier.

They arrived at around seven o'clock, with Peaches' unmistakable, startling pounding on the front door. *I wish she wouldn't do that!*

I walked to the front door, preparing my face to go along with the lecture that I was about to give Peaches—and knowing that she wouldn't give it a second thought. "You scared me half to death, beating on the door like that."

"That way you know it's *me* and not some crazy *maniac.*" She exaggerated her words with bulging eyes.

"That's debatable," I teased her. She hugged me, and I was instantly engulfed in her expensive perfume. Peaches wore a staple white blouse with fitted black slacks and a cute little narrow pair of slip-on heels that I know would have had my toes stacked one on top of the other.

"Hi, Deniessa." She hugged me, too, and I welcomed both of them into my home. "Make yourself at home, girls. It's just us tonight."

"Thank you," Deniessa said, taking a big breath. "I need a good talk with some girlfriends tonight."

"By the way, I love your hair!" I remarked, tugging at

the lengthy braids that bounced freely from the twist on top of Deniessa's head. "When did you get it done?"

"About a month ago."

"Girl, this looks so good. How long did it take?" I asked.

"Ten long hours." She shook her head and added, "But it was worth it. My curling irons have been under the sink for four weeks, and I get an extra half hour of sleep every morning. These microbraids are priceless. I'm spoiled."

As we talked, Deniessa picked up on Peaches' cues and imitated her make-yourself-at-home gestures. She took off her tennis shoes, and they both removed outer layers of winter clothes. Deniessa raised her bulky pink and green AKA sweater over her head, folded it, and tossed it onto her purse.

"Yeah, you sure *do* need to take that off," I teased her.

"Don't hate us because we're beautiful." She swung her pinky finger around and flashed a placid smile.

"Whatever!" Peaches held out her hand.

I helped Peaches put the food into the refrigerator, and we watched a little B.E.T. while we waited for the spaghetti to boil. I curled my feet up beneath me on the sofa and contributed my two cents of chitchat before Peaches got down to the real nitty-gritty with Deniessa. We turned the channel to a smooth jazz music station and listened while we talked.

"Okay, Shondra, Deniessa would like a third opinion about her relationship with her boyfriend, Jamal."

"Ex-boyfriend," Deniessa corrected her.

"So-called ex-boyfriend." Peaches smacked her lips and looked at me out of the corner of her eyes. "Anyways, she wants to know if she should try to patch things up with him."

"What happened?" I faced Deniessa to get a firsthand account.

Deniessa swung her braids over her shoulder and waved her bright red acrylic nails. "Well, Jamal and I have been together for four years now."

"What kind of together?" I asked.

"We've lived together for about three years—dated for almost a year before that. Anyways, I let him move in with me with the understanding that it was a temporary arrangement. We agreed that as soon as he got on his feet, we would either go back to our own places or get married. Weeks turned into months and now years—I just can't take it anymore. I knew it wasn't right when I agreed to let him move in. But it took me three years before I gave him this ultimatum. Now he's saying that he'll be out by the end of the month." She gave me a blank stare, lips open.

"Okay, back up, back up. Does he work?" I asked. "By 'work,' I mean, is he steadily employed?"

"Not really."

"Aw, girl, he did you a favor." I slapped hands with Peaches.

"Good riddance!" Peaches said.

"But he's leaving with four years of my life," Deniessa said, holding her head out on the end of her neck like a flag on a flagpole.

"Okay, but you *gave* him those four years," I said. "It's not like he stole them from you. But you'll be okay, girl. You live and learn. A lot of us have been down that road before, and we've learned what to look for in a good man.

"Listen, what I learned through my experiences was that I want somebody who knows the Lord and loves Him so much that everything he does reflects his relationship with Christ." I laced my fingers behind my head, eased back on the sofa, and closed my eyes. "My Mr. Right will *add* to my life, not subtract. He's secure. He's considerate. He knows how to treat a lady, but he's not a ladies' man. He handles business and he does right because it's just *in* him, you know? He's not perfect, but his heart is in the right place and his intentions are good." I opened my eyes and returned to reality. "It would also be nice if he was tall, double-dipped-chocolate dark, and slap-the-judge handsome."

"Ooh-wee!" Peaches fanned herself. "Girl, y'all would have to pick me up off the ground if I met a brother with all that on his résumé. Tall, dark, and handsome, too?"

"Right about now I'd take the short, white, and ugly if I could recoup the last four years of my life," Deniessa said as she folded her arms across her chest and laughed.

"I could do the short and ugly, but I don't know about the white," Peaches said with a scowl on her face. "White men just don't turn me on. They've always got those big, pale, hairy feet in some sandals. They need to cover that mess up."

"Get real." Deniessa shoved her. "White men can be just as good or as bad as the brothers."

"I wouldn't know and I am not trying to find out." Peaches shrugged.

"I just couldn't see myself with a white man." I bunched up my lips. "That would be . . . I don't know . . . like going against myself."

"I dated a white man once, thinking things would be different," Deniessa admitted. "I actually thought that because he was white, he had money lying around somewhere that he could borrow against to repay the series of small loans I made to him. Shows you how ignorant I was—that joker turned out to be the biggest overgrown mooch that ever lived."

"Deniessa, I don't know you very well, but I'm gonna tell you something that it took me several heartaches to learn: you teach men how to treat you. You taught Jamal that you were available to him in every way, with or without a commitment, and you probably taught that white guy the same thing."

"But is it my *job* to teach a full grown man?" Deniessa sighed. "Why can't they just come ready?"

"See, that's what I'm talkin' about." Peaches nodded her head. "I want me one that's already housebroken, okay?"

"That's why I'm waiting on my Boaz." I nodded and smiled. "He's the epitome of my Mr. Right. I figure, if God can make a Boaz for Ruth, He can make another one for me."

"Who's Boaz?" Deniessa asked.

"Boaz was a man in the Bible—the Book of Ruth, to be exact," I explained. "The original knight in shining armor. Boaz was an honorable, compassionate, rich man."

Deniessa stopped me. "Okay, see, we already got a problem right there. How many rich men—or semiestablished men—still have honor? Nine times out of ten, he's had to stomp on a few heads to get to the top."

"That's how it goes with your *average* man. But not with a Boaz. See, Boaz was wealthy, but he treated his servants well. He even took consideration of the people who came around to glean the fields after his servants had gathered the harvest. That's how Ruth, a widow, crossed his path. Boaz liked what he'd heard of Ruth's commitment to her mother-in-law following the death of the men in their family."

Deniessa jumped in. "Oh, I'm starting to remember this story. Didn't he tell his servants to leave extra for Ruth to gather and not to embarrass her?"

"Not only that," Peaches added, "but he told the men not to mess with her and to let her drink from their water jars when she got thirsty. Ha! See, that's what I'm talking about. Look out for your *woman*!"

"I know, girl." I placed a hand over my heart. "That brother has got to have my back, okay?"

"So what happened next?" Deniessa squinted her eyes, as though she might already know the wonderful ending.

"Well, to make a long story short," I continued, "even though nothing happened between Ruth and Boaz, they had a little chemistry going. I mean, it would be hard not to like somebody who's always doing nice things for you. So Ruth let it be known to Boaz that she was his servant for life and that she wanted him to make her his woman since, legally, he did have a right to her. Now, you have to understand: this conversation took place in the middle of the night while the two of them were all alone." I raised my eyebrows.

"Talk about your temptation." Peaches smiled.

"But Boaz made a decision to honor her by going through the proper channels before taking her as his wife. Back then, when a woman's husband died before they had a son, the man who was next of kin was supposed to marry that widow, and their firstborn son would carry on in the dead man's name. Boaz was kin to Ruth, but there was another man who was more closely related to Ruth's husband, so Boaz had to clear up that matter first. Boaz didn't waste any time—he got up and found that man the very next morning and asked him if he was going to purchase the land and perform the duties of the next of kin for Ruth. Only after the closest kinsman declined to purchase the land, with Ruth, did Boaz make his move and take Ruth as his wife."

"That's what makes the difference," Peaches commented as she turned to face Deniessa. "A real man, like Boaz, treats people right—from the servants to the family. That man could have and probably wanted to get down and dirty with Ruth that night. But Boaz knew that he had a conscience to deal with and a God to answer to. You can't beat integrity, girl."

"That's what I mean when I say I'm waiting on my

Boaz. I want someone who's gonna treat me right and act right. Now, is that too much to ask?"

"I hear you," Deniessa added. "I need me a Boaz, too."

I pulled my knees into my chest and wrapped my arms around my legs. "A modern-day Boaz has been through enough tests to know that God is his source, and he knows a woman of God when he sees her—I, of course, am that woman." I released my knees and pointed at myself. Peaches and Deniessa laughed at my fake princess wave. "I'm gonna be like, 'Hey, baby, you found me!'"

"Okay, that's what you want him to be like on the inside. But you'll never get to the inside if you don't like what you see on the outside." Deniessa snapped her fingers. "Let's be for real here: unless he comes up to you with a Bible in hand and his suit coat draped over a puddle of water, you won't know the first thing about what's going on inside without first working through what you see. Keep it real, now."

I took a deep breath and gave in to her. "Okay, okay, okay. If we can become friends first, and I get to know him without the pressure of an exclusive dating relationship, then the face-and-body thing will be secondary."

"So what you're saying is, a relationship with an ugly brother would have to kind of sneak up on you?" Peaches summarized.

"You did not have to say it like that." I rolled my eyes at her.

"It's the truth!" She teased me.

"It's the truth with you, too," I laughed with Peaches.

"Hey, I'm not the one up here saying he's got to be Jesus' little brother for me to get with him. As far as I can tell, your main physical request is that he's a black man."

"Well, that part goes without saying," I said, sighing. "I just want the right man, you know? The man God has for me."

"Well, the pool is getting pretty shallow. Half our brothers ain't tryin' to get with sisters," Peaches pointed out.

"Whatever." I shook my head. "That's their problem. I'm holdin' out. They say there's somebody for everybody. I believe that."

"It's just so hard, you know?" Peaches commented in all seriousness. "Trying to live right and date seriously in this world today. On one hand, you want to do God's will. On the other hand, you just want to get this whole dating thing over with already. I don't know about you two, but I get tired of wondering what's gonna happen. If somebody would say to me right now, 'Peaches, you're gonna be single all your life,' I would have no problem whatsoever with that. I would put a whole lot more into my retirement; I'd go ahead and buy a house for me and my son; I would find a good travel agent and get set to live my life as a single woman. No problem. But I feel like I'm in limbo now."

"Yeah, that limbo ain't no joke. I really thought that letting Jamal move in would speed me on down that aisle. It went against everything I was taught. My grandmother always said that 'shackin' up' was synonymous with living in sin. I've lived these last three years in constant denial spiritually. It would be different if I had seen my aunts and cousins living with men, but that was not the example set before me. I *knew* better. But it just seems like none of my grandmother's warnings could compete with the comforts of a man."

"Oh, girl, I feel you." I gave her a high five. "Once your flesh gets hooked on that feeling, it's hard to stop."

"Mmm," Peaches let out a judgmental moan and stuck her lips out.

"Ooh, Peaches, don't even go there," I confronted her. "Let the record show that I tried to tell you that you were out there with Raphael, okay? Wide open! Whipped!"

"No, I'm not the one who was whipped; it was this one here!" Peaches pointed at me. "This girl called in *sick* on several occasions so that she could lay up with—what was his name?"

James Perkins. "I'm not saying his name." I put my head in my hands, laughing and dreading the memory simultaneously. I met James when I was twenty-two—just out of college and barely into my own apartment. Ours was a relationship that started out appropriately enough as fellow Jarvis Christian College graduates who'd learned that we would be working in the same school district. We'd exchanged phone numbers and, during the first semester of teaching, spoke often about the challenges of being a first-year teacher. What started out as shared employment quickly became shared bedrooms as I allowed the relationship to progress further than I intended, with the excuse that we were "there for each other." The intense pleasure of sharing sex with someone I knew made it seem "okay." Like it couldn't be that wrong, especially if I cared about him.

If there was any one "gateway" relationship that started my spiritual hiatus and consequent heartaches, it was the one I had with James Perkins. I wasn't a virgin when I started sleeping with James, but he was the first to send off all the bells and whistles in my body. The short-lived relationship that I had with James Perkins opened a can of worms that almost cost me my life. *But God . . .*

"It was James Perkins!" Peaches exclaimed after a few moments of thought. "Yeah, that's right. Old Perky." Peaches erupted in laughter, and I had to join her. God had brought us a long way.

"No, you're the one who all but kicked me and your family to the curb because we tried to tell you that Raphael was nothing but trouble. But no! You wouldn't hear of it!"

Peaches yelled, "Don't talk about my baby's daddy!"

"No," I stopped her, "don't bring Eric into it. This is about hardheaded Patricia Miller. We told you Raphael was runnin' game, but you were 'in love' and he was 'fine' and he was the first one to tell you that you were 'fine' after you lost all that weight."

"I knew I was fine *before* I lost the weight."

I continued, "Matter of fact, we almost got ourselves killed goin' up in that club with you to confront that woman he was seeing—like we had guns or something in our purses. Know good and well if that woman had said 'boo' we would have both jumped back!"

"Okay, okay, okay," Peaches gave in. "You're right. I was hardheaded. But not anymore. Through that experience, I learned to seek out and take heed of wise counsel."

Peaches caught her breath and got back to Deniessa. "So now you're the one with the issue. What did Jamal say when you told him to hit the road?" Peaches jerked her thumb to one side.

"I didn't exactly tell him to hit the road, Peaches." Deniessa wagged her head. "I told him that I loved him and that I cared about him, but we just couldn't live together indefinitely. He said, 'So is this about the *M* word again?' And I told him that it was. Then we went around and around about how old-fashioned the whole thing was. The whole time I was thinking to myself, If I'd been a bit more old-fashioned to begin with, we probably wouldn't be in this mess now. I didn't even respond to his comments, because I was *so* close to kicking myself for letting him get so much free milk for so long. Besides, I didn't want to say a whole bunch of things that I might regret later." Deniessa gave a hopeless grin. "And that's what happened."

I sensed her despair, knowing that what she did was right yet unpopular. Knowing that she'd ultimately done the best thing but immediately inconvenienced herself.

I didn't know exactly where Deniessa stood on all the

hot dating issues, but I'd cut off sex altogether when I put my foot down on the kind of mess that I would no longer accept in my life. The vow to become celibate seemed overwhelming at first. After years of sexual activity, celibacy felt as if I were giving up womanhood itself.

"I think I can relate to at least part of what you're going through," I shared with her. "Peaches, you remember when we first started talking about celibacy? That was what—two or three years ago?" Peaches nodded. I faced Deniessa. "Girl, I thought I was going to fall out on the floor at the thought of celibacy. I had that booty-call phonebook right in my nightstand. I mean, I had some top performers on standby, okay?"

"Well, I wasn't getting any to begin with, so it wasn't a problem for me." Peaches pursed her lips. We laughed at Peaches as she continued with her testimony. "After I had Eric, I closed up the shop. Twenty hours of labor will do that for ya, you know?"

"Ooh, please, not the twenty hours again," I begged her.

"I cannot wait until you give birth." She eyed me. "I am going to record every single hour of it."

The finale for the evening was dinner, which we made together in the kitchen. We prepared spaghetti, corn, garlic bread, and Peaches' marvelous Caesar salad. I tried to see what she had going into that salad, but she brought the ingredients in a brown paper bag and refused to let us in on her secret recipe.

"Get back." She threatened with the tongs.

"I've got my eye on you," Deniessa told her.

"You're about to have these *tongs* on you." Peaches waved them around and turned her back to us again, hunching her shoulders over her corner of counter space.

I don't know why we tried to eat while we were talking. It was a miracle that none of us choked on anything, as much as we laughed about life and work as black women in America. Deniessa told us how she almost got into it with a woman at Walmart.

"So I was in the express line and the sister in front of me has, I know, a good forty items in her basket. This white lady behind me said something about counting items and reading signs, but the sister in front of me thought *I'd* said it," Deniessa clarified. "Next thing I knew, she was like, 'You got something to say, you need to say it in my face.' I just kind of smiled and told her that I didn't have anything to say. The white woman behind me who *really* said it was as quiet as a mouse. I don't think she meant for her comment to be heard. If I had told that sister in front of me that it was the white woman behind me who'd said it, it would have been all over in that store."

"I bet she'll think about that the next time she's standin' behind a black woman in the express line," I smirked, climbing onto my racial soapbox. "White folks could stay out of a whole lot of trouble if they would just keep their opinions to themselves. They always got somethin' to say, but when somebody checks them on it, they get scared."

"That's true," Deniessa agreed, "but sister-girl was wrong for having forty items in the checkout lane. You know, *we* can be pretty bad about following directions sometimes."

"Girl"—Peaches raised her hand to tell us a tale of woe about her world in human resources—"I was training one of the HR representatives last week, and we sat down with a brother who didn't realize that he was making almost fifty cents an hour less than his manager told him he would be making. He had worked *six months* without ever sitting down with his paycheck and a calculator to make sure that he was actually making seven twenty-five per hour. I couldn't believe it. Girl, that's the first thing I do when I get my printout. I make sure it's *all* there!"

"Maybe he just didn't know how to figure it out," I said. "You would be surprised what people know and don't know."

"But black folks know our money if we don't know nothin' else," Peaches countered me. "He was just being lazy."

"I'm with Peaches on this one, 'cause any other black person wouldn't have even made it out the door without seeing that," Deniessa said. "I know I wouldn't have."

"I just know that some of the things we take as common knowledge isn't common to everybody else," I said. "I sit down with parents every day who don't know how to average their child's grades. It all boils down to education in America. The system has done a poor job of teaching people what they really need to know. Especially when it comes to educating *our* kids."

"Yeah, but some stuff can't be taught," Deniessa said. "Nobody should have to *tell* you to check your check. If you don't know how to do it, ask somebody. It's that simple. Well, let me take that back. We *are* talking about a black man, aren't we? You know a brother ain't tryin' to ask for help."

"Oh, no, you didn't go there on the brothers," Peaches scolded her. "I won't hear of it!"

"Anyway! You didn't start with all this until you had Eric. You know you were the main one dogging brothers out until you had a son. Now, all of a sudden, it's 'Don't talk about the brothers.' Girl, please, I just call it like I see it."

"I have to recognize"—Peaches took a bite of her breadstick and used the remainder to conduct her words—"Eric is a husband in training. Somebody's gonna have to put up with him once he leaves my care. I refuse to make him another sister's burden."

"What if he doesn't marry a sister?" Deniessa joked.

Peaches closed her eyes and swallowed the bread in a hurry. I smiled, waiting for what would surely be some outrageous statement. "I wish Eric *would* bring home a white woman! It wouldn't be nothin' but a whole bunch of ugly. No, ma'am, I'm raising Eric to be a black husband to a black wife and be a black father to some little black kids. I want naps on my grandkids' heads. I'm talking beady-beads, okay?"

"Okay, I don't know about the beads. But I do second that *black* thing," I agreed.

"Speaking of black things, I'll let you two know the next time the undergrad chapter I sponsor steps at Paul Quinn's Greek show. It'll be fun," Deniessa said by way of invitation.

"Just let me know," I said.

CHAPTER 3

Our first place, an apartment, was on the wrong side of the tracks. Well, come to think of it, we were always on the wrong side. But we used to be on the wrong side of the wrong side a long time ago. It was a two-bedroom, one-bathroom deluxe cheap apartment complete with shag carpeting and lime green psychedelic lava lamps in every bedroom. I shared a room with Jonathan, who always got up at the crack of dawn, fooling around with toys or watching cartoons. Other than that, I enjoyed living at the apartment. It was close to my school, and sometimes Momma would take us to the school playground to play on swings that actually had the seats in them. The playground at our apartment complex was always being vandalized by teenagers, most of whom weren't even residents.

I was happy to see a moving van parked near our building, but Daddy said it was high time we moved when our last set of upstairs neighbors moved in. "I refuse to live right next door to a clan of Mexicans!" he declared.

At the time, I didn't know what a Mexican was. From the way Daddy talked, I thought Mexicans were bears or something.

"We gon' have roaches before you know it." Momma shook her head. "You mark my words! Jon Smith, we better hightail it out of here!"

It was one of the few times they openly agreed on something.

Watching them pace around the room as the Mexicans moved their furniture upstairs was rather exciting from my perspective. When I got the chance to peek between the slats of our blinds, I saw a little girl. Finally, a girl! I went outside to play with her that evening, and we played dolls until the lamps came on. Never mind the fact that she didn't speak a word of English and I didn't speak a word of Spanish. That wasn't important. Smiles, hand gestures, and laughter were all the communication we needed to have a good time.

Momma told me to make sure I took a good bath that night. "Those Mexicans are nasty," she told me. "It's all right to play with that little Spanish girl outside, but don't think you're gonna spend the night over there with her and her kind. Don't even ask."

"What's Spanish?"

"It's the way they talk. It's a different language," she told me as she double-checked my scrubbing efforts.

"How come she speaks a different language?"

"'Cause she ain't learned English yet."

"Is she ever gonna learn it?"

"I don't know. Probably." Then Momma said under her breath, "She should have learned it before she got here. They ought to make 'em all learn it before they cross the border. That'll cut out a lot of this mess."

I envisioned a group of teachers meeting the Spanish girl and her family at a bus station and then teaching them English in a matter of minutes. "Can I teacher her English, Momma?"

"You ain't got time to teach her English." She stood me up and wrapped a towel around me before lifting me out of the tub. "You need to worry about your own education first."

⊡ ⊡ ⊡

The answering machine blinked the number *2* when I got home. The first message was from my brother, wishing me a happy birthday. The second was from my mother, checking to make sure that I was coming over for dinner.

I picked up the receiver and called to assure her that I would be there in a few minutes.

"You gonna bring the rolls?"

"Yes, ma'am," I replied.

"Well, come on, then. Me and your daddy'll be waitin'."

I hung up my church clothes and put on an all-season denim dress with a split up the back. Too risqué for my church, but fine for Sunday dinner with the parents. I slid into a pair of low-heeled mules and pulled my hair back behind a headband.

I took the old familiar back roads to "the hood." It was beautiful scenery—always had been, until you got across the tracks. I glanced down at my panel, making sure that my doors were locked. As much as I loved the hood and my people, I couldn't deny the uneasy feeling I had in this twenty-first-century Brockmoore neighborhood. It wasn't the same since most of the original homeowners moved out. The new owners, younger and poorer, didn't give two cents about their property or the neighborhood. Their yards were unkempt, their nonfunctioning cars sat propped up on bricks in front lawns, and dangerous-looking dogs were chained to stakes in the ground.

And yet, it was my hood, my stomping ground. I had roots there, even if the ground was less than desirable. *If I can't fit in here, where do I fit in?* It had all been so simple when I was a teenager. Everybody knew everybody. I wasn't allowed to socialize with all the kids in the neighborhood, but I did know their names and they knew mine. I could ride my bike and pump Jonathan on my handlebars without worrying about some strange white man kidnapping us.

Now almost everyone looked strange. Addicts as skinny as the hungry African children on television walked the streets, giving me gestures and then blank stares. They wanted to know if I sold drugs. Their beckoning made me feel blessed and ashamed at the same time. Blessed because it could have been me. Ashamed because I thought, could I have done something to change this? It also made me wonder how much of the problem was due to addicts' bad choices and how much was environmental, system-oriented.

My parents' house looked as if it had landed on the wrong street, with its new coat of paint and well-tended lawn. The chain-link fence around the front yard kept the neighborhood kids from making a shortcut across their corner lot. Momma and Daddy had put their everything into that house and refused to move, even after someone tried to break in a few years earlier. They were getting old, and I feared for them sometimes, but 700 Dembo was their little piece of America.

When I got to my parents' house, I could smell Daddy's mouthwatering fried chicken from the porch. Lord knows, if that man couldn't do anything else, he could *burn*. Everything he made tasted like heaven.

The screen door gave me a quick swat on my behind as I crossed the threshold, and I followed my usual path to the kitchen. Past the off-limits living room and the hall bathroom was the large central kitchen. I wasn't much of a cook, but I liked the feel of that room; it seemed to branch off into the other rooms of the house. The kitchen's aromas roamed into every passageway and every corner. Some of the kitchen's old tiles were torn, but they had been worn so much that they'd smoothed out with time; as though they were supposed to be that way, ripped edges and all.

Jonathan and I had tried to convince Momma to resurface her counters, but she'd refused. Aside from the refrigerator, everything in that kitchen was at least fifteen years old. The cabinets were dull olive, and the wallpaper was a sad pattern of flowers and teapots. All of Momma's pans, some of which were on the stove, were missing their handles. But she said she wouldn't dare part with them. "That's when they get good," she'd said. The ever-present supply of leftover grease in the Crisco can sat between the stove's eyes, ready to fry up anything at a moment's notice.

"Hello!" I called.

I heard the television blaring and figured Daddy was in the middle of watching some football game. With the chicken finished, he'd already done his part.

"Hey, baby," Momma called as she came from the back bathroom. She shuffled into the kitchen toward me, her graying hair pulled back into a soft bun. I could still see the impression that her Sunday hat made on her light bronze forehead. She would not be caught dead at Sunday service without a hat on. She had a dash of her latest discovery, lipstick, on her lips. When I was growing up, Momma had always said that she wouldn't paint her face. But lately I noticed her branching out, though not so far as to cause the saints to speculate.

Her bifocals dangled near the edge of her nose for just a moment; then she pushed them up with a forefinger and wrinkled up her nose to hold them there for a second and get a good look at me. Her light brown eyes met mine and checked me, as they always did when I saw her. She could decipher my mood with one glance. She could tell that I was fine, and unwrinkled her nose so that her glasses could begin their descent into the soft, pink groove near the center of her bridge.

Her thick arms embraced me, but only for a moment. There was work to be done. I hung my coat on the coat-rack and rejoined her in the kitchen. I put my purse down in a chair, washed my hands, and grabbed an apron from the stove handle.

Daddy came in and stood over me, scrutinizing my

every move. His favorite belt buckle, an oversized silver mold of Texas, pressed into his round stomach. He'd never give it up, even though it was on the last notch. In fact, I think he'd poked another hole in it, just to keep on wearing that belt with his name stamped into the back in big brown capital letters: *JONATHAN*. His wardrobe was much like the kitchen decor—old-fashioned and so outdated that it was just about back in style. He wore blue jeans and a T-shirt bearing the Coca-Cola emblem that I recognized from a Christmas long gone. His salt-and-pepper hair had been brushed back with a few unfocused strokes. The deep brown skin poking out at the top of his head shined like a lightbulb, as though he had a bright idea.

My father might have been a fashion disaster waiting to happen, but he always smelled good. He splurged on cologne, though he rarely went anywhere since retiring. He said that Grandmomma Smith always taught him that you might be poor, but you didn't have to be dirty or stinky.

As was routine, I ignored his inspections and continued with my duty.

"Hey," he prodded, "what kind of rolls did you make?"

"I bought 'em at the store," I said in answer to his *real* question, pulling a cookie sheet from the cabinet beneath the counter.

"Hmm," he said with a frown on his face.

"What's wrong with the rolls, Daddy?" I asked him, sighing and placing one hand on my hip.

"There's nothin' wrong with them. I'm just waitin' for the day you start makin' them from scratch," he said.

"Daddy, I don't even know where 'scratch' is."

"That's the problem, now," he said, looking down his nose at me. "How do you expect to get a good man without knowing how to cook? You watched your momma and me make plenty of meals that you claim you can't whip up now. Don't you know the Bible says that the way to a man's heart is through his stomach?"

Momma contradicted him. "That ain't in the Bible."

"It ought to be," Daddy said with raised eyebrows. He pushed his stomach forward indignantly and let his arms dangle at his sides. "They sure left a whole lot out if *that's* not in there, 'cause it's the truth, so help me God."

"Well, if you would read the Bible for yourself, you'd know what's in there," Momma said as she spread low-fat margarine on top of the unbaked rolls.

"See?" Daddy pointed. "Stuff like that—fake butter—probably has all kind of chemicals and preservatives. That's what's makin' people so sick these days—givin' everybody cancer. I swear, we didn't have all these problems y'all have today. Now, we had high blood pressure and arthritis, but we didn't have all these no-name quick-killing diseases y'all have today. You know why? Because we used natural fat!"

"What should we be using, Daddy?" I opened that can of worms knowing that he'd bring up something utterly ridiculous like using apple butter in place of light syrup.

He proceeded to tell us, for what was probably the hundredth time, the Vaseline story. He repeated it as though he'd never shared it with us before. "I swear to God." He held up his right hand. "One day your grandmomma Smith was in the kitchen about to cook us breakfast. She barely had enough stuff to make the pancake batter—probably just some flour, eggs, water, and powdered milk, but we were gonna eat it because that's all we had. Momma looked in the cabinets for some shortening or some butter to fry them pancakes up in, but we didn't have any. All we had was some Vaseline from when she did Debra Jean's hair, so that's what she used. And it tasted just fine. I ain't lyin'! Call my momma on the phone right now and ask her! She'll tell ya! We ate whatever we had."

"Ain't nobody fixin' to call your momma." Momma shook her head.

"Momma told me about you light-skinned women," he teased her. "Y'all worked in the kitchen. Don't know anything about *real* cookin' for black folks." Daddy sauntered back toward the living room to watch more of his game. "But you turned out all right, gal; you grew on me after a while."

"Jon, please. Your momma said that I was the best thing that ever happened to you. According to her, I rescued you." She turned from her cooking and looked at him above the rim of her glasses. "And I thank God every day that I never had to work in another woman's kitchen."

"Well, you can thank God *and* me. Somebody had to work around here." Daddy headed toward the living room.

"I worked right here in this house! Matter of fact, I'm still workin'. They ain't come up with a retirement plan for full-time mothers yet," she fussed. "And anyways, *your* mother didn't work."

"My momma knew how to make money stretch, though." Daddy stopped in his tracks and pivoted to address any concerns Momma had about Grandmomma Smith. *Please don't get this man started on his momma.*

"Watch out, now. We don't want to talk about mommas," Momma tempted him.

Daddy marched back into the kitchen. "I'll call my momma up right now. I betcha she'll hop out of that wheelchair and whip *anybody* try to jump bad with her."

"So what are you saying, Daddy? You want us to use some Vaseline for the rolls?" I asked.

Daddy waved his index finger at me. "Be careful, girl. You never know what you might have to do in a bad situation. You see how these white folks fixed that election back in two thousand? They never intended to let Al Gore become president. Had all those people in Florida countin' ballots like they were little elves or somethin'. If the blacks don't get off their butts, we're gonna be back on the boat!"

"Momma, is he still talkin' 'bout that election?" I asked her.

"Just like it was yesterday," she sighed.

I set the table while the rolls browned. We used Momma's best dishes every Sunday. The main platters had roses in full bloom splattered around the edges, while the plates and saucers had tiny buds sparsely placed near the rim. The silverware was engraved with the letter *S*. Momma said that we used them every Sunday because we never knew when it would be our last. She put the food in serving dishes, and Daddy went back to his lounge chair in the living room, looking over his shoulder every few minutes to see if we were ready yet. In the natural process of bending over to get the rolls out of the oven, I must have given my mother an eyeful of my thighs and behind.

"You ain't got no slip on under that dress?" she asked me, squinting to find a trace of silk or lace.

Why is she watching my behind? "No, Momma, I'm not wearing a slip."

"You got on a girdle?"

"Momma, people wear shapers and control-top pantyhose. Most women don't wear those heavy-duty girdles anymore."

"I don't know who told you that!" She turned her back as she finished preparing the table, and talked to me over her shoulder. "In my day we didn't like all our stuff showin' and jigglin'."

"I'm jigglin', Momma?" I managed to laugh through what I considered an outright insult, the kind that only your mother can get away with.

She sensed my dismay and compassionately explained her position. "It ain't nothin' wrong with you, Shondra.

You're a woman. You got the curves and lumps God gave his most beautiful creation on earth. But that ain't for everybody to see. Shouldn't nobody but you and your husband know the shape of your thighs, chile."

"This dress is denim, Momma. I don't need a slip under it. Nobody can see my 'lumps' through this."

"You're supposed to wear a slip under *every* dress," she fussed, taking hard breaths and willing her blood pressure to stay low. "I hope you ain't goin' 'round the saints at your church like that, shakin' your goodies and provokin' the men. They gonna think I didn't teach you any better. They haven't pulled you to the side and talked to you about it?"

"No, Momma. I don't think I've ever seen anyone being taken to the side," I said. "Are they still putting handkerchiefs over people's knees at Gethsemane?"

"Any time we need to." Her chin shook as she declared her church's stance. The bun at the base of her head took on a life of its own, bobbing up and down as she continued her lecture. "Only reason your church ain't doin' it no more is because y'all got that new pastor. That church ain't been right since your old pastor died. Now, *that* man knew the way."

"Leave her alone," Daddy called from his favorite seat. "Your church's got more devils runnin' around in long skirts than anything."

"How would you know?" Momma called back to him, rising up from her slump over the stove and putting her hands on her hips.

"They've always been a bunch of fakers and shakers," he teased.

"You be careful what you say about the saints." She resumed the task of scooping macaroni and cheese out of the pot and into a quart-sized serving bowl.

It took me a while to figure out that the petty disagreements my parents had on a daily basis were actually how they communicated with each other. Despite the outward appearance of constant dissension, I don't think either of them would have had it any other way.

At times like those, I wished that Jonathan were home. He was the only other human being who'd grown up at 700 Dembo Street. He understood the atmosphere, the aura, the smells, and the memories there. He knew why the fourth canister was missing. He remembered the day I messed up the ceiling fan when my balloon flew up too high. We'd gotten whippings together with "the brown belt." He knew that sometimes you had to turn the door-knob backward to open the front bathroom door. Jonathan also knew that no matter how much Momma and Daddy fussed, they had done the best they could to give us what they thought we needed.

Since we were kids, I'd envied Jonathan. It seemed that he could get away with murder. As young adults, he seemed light years ahead of me spiritually. But since the Lord had begun working with me, I'd found Jonathan to be one of the most prudent people to talk to. I valued his insight, and I admired his wisdom at such a young age. I told him that once, and he told me, quite frankly, that he'd received it from God and that there was more than enough to go around. With anyone else I would have been offended, but my little brother loved me. I knew that. I appreciated Jonathan, and I missed him dearly. The house wasn't the same without him.

Momma said a prayer over dinner, and we began eating. I enjoyed my parents' company, for the most part. Though our time together sometimes reminded me of a roast, it was routine. Momma, on my left, could be hard to get along with, but she had good intentions. Across from me, a man who had worked hard all his life to provide for Jonathan, Momma, and me—and complained the whole time, although he wouldn't have it any other way. I'd overheard him tell one of our neighbors that he had a good thing at home.

However, sitting there with them Sunday after Sunday made me all the more curious about my future. *Who will I eat Sunday dinner with when* I'm *sixty*? If it was nothing more than a few girlfriends, I wanted to eat with somebody. *Maybe by that time I might know how to make a decent pan of corn bread.*

"Have you been seeing anybody?" Daddy asked me. He had a knack for starting in on me without warning. Daddy planted his elbows on the stained oak table, awaiting my answer.

"No, Daddy, I'm not seeing anybody." I endured his line of questioning.

"What's the holdup, gal? You're not getting any younger. What are you now—thirty-five?"

"You know I'll be thirty-one, Daddy. Where did you get thirty-five?"

"You're gonna fool around and be an old maid," he said. "Better quit being so choosy."

"You leave her alone." Momma jumped to my defense. "She needs to be choosy. We don't want her with just anybody. Besides, women these days have other things on their minds. They've got a whole lot more opportunities than I had in our day, Jon."

"Okay, am I not sitting right here?" I asked as they talked over my head.

"Maybe she's looking in the wrong places." Daddy took a bite of his chicken, letting the grease run a moment before grabbing his napkin and wiping the trail.

"We need more choosy women with some kind of sense," Momma laughed, getting up from her seat to get more ice. "Some of these girls today just don't have any kind of standards about themselves. Just hop in the bed with anybody."

My stomach leaped and I kept my head down low, chomping away at my food. I'd done a good job of keeping my business off the streets and out of the COGIC. Aside from the time Momma accosted me about the spread of my hips when I was a senior in college, there had been no other discussion about sex and me.

Momma went on, "And these Negroes today are just sorry! I don't know how you do it, LaShondra. From what I see on this TV, there ain't hardly any good men left. But don't worry, baby. God's got somebody for everybody."

"Somebody like me, for example," Daddy added. His humorous side, my favorite, came forward. "I'm telling you, Shondra, there are a lot of good black men up at the Postal Service. Who's your postman?"

"I know you don't think I've been sitting outside waiting to find out who delivers my mail. What am I supposed to do—take him a glass of lemonade?" I sassed.

"That's how your momma lucked up on a good man like me," he bragged.

Momma let out a sneaky laugh at the freezer door. "Hee-hee-hee-hee-hee."

"Yeah, I said it. I know I'm a good man."

"Who told you that you were a good man?" Momma put the pitcher of tea back into the refrigerator.

"Nobody had to tell me. I already knew that." Daddy slapped Momma on her behind just as she lowered herself to the seat. "Jonathan Smith, you stop that!" she said as the corners of her lips turned up.

"How are things going at your job?" Momma asked me.

"Oh, the same. Just handling problems with kids and teachers and parents." I shrugged.

"White folks?" Daddy asked.

"All kinds of people, Daddy." As much as I respected my

father's position on race relations, he could be a bit overbearing. I did agree with him regarding the need for black people to learn to stick together before we undertake the task of becoming a part of America's melting pot, but I picked my battles with him about exactly how the goal should be reached. Actually, I don't think jumping into the melting pot was on Daddy's list of things-to-do-as-an-African-American-man. I didn't foresee myself jumping in the pot, either. But I did want it for the future, maybe generations from now, after all of us who still had reservations died off. It might happen, I guessed, but not in his time.

He'd lived through everything I read about when I studied Martin Luther King Jr. in school. And I figured there were enough white people who came of age in my father's day to duly influence their offspring for another two or three generations. Those like me—the first generation to be legally recognized as U.S. citizens with all rights and privileges therein—still had our doubts. We'd heard things from the horse's mouth. And those we loved and trusted had taught us to be suspicious. Careful and protective.

"You just keep your nose clean at that school, you hear?" Daddy pointed his fork at me.

"I always do," I said in a monotone voice.

"All right"—he let his voice swing up—"you think you know everything. Can't nobody tell you nothing. Not that much has changed in forty years, you know."

"I know that, Daddy."

"What exactly is she supposed to be doing, Jon?" Momma asked.

"Just go to work, do your job, and come home. That's exactly what I did for over thirty-five years with the United States Postal Service. Only problems I ever had with my work were with dogs. I know those higher-ups overlooked me for promotions because I was black, but they always wanted me there because I was a good worker. Didn't miss a day unless it was absolutely necessary. Rain, shine, sleet, or snow."

"Thanks for your hard work, Daddy," I half thanked, half patronized him. I don't think he could have withstood actual gratitude without throwing some kind of desentimentalizing twist on it. "I appreciate it, and so do the white people at my job."

"Mmm-hmm," he moaned, bringing a margarine-laced roll toward his mouth and taking a bite. "You think that's funny. Just keep on livin'. You gonna learn that white people don't mean you any good."

"Not a single one of 'em, Daddy?"

"There's always one or two, but you don't have any way of tellin' which ones are really okay and which ones are just tryin' to stab you in the back or ease their minds about what they did in the past. Just no way of knowin'. It's best to just steer clear of 'em. Keep to yourself and do your job."

"Ooh, can we please talk about something other than white people?" I asked him. "You would think white people *live* here as much as you talk about them."

"I'm not talking about white people. I'm talking about *you*."

"What about me, Daddy? I work with people of all different colors every day." I was getting more and more irritated with his insinuation that I was selling out.

"And you like the whites just as much as the blacks?"

"When I deal with kids, it's really not about color, you know?" I turned toward my mother, who might have been more receptive to my case.

"Kids grow up." Daddy demanded my attention. "And I'll betcha some of those same kids' parents tell them not to listen to that old *black* vice principal."

"Well, I don't know if they do or not, Daddy." I shook my head and continued eating. *Perhaps if I stuff my mouth, he might leave me alone.* Talking with Daddy about white people wasn't like talking with Peaches and Deniessa. We laughed, we joked, and we went on with our conversation. But with Daddy, it was serious. I'd realized very early on that he was all consumed with race and discrimination and prejudice, as though that were all there was to life.

I ate, drank, and breathed race at 700 Dembo Street. With that came a sense of pride and damnation all together. Grateful to be at a point in time where I could dream, but perhaps damned to a life of overexertion in my efforts to be all that my ancestors could not be. These privileges, these rights that many before me had bled and died for, came with such responsibilities. With so much more at stake than my white counterparts, I was resentful. *Why do I have to put forth 110 percent while the white woman next to me gives maybe 75 percent? What makes her so special?* Looking at white people—particularly white women—and feeling that they thought the privileges of this country *belonged* to them set up a kind of grudge. Not intentional, I reasoned, but an inevitable byproduct of slavery.

CHAPTER 4

What's your name?" I asked the new girl when we went out to recess.

"Patricia," she barely spoke. I watched her shift the dirt with her patent leather Buster Brown shoes. With her head down, I could see the zigzag part between her ponytails. I'd asked Momma to do that for me, but she never had the time.

She still hadn't looked me in the eye. I noticed the way her legs bulged out of her socks just above the elastic. Then I thought of my own scrawny, chicken-looking legs. Mother Dear had said that I looked "po'."

"Are you rich or somethin'?" I asked her.

"No." She finally looked at me. "I don't think so."

"Well, how come you got so much meat on your bones?"

"My momma said it's 'cause my tabulism is so slow," Patricia told me.

"How do you get your tabulism to slow down?" Maybe if I could slow mine down, Daddy would stop calling me "tooth-pick."

"I don't know. My momma said it's from my daddy's side of the family," she said. Then she held her hands to her lips and whispered, "Sometimes I get up at night and sneak chocolate chip cookies."

Okay, I did that, too, but it hadn't helped me any. I was convinced that she had to know more than she was confessing.

"You want to swing together, Patricia?" I asked her.

"Sure." Her cheeks almost pushed her eyelids closed as she smiled. "And you can call me Peaches."

That happened right around the time our teacher, Mrs. Schumacher, divided our kindergarten class into two sections: the butterflies and the rainbows. It didn't take long before we all figured out that the butterflies were "smarter" than the rainbows. Being a butterfly meant that you used crayons less and wrote more often with big, round pencils. Butterflies read from certain books with the "real" teacher while rainbows assembled around the teacher's assistant, being drilled over and over again on the letters of the alphabet. I couldn't have explained how happy I was to have another brown face in my group. We quickly became inseparable.

I met Peaches for dinner on her side of the city. She picked a quaint, elegant little restaurant well known around town for its pricey but hard-to-find specialties. The clatter of silverware against plates and glasses attested to the upper-class atmosphere, putting us both on dialect alert as we waited to be seated. My Boaz look-alike rushed in through the restaurant doors and accidentally knocked over my purse. "Oh, excuse me, sister," he said, bending down to hand it to me. *Ooh, he called me 'sister.'* I got that warm, familiar feeling inside that I wouldn't have to start from square one with him. "It's okay." His skin was likened unto Hershey's with a smile that said, "I see my dentist regularly." Granted, he was a bit clumsy. But he'd stopped in his hurried tracks to make it all better. *Can we get some violins here?* He nodded and smiled at Peaches and me, then rushed past us toward the waitress's podium.

I hated moments like that—the ones that leave you thinking, *I should have said something,* days after the opportunity has passed.

"I see my party over there," he said as he pointed to the bar. Then he waved. Peaches and I looked clear through the minigarden and two other panes of glass to see his party. A black woman in a blue dress and blue pumps waved seductively in his direction. *So much for the violins.*

"Girl, I could feel that in my bones. That was a *good* black man," I said, shaking my head.

"A *taken* good black man," she added.

Our waitress, a young white lady with a vibrant smile, ushered us to a booth for two. Peaches relieved herself of her sweater, revealing perfectly toned arms and the bones that protruded just below her neckline. I'd seen her in that dress before, but it always amazed me to see the degree of transformation the human body can undergo given a change of habits. Her makeup was perfect, as usual, and her handbag matched her red, strappy shoes.

"Are you going to the retreat?" she asked me later, twirling pasta around her fork. Her church always held a dynamic Spirit-filled women's retreat in early December.

"I don't think so. I'm in charge of career day at the school next week. I'm missing confirmations from some of the firms. And I'm still looking for someone with a career in math or science—preferably an engineer."

"Well, if you find one, give him my number."

"Girl, please—you! What about me?" I held up my hand to stop her. "Anyways, I think I'm gonna invite a female engineer. And an African-American one at that," I informed her.

"You go, girl." She leaned back and smiled, dabbing the corners of her lips with a white linen napkin. "I wish they would have brought in some black people to talk to us when we were in school. Maybe we would have had a little more vision."

I echoed her sentiment with a touch of natural black attitude in my voice. "Be for real, Peaches. Those white folks wudn't thinkin' 'bout us. They wouldn't even hire a black teacher, so you know they were not about to bring in no black role models makin' mo' money than them."

We shared a laugh and carried on, catching up on each other's lives. I watched her brown eyes light up and dance when she told me about Eric's upcoming basketball season and how she had found the cutest little high-tops for him. She also let me know that Raphael made good on a promise to take Eric to Six Flags.

"Really?"

"But why did he come up to my doorstep with another woman?" She glared at me with her neck and lips stuck out.

"What?"

"Some girl from his job, he said," she went on. "I think Raphael is just using Eric to win her. You know, trying to make it seem like he's the good type of brother doing the right thing for his son. But I'll take it for what it's worth. God is doing His thing in His own way in His own time. All Eric knows is that he spent the day with his daddy. Oh, girl, let Eric tell it, they had the best day on earth." She'd tried hard, but the sarcasm still came through in her tone.

"I'm proud of you, girl," I encouraged her. "The *old* you would have snatched Raphael up in a heartbeat! Isn't it funny how we're changing?"

"It is." She grinned with me. "But I know that no matter what I think about the situation, what matters most for Eric is that he has a relationship with his father."

"And that is so important." I tossed my curls back and leaned in to her. "Our men already have issues. Every black boy needs a black male role model."

"A *good* black male role model," she clarified, striking the air with her fork. "My brothers already do a good job of mentoring Eric. Whether Raphael is the best role model for Eric is still questionable. I just want my son to know his father, for whatever it's worth."

We ordered light desserts and savored the familiarity a little longer. The restaurant filled quickly as the dinner hour progressed. The same waitress seated two white men at the table next to Peaches and me.

"Don't look now"—Peaches lowered her voice—"but one of 'em is staring at you."

"Girl, please," I sighed. "He ain't about to get none of *this* chocolate drizzled on his sundae."

"You betta get that white man," she teased.

"There is nothing a white man can do for me except fix my computer, okay?"

"So what's been going on with you?" she continued, not giving their table another look.

"Girl, the Lord has got me reading a lot of stuff on love," I told her with the same puzzled look that I had when I discovered, through the process of straightening up the books on my bookshelf, that I'd begun collecting books on love. "It's really interesting because it's like, I always thought I knew what love was. I mean, I work in a school and teach children's church—how can I *not* be a loving person? But the more I learn, the more I find out that I didn't know."

"That's serious."

"I know. There is so much work to be done," I admitted. "But I know He's gonna do it."

"Look, if he can deliver me from chocolate, anybody can be delivered from anything!" Peaches roared, and the other customers looked at us like we were a little crazy. You had to know Peaches to understand how much chocolate meant to her. It was the one thing that had kept her overweight more than anything else. She believed God for perseverance in diet, endurance in exercise, and deliverance from chocolate when she lost eighty pounds. Of course, that led to the other stuff with Raphael.

Next I began telling Peaches about my battles at work. As a vice principal, I often felt pressured to uphold so many ideals and principles as a Christian, a woman, an African-American, a role model, and a supervisor. Actually, the students weren't the problem. Most of my conflicts involved parents or colleagues.

"Girl, I had this woman, Mrs. Donovan, up in my office last week talking about how she's gonna go up to the board because her daughter flunked math and can't play basketball for the next three weeks." I stuck my lips out and waited for Peaches' question.

"And?"

"That's exactly what I said! She can go to the board, the superintendent, the Lord Himself, but a rule is still a rule. The girl had a fifty-eight. She wasn't even close to passing!"

"Then what did she say?"

I put on my best prissy, proper voice to imitate Mrs. Donovan: "'Miss Smith, I don't know if you're aware or not, but my husband is a major contributor to the booster club. We do a lot to support this school.'"

"What color was she—white?"

"You know she was." I stuck my neck out and gave her a smug stare. "I told her, in so many words, that her daughter's education was not for sale, and that the little girl would have to bring up her average in math before she would be allowed back on the court again."

"She was hot when she left, wasn't she?" Peaches grinned.

"Girl, she was hotter than fifty Mexicans in the front seat of a Pinto."

Peaches almost choked on her water. That was right about the time that a still, tiny *Ding! Ding!* of a warning bell went off inside me. I felt it, almost tangibly. But why? This old joke had never caused the bell to go off—until now. So I decided to talk about something else.

"Then I had this little black boy that this white teacher sent down to me for having a straw in his mouth."

"What?"

"A straw, girl. Like it was a knife or something."

"That's crazy."

"I sent him right back up there with a little note to her saying, *Handle this with your classroom consequences.*"

"When are you gonna quit that job and come to Northcomp?" Peaches asked me. "You know I'm director of personnel. You could be making two or three times what you're making now, with half the stress," she offered for the billionth time.

"Because *our* kids need us," I replied, running a finger across my forearm. "I'm the only spot in administration at the school. It's important for our kids to see somebody black running things. I wouldn't trade it for a million dollars. Education is my calling. You know that. Besides, I don't have the degree for your field."

"Girl, please," she fussed, waving her hand. "All those white people up in there with little or no education! And even the ones who have degrees aren't necessarily competent. They made up the buddy employment system—it's about time *we* got some people in high places so we can have it like that, too."

As we rose to leave the restaurant, the white man that Peaches referred to earlier quickly cleared the corners of his mouth with his napkin and stood as well. He took a few steps toward me and held out his right hand, shoving the left one deep into his pocket.

"Hello. My name is David Moore."

I'm sure my face said, *"And?"* but in the interest of my good home training, I shook his hand and introduced myself as well. "LaShondra Smith."

"I . . . I was just admiring your smile."

Peaches poked me hard in the back and almost caused me to have a muscle spasm. "Ow—oh. Thank you." He stood there for another moment before it dawned on him that I had absolutely no interest in pursuing the conversation any further.

"Well, it was nice meeting you, Miss Smith," he said with a quick nod.

"Same here, Mr. Moore."

"You have a nice day."

I watched him return to his table and grab his glass. His hopes of a fling with a black woman were dashed.

It was still early when I got home. My soul was both thirsty and curious. Why had I heard that little voice in my heart over something as innocent and familiar as our Mexican joke? I'd never felt bad about it before. *There really isn't any harm in two old girlfriends sharing an inside jest.* Or was there?

I had been talking and thinking and meditating on love lately. And I'd begun to feel uneasy instead of peaceful about an area that I had always thought was pretty well covered in my life. *What am I misunderstanding about love, Lord?*

When I got inside, I called Peaches to let her know that I'd made it home. After washing my face, brushing my teeth, and tying my hair in a satin scarf, I made my way to the prayer closet for my last words of the day with the Lord.

I approached the room with some degree of apprehension. I didn't like feeling as though I was missing out on God's voice. I fell to my knees and started out with praise; thanking God for His blessings and praising Him for who

He is. Then I got into my groove at my desk and asked the Holy Spirit to take me where I needed to go in the Word. Since God had been teaching me about love, I knew that I needed to be there. I just wasn't exactly sure. I searched the subject index of my NIV Women's Devotional Bible, and I began going through the writings that had to do with love for others. Still beseeching the Spirit for guidance, I went through the indicated pages and read until I felt the Word speak to me. Halfway down the list, I realized that I was still "cold" on the trail. I let my eyes wander to the adjacent page and then I saw it: *PREJUDICE.* I flipped to Galatians 3:26–29 and read:

> *You are all sons of God through faith in Christ Jesus, for all of you who were baptized into Christ have clothed yourselves with Christ. There is neither Jew nor Greek, slave nor free, male nor female, for you are all one in Christ Jesus. If you belong to Christ, then you are Abraham's seed, and heirs according to the promise.*

My heart sank as I rolled this scripture over in my mind. I tried to find a loophole—anything to unjustify what the Word was saying about prejudice. After all, I had good reason to be prejudiced. Mexicans were taking over. Middle Easterners were always bombing people. Asian people made me sick following me around their little dollar stores as if somebody really wanted to steal a cheap plastic yo-yo. The Native Americans were getting a free ride, though they deserved it. *And white people.* They stole my ancestors, sold them, used our backs to build their own wealth (mind you, never paid us for it), and the list went on and on.

I thought aloud, "It's so hard for me to love white people." But as quickly as the confession escaped my mouth, I knew that I could have just as easily substituted the word "black" because I truly had a hard time dealing with my own kind, too. I mentally ran down the list of our issues:

Black people could sure enough get on my nerves making us all look bad. Always running on C.P. (Colored People) time like the world revolves around us. Not checking over our kids' homework, let alone coming to PTA meetings to find out what's going on up at the "schoolhouse." Then we want to come up and act crazy when our children get into trouble. Empty promises, half-steppin', all talk and no action. Kids dressed to kill in Tommy Hilfiger and CK, but they're on free or reduced lunch. We don't support our own, we're always pulling each other down, we don't vote, and we could sho 'nuff get "ig-nut" over some money. Leave it to black folks to start a friendly family game of dominos and have it end up with somebody getting shot over fifty cents.

Yes, we could be called a lot of things, but much of it was due to the fact that we are still trying to find ourselves in America. After all, I was in the first generation of African-Americans to have both freedom and civil rights, the first to be able to live out my dreams with the law on my side.

With my justifications for prejudice still fresh on my mind, I closed my Bible and got back on my knees to have a little talk with Jesus. What, exactly, was He asking me to do? Was He asking me to ignore all the facts? Was He asking me to forget about the cause of black equality? Did He expect me to just put down my guard when dealing with people who, collectively, intended to remain on top by keeping others down? Was I supposed to make friends with whites and Hispanics and every other type of person on the globe?

And what of blackness itself—the pride, the attitude that came with my heritage? I *liked* black things—Juneteenth, *Essence* magazine, hips, our sororities and fraternities, our churches, and those little shirts we used to wear that read: *It's a* black *thing—you wouldn't understand.* I paid my NAACP dues, and I was committed to making sure that every child in my church got the help they needed to be successful in school. So what if those kids happened to be black? I'm black. I wanted to help my own.

Truly, this thing in my spirit was an assault on my fabric. I prayed my own words and ended the conversation. I left my prayer closet that night without any answers, only a conviction that I did not feel was a fair one, given the history of the very land that I stood on.

CHAPTER 5

When Jonathan made the announcement that he was going into the navy, Momma was a little frightened—as any mother would be. But my parents were in no position to turn around and put a second child through college. They had already taken out several loans to pay for my education, and it was no secret that Daddy postponed his retirement to make sure that I could finish school without owing anything. Initially, Jonathan went into the military so that he could see the world and get a free college education. As it turned out, he enjoyed military life so much that he reenlisted for another four years. This time he was off to Germany indefinitely.

Momma had that first, awkward-looking military photo hung high above the mantel. I don't know what they do to those soldiers just before snapping that first military picture, but those people always look starved, worn out, and homesick. Jonathan was no exception. I almost cried when I saw my brother in that photo. Momma did *cry.*

"Stop all that cryin', girl. They just makin' a man out of him," Daddy said proudly.

"That was your *job!" Momma yelled. Then they got into it again about how they would have had enough money to put us both through college if Momma wasn't giving so much money to the church or if Daddy would stop playing the lottery. Let them*

tell it, they would have been billionaires if only the other one hadn't been doing this or that.

They did, however, agree that Jonathan needed to remember at all times that he was black. The day before Jonathan left, Daddy sat him down and had a long talk with him. I heard the whole thing from the living room. Jonathan was told, in no uncertain terms, that he was not, under any circumstances, to come home with any woman who was anything other than black.

"I don't care what you see going on around you. I don't care what a white or Korean or whatever girl says to you, you remember—if she can't use your comb, don't bring her home!" Daddy told him with conviction.

"You know your great-uncle Eddie George got killed behind a white girl," Daddy said. "And he was the only uncle I had on my momma's side."

Momma was washing the dishes and butted in the conversation. "Eddie George got killed 'cause he was messin' with a married woman."

"She was white!" Daddy yelled. "If she woulda been a black woman, my uncle woulda been alive today."

"He woulda been a hundred and ten years old!" I yelled from the couch.

Daddy wasn't having it that day, though. He was serious about his talk with Jonathan, and something in me was struck by Daddy's desperate plea to my little brother. The fear and anger in his heart made his voice tremble. Jonathan listened intently as he never had before, and Momma stopped sloshing the dishwater. Daddy poured out his life's understandings, and the heat of his words spewed out of his mouth like steam, thickening the room's air.

"The hardest thing in the world is being a black man in America. Nobody will ever understand that but black men. The best thing we got going for us is our women and our families. You can go off into this navy and bunk up right next to a white man, but don't ever think he's got your back. 'Cause if push *comes to shove, and he's got a choice between saving you and saving a white man, he'll save the white man every time." Daddy stressed every syllable by slamming his fist on his knee.*

"Everywhere the white man goes, he destroys people. America is the greatest example of the white man doing what he does best. He killed off the Indians; he got the Mexicans over here to work the fields in World War Two, but now he's trying to send them back with nothin'; and he worked the blacks to the bone for his own gain. And they've never paid any of us back. Now, you take this money they give you from the military and use it to help you and yours. But don't ever turn your back on a white person, Jonathan. They will stab you in the back every time."

Those words were meant for Jonathan, but they seeped deep into my spirit.

Unlike workday mornings, I liked to get up in plenty of time to prepare for church on Sunday. I sprang out of bed, quickly prayed, and got ready for service. As I pulled up my loathsome off-black pantyhose, I let out an indignant sigh. I hated wearing pantyhose, but I knew that many of my children's church students had been told that when they grew up, they would be expected to wear pantyhose to church. I didn't want to cause any discord, so I suffered that nylon and threw on black pumps, a black skirt, and a sweater.

I still had to stop by the grocery store and get snacks for my children's church class, so I rushed out without eating breakfast. Most of the R & B radio stations played gospel on Sunday mornings, so I gave my CDs a rest and listened to the latest in gospel music while driving to church.

Something about the drive to church always calmed me. It was as though I were going to an old friend's house—a place I had always known and cherished. A place where I could be me, only better. Sometimes, if I lay in bed too long, I would consider skipping a Sunday or two. And even if I did stay home for whatever reason, the part of me that longed to be in my Father's house couldn't rest well knowing that there might come a time when I couldn't get to a church and then I would regret all the times I'd lazed in bed on Sunday mornings. No, I had to be there.

Once at the church, I made a few copies in the front office and set up my classroom. I turned the lights on, listened to the buzz, and waited for the lights to pop on, one square at a time. It was my classroom, my canvas, the place I could paint perfect. Since becoming a vice principal, I didn't have the opportunity to stand before children and watch them discover and learn and love life the way I did when I was a classroom teacher. Tutoring on Wednesday nights was productive, but there's also something blessed about presenting an actual lesson, looking down at tiny little brown faces and telling them how much they are loved. Teaching children's church on Sunday mornings gave me the opportunity to use my gift as an educator for God's glory.

As I filled the plastic cups with crayons and scissors for the project we'd be creating, I turned on the intercom and listened to the service going forth in the main room. The praise team was singing a medley of "Jesus Is Mine," "You Don't Know Like I Know," and "Victory Is Mine."

I had a surprise that morning when the children filed into the classroom. A little white girl visited our class. Maybe at another church, a white child wouldn't stand out. But in our African-American southern Church of God in Christ, having a white face among the crowd was not a regular occurrence. I never really stopped to ask myself why, because I rather enjoyed being "at home" in church. As far as I was concerned, the less I saw of white people, the more I could be myself.

The little girl's name was Emily, and she told us that she was visiting with her mother. Her pale face was sprinkled with outstanding brown freckles, which were upstaged only by her bright, contagious smile. There was always something about children—the innocence of their beliefs, the blindness of their love—that made me stand in awe of how close they are to ideal.

Emily participated in the discussion and drew an awesome depiction of herself praying. When we finished class, I made my usual call for students who wanted to accept Christ in their lives. Emily came forward with a few others. We all clapped for them and asked them to repeat the prayer of faith. Then we hugged them and officially welcomed them to the body of Christ. It was always a great feeling to know that I had been used to bring another soul to Christ, regardless of color or background. Every soul needed to be saved. Period. After serving the snacks, I had the ushers assist me in getting the children to their parents. A few of my former students, now in the junior class, helped clean up the room, and then we all went back into the sanctuary.

The Spirit was high, and Pastor Williams was whooping—preaching hard and catching his breath between the organ's hits. Everyone was on their feet, giving him the impetus he needed to go higher and higher. I stood and joined in, catching on to the last part of his sermon and praising God right along with the congregation.

"I stopped by to tell you this morning . . . that God is able . . . to deliver you . . . mmm hmmm . . . from whatever is stopping you . . . from receiving the fullness . . . of His blessing!"

"Yeah!" The Mothers on the front row cheered him on. Most of the congregation was standing, with the older sisters waving their white linen handkerchiefs. "Go 'head! Preach, Pastor!" The Pastor's mother, too ill to stand, sat with her hands in her lap but showed her involvement by poking out her lips and tossing her head left to right with such fervor that her whole body swayed. Pastor was preaching so intensely, even some of the deacons got up off their bench, crossed their arms, and nodded.

After the altar call and prayer line, we were all in a good, peaceful mood to be dismissed. Pastor made his usual comments about our minds turning toward food and football, and the congregation laughed. Then he asked the head usher to come again and recognize the first-time visitors as well as those who invited them. I saw a white woman, unmistakably the only visitor left in the crowd, and obviously Emily's mother. I'd catch her after service, I figured, to tell her what a wonderful student Emily was and invite her to come again.

Sister Wilson, dressed far too stylishly to be an usher, smoothed out her white gloves and spoke from behind the white veil poking out of her hat. "Pastor, this is Shannon Potter. She is a guest of Brother Paul Pruitt."

The congregation clapped as Shannon pushed herself up and nodded graciously. Paul stood up next to her—I hadn't even noticed that he was on her pew. He closed in the space between them with his body and smiled broadly.

"Would you like to have words?" Sister Wilson asked Emily's mother.

Shannon smiled and flipped her blond hair in that white-girl fashion as she spoke. "My name is Shannon Potter, and this is my daughter, Emily. We're members at First Methodist of Dallas. I have really enjoyed myself today. My daughter and I are guests of Paul Pruitt." She smiled at Paul.

"Old Pruitt," Pastor teased. "You finally brought you a woman to church!" Brother Paul gave a sheepish grin, consistent with his low-key manner.

People laughed, but I knew there had to be a good majority of us who felt exactly the way I did: *I know he didn't!* If *ever* there was anything that could get my blood to boiling, it was to see a black man with a white woman. Well, let me qualify that. When I saw what appeared to be a kind, decent-looking, gainfully employed brother hooked up with a bologna-fryin', no-shoes-in-the-grocery-store-wearin', wanna-be-black-actin', Ebonics-fakin', nose-up-turnin' white girl, *that* burned me up.

Now, if he was broke and busted, I didn't mind him being all hugged up with a white girl. Nine times out of ten, a broke brother had tried to get with a sister but got kicked to the curb. And if she was a really pretty white girl, I could almost see it—but only on the grounds that the brother was disillusioned by the media, white-actin' himself, and/or carrying out some secret taboo passed down to him through slavery. In either case, a sister really wouldn't want a brother like that. The white girls could have him.

True, I didn't want Paul for myself, but there had to be a sister out there somewhere who would jump at the chance to be Mrs. Pruitt.

This Shannon, with the hair flips and high-squeaking voice, seemed like the kind of white woman who just wanted to get with a brother and find out if all the rumors she'd heard from her girlfriends about black men were true. She was one of those kinds of white girls that spelled nothing but trouble for a black man. Any brother with half a brain should have been able to check that from the beginning.

Why, Brother Pruitt? He seemed like a *real* brother; mentoring the young men of our church and playing on the church's basketball team when he got the chance. He didn't fit the bill for the white-girl type of brother. You know, the ones that jog outside in the heat of the day. No, Paul was solid. What kind of message was he sending to *our* boys now that he'd trampled up in the church with this white woman?

It was well past time to dismiss church, as far as I was concerned. My spirit was messed up after seeing that junk. Yes, Lord, the button had been pushed.

After church I went back to my classroom to make sure I hadn't left anything. Emily caught up with me and gave me a big hug.

"Are you Sister Smith?" Shannon asked me, walking up behind Emily.

I put on my best white folks smile and said, "Yes. You must be Emily's mother."

She nodded, and we shook hands. Blue eyes. Pale skin—no tan to speak of. Dark brown roots peeking out from under her limp, bleached-blond hair. "Yes, I'm Shannon Potter. Emily really enjoyed your class today. I don't know what it is about you, but she just loves you to death."

I accepted the compliment, since it had come from an innocent child. I relaxed the corners of my mouth a bit and settled into an authentic grin. Emily hugged me tighter and looked up, flashing a big snaggle-toothed smile. "I had fun!"

"Well, I'm glad to hear that you had such a great time." I returned her hug.

"Emily accepted Christ today," I told Shannon. "Did she tell you?"

"Oh, girl, I think Emily accepts Christ every day." Shannon laughed. "She's a Christian at heart."

Did she just call me 'girl'? "Oh, just call me Sister Smith. And I agree, Emily's got a heart of gold."

I turned from Shannon because I didn't know exactly what my face was saying. "Emily, I hope to see you again soon."

"Oh, I'm sure we'll be here again. Paul and I are alternating between churches," she informed me. "We're not sure exactly where we're going to end up. I think we both enjoy each other's churches so much."

See, here she goes with too much information. Did I ask her where she and Paul were going to church?

Just then Brother Pruitt walked up behind Shannon in his dark three-piece suit and crisp white shirt. He placed his left hand on her shoulder and offered his other hand to me, greeting me with a smile, looking like a big, sorry something. I shook his hand, but I didn't want to. What was his problem, standing there with his arm around Shannon's shoulder like somebody *really wanted* that white woman?

Emily released herself from my side and pushed her body into the side of Paul's leg. He picked her up and kissed her on the forehead, then placed her down beside her mother. "Are you ready?" he asked Shannon.

"Yes," she said to him. "It was so nice meeting you, Sister Smith. We'll be seeing you again."

"Great." I smiled at Emily. It was the only thing I could do to try to hide the anger that was welling up inside me. "I'll see you next time, Emily." And then the three of them turned and walked away. Emily's ruffled, pink dress bounced with every step she took between her mother and Paul. Halfway down the hall, Paul took hold of Shannon's hand. His deep ebony skin seemed to clash with her milky-white complexion. As though she knew I was still watching them, Shannon turned back and gave me one last smile, swinging her chin just above her shoulder. I gave her the finger wave: fingers fluttering, palm motionless.

On my way out of the church, I stopped to relieve myself in the ladies' room. I'd been holding it all morning, it seemed, but the heaviness in my bladder had taken a backseat to my anger following Shannon's introduction. The church's restroom was small and only semiprivate, with one stall, which had a shower curtain rather than an actual door. With two older women inside, the room was already crowded, but I waited inside anyway because I didn't know if my bladder would tolerate much movement. I tapped my heel, ever so slightly, as I waited.

"Yeah." Mother Alderson shifted her hat on her head. "You're right about that, Marlaine. The only reason that white woman is with him is 'cause she couldn't find a white man who had just the same going for him. I'm sure she would much rather be with a white man—just wasn't one out there that could match Pruitt. I sholy hate to see that, though. And I know Jannie 'nem ain't too happy about it."

Mother Alderson looked away from her reflection and gave me a sympathetic grin. I grinned back and then looked down at my feet, expecting to see a pool of urine form around them if Mother Marlaine Cook didn't hurry up and get out of that stall. They had been talking about Paul, I knew, and I wanted to jump in with my two cents' worth, but it didn't seem the right thing to do. At least not in church, anyway. Maybe, somewhere out with Peaches or in the car, I could say all the things I felt. But not in church.

I thought about Emily as I traveled home from church. She was a child, now, but what would she be like when she grew up? Would she still hug black people? Would she still accept a black man kissing her on the cheek, or would she be one of those white girls who would tell the principal when a black boy expressed an interest in her? Would she like black boys? Would she follow her mother's example and date or marry a black man? I wondered next how Emily's father must have felt about a black man kissing his daughter. *Hmm.* I betcha it would burn him up that his little angel was in the company of a black man. He'd probably sue for custody!

CHAPTER 6

Daddy had his reservations about letting me join the debate team, let alone going off to competition with them. "How many black kids do they have on that team?"

"None. I'm gonna be the first."

"Hmm." He'd rubbed his chin with his thumb and reread the permission slip I'd given him. I sat across from him at the kitchen table, waiting for the verdict. Beneath the surface, I crossed my fingers and forced my feet to stay still. "Well, I guess you can sign up. There's bound to be some more black kids who'll want to get on this debate team in the future. It's important that you open the door—but don't forget your way back out! And keep lookin' over your shoulder, that's for sure. White people get real crazy when it comes to competition."

I rode with Amy Baltensperger and Judith Pinchowski to the movie theater following our debate team's victory at Marley High School. We'd worked together long and hard on our arguments and impromptu chemistry, bringing in the crucial points that led to our team's first-place trophy. "LaShondra, you were awesome," Amy complimented me, her braces shining like flashlights in the front seat. "When they called our name for first place, I was like, hell, yeah, thanks to LaShondra. Nobody from those other schools knew we had someone new on our team. You're like our secret weapon."

Secret weapon. I liked the way it rang, but didn't know if I liked the connotation. Nonetheless, we'd won the tournament, and these two were my teammates.

"Did you see the scores the judges gave us?" Judith asked. "I mean, I swear, they were so high I was freakin' out." She went on and on about how great it was that we were a team, especially since we were all juniors. "Next year, we will dominate!"

Judith pulled into the theater parking lot and took a space next to her boyfriend Daniel's car. Daniel worked in the theater's box office and had promised to get tickets for Judith and her friends after the competition. They bounced out of the car, and try as I might, I could not match their enthusiasm. Their bubbly personalities could be observed from the flouncing of their spiral curls to the spring in their steps. I didn't have anything against being friendly, but Judith and Amy took it to another level. I couldn't help but hope that next year there would be other black students on the team.

We approached Daniel's booth, and Amy happily informed him of our victory. "First place!"

"Cool!" he said. And then he saw me. "Who's she?"

"Oh, babe, this is my friend LaShondra. She's on our team." Judith introduced us.

His eyes traveled my body in disgust. "I don't have a ticket for her."

"Daniel . . ." Judith looked at me and then back at him. "I thought you said you could have as many as—"

"Not for coons," he said.

"Oh, my God, Daniel! I don't believe you just said that!" Amy shrieked.

"I don't have a ticket for her," he repeated, and smiled, swinging his brown hair away from his eyelashes. He refused to look at me and spoke as though I weren't standing right there in his face.

I have replayed that instant a million times, thinking about what I should have said or done at that precise moment. How I should have spoken up for myself. How I should have approached that glass as though I were going to purchase a ticket and then reached through that hole in the glass and popped him dead in his face. But I didn't. I just stood there, frozen by his ambush of insults.

Judith and Amy apologized the whole way home for Daniel's behavior. "I can't believe he said *that," Judith kept saying.*

Amy kept shaking her head. "I didn't know Daniel was like that."

When they dropped me off, I faintly waved good-bye and went to my bedroom. I cried with anger and disbelief. Somebody actually called me a coon? In the '80s? The only thing that made me angrier was to learn that Amy and Judith had gone back to the theater later and watched that movie using Daniel's free tickets.

I never signed up for debate again.

◘ ◘ ◘

I was ready to go back to work after the long weekend. I woke and spent a good half hour in prayer and meditation before beginning the week. Following prayer, the rush was on—shower, brush my teeth, do my hair, put on a dab of makeup, and eat a bowl of cereal if I had time. For a single person with no kids, I *should* have had the morning thing down pat. Nevertheless, I left seven minutes later than I wanted to.

I listened to a compilation of greatest gospel hits as I drove in to work, but my mind was far from the familiar tunes that came across the speakers. Rather, I was consumed in thought about the previous weekend. Since Saturday night, I had been perturbed about this race thing. I could feel myself sliding, albeit minimally—a gradual distancing from . . . my Father. I felt it, much the same way you feel a void when a friend has moved out of town. Perhaps it's not so bad the first day or the second day. But as time goes on, you miss that person, begin to know how much their presence meant to you. I knew then that God meant business about what He'd shown me in Galatians.

I wondered how, if ever, I could see past a white person's skin. *How do you see someone and not see what color they are?* I knew, theoretically and morally, that labeling people was wrong and there was always an exception to the stereotype. I didn't appreciate being stereotyped any more than the next person. But it was a fact—a reality of life in twenty-first-century America. I wasn't as adamant about things as Daddy, but I did believe in Blackness, in unity, and in the power of our solidarity.

An even greater question was whether I *wanted* to start dealing with white people beyond casual and professional acquaintanceships. Miss Jan, my secretary, was okay, and most of the white people on staff were fine. I cared deeply for every student on the campus, regardless of race. Bottom line, I did love everybody. *Don't I?* I mean, I wouldn't kill or hurt someone just because they were white or Hispanic, and I didn't wish anyone any harm.

Still, I knew Father well enough to understand that He wasn't talking about the cordiality that most of the population extends to every other human on the planet. He was after my heart.

"It's just a matter of time, LaShondra," I said to myself, breathing in and then exhaling until I couldn't stand it anymore. I had no idea what I was getting myself into, but experience had shown me that the best thing to do when convicted by the Word is to surrender. "Okay, Father. I submit to Your will."

Well, the devil always gets extra busy when you start breaking down a stronghold. Can I get a witness? He met me bright and early when I walked into my office. "Ms.

Smith, the Donovans are waiting for you in your office," Miss Jan forewarned me.

"Why didn't you have them wait out here?" I asked her.

"They insisted on waiting inside," she said with her head down. *Mental note: Miss Jan needs to attend a workshop on assertiveness.*

"Good morning," I said to Mrs. Donovan, and held my hand out to greet both her and Mr. Donovan. Neither of them shook my hand. *How rude.* Mrs. Donovan sat upright in her chair, legs crossed at the knee, exposing her six-inch heels in their entirety. Mr. Donovan was stony in his dark suit and personalized cuff links. She had a little too much bosom to be natural, and his hairline was unnaturally advanced—both evidence of how money can retard the aging process.

I put my things down and sat behind my desk. The details of Katelyn Donovan's issue were still fresh in my mind: state law mandated that if a student failed a course for the six weeks, he or she was ineligible to participate in any extracurricular activities.

Mr. Donovan started on his spiel about poor Katelyn and how she'd really learned her lesson and didn't need to be suspended from extracurricular activities. When he seemed to be at a stopping point, I told him blankly, "Mr. Donovan, when I spoke with your wife last week, I explained to her that our state does not allow for a student to turn in late work beyond the end of a six-weeks period unless there are extenuating circumstances such as illness or a need to travel out of town for a funeral—things of that nature."

"I'm asking you to make an exception for Katelyn," he said with no hesitation.

"On what basis?" I asked.

"On the basis that I'm telling you to," he said. His jaw flinched, and his lips pulled in tighter.

My neck must have done a flip, because all of a sudden Mr. Donovan looked as if he was sideways to me. "Excuse me?"

"Miss Smith," Mrs. Donovan added, "we are very well connected people within this school district and this city. If you value your professional reputation and your paycheck, it would be in your best interest to allow Katelyn to continue to practice and compete. I can assure you that she will make up any work or do whatever she needs to do to bring up her failing grade. We're not asking you to let her off the hook with no repercussions—she *will* make up the work."

"It's too late to make up the work. The grading period is over," I told her without the least bit of fear or trembling in my voice. "And I will not be threatened into defying the orders of the state of Texas."

"You would do it for a black kid, wouldn't you?" Mr. Donovan asked me.

"I'm afraid this meeting is over." I stood up.

"Not quite." Mr. Donovan remained in his seat. "Chauncey Sarrington, in Ms. Ashton's class. You made Ms. Ashton change Chauncey's grade. Those were her very words. You *do* have the power, Ms. Smith."

"I do not have to answer to you for the actions that I take as an administrator." My hand flew to my hip, and my neck was working. "Mr. and Mrs. Donovan, I'm going to have to ask you to leave my office."

Mr. Donovan stood and stormed past me, saying something to the effect that he would be getting with the principal and the school board. His face was red, and his jowls shook as he ground his feet into the floor with every step.

Mrs. Donovan stayed a few steps behind and pleaded with me when her husband was out of earshot: "Miss Smith, for God's sake, just do what he says. There's a lot more at stake than you know. He can ruin you." I felt almost sorry for her. She really thought her husband had power over people's entire lives.

Then I held my head up high, did one of those white-girl hair flips, and told her, with every intent to chase that spirit of fear right out of my room, "Mrs. Donovan, your husband does not possess the power to make me or to break me."

Mrs. Donovan left without saying another word.

After I'd closed the door, I heard myself say, "Ooh, these white folks ain't got the sense God gave a fly." I was fuming mad. *Who does he think he is, comin' up in my office tryin' to intimidate me with his money and influence? He is messin' with the wrong black woman!* This situation had politics written all over it, and I was no stranger to the ins and outs of the game. I needed to have my behind covered both spiritually and professionally.

I calmed myself by pacing the room a bit and then watering my plants. I had been enamored of that office when I first moved in: cherry wood desk and shelves, leather chair with antique gold tacks in diagonal rows across the back. All the things that make an office an office. I'd done my best to make it serene by bringing in the plants, miniature waterfall, and crystal figurines. But none of that was working. The job was stressful, and I was feeling every ounce of it.

My plate had quickly filled itself. I took a seat at my desk and documented the meeting right away, then printed a hard copy of my notes for my records. Next I thumbed through the master schedule to find out when little Ms. Ashton would have her conference period. We needed to have a talk. Afterward, I quickly checked with Miss Jan about the arrangements for career day. She informed me that everything was set—except the engineer.

"What happened?"

"She canceled. That's one of the messages I put on your desk."

"Okay. See if you can schedule another engineer so the people in the math and science departments don't feel underrepresented at the job fair."

"Which firm?"

"I don't care."

"I mean, I thought we were trying to achieve a certain number of . . . well, I thought we were going for diversity." She said it like it was a score.

"Right now I don't care who you call, Miss Jan. Just pick the first one in the phone book."

I closed the door to my office and made a call to my building principal's private cellular phone. He was out of the building this morning, but I knew he always kept his cell turned on. "Mr. Butler, this is Miss Smith. I need to speak with you about a situation involving a student who failed a class and isn't able to participate in sports."

"Is it the Donovan girl?" he asked.

"Yes, as a matter of fact it is."

"Donovan called me just a few minutes ago. You and I will need to sit down and discuss the circumstances of the situation this afternoon." He rushed me off the phone.

"Okay," I agreed. "I'll see you then."

I knew then that they were on the same side.

"Ms. Smith?" Miss Jan poked her head into the door. "I've got the engineer on the phone."

Why can't she schedule this on her own? "Okay," I told her. "Go ahead and transfer the call."

"Hello, this is Miss Smith," I said in my most professional tone, trying with all my might to hold back any hint of annoyance.

"Hi, Miss Smith, this is Stelson Brown." Okay, this was a man with a super-dee-duper deep voice, but I couldn't quite catch the race by his diction or voice quality. "Your secretary tells me that you're in need of an engineer to present on Thursday?"

"Yes, we are." I lowered my voice an octave, hoping that he'd pick up on my blackness and then, perhaps, feed me a phrase or two to let me know that he was a brother. "We're having a career fair, and we're looking for presenters in the fields of math and science. I know it's rather short notice, but if you could spare a few hours Thursday morning, we would greatly appreciate it."

"Certainly," he said cheerfully. "I'd be honored. Will you have a booth prepared, or will I need to bring my own kiosk?"

"We'll have a booth ready for you," I said. "All you need to do is bring a few brochures, flyers, and perhaps a model to display. Other than that, just be ready to answer students' questions about your field as they come by."

"Sounds great," he said. I could tell that he was smiling, but I still couldn't pick up on his ethnicity. "What time should I be there?"

"You can probably start setting up at around seven-thirty. We'll be closing off the exhibit at noon."

"Okay, I guess that's everything I need to know," he said.

"Oh," I said, "I need the name of the firm that you represent, so that I can put it on the bulletin."

"It's Brown-Cooper Engineering."

"Brown-Cooper Engineering," I repeated as I wrote it down. *Was that Brown, as in Stelson Brown?* "Okay, Mr. Brown. Thanks so much for being such a willing participant."

"Thanks for having me," he said. "I look forward to meeting you, Miss Smith."

Not a hint. Mr. Brown would have to wait until Thursday.

Ms. Ashton came to my office at 10:30, as I'd requested.

She pranced in there with her teacher clothes on (denim jumper with rulers, apples, numbers, and the alphabet embroidered across the bodice). She crossed her ankles and her arms to go along with her cross attitude. For a first-year teacher, she sure had a lot of nerve coming up in my office like she had her act together.

"Ms. Ashton, I'd like to speak with you about a serious matter that has recently come to my attention." I weighed my words carefully as she sat across from me, her eyelashes fluttering. "I was speaking with a parent, and that parent repeated some very confidential information about a student who was not his child."

She shook her head, and her face remained expressionless as she lied through her teeth. "I don't know what you're talking about." Her jaw tightened.

"Ms. Ashton, let me just get to the point here." I put my pen down. "The Donovans came in this morning to speak with me about Katelyn's failing grade. In the process, Mr. Donovan let me know that you discussed Chauncey Sarrington's situation with him. You are aware that student confidentiality is paramount."

"I was just stating the facts. I let him know that apparently grades can be changed under certain circumstances for certain people." She shrugged, with her nose still in the air.

"Ms. Ashton, I thought we were clear on why I advised you to change Chauncey's grade." I ran down the list to refresh her failing memory. "First of all, Chauncey is a special education student, and you made no effort to make the modifications that he needed. Secondly, you only took seven grades the whole six weeks, while district policy states that teachers must record a minimum of twelve grades to average in a six-week period. You made no effort to contact Chauncey's parents and let them know that he was performing unsuccessfully when it was apparent early on, according to your own calculations, that Chauncey was failing.

"And, for the record, I did not instruct you to change Chauncey's grade. I *advised* you to do so. Now, off the record, Ms. Ashton, I made that recommendation to you to save *your* face, not Chauncey's. Had you gone before the special education committee with your shoddy documentation, they would have eaten you for lunch, and they would have had a nice little note put in your personnel file. Did you tell the Donovans all *that*?"

She let out a loud, airy breath and checked her watch. "I've got a parent conference in five minutes."

"Ms. Ashton," I said calmly, "every student has the legal right to privacy. This is not what we expect of our teachers here at Plainview Middle School."

She cut me off. "So what are you saying? Are you going to report this to somebody, or something?"

I took a deep breath. "I have to find out what is customarily done in circumstances such as these."

"Uh . . ." She had that gag-me-with-a-spoon, Valley-girl look on her face. "This is not that big a deal."

"The Donovans seemed to think so." I gave her the look that cashiers give when they tell a customer that the card has been declined, complete with my closed lips rolled in between my teeth and my head cocked to the side. "They're ready to use this confidential information to pursue their daughter's case. If this quest gets very far, the source of their information—you—will inevitably be uncovered. And if I don't reprimand you now, who knows? The school board may do so when they begin their investigation."

I stopped for a moment and read her. She'd gotten the message, and she was afraid. She unfolded her arms and threw them helplessly over the sides of the chair. "You didn't think about all of this, did you, Ms. Ashton?"

"It's not like I meant to tell them," she said, "I was just angry about what happened with Chauncey, and . . . I don't know what made me tell them all of that. Katelyn's not even in my class, but for some reason Mr. Butler sent them to talk to me—"

"Mr. Butler told you to talk to them?"

It suddenly occurred to me that she was being used in all this.

"Yes, Miss Smith." She looked around the room for a second and then established eye contact. "It was weird. Mr. Donovan came up to me and said something like 'I understand that you know how a person's grade can get changed around here,' and I told them about Chauncey and what happened with his grade."

The light went on in her head. "Oh, my God. How could I have been so stupid?"

For the record, I could neither deny nor confirm her suspicion. She balled one of her fists and used the other hand to grab the paperwork that she'd brought in with her. "Don't worry, Miss Smith. This kind of thing won't happen again." She averted her eyes and dismissed herself from the office.

When Mr. Butler returned to the building, his secretary called me, and I went to his office. His shelves were lined with paraphernalia boasting of his golfing and sporting achievements. Nothing recent to show, however. I sat down and listened as he explained that the Donovans were planning to take the issue before the associate superintendent.

"Exactly what grounds do they have to press this issue?" I asked him. "I thought we were all clear on the no-pass, no-play laws."

"Well, uh . . ." Mr. Butler sat back in his chair, crossed one leg over his knee, and brought one hand to his chin. "The Donovans are going to pursue it because you, being the seventh-grade principal, have a history of making exceptions for black students."

I needed more from him. "Go on."

"Actually, Miss Smith, several incidences have been brought to my attention. I've been meaning to talk with you about this myself." He reached into his top desk drawer and pulled out several files. "This one here, James Woodall, an African-American student. He was sent to your office for not bringing in homework. You sent him on to his next class and called the teacher in on it. Then this one here, Shaniqua Adams, also African-American. Mr. Frazier sent her to you after she had an argument with another student. You only assigned her to two days' after-school detention. And there are many more. Shall I go on?"

"Mr. Butler, both of those students' situations were handled successfully. James's parents were notified of his lack of homework, and that student hasn't missed an assignment since. And, in addition to assigning detention to Shaniqua, I utilized our peer mediation program to help her learn the skills she needs to talk through her problems both now and in the future. Mr. Frazier hasn't had any more problems with her. I fail to see how either of those situations, as successful as they were, relates to Katelyn Donovan's situation."

"We're starting to see a pattern, Miss Smith." He nodded, his eyes darting to avoid mine. "These are not random incidents here."

"Exactly what *is* that pattern as you see it, Mr. Butler?"

"Seventy percent of the African-American students who come through your office are given rather lenient punishments, while the white students who come before you are not treated as favorably." He opened up another manila file folder.

"This student here, Ashley Taylor, white. She was sent to

your office, and you suspended her for three days." He quickly closed the folder.

"She stole money from her teacher's desk, Mr. Butler."

"Like I said," he breezed past my point and cleared his throat, "this is a pattern."

"Mr. Butler, has it ever occurred to you that while our student body is less than fifty percent African-American, black students make up over three-fourths of the referrals that come across my desk? *That's* the pattern we need to be looking into."

"Miss Smith," he said, "I have talked to several seventh-grade teachers who feel that they can't trust you to back them with discipline. Your actions are creating a serious gap between you and those teams of teachers."

"I will go to the wall for any teacher who has done all that he or she can do to help a student be successful. Ask Mrs. Holloway. Ask Mr. Levian or Miss Gallahan. I have gone through the fire for them all recently. But my loyalty to the teachers does not override a student's right to be treated equitably. That includes Katelyn Donovan. What kind of message are you all trying to send her—that her father's money can buy her out of any situation? That grades and teachers and administrators are for sale?"

He turned his head sharply, eyes widened. I watched his face turn from pink to white. "Miss Smith, you are out of line."

I didn't say anything. He was waiting for me to go off, I think, but I didn't. The silence was very uneasy, but I withstood it, waiting for his next words. He thrust his hands into his pockets. I watched him pace twice before his color returned. He sat down at his desk and faced me head-on.

"If you don't instruct Mr. Miller to change Katelyn's grade, I will. And if you have anything to say to the contrary, I will launch an investigation into your administrative practices here." His last sentence came out slowly, one syllable at a time. "I can make things happen or not happen."

The look on his face said *get out of here,* so I did.

After lunch, it was my turn to go to the administration office for a meeting. I had time to sit down and crunch numbers with my colleagues. The results of the preliminary data showed that our school's standardized test scores were looking good. We would only be rated 'Acceptable' by the Texas Education Agency, but there was some improvement, and I was glad that I'd have good tidings to relay to the staff. Mr. Butler usually left that responsibility to me.

I went back to the campus to close out the day. "How did the meeting go?" Miss Jan asked me.

"Oh, it was fine," I told her. "Our scores are looking pretty good."

"That's great news," she said, handing me yet another student referral that I'd have to deal with first thing in the morning.

Peaches called me at around five o'clock. "Hey, girl," she said.

"Hey, what's up?"

"Nothin'," she said. "I was just calling to see how your day at school went."

"Crazy as usual," I laughed as I turned down the volume on my television. "How about yours?"

"Girl, I'm just on white-folks overload right about now," she laughed. "Tired of smilin' and chirpin' and laughin' at stupid jokes and observations."

"And you want me to come work with you?"

"They can't be any worse than the white folks at your job," Peaches remarked.

"I hear you."

"You want to go running tonight?" she asked.

"Girl, please. You know I don't run. I might *walk* with you."

"I'll meet you at the track in half an hour."

My poor little athletic shoes were longing to be worn. Exercise was not high on my list of priorities. I knew, however, that I needed to get into some kind of routine to preserve my body. The best things I did for my body on a regular basis were to get my checkups and take a women's daily vitamin. Every so often, Peaches got onto me about exercise. I was thankful for her perspective on health. Because she had made a change in her diet and exercise, it affected what we ate when we were together. That alone probably added another ten years to my life.

Peaches pulled up in her Mercedes and waved as she got out. Her short, cropped haircut was perfect for the active lifestyle she led. Dressed in Nike from her hooded fleece to her cross-training shoes, she looked like an advertisement.

Eric ran straight to me and gave me a big hug. "Hi, Auntie Shon."

"Hey! You almost knocked me over, man." I took a few steps back, exaggerating his strength. He looked up, laughing, and then ran to the playground within view of the track.

Peaches started stretching, and I followed suit. She looked as if she were releasing the weight of the world as she inhaled and exhaled slowly to the silent count of eight. I let her lead me in the counts and the movements. Then she pushed a button on her stopwatch, and we took off walking.

"So what happened today?" I asked her.

"My team and I had to work up a settlement package to sever an employment contract due to embezzlement," she said. "The kind of stuff a black man would have gone to jail over."

"Why would you need to offer a settlement package for an employee who was stealing?" I asked.

"The company would have spent twice as much in attorney's fees and court costs if he hadn't accepted our offer to leave uneventfully. It's white-folks'-world stuff. Happens every day. What's new with you?"

I filled her in on the latest details with the Donovans. "What do you think I should do?"

"Write her up," Peaches said with a straight face, puffing air between strides. I gave her a puzzled look. "Trust me—write it up, leave it in her file for however long you have to leave it in there, and then discard it when it expires. If she does it again, you'll have a paper trail of her patterns, and a leg to stand on when you get ready to fire her. If she doesn't, there'll be no additional harm done. Furthermore, she won't be able to say that you knew she had this problem but didn't inform her that it was inappropriate."

"Do you think it's that serious?" I asked Peaches. "That I could end up in court behind it?"

"Pulleaze! Girl, people go to court every day wishing they'd documented their evidence more carefully. If I were you, I'd get in touch with one of those union attorneys and cover your behind completely."

The thought of having to call an attorney for legal defense frightened me. I'd never needed to call an attorney before. The only time I'd ever really mention the word "attorney" was when someone was joking about whiplash. I guess I always figured that if I did the right thing, I would never need counsel to defend me.

"You ready to jog now?" Peaches asked.

"You go ahead. I'm gonna walk today." I was already panting from trying to keep up with her warm-up. She went ahead of me, her hood flapping in the breeze produced by her speed. Her "jogging" always looked like running to me.

After talking with Peaches, I knew I had a lot to do. *Call the union. Write up Ms. Ashton. Pray.*

CHAPTER 7

Peaches sat on the floor, and I sat behind her on my bed, brushing, pulling, and pinning her hair into a French roll. The style was far too elevated for my taste, but Peaches liked her French rolls as high as I could possibly get them. She said the higher it was, the skinnier she looked.

In a minute she'd take her turn behind me, sitting on the polish-stained bedspread beneath my poster of Michael Jackson. I liked my hair set with mousse so that my curls would dry quickly and I wouldn't have to sleep with all that hard plastic in my head.

"Hold your head down," I told her.

"Look—here's an article about finding the right kind of guy for you," she said as she thumbed through the pages of a Young Miss *magazine.*

"Find something else," I mumbled through the bobby pins I'd carefully placed between my lips. I pulled one from my mouth and placed it at the base of the French roll, shoving it in as far as it would go.

"Here's one about that guy in that movie Risky Business,*" she said.*

"Tom Cruise?" I asked, peeking past her shoulder.

"Yeah. Says that he is the number one heartthrob according to last month's poll," she summarized. "You want me to read it to you out loud?"

"Naw, he ain't cute to me." I realigned myself with her head and continued my work. "I think he's kind of skinny, too."

"Hmm. Let me see . . ." Peaches sized him up, turning his centerfold picture vertically. "I don't think he's ugly."

"He looks like he needs a haircut every time I see him on TV," I said. "I don't see what all those white girls see in him. Then again, white people are always sayin' somebody is cute when they look just as plain-Jane as the rest of 'em."

"Yeah, you're right about that. To me, the only time a white person is really cute is when they've got somethin' else mixed in 'em," Peaches observed. "Otherwise, they're just white with that do-nothin' hair that they're always tryin' to tease so it'll stand up like ours."

I agreed, putting the last pin in place.

◘ ◘ ◘

I spent hump day in team meetings, listening to a variety of teacher concerns from problems in the cafeteria to curriculum issues. I took note of their concerns and put them on my lists of things to investigate, do, or delegate. I closed each meeting with the good news about our test scores and with reminding them about the next day's career fair. I got moans and groans when I asked the teachers who were off during the morning to drop by and monitor for just a few minutes during the exhibit.

Eighth grade was receptive to me, but I could tell that something was going on with seventh grade. Especially with Ms. Ashton's academic team, the Pacers. They didn't give me the courtesy of letting me know that they had changed their meeting place, so I ran around the building for a good twenty minutes looking for them. Then they scheduled a parent conference for the second half of the period, and the team secretary claimed to have misplaced the agenda that I e-mailed them the previous week.

I couldn't put my finger on which of them was the ringleader, but they were all in on this display of group unprofessionalism—griping about their duties, complaining about this and that, but offering no alternatives to solve problems. I explained to them that it was okay to complain about a problem, but it was also incumbent upon the complainer to suggest a solution.

"Isn't that your job?" Mr. Baudin, a language arts teacher, asked.

"That job belongs to all of us. We're a team," I answered slowly.

After I met with them and their nasty attitudes, I was just about ready to call Peaches and tell her that I was ready to come to Northcomp because I was fed up with being a vice principal. I went in every morning trying to do my best, but it was never good enough. For as much as I got done, it seemed there was twice as much left on my to-do list by five o'clock. Bottom line, I was frustrated and I wanted to quit that morning.

You know how it is sometimes? Sometimes one little thing can make you just want to run off to Mexico, build a hut, and set up a jumping-bean store—anything to get away. You just get sick of it all.

When I got back to my office, I slammed the inner door and prayed at my desk. The enemy was getting on my last nerve, and the week wasn't nearly over. I needed strength. And even before I was finished praying, I heard the words of an old Clark Sisters song, "Count It All Joy." I laughed at myself as I stood again. I knew that someday I would look back on all of it and be able to see what was happening and why the Lord had put me on a staff that needed so much work (myself included). I couldn't think of a trial to date that hadn't worked to my advantage in the end, and I knew that working here at this school, even with Mr. Butler, would be manipulated for my benefit.

When I got home from work, I found a package on my doorstep. It was from Jonathan. I grabbed the box and unlocked the door. An all-too-familiar smell assaulted my nostrils as I realized that I'd forgotten to take the trash out again. I set the bags back into the garage. They'd have to wait there until Monday. I could almost hear Daddy in my ear: "See, if you had a man, you wouldn't have to worry about that."

I ripped the box open, knowing that there would be some thoughtful gift enclosed. Jonathan had a knack for finding just the right things to give. I tore through the paper with no regard for the beautiful print. He hadn't let me down.

"Oh!" I put my hand before my lips and gasped. It was an old picture of Jonathan and me outside, leaning over the balcony, when we used to live in the old apartment. It was blown up, framed in antique gold, and the frame was engraved:

To My Big Sister,
LaShondra
I'll Always Look Up To You
God Bless,
Jonathan

He'd attached a sticky note on the back of it:

I found it while going through some old stuff. Hope you like it!

My hand fell on the bed as I revisited the picture. It had been probably twenty years since I'd seen it. Jonathan, with his chubby stomach hanging out of the bottom of his shirt, pants too tight, button screaming to be loosened. Then me, with untamed pigtails, snaggleteeth, and ashy knees. I remembered that day at the old apartment complex clearly. We'd been playing outside in the sandbox when Daddy came out to call us up for dinner. We'd just gotten the new camera. There had been a big fight about it only moments before.

"Daddy," Jonathan asked, "can you take a picture of me and Shondra?"

"We don't have to take pictures every five minutes," Daddy bickered.

"Well, what you think we got a camera for, Jon?" Momma stopped washing dishes and asked.

"For important stuff."

"What's more important than our kids?" she asked.

"Nothin'. Just, we don't have to act like we've never had anything every time we get somethin' new," he said, shaking his head.

Daddy had told us to go on outside and he'd take a picture of us later. We were thrilled when Daddy came to the apartment's playground to get us. "Is it time for the picture yet?" I begged to know.

"Go on upstairs," he said softly, with a hint of mischief in his tone. I knew he was stalling.

Jonathan and I got all the way to the second floor when he called, "Hey, look down!" He pulled the camera from behind his back.

We ran to the balcony, linked arms, and smiled as Daddy snapped the shot. This shot that I hadn't seen or thought about in so long.

I called Jonathan later that afternoon. "Hey, Jonathan, it's me. Thanks for the picture! That took me wa-a-ay back."

"Yes, I know," he laughed. "I forgot how chubby I used to be. So, what are your plans for your birthday?"

"Nothing, really. I think I'll just relax, you know?" I lay back on my sofa and let my head rest on the pillows.

"That sounds good. So, no man, huh?"

My neck tightened. "You sound just like Daddy."

"Yes, I know. I talked to him the other day. He's been on my case, too. Says I should have settled down by now. I told him I could settle down if he didn't mind me doing so with a German woman."

"Ha!" I screamed. "What'd he say?"

"He said he'd give me some extra time since there aren't as many black women out here."

"How fortunate for you," I teased him. "It must be nice to have your harassment postponed. It's getting so bad that I almost don't want to go over to eat with them on Sundays."

"I'd trade places with you in a minute for a piece of Daddy's fried chicken," Jonathan offered.

"I can't argue with you on that one." I smiled. "Hey, when are you gonna come home?"

"Maybe in the summer—July," he said. His speech was so standardized now, no hint of the southern drawl. "So, what else is up?"

I thought of telling him about the mess at my school, but decided not to burden him with something that I wasn't sure would amount to anything. "Same old same-old. Working, going to church. What about you?"

"Well, actually, I've been doing a lot of reading and thinking and praying. I'm debating on whether or not to reenlist after this term. Maybe Daddy's lectures are getting to me." He gave a troubled laugh.

"But I thought you really enjoyed the military."

"I do. It's just that—I think it's time for me to move on. This experience has taught me a lot, and I think it's time that I took this knowledge and applied it in some other field. Maybe teaching."

"Are you serious?" I envisioned my little brother dressed in slacks, dress shirt, and tie, standing in front of a classroom full of little black faces, filling them with knowledge and hope. I was proud already.

"Yes. But I'm still praying on it."

"You'd make a great teacher. And black boys need role models and structure like nobody's business," I encouraged him.

"Well, that's just the thing," Jonathan said. "It's a black thing, and then it isn't. I know that black boys need to see black men doing things. But by the same token, people need to help people regardless of race, you know? It's not nearly as much about color as I once believed. At least that's what I've learned in the military."

Okay, I'm cool with the whole humanitarian thing. But the fact still remained, in my book: black men needed to be in classrooms primarily for black reasons. *Jonathan ain't thinking black and white, because he ain't in America.* "Well, I do hope that you give it considerable time and prayer. We could definitely use you in our field."

"Thanks. I'll keep that in mind."

"Well, speaking of the field of education, I've gotta go. It's Wednesday night—that means tutoring at True Way. It'll be a madhouse, but I'm enjoying it."

We ended our conversation with love and promises to talk again soon.

True to my prediction, I was completely swamped at Wednesday night tutorials. We were nearing the end of the three-week grading period, so kids came from miles around to get help. I was almost sweating from the immense pressure and the physical demand of buzzing around the crowded room. At one point, some of the kids became so frustrated with having to wait to ask specific questions that I had to tell them to come back after the service and I'd help them when church was over. I ended up staying another half hour, working with the kids whose parents were willing to let them stay late and get the extra help.

The last student, Reshawn, asked me to pray with her because there was a very good chance she'd end up in summer school if she didn't pass her next test. Reshawn, her father, and I prayed, touching hands and agreeing that Reshawn would be successful through Christ. They also prayed for me, that the Lord would send me help with Wednesday night tutoring.

I went home and rejoiced. *Thank you in advance for the help, Lord.*

Thursday morning I rose a little earlier due to the career fair. I put on my best red pantsuit and took time to apply my makeup neatly. Days like these, when our campus had visitors, I felt as if I was on display. I had to represent on so many levels: women, African-Americans, the best that the field of education had to offer. By the same token, it was also my time to shine and to proclaim to the world: "I'm a black woman thriving in a white man's world. How you like me now?"

I was pleased to find the kiosks already set up when I got to work. Miss Jan had directed most of the representatives to their slotted spaces just beyond the foyer. Some of the presenters were already networking, exchanging cards and talking over coffee. The students weren't in the building yet, but there was already an electricity in the air.

I wasn't running late, but everyone else seemed to be running early. I overheard Miss Jan talking to one of the teachers, Miss Gallahan, about one of the presenters.

"Did you get a look at him?"

"Yes," Miss Jan cooed, "he certainly is good-looking."

"If I had known that we were going to have centerfolds here, I would have worn my blue dress," Miss Gallahan laughed.

"Good morning, Ms. Smith." Miss Jan finally noticed me looking at the papers in my In box, only a few feet away. She handed me a name tag to stick on myself so that the visitors could easily identify me.

"Hi, Miss Gallahan. What's all this talk about a handsome man?" I asked casually.

"That engineer from Brown-Cooper. He's a dream. Dark brown hair, blue eyes, and the body of a god. Absolutely gorgeous." She smiled. Her flaming red hair framed her face in perfect little innocent ringlets.

"Well, what are you doing in here? It's your conference period—get out there and go learn about the wonderful world of mechanical engineering," I teased her.

She blew a puff of air that made the ringlet on her forehead flutter. "Like he'd really want *me*."

"Don't knock yourself." I shook my head. "There is no reason on earth why he wouldn't want *you*." I truly didn't see anything wrong with Miss Gallahan. She was just as cute as the next white woman in line. And it turned out that there were several. The women's restroom looked like backstage at a cheerleaders' competition: hairspray clouding up the room, perfume clashing, and not an inch to spare in the mirror. I said a quick "Good morning" and then rushed into an empty stall. A few of them joked about all the eligible men present in the building, but the engineer was obviously the catch of the day.

"He is so gorgeous," I heard one of them say. "I could drink his bathwater." The other teachers in the restroom laughed with playful shock.

"He's probably gay," someone said. "Men *that* gorgeous are *always* gay."

See, Lord, this is why I don't get involved with white women. All this "oh-my-gaw!" It never failed—every time I tried to sit down and have a heart-to-heart with a white woman, I could not relate. The stuff that happens to us every day is just life-altering for them. So your husband got a ticket? So your son didn't get into the college of his dreams? So you didn't get the mortgage? And? Life goes on—but not to them. They think everything is supposed to be handed to them on a silver platter. Maybe because it usually is; who knows? This business of a whole bunch of 'em crowded up around a mirror to meet one man is just another example of the kind of stuff I can't get involved with.

I left the restroom, striding confidently into the main foyer of the building. One foot in front of the other, shoulders thrown back like a runway model. My shoes hit the floor with the distinctive pattern of a woman taking sure steps: no dragging of the heels, no short skips. There was too much at stake.

It didn't take long before I saw this man that they were all making such a big fuss about. As he busily rearranged the brochures at his table, I noticed that there was a picture of him clasping hands with an older black man. He *was* the Brown of Brown-Cooper Engineering. It was Cooper who was black.

As I got closer to the Brown-Cooper display, I found myself giving this man his props. Okay, he was up there with the best of the white men. He was action-movie fine. Muscles, nice tan, wavy hair. *He aiight.* Then I got a whiff of his cologne. Okay, I had to give it to him—he had it going on, for a white man. To my surprise, I felt my stomach tighten.

"Miss Smith?" he asked, extending his hand.

"Yes," I said, shaking his smooth hand. *Never worked a hard day in his thirty-something years.*

"I'm Stelson Brown. We talked the other day. It's nice to finally meet you," he said.

"Same here," I said before he released my hand. "Looks like you're just about finished setting up. Is there anything I can do to help?"

"Oh, no, thanks." He smiled again. My eyes caught the little tattoo on his upper arm. A small blue lion with a banner underneath bearing the initials *S.A.B. What kind of mess is that?* I didn't want him to know that I was looking at it, so I willed myself to stop staring and start talking.

"Well," I continued, trying to remain strictly professional, "the students should be down to visit the exhibits in about another ten minutes. Be sure to let either myself or Miss Jan, my secretary, know if you need anything."

"Thank you, Miss Smith," he answered. "I'll be sure to do that."

I moseyed on down the aisle of vendors and continued greeting the businessmen and women who were setting up their kiosks and booths. The displays and handouts were colorful and intriguing, sure to keep the interest of the students—though none of the other representatives were as cordial as Mr. Brown.

Later in the morning, Miss Gallahan came to the exhibit with her class. "See what I mean?" she asked, referring to Mr. Brown.

"You were right." I played it down. "He is attractive."

She whispered, "Look at how everyone is just throwing themselves at him." Though the students were busy visiting every booth and stocking up on freebies, most of the teachers were clustered at or near Brown-Cooper. Fresh makeup, hair released from ponytail holders and clips. It was ridiculous. I would have been embarrassed, except for the fact that Mr. Brown was so wrapped up in talking to the kids that he wasn't paying much attention to his admirers. I got the feeling that he was used to women flocking around him. Maybe it was in the way he smiled at the teachers casually but engaged himself in meaningful conversation with the students. I was impressed with the way he handled himself.

At a quarter till twelve, the exhibit was officially over. Presenters packed their materials as the cafeteria lunch shifts began. I returned to my office to call personnel regarding a long-term substitute for a teacher who would soon be out on maternity leave.

Just as I was about to make the call, my phone rang once, and then I heard Miss Jan's voice through my phone's speaker. "Miss Smith, Mr. Brown would like to have a word with you."

"Oh, okay. Send him in."

He knocked politely as he entered. "Hello."

"Well, how did it go?" I looked up from my paperwork, tapping my pen on my desk.

"It was great," he said, "I really enjoyed myself with these kids, and I owe it all to you. I'd like to take you to lunch."

I stopped tapping my pen. "I'm sorry?"

"I'm asking you out to lunch."

Did this white man just ask me out to lunch? "Um. Oh."

"I mean, if it's okay." He waited for my answer, shifting his weight from one side to the other.

My first thought was to turn him down and let this little white man go on his merry way. I might even let him down easy—tell him that I'll take a rain check. But something caught my eye in the window just beyond him. There, in a little huddle, was a small congregation of white women "casually" waiting near the exit doors for their handsome Mr. Brown to walk by in hopes that one of them might actually get to talk to him personally. Even Ms. Ashton had herself out there on display.

And then it hit me—this was the chance of a lifetime. I had the opportunity, for once, to show white women what it feels like to have one of your most eligible bachelors snatched off the market right before your very eyes. Then maybe they'd tell two friends. And so on and so on and so on, until *we* got *our* men back. Well, that was a long shot, but it would certainly feel good.

A stealthy grin spread across my face. "I'd love to, Mr. Brown."

You couldn't beat me slinging my coat on to walk out that door with him. "Miss Jan, Mr. Brown and I are going out to lunch."

Her mouth dropped. "Okay. Okay. Okay."

The look on her face was priceless. We waltzed past her and on to the main entrance, where Mr. Brown's newly formed fan club was all smiles until they saw me by his side. My long, proud strides made my hair bounce up and down like somebody on a shampoo commercial. The whole scene went by in slow motion. Elation at his presence. Confusion at mine. Disappointment that Mr. Brown was obviously in my company.

"Thanks for inviting me to lunch, Mr. Brown. I'm starved," I said aloud.

Mr. Brown, oblivious to the drama going on around him, replied, "You're welcome. And please—call me Stelson."

I turned my head just in time to give Ms. Ashton a mouthful of smiling teeth. Unfortunately, that smile also extended to Miss Gallahan. I did feel a little sorry for her—she was a nice woman who was on the lookout for a decent white man. Earlier that morning, I'd encouraged her to approach Mr. Brown, and here I was leaving the building with him. But it didn't really matter—I didn't want him. She could have him back later.

"Oh, you can call me LaShondra," I said casually. Once outside the building, I suggested that we go in separate cars so that he could get back to his business before too long.

"That's fine," he agreed. "I'll follow you."

I hopped into my Honda and waited for him to pull up behind me near the exit. Stelson followed me in a white

Ford pickup bearing his company's logo, and we were on our way to Chester's Bar and Grill.

At the restaurant, the lunch crowd was in full swing, and we were told that we'd have to wait a few minutes to be seated. Stelson gestured toward an empty bench, and we sat waiting for our table. Having already achieved the desired effect I wanted with the teachers on campus, my business with Stelson was officially over as far as I was concerned. Okay, I knew it was wrong to use him in my vengeful plot against white women. *Forgive me, Lord.*

An older white man with white hair and a ranch-style mustache came into the restaurant next and put his name on the waiting list. "Dunley," I heard him say. He took off his hat, revealing a bald crown with a few lonesome strands of hair combed over the otherwise smooth dome. Then he looked around for a place to sit. He approached the bench where Stelson and I were seated, and commenced squeezing in between us.

"Excuse me." Stelson stopped him. "We're here together."

"Oh, I'm sorry." The man hopped up and apologized again. "I just assumed . . ."

Stelson took in a deep breath and seemed to be daring the man to say *one thing* out of line. "You're welcome to sit *beside* us." Stelson slid close to me and offered the empty space created by our close quarters. But the man refused, still offering his apologies. He found a corner and stood.

"Brown," one of the waitresses called.

On the way to our table, I felt a sensation in my body that felt like attraction. I was a little upset with my body for betraying me, conjuring up this uncomfortable feeling that would be going absolutely nowhere quick with this white man. I convinced myself that the attraction was universal—a boy-meets-girl thing.

I ordered sweet tea, and Stelson ordered a Coke. We

took the next few minutes to peruse the menu. I knew that menu backward and forward, but I didn't have anything to say to Stelson. When the waitress returned with our drinks, we placed the orders for our food. She took up the menus, and there we were. Me and this white man, Stelson. The incident with "Dunley" was just another reminder that I was in the wrong place with the wrong person.

"So, LaShondra," he began the conversation, "do you enjoy being a principal?"

"Very much so. And you—do you enjoy engineering?"

"Yes, but I think I might have caught the teaching bug today." He laughed.

"Well, if you ever decide to change fields, there will always be a place for you," I assured him.

The women next to us were whispering and glancing our way. The younger woman, a brunette dressed in casual shopping clothes, pointed her pinky finger at Stelson. It was done so carelessly that it was obviously intentional.

"I was so glad you guys called and asked me to be a part of the career fair. I had my secretary reschedule a few appointments so I could make it. The students were great—nothing like what I read about in the papers."

I smiled. "You know, Mr. Brown, it's a well-kept secret that children aren't much different today than when we were children. They just want to have fun. Problem is, most adults have conveniently forgotten what it's like to be a kid."

"It's easy to block the rough years out," he agreed.

A black couple on their way to being seated looked us over twice as they passed. The man, short and chubby with a clean-shaven head and a sharp goatee, looked mostly at me—as if to ask, *why*? And the woman, short and chubby to match, gave me that I-ain't-mad-at-you look.

I placed the red linen napkin across my lap and mentally ran down the rules of etiquette: no elbows on the table, knife at the top of the plate, short fork for the salad. When our food arrived, the waitress was especially careful to avoid eye contact with either of us. *What is her problem?* Come to think of it, I was beginning to wonder, what was *everybody's* problem? Maybe that weird feeling I had wasn't attraction but the judgmental vibes from people staring at me. Either way, I didn't like it and I was ready to leave.

"Do you mind if I say a blessing over the food?" Stelson asked.

I was caught completely off guard. "No. Go ahead." *He offered to pray?*

"Father, we thank You for this food that has been prepared for us. Bless the hands that prepared it, and let it be a blessing unto our bodies. In Your Son Christ Jesus' name, amen."

"Mmm." That escaped from my throat before I could catch it.

"What was that?" he asked.

I bit my lip and then answered honestly. *What have I got to lose?* "I was just thinking, when you prayed, you pray like you know who you're talking to."

"I do," he said without hesitation.

I smiled, pleased to be in the company of someone who wasn't shy about proclaiming his faith. My shoulders relaxed, and that tense feeling in my stomach subsided, though I could still feel the butterflies. It was interesting for once, to eat lunch with another professional who actually blessed his food. If nothing else, he put up a good front. I had no intentions, however, of delving beneath it.

We talked a little more about my job as an administrator and his company's expansion before I looked at my watch and discovered that I was going to be late getting back to the school.

"Oh," I excused myself, "I'm sorry, Stelson, I've really got to go."

"It was really nice talking to you," he said. An ambiguous moment passed, with the clink of dishes and silverware the only noise to be heard. Then he blurted out, "I'd love to see you again."

"Oh . . ." I looked around the room for something to say. "You've got my number?"

"I've got your *office* number," he hinted.

"Okay," I chirped, clutching my purse and standing. *I'm not about to give no white man my personal information so he can come serial-kill me.*

He stood, too. "I'll walk you to your car." We faced each other at the end of our booth. I noticed just then that he was a good five or six inches taller than me.

"Oh, stay," I told him. "You're not finished eating."

"Are you sure you don't want me to walk you to your car?"

"I'm fine," I said, shaking my head. "Go ahead and finish."

"Okay," he relented. He took my hands gently, leaned my way, and then planted an innocent kiss on my cheek. You know, one of those friendly kisses that white people do on TV, the ones that always serve as the precursor for the man to run off with the wife's best friend, that kind of mess. "Thanks again for joining me."

"Good-bye."

"Good-bye, LaShondra."

When I got in the car, I called Miss Jan to let her know that I was on my way back in.

"How did it go?" she asked.

I chose my words carefully. "Just fine."

"Okay . . ." She must have been hoping for more information. "I . . . I guess I'll see you when you get back."

Driving back to school, I thought about the lunch with Stelson. Little things he did flashed through my mind: holding the door open for me, refusing to let Dunley sit between us, praying before we ate, and the respectful way that he treated me. He was very nice. Well, actually, *nice* wasn't the word for it. Anybody can be nice. Stelson was kind. Kindness is something that comes from the inside.

Miss Jan gave me my messages and tried to pick me about the lunch with Stelson. "So, did you have a good time?"

"I had a salad, Miss Jan." I gave her a fake smile and blinked my eyes a few times.

"Okay, okay." Then she asked, "Is he married?"

"I don't know, Miss Jan. We didn't discuss that."

"Everybody wants to know." She followed me into my office.

"It was a lunch, Miss Jan. That's all there was to it. Mr. Brown is very nice; he enjoyed himself with the kids today . . . What else do you want me to say?"

"Was it business or pleasure?"

"Strictly business."

"He didn't look like business when he asked to speak to you personally," she said implyingly.

"Well, I don't know what it was on his part, but it was business on my part. Keep his number so that we can call on him again for next year's career fair.

"Did you get a chance to contact Mr. and Mrs. Shuling about Melissa Shuling's absences?" I changed the subject abruptly.

Truth was, I liked Miss Jan. But there were times when she got on my nerves, always wanting to talk about irrelevant stuff like recipes and gardening secrets. She was always telling me how much she wished her hair was like "ours" because we can do so many things with "our" hair. But when I practically pushed her out of my office that day, I felt a twinge of remorse. In my heart of hearts, I knew that Miss Jan never meant any harm by the things she said. And she only told me about recipes and gardening secrets because that was a part of her life that she was trying to share with me. I opened my office door once again and hung my head out.

"Yes?" she stopped working and asked softly.

"Thanks for setting everything up this morning. The career fair went very smoothly," I said.

"Oh, you're welcome." She beamed.

"And my lunch with Mr. Brown was just fine. He asked to see me again."

"I knew it!"

"But don't get your hopes up. He's not my type."

CHAPTER 8

Someone came up with a plan to celebrate Juneteenth in the community, and the Purity class of Gethsemane Church of God in Christ was called into action. Year after year we marched down Main Street in the hot sun wearing our African colors, with maybe an American flag or two somewhere in the background, celebrating the announcement of slavery's end in Texas. Even Daddy came out to support the annual Juneteenth celebration.

The keynote speaker changed every year, and this particular year it was our pastor's turn to deliver a call to the community: we need more unity and progress.

"Juneteenth," he said, "is a great time of reflection for us as black people and as Christians. It's a time for us to sing both 'Look Where He Brought Me From' and 'We Shall Overcome.' For as much as we have overcome, there is just as much to conquer. But rest assured that by the power of God, we have the victory!"

The crowd spent what little energy we had left and applauded my pastor. At times like these, there was an unmistakable quality about blackness and religion: that somehow, because of the African-Americans' plight, Jesus belonged to us just a little more than to anybody else. We *had been right, and* they *had been wrong, and righteousness ultimately prevailed—as it always did for those who were on the Lord's side.*

I heard those messages, from church and home, and formed a sort of black vs. white, good vs. evil battle in my head. As circumstances and situations ran through my life, they were sure to sift through the black-white filter. My world didn't revolve around it, of course, but it was present, ready to give its interpretation of any issue.

"Thank You, Lord!" I called out. "Thank You for another year!"

It was my birthday, and I felt especially blessed. I made my way to my prayer closet, still making a joyful noise. Once inside, I shut the door and got down on my knees. I praised Him freely, with my arms raised high and tears marking fresh trails down my cheeks. My life flashed before my eyes: the time I almost hit a bus head-on, the fibroid I'd had removed from my uterus, the nights that I should have been at church but I was at the club—all that time I was running from the Lord and He'd still been watching over me. He'd still sent an angel to keep me even when I didn't want to be kept. And He'd completely forgiven me despite all the things I'd willingly done against Him.

"Yes, Lord!" I'd called out. "Yes, Lord! Yet will I serve You, Lord!"

I finally got to a sitting position to read the Word and speak the Scriptures of deliverance that God had given me. I found the next page in a women's devotional that I read weekly. The day's verses were Proverbs 31:26: *She opens her mouth in skillful and Godly wisdom, and on her tongue is the law of kindness.* And Psalms 141:3: *Set a guard over my mouth, O Lord; keep watch over the door of my lips.* It had been a while since I'd read either of those verses, and for some reason they touched me in a different way. I repeated the verses several times, letting them sink into my soul. My heart was full of expectation. The feeling of victory was so tangible I could hardly contain myself. God had been so good to me!

By the time I came out of my prayer closet, I felt as if I'd been to the mountaintop and seen glory with my own eyes. It was at times like those that I didn't care what was going on outside my closet. Satan himself could have been waiting to take my life once I walked out of that room, and I wouldn't have flinched. That would just be all the sooner I could see Jesus face to face. Sometimes I longed for my heavenly home, to be physically present with God and leave the cares of this world behind. Can I get a witness?

I greeted Miss Jan with a big smile: "Good morning."

"Good morning, Miss Smith. How are you today?" She matched my enthusiasm.

"Great!"

I waded through data and documents and students' files and teacher absentee forms that morning. Nothing too stressful, just stuff that I'd saved for a rainy day. Since it was my birthday, I kept my calendar clear. The staff usually did something for me at some point during the day as part of the tradition.

Just after eleven, a small crowd gathered outside my interior window. I peeked through the blinds and saw Mrs. Harmon's gospel chorus assembling along with Mr. Matthews and Mrs. Turner (sixth- and eighth-grade principals) and a few other teachers who were on conference.

"Get away from there!" Miss Jan scolded me. "This is supposed to be a surprise!"

I ran back to my inner office and waited with anticipation.

After the students were assembled, Miss Jan walked into

my office and said with flair, "Ms. Smith, could you please come with me?"

The students were perfectly silent as they waited for the magic moment.

"Surprise!" they screamed. "Happy Birthday, Miss Smith!"

I put my hands up to my mouth and held my breath. "Thank you, guys!" Even though it wasn't a surprise, it still felt good.

They sang Stevie Wonder's version of "Happy Birthday," and I swayed with them, acting as young as they were. It probably wasn't what a vice principal was supposed to do, but I raised my hands in the air and swayed to the music. Mrs. Harmon almost knocked me over with a deliberate whack of her hips. She did it twice before I gave in to her cheerful persuasion and joined her in the bump. All the kids got a big kick out of it. Being in their midst reminded me how much I missed their youthful energy and the direct influence of being a classroom teacher. I hugged several kids and thanked them again for the serenade.

"Girl, you so crazy," Mrs. Harmon said in a whisper. "You know we have absolutely no business out here doin' the bump with all these white people around."

"Please . . ." I waved my hand. "If they haven't seen us dancin' by now, they have other, more pertinent childhood issues that need to be resolved."

Out of the corner of my eye, I saw someone on the second-floor balcony move. It was Mr. Butler. He'd obviously been watching the celebration but hadn't come to participate. Mrs. Harmon saw him, too.

"Don't look now," she said.

"I already saw him," I snickered. "He'll get over it. Nobody said anything when all those teachers got sloppy drunk at his birthday party last year. They did a whole lot more than just the bump!"

"Ooh! You need to quit!" She smiled.

"Thanks for bringing the kids to sing to me," I told her again. "You have really blessed me today."

"Any time, my sister!"

I truly liked Mrs. Harmon. Her natural Afro and earth-tone makeup complemented her down-to-earth, genuinely good attitude. She was dedicated to her work and her students. I never knew that a music teacher could squeeze standardized test material into her curriculum, but she did. I wished that I could spend more time with Mrs. Harmon, but her life was far too busy. She was a newlywed, new to Texas, and they had a brand-new baby. Somehow, she still gave those kids her all. I was glad to have her on our staff.

When we interviewed for new teachers in the spring, I tried to snatch up as many black teachers as possible. Mr. Butler didn't seem too happy about that. Yes, I know I have to try to pick the best person for the job, but when you're hiring new teachers, you don't know who's good and who's not. Grades and certificates don't tell you who can actually convey his or her knowledge while managing the classroom. With the teacher turnover rate as high as it was in our district and across the state, I figured it couldn't do any harm to give a brother or a sister a chance. Maybe I was right; maybe I was wrong—I didn't give it much thought.

I took Miss Jan up on her offer to treat me to Chinese food for lunch. She ordered, and we spent the lunch hour in my office talking about my thirty-first birthday. Though everyone referred to my secretary as "Miss Jan," she had been married for more than twenty years. She was forty-five and didn't look a day over thirty-eight. "I hope I look as good as you when I get forty-five," I often told her. I could be nice to Miss Jan—when I wanted to.

"Well, if it weren't for your business suits, I'd think you

were one of the kids," she said. "You're gonna look great at forty-five."

The residue of my morning worship was still on me, so I made an effort to squeeze in a little casual witnessing during the lunch hour, telling Miss Jan how thankful I was that God had blessed me with such a rich, full life. She sat quietly, smiled, and nodded her head as she always did. Her brown hair was interrupted here and there by strands of gold and red: her highlights caught the glare from the overhead illumination perfectly. The telltale signs of aging were in their infancy: thinning lips, crow's-feet near her eyes. Her slightly tanned skin was just the slightest bit loose on her arms and neck. Were it not for her clothing, I would have given her the thumbs-up for presentation. But the one-piece clown suits and ruffled collars gave her away. Miss Jan was stuck in the eighties from the neck down.

I stuffed my mouth with food, allowing Miss Jan the opportunity to say something.

"Your life is so great," she said, looking down. "You've got everything already, and you're not even forty."

"Hey," I said to her, "your life looks pretty good to me, too. You've got two great teenage girls, your husband adores you, and you only work because you'd be bored at home."

"Well . . ." she smiled, still looking down. "I'd trade places with you in a minute. I mean, my life is more than halfway over, and I really haven't done anything with it, you know? Let me ask you: how did you know what you were supposed to be doing? And how do you get past the fear of failure and just go out and do things? I've seen you do so much stuff here—things that people had been *saying* they were going to do but never got done. You just came in and did it without ever looking back. It's like—you're so amazing."

Her eyes were big with awe, and I knew that she meant

well, but I was a little agitated. What did she think I was *supposed* to be doing? Sitting up somewhere on welfare with five kids and five different babies' daddies? But I wouldn't go there. Instead of telling her what I wasn't, I'd tell her Who is.

"Well," I said, slowly, "the key, Miss Jan, is in a *real* relationship with God. When I gave Him full control, He also assumed full responsibility for me. After all, I am His child. Whatever success I have, whatever trial I have, whatever comes my way, God gets the glory out of it."

"Wow!" She smiled again. "I hope my girls grow up to be as strong in their faith as you are. You know, Christina asks about you all the time."

Little did Miss Jan know, she'd just twisted my stomach in knots and caused the Spirit's warning bells to go off. I took another huge bite of sweet-and-sour chicken and washed it down with remorse. I had taken something as simple as a compliment and turned it into a racial incident *that quickly* in my head. Regardless of the root of Miss Jan's comment, there was no malice in her accolades. *Quit trippin', Shondra. Get a grip.*

Mr. Butler called an after-school faculty meeting to discuss end-of-semester disciplinary issues that had been simmering on campus. Afterward, he asked to see me. I met him in his office and immediately sensed that he was up to no good. He closed the door behind me and took a seat.

"There is still the matter of the Donovan girl and your disciplinary strategies, Miss Smith," he said in long-drawn-out words.

"Is there something I should know, Mr. Butler?"

"They have contacted the board, and I'm sure the board will be getting in touch with you in turn." He was close to smiling.

"I've been in contact with my legal advisers," I said. He wanted to know more, but I wasn't about to lay all my cards on the table. I walked out of there as if I had a full house—whatever that is.

Miss Jan was still at her desk long past four o'clock. "Working late today, aren't you?"

"Oh, yeah . . ." She smiled and faced me. "I decided to stay and finish up some things. Christina's got a late basketball practice today. I thought I might as well hang out here instead of going all the way home and have to get back out again to pick her up.

"By the way, Stelson Brown called for you."

"Who?"

"Mr. Brown. From the career fair."

"Oh, did he say what he wanted?" I took the yellow message slip from her.

She batted her eyelashes. "Obviously, he wants to talk to you, missy."

"Just take a message the next time he calls," I said.

Miss Jan was never good at following directions. When Stelson dropped by the next day, she led him right to my office, with very little notice.

"Miss Smith, hi! How are you?"

"I'm fine, Mr. Brown. And you?" I shook his hand at the door to my office. He looked different underneath the bright lights of my office. He hadn't been in the sun lately; that was for sure. But even though his skin was about the business of returning to its natural shade, he was still handsome.

"Great."

"How can I help you?"

"Well, I was doing some work in this area, and I decided to stop by and ask. . . . I was wondering if we could get together again."

I invited him into the office and closed the door quietly to save him the embarrassment. "Mr. Brown, I . . . I don't think that's such a good idea."

"Would it be too much to ask why?" he probed gently.

I put my head down and hung my hand on the back of my neck. *To be truthful or to be rude?* I at least owed him an honest answer. "Mr. Brown, I don't know what you're going to make of this. I think that you're a nice, friendly person, and this is all very flattering, but I'm attracted to African-American men."

"Exclusively?"

"Pretty much."

"Hmm." Stelson took the liberty of seating himself in the hot seat. He motioned for me to sit down across from him.

You got your nerve! "No, thanks. I'll stand."

"You see, I'm only seeking a certain kind of woman. She's got to be strong . . . secure . . . positive. And a woman of God," he said. "I, too, have discriminating tastes."

I waited for him to go on, but he didn't. A charged silence hung between us. He watched me as I fidgeted between being annoyed and intrigued—his confident aura was magnetic. *Reality check, Shondra! White men with money think they have the power to push other people around.*

"Mr. Brown, this isn't going anywhere." I walked toward the door.

"LaShondra"—I was startled to hear him speak my name—"can you give a *brother* a *chance*?"

I laughed at him, sitting there in his khakis and heavily starched button-down polo shirt and looking like white America's poster child. I couldn't believe that those words had come from his mouth. "You are *not* a *brother*!"

"If I'm not mistaken, I *am* your brother—in Christ. Doesn't that count for something?" He stood and approached me at the door.

"Who taught you that 'give a brother a chance' line?" I grinned against my will.

"You're not the only black person I know, Miss Smith."

"Look, you're not earning any brownie points with me by trying to act black, okay?" I shook my head. He was closer to me than he should have been, but I traded my personal space for the pleasant drift of his cologne.

"I'm not trying to earn points with you. I just want you to know that you don't *know* me until you *know* me." His voice deepened with sincerity.

"Are you a serial killer?"

"No."

"A stalker?"

"No. I don't have time to stalk people. In fact, I barely have time to be here now." He shook his arm and looked down at his wristwatch. "So what do you say, Miss Smith—dinner Saturday?"

I raised one eyebrow and crossed my arms. "Dinner. Saturday. I'll call you. Leave your number with my secretary."

"I'd rather leave it with you."

When I got home, I took a few minutes to eat a snack, unwind, and catch my breath before getting ready for singles Bible study at Peaches' church.

Peaches got to my house at ten minutes after six in her usual rush, honking her horn to signal her arrival. I grabbed my purse and my book bag, setting the alarm before I walked out. Peaches was bouncing around in the car, flailing her thin arms to something with a fast, heavy beat. You would never have guessed that she was one of the youngest high-powered executives at Northcomp by day.

When we got to the church, we sent Eric on to the children's class. Peaches and I walked down the east hall and greeted our classmates in the biweekly singles fellowship/Bible study. Our desks were small, obviously meant for school-age children. But we suffered through the downsized furniture for Brother Johnson's priceless wisdom. He was in his late forties and recently married for the first time. And even though he'd considered turning the singles class over to another teacher due to his change in status, we'd successfully begged him to stay and help us on to the other side.

"I'll be so glad when I can stop coming here," Peaches teased me as we took our seats. "I'm ready to graduate to the couples ministry. I want to know what they be talkin' 'bout in there."

"Peaches, be quiet," I shushed her.

Brother Johnson led us in prayer and then asked us to pull out our notes and Bibles.

"Your homework was to describe your ideal mate and list some attributes that you would especially like to have in your future spouse. I also asked you to spare no details. Whether your desire is biblically based or not, I want you to let us know exactly what you are looking for. Tell the truth and shame the devil," he said.

"The whole truth?" Brother Robertson asked. There was a light chuckle in the audience.

"And nothing but the truth. You may go first, Brother Robertson," Brother Johnson volunteered him.

Brother Robertson stood and cleared his throat in a humorous effort to get our attention. He pulled a list from his tattered Bible. "I'm looking for someone who's a woman of God, who exhibits all the fruits of the spirit, who will share in some of my hobbies, who loves to cook. And . . ." he paused. "She should be physically active."

"In other words, she needs to be thin," Peaches jumped in.

"She's got to be if she's gonna keep up with me," he said, throwing his shoulders back and inflating his chest.

Peaches cocked her head, squinted her eyes, and gave him a look that wasn't totally appropriate for church. Then she rolled her eyes. The other class members and I let out a collective "Mmmm."

"Peaches," Brother Johnson asked, "what's on your list?"

Peaches cleared her throat and shook out her paper a few times, flashing her French-manicured nails. "Okay, I have this broken down into categories. Category one: spiritual. He must have accepted Christ in his life, he must attend church regularly, and he must actively study and apply the Word of God. I think if he's doing all that, we will be able to get along no matter what his basic personality type is. Category two: family. He must accept my son as part of the package, he must have a good relationship with his own mother, and if he has a child, the romantic relationship with his baby's mother must be completely severed and she cannot be crazy. He must also be active in said child's life. Category three: financial. He cannot be threatened by my success, he must have good credit, and he must have a good work history." She looked around at us all, "Failure to maintain steady employment is the quickest way to get x-ed off the list."

"Aaay-man!" one of our older female classmates interjected.

"And," Peaches continued reading from her paper, "last but not least, category four: physical. He must be at least four inches taller than I am; he must be physically active . . ." She eyed Brother Robertson for a second before going on. "I can't really say exactly what a man needs to look like, because there are a lot of different things that I am attracted to, but I do know that he needs to be black. And the blacker the better."

"Girl!" one of the sisters called out. "Get me a copy of that list!"

I was the next to disclose my list. "Okay, I also have mine broken into categories, but they're a little different. I insist that he is a man of God and that he expects me to be a woman of God, because I know that we'll help each other grow in Christ. I also insist that he is employed, although I really don't care what kind of work it is. I prefer that he not have any children and that he has not previously been married. I also prefer a tall, dark, handsome man with no gold teeth."

"What if he did have gold teeth?" a gold-toothed brother asked with a bright, shiny smile.

Oh, my. I put my hand over my mouth. "I would have to pray on that."

"That's a good question," Brother Johnson probed. "What difference does it make if he has a gold tooth or not?"

"Well . . ." I was trying to think of a tasteful way to say "that's ghetto." I answered with, "If he has a gold tooth, we probably don't have much in common."

"Maybe we just don't have the same tastes," Brother Gold-Tooth responded.

I shrugged. "And if we disagree on something as simple as gold teeth, there's no telling what else we won't be able to see eye to eye on."

After everyone else had the opportunity to make his or her list known, Brother Johnson led us into the Word. "Keep your lists handy as we cross-examine them with God's Word."

I thought I would fall out of my chair when he went to many of the verses that I had highlighted in my Bible—those verses that I'd marked for deliverance from prejudice. Brother Johnson made us recognize that even though we had all first claimed that we wanted mates who were Christian, we then went on to define exactly what *kind* of Christian we wanted. We had done everything from placing restrictions on what kinds of sins he or she must not have committed (prior to accepting Christ) to how he or she must appear to our physical eyes now.

We got stuck, however, on Acts 10:34–35: *Then Peter*

began to speak: "I now realize how true it is that God does not show favoritism but accepts men from every nation who fear him and do what is right."

"But we're not talking about every man," one of the sisters said, "we're talking about *my* man."

"That's a fact," Brother Johnson said gently, "but the real truth is that if you are looking for a sinless, perfect man or woman with a history as clean as a whistle, you may miss what is right under your nose, maybe even right here in this room."

I saw Peaches' eyes dart to Brother Robertson, but I was too busy nudging her to see if he was looking back at her. "These are the verses I've been studying."

"Regardless of outward appearances or past experiences," Brother Johnson eloquently explained, "a person in Christ is a new creature. We've got the whole 'unequally yoked' thing down, but we now have to learn to see our brothers and sisters in Christ as a part of who we are, because we all make up the body of Christ.

"Now, let me clarify some things here. You can expect God's people to bear fruit in their lives and be respectful, productive people. But every part of our lives—even down to the selection of our mates—needs to be turned over to God so that His perfect will can be carried out in your life. So if your personal preference is not in line with God's plan, you've got some rethinking to do."

We talked for another half hour before Brother Johnson made the call for final questions. Then he asked if there was anyone who would like to accept Christ in their lives that evening. When no one stepped forward, he asked us to join hands. We went around the circle making special prayer requests known before he led us in the closing prayer.

I saw Brother Robertson making his way over to Peaches, so I tapped her on the shoulder and let her know that I was going to get Eric from the children's class.

"Okay." She winked at me.

When we got in the car, I asked Peaches about Brother Robertson. She spoke softly so that Eric couldn't hear our conversation. "Well, we've been kind of doing the eye thing for the last couple of meetings. He's a new member; he's from D.C. He just got transferred with some insurance company.

"Anyways, we've got a date for Friday night. Can you do me a biiiiiig favor and watch Eric for a few hours? Raphael doesn't get off work until eight. I'm sure he'll pick him up by eight-thirty."

"Aw, girl," I teased her, "I can't. I told Shamar Moore that I'd meet up with him at around seven."

"Don't play, Shondra." Her voice was charged with the electricity of her new relationship. I was happy for her, but couldn't help wondering when I would have my turn.

CHAPTER 9

I watched in amazement as Vanessa Williams made it past the first, then the second round of eliminations for the crown of Miss America. Every scrap of hope within me yearned for her to win it—for us. *My entire family gathered near the television—me, Momma, Daddy, and Jonathan—our faces aglow from the screen's reflection. Daddy sat on the edge of his chair with his balled fists fastened to his knees. And when they called her name, Daddy leaped so high his glasses fell off. We hugged and hollered as though a member of our immediate family had cashed in a lottery ticket or reclaimed a lost treasure.*

Later, I felt her shame as she was forced to relinquish her crown. For weeks, the media mashed our faces in her disgrace.

"That's a shame," Momma said, stopping from her chores just long enough to catch the latest news on the issue. "Yeah, those white folks took the crown away because she did something she shouldn't have. But I'll tell you what: when that nasty *magazine comes out with her pictures in it, I'll betcha every white man in America'll have a copy under his mattress, settin' their eyes on a black woman's body. That's all they think about—how to get somethin' they ain't supposed to have. White men are just* nasty-thinkin', *'specially when it comes to black women! That's how she ended up in this mess to begin with—some white man and his nasty old fantasies."*

◙ ◙ ◙

Peaches called me later that evening to see if I wanted to work out with her at her gym, on a guest pass. "No, not tonight, Peaches."

"What's up, girl?" she asked. "You okay?"

"Yeah. Just tired. This change in the weather is wearing me down. I think I'm gonna sit myself down at church tonight. We're having a revival—I could use a good reviving."

"Thanks for telling me about it," she said sharply.

"I'm sorry. I just thought you'd be too busy with your Brother Robertson."

"Girl, please. We got into a big argument last week."

"About what?"

"He wants to get to know Eric, and I told him it was too soon."

"Well, at least he does recognize that you two are a package deal," I said.

"Yeah, but Eric is my baby, you know? I can't have him getting hurt every time I get hurt." She stated her case. "Besides, Eric is just now getting to know Raphael. One new relationship at a time is enough for anybody, let alone a child."

"You're right about that."

"What time does service start tonight?" she asked.

"Seven."

"Okay. I'll be there around eight-thirty," she said. "I know y'all don't start on time anyway." I couldn't argue with her on that one, either. Nothing at our church *ever* started on time.

The guest minister's choir was singing an older song of praise when I entered the sanctuary. "I am changed, Lo-o-o-o-ord, to love You. I am cha-a-a-anged to bless You. I am changed, Lo-o-ord by this, Your word, fore-e-ver to wo-o-o-orship Thee."

After their selection, the ushers directed the congregation in giving a love offering for Minister Jackson. Peaches jumped in the line behind me and marched around the table, giving her offering and then sitting next to me on the fourth pew.

"Hey." She pulled her Bible from her worn canvas bag.

"Hey."

Following a second selection, Minister Jackson took the pulpit. He adjusted the microphone to accommodate his short frame and asked the congregation to stand for prayer. Minister Jackson's prayer came out like a song. It reminded me of the prayers of David and Solomon, rich with praise and wisdom. His voice was smooth and steady as he pleaded for the guidance of the Holy Spirit in delivering a word from God that would bless the entire congregation.

"Amen. You may be seated in the presence of an awesome God." Minister Jackson was one of those preachers that my mother wouldn't have approved of. He was far too casual in his demeanor, not approaching his duties with the stiff reverence that she was used to in the old church: three-piece suit and tie, oversized crucifix hanging about his neck, and the tips of his something-skin shoes buffed and shined to perfection. Minister Jackson wore black slacks, a navy blue dress shirt, and a black tie. Yet, his salt-and-pepper hair spoke that he had a wealth of experiences to bring to the pulpit.

"For those of you who are attending this revival for the first night, I must let you know that we have been tackling several issues that I believe have plagued the body of Christ for centuries. Tonight I want to talk about something that I think we as Christians are extremely guilty of. This is not a popular message, especially not amongst our particular denomination. So, if you don't agree, just raise your finger and tip on out. I'll understand."

The congregation gave a collective laugh.

"Tonight I want to talk about voluntary separatism."

"Mmm hmm," we moaned.

"You see . . . uh . . . since man can remember, we have set ourselves upon creating groups, cliques, and boundaries. While I do understand that sometimes . . . these things are necessary to maintain a civilization. After all, you can't very well have people running in and out of other people's homes and expect to maintain order. Somebody would end up hurt if we didn't have boundaries.

"But I'm not talking about the world. The world has to maintain a lot of rules and regulations on the books in order to force people into what it believes they should do. Tonight I'm talking about the body of Christ. We have to begin to look at the boundaries and walls that we have set up between God's children, which hinder the spread of the gospel."

"Well," one of the deacons called out.

Ding! Ding! sounded the internal bell. I knew that Minister Jackson's message was meant for me. He'd hit the nail on the head, bringing the same issues—love, unity, Christianity—to the forefront.

I talked with Peaches quickly outside after the service, thanking her for her company and letting her know that I'd be in touch later in the week.

"Thanks for inviting me. That minister was really preachin' tonight. You know how black folks are—always trying to pull each other down. Always creating boundaries with our economic cliques and sororities and denominations. We really do need to come back to the Lord as one," she said as we walked toward the lot.

"Yeah, that's true," I agreed. "But do you ever think

that maybe we need to do the same with everybody—I mean, people who aren't black, too?"

"I don't know about all that." She gave me the eye. "I think our first priority is to love ourselves enough to help one another. We have to learn to deal with our own kind before we can worry about dealing with outsiders. Maybe that's a job for the next generation."

"Hmm." I felt her, but I was on another page.

The message *I* received was about race, love, and the body of Christ. In fact, the rest of the week's sermons poked and prodded me. Night after night, the Holy Spirit convicted me of prejudice. I saw it in myself—a short temper with the white woman behind the counter at a drug store. I heard it in my conversation with Peaches. I felt it when I was uncomfortably alone on an elevator at the mall with a man of Middle Eastern descent.

The conflict inside me was a war of words and emotions, as though an angel sat on one shoulder and the enemy sat on the other. One whispered messages of love and peace, while the other whispered horrible, discouraging facts and realities about life, people, the way things were and had been for hundreds of years.

I wept at the altar, surrounded by missionaries and other altar workers who felt my undeclared battle. "Just give it to Jesus," they whispered in my ear. Their hands made warm paths up and down my back. They encircled those of us who had come to have Minister Jackson lay hands on us, agreeing in the Spirit that God would deliver us from mental and physical afflictions. "Just leave it here at the altar. He is able."

Saturday sneaked up on me before I had the chance to fully develop an excuse *not* to call Mr. Stelson Brown. But when I got in the Word and reviewed the notes from Minister Jackson's sermons, I put the excuses aside. I decided to call him early, figuring that he wouldn't be home, because most people try to run their errands before noon. Then I could leave a "sorry I missed you" message, screen my calls (if he got my number from caller ID), and conveniently miss him until it was way too late to go out.

"Hello," he answered the phone at nine o'clock in the morning.

"Hi, may I speak with Stelson, please?"

"This is Stelson."

"Stelson, this is LaShondra Smith. How are you?"

"I'm great . . . great." He seemed glad to hear my voice. "How about you?"

"Fine as well. I'm calling to take you up on your offer." I laughed.

"Okay"—he laughed, too—"I'm glad you did. Um, let's see . . . do you like Mexican food?"

"I love Mexican food."

"I've got just the right place in mind. There's a Mexican restaurant named Abuelita's on the south side of town—off Industrial and Ninth. It's a tiny little place, but they've got live entertainment and the best Mexican food on the entire globe."

"Mmm," I said, "I think I've heard of that place, but I've never gone there. I'd like to try it."

"What time shall I pick you up?" he asked.

"Uh, no offense, Stelson, but I would prefer to meet you there." I imposed my standard residence rule: don't let a man know where you live until after the third date.

"None taken." He didn't skip a beat. "I can meet you there at eight."

"Eight is fine. I'll see you there."

I scoured my closet for the perfect outfit and settled on an indigo pants set with a pair of black low-heeled boots. I swept my hair up into a twist and let what was left of my curls sweep across my forehead and on top of my head. The hairstyle was a bit more formal than I wanted, but I didn't have much choice.

Eight took its sweet time coming but found both Stelson and me being seated at a table for two. "You look great, LaShondra," he said to me as he placed his jacket on the back of his chair. Any other time, I would have mentally twisted his compliment to the point that it was perverted. But not tonight.

"Thank you, Stelson."

Once again he was wearing that cologne that I had come to associate with him—not too strong, definitely masculine. His hair had grown out a little, maybe into what it was supposed to look like at its best.

The smell of authentic Mexican food filled the atmosphere, along with the energy of the mariachi band. Every song had the distinct, three-count beat of Latino rhythm. Waitresses dressed in sombreros and bright, colorful skirts whisked through the crowd with platters of sizzling fajitas giving off their mouth-watering aroma. It was different, but I liked it.

I almost hurt myself on the biggest, spiciest, most delicious chicken burrito I ever tasted. Stelson laughed at me when we were finished, because I just sat there, too full to move.

"Just give me a minute," I said, loosening the drawstring on my pants. After the way I threw down on that burrito, I was well past manners. "Okay. That's better. I'll be all right in just a few minutes."

"I told you this place was awesome." He smiled. A clump of his dark hair fell out of place, and touched his eyebrow. He forced it back to its rightful spot by yanking his head back and shaking it slightly, like it was really going to stay in place now. *There goes the white-girl flip.*

"'Awesome' is an understatement," I said, willing myself to ignore the hair thing.

"We'll have to come here again," he suggested.

"Definitely." I had inadvertently agreed to another date.

"So, Miss Smith," he teased, "tell me all about you. What goes on in a typical week in the life of LaShondra Smith?" he asked.

"Not too much. I spend a lot of time at work. I usually go to a singles Bible study on Tuesday nights, tutoring on Wednesday nights at my church before midweek service," I babbled freely, "but that tutoring takes a lot out of me because right now I'm the only one on who's tutoring. Every once in a while, someone will come back to volunteer and help, but for the most part I'm roughing it alone. I've been praying that God will send some help—anybody.

"The rest of the week I'll probably lounge around. Check out a few bookstores, do a little shopping. Go to church Sunday morning." I shrugged.

"Tell me about your church," he requested. "I mean, what denomination is it? What's it like?"

"I attend True Way Church of God in Christ, where my pastor is the Reverend Billy Williams." I gave my spiel.

"You're kidding!" he exclaimed. "Church of God in Christ?"

"Yes, Church of God in Christ. Pentecostal. Holy rollers, open expressions of praise, tongue-talking, let the Spirit take lead in the service. That kind of church."

"You're kidding me," he repeated.

"No, I'm not. What's so incredible?" I asked him, waiting for him to say something derogatory about my denomination. I'd be the first to admit that COGIC wasn't perfect. But if Stelson said one bad thing about my church, I would have to go left.

"Did you know that your church and the church I was raised in were once the same denomination?" he asked. The look on my face answered his question. "It's true. The Church of God in Christ and the Assemblies of God were once one church. The founders of your church and the founders of my church worked together up until the early nineteen hundreds."

My ears heard it, but I couldn't really imagine it. Blacks and whites together in the early 1900s for *any* reason was highly unlikely.

"LaShondra," he continued, breathing hard with excitement, "The Church of God in Christ was part of the Apostolic Faith movement that started in America in the late eighteen hundreds. I mean, my church's founders and your church's founders were both present at the Azusa Street revival in 1906."

"I've heard of Azusa Street. They still have the convention every year," I commented. "But what makes you think that the Church of God in Christ, founded by Bishop Charles Mason, and the Assemblies of God were ever one?"

"I've researched this, LaShondra. The Church of God in Christ had huge, absolutely phenomenal growth. At one point, there were as many white Church of God in Christ congregations as there were black ones—all of them with Bishop Mason's stamp on them. People were beginning to see that God was alive in everybody, with no regard to nationality or race or class. It was amazing. And it went on until around 1918 or so."

"What happened?"

"It split up," he said, bowing his head and lowering his voice. "It got divided right down the middle."

"Along racial lines, huh?"

"That among other things," he said. "That's how we ended up the Assemblies of God and the Church of God in Christ. Two separate denominations that shouldn't have *ever* been apart. The truth is, you and I go way back, LaShondra."

"Well, why haven't I ever heard about any of this?"

"I didn't hear about any of it, either, growing up. It

wasn't until I started looking for a church home in Dallas that I got into the church's history. I guess it's just one of those things that isn't discussed."

"Are you still in the Assemblies of God?"

"No. I belong to Living Word. It's nondenominational."

"So how did you end up in a nondenominational church?" I asked him. "If you were raised anything like I was raised, you know it's a serious thing to leave 'the church.' "

"I didn't really make the decision to be nondenominational. I just asked God to send me to the church where He wanted me to serve and give. That's how I ended up at Living Word Church. That church has been such a blessing to me. There is so much love in the congregation—probably the same love that was once shared between the Church of God in Christ and the Assemblies of God."

"You are right about it, nobody discusses that kind of thing," I said. "I mean, I can probably count on one hand the number of white people that I know of who were members at a Church of God in Christ. Every once in a while, we have a white visitor or something, but that's about it. If we're supposed to have been so close, why are we so far apart?"

"That's a good question."

"What about at the Assemblies of God? Is the congregation still all white?"

"No, not any more. I mean, it's predominantly white, but in the past twenty years or so, with interracial couples and fellowship with churches of different denominations, we've gotten somewhat diversified. Most of the members who aren't white are younger. It's funny how kids don't seem to care about race as much as adults do."

"I can second that," I agreed with him.

He still had that excited and happy expression on his face.

"What?"

"Why are you looking like that?" I asked him.

"Looking like what?"

"Looking all happy."

"I'm happy to finally meet someone who understands where I'm coming from. Someone who knows what it means to take communion, to let the Spirit of God lead you, to be set apart from the world. All the stuff that you and I were both raised believing." He beamed as though he'd found a long-lost friend.

"Stelson, you don't understand." I tried to brace him for my less-than-joyful interpretation of this slice of history. "You can be happy about it, but I'm not. I don't see anything exciting or happy about finding out that my people and your people used to get along but stopped getting along because of race. That is no comfort to me."

"We're all God's people, LaShondra. There are billions of Christians who are divided for unexplainable reasons. I do know, however, that it was never God's will for his children to be split up. No parent would ever want that for their children. You and I both know that God isn't about division. He's about unity. We were chosen long before 1918."

"I know you're right, Stelson. It's just that maybe it's easier for you to disregard the particulars when you weren't the one on the short end of the stick, you know? And I don't mean you, I mean your people." The conversation had turned into a debate of sorts, but it was respectful.

"*You* are my people, LaShondra," he said forcefully. "Every last church that's divided up is my people because the church is the body of Christ."

It took a second to accept that fact. That truth. The same truth that Minister Jackson preached about only days before. I'd known, that day at Chester's, that Stelson was my brother. I'd known all along that there was something about him that I was drawn to. Perhaps it was the whole truth: that part of him was part of me.

My mind was running in circles. I felt a tug-of-war going on inside of me, an internal conflict pitting everything I thought I knew about myself against an emerging image of who this child of God (aka LaShondra Smith) truly was. *This is too hard, Lord.*

I sat back and took in the restaurant again. Despite the noise level, I'd heard every word Stelson said. More important, I'd felt them. For the first time, I saw the flecks of black in his otherwise crystal clear blue eyes, the outline around them. I noticed the slope of his nose—steady and steep. His lips were not quite pink, not quite peach, but something in between.

"And what goes on in a typical week for you?" I changed the subject.

"Meetings, meetings, and more meetings at work. Every other Saturday I volunteer for the Saturday Night Live program at our church. Um, what else? I read, I work out, I pray, I study the Word, I go to church. I sleep. And all of that in no particular order," he said.

"Sounds like a pretty busy life."

"Busy but not full. There's more to life than working hard but having no one to share success with," he said with a blank expression.

Relieved that he was not making any premature hints about a relationship, I agreed with him. "I understand. I mean, I love being single. I do my own thing without having to consult with anybody else's schedule. If I don't want to clean up today, I don't clean up."

He nodded, "I know what you mean. Coming home to peace and quiet after a long day's work does have its rewards. But then again, so would coming home to a foot massage."

"Ooh, that sounds good," I agreed. "I don't know, Stelson. I think that by the time I meet the right person, I might be too set in my own ways, you know? I can't wake up in the morning, pour a bowl of cereal, and find out that all the milk is gone because somebody else in the house drank the last drop and didn't tell me. That kind of thing would irritate me."

"More than the irritating comments from family members—'Why aren't you married yet?' and 'When am I gonna have my grandkids?' "

"Your family, too!" I gasped.

"Oh, yes. My mother especially. She lives in Louisiana, but she tries her best to keep close tabs on me. I have no doubt that seeing me married is at the top of her prayer list."

"I didn't think many men had that kind of pressure. I mean, it's obvious that women have external pressures, but the fact of the matter is, our biological time clocks tick much faster than men's. We can't wait until we're fifty to make a move."

"Well, who says you've got to have kids?"

"Nobody." I rested my elbows on the table and laced my fingers together under my chin. Stelson leaned in to listen more closely. "I mean, I'm not one of those who absolutely has to have kids. But it would be nice, granted that I had a husband to raise them with—which brings us back to square one."

In the parking lot, Stelson walked me to my car and saw me in safely. I lowered my window. "Thanks, Stelson. I really enjoyed this place."

"Thanks for joining me." He smiled, his hand on the hood of my car. "LaShondra, would you mind if I had your phone number? I really enjoyed your company, and I'd like to talk more some time."

After the great time we'd had at the restaurant, the question seemed almost silly. And, come to think of it, maybe the game I was playing with Stelson was a little silly, too. White as he was, he'd gone through the entire evening without setting off any of those internal alarms. You know, when a guy says or does something on a first date and you immediately know that he is *not* the one? "Sure, Stelson. I think I'd like that, too."

When I got home from our date, I jumped onto the Internet. I believed what Stelson had told me about our church, but I wanted to read it for myself. Our denominational Web sites didn't list much about the split, but I did find that the doctrines were similar. A more detailed search of several historical and theological research engines yielded the confirmation that I needed. My church and Stelson's church had indeed been united almost a hundred years earlier. We'd been divided by the work of the enemy.

CHAPTER 10

I had already asked Momma if I could go to the freshman dance with Reginald, but she said that she and Daddy had to meet him first.

"Do you want me to invite him over?" I'd asked.

"No, I don't want him over here. Invite him to church." Her eyes got real big, and she nodded down toward me. "If he can't come to church, he ain't worth a quarter."

I thought to myself, "Daddy don't have to go to church, and you married him." I could think whatever I wanted to, but I knew better than to say it.

"What's his name?" Daddy wanted to know.

"Reginald Devereaux."

"Reginald what?" He jerked his head back.

"Devereaux, Daddy. It's French."

"Ain't that something—a tough black name like Reginald mixed up with a soft-sounding French name. What's he look like?" he asked.

"He looks black, Daddy." I shook my head. I'd wondered, even then, what that *had to do with anything. I thought that the question at hand was whether I could go.*

I followed Momma's orders and asked Reginald to come to church. He wasn't actually my boyfriend, but we were "talking," as we used to call it. I knew his cousin, Renita, a mixed girl in my Spanish class. I'd seen his picture in her photo album and asked about him. Since then, Reginald and I had been passing notes via Renita. I'd also sneak on the phone to call him from a friend's house, or from the living room if I happened to be home alone. Despite the fact that I was not supposed to be talking on the phone to boys, I managed to carry out a very active social life with both sexes. In retrospect, that no-talking-on-the-phone-to-boys rule probably ended up being the most harmful because I never formed the concept of letting the young man chase me, rather than the other way around. Old habits die hard.

Momma was impressed with Reginald Devereaux. He had introduced himself politely after church and then asked her and Daddy if he could take me to his school's freshman dance. Both his parents had come to church for the occasion as well, and I was thankful that they both looked as black as Reginald did. My parents finally gave us the green light to attend the dance.

His parents drove us to the dance and dropped us off, telling us that they'd be back at eleven to pick us up. We both let out a sigh of relief when they drove off.

"I thought they'd never leave," Reginald whispered in my ear as we walked through the gymnasium doors. His breath tickled my ears when he talked, and sent a tingle down my spine. We danced throughout most of the night, touching innocently yet purposely. His smooth, light complexion was bronzed just enough to bring out the unmistakable African heritage in him. I'd wondered before if he was black enough for me. Not just in terms of his complexion, but by his persona. I hadn't really seen him except in pictures and that one time at church. There, on the dance floor, he put my anxieties to rest. He could prep, he could cabbage patch, and he could Reebok. Yes, he was my kind of black boy.

The DJ announced the last song at around ten-forty-five. "Everybody grab somebody. This is the last dance. Make it count!" Reginald and I had taken a break to get chips and punch, but we quickly took a place on the dance floor.

Reginald pulled me close, and we danced to Atlantic Star's

"For Always." *He put his cheek against mine and kissed me. I closed my eyes.* Ooh, please don't try to kiss me on the lips. I don't know how to kiss. *I was terrified and excited all at once. Reginald's mouth moved toward my lips. Slowly. Until finally, they landed on top of mine. I was prepared for the little pecks, no problem. I'd practiced those on my stuffed animals. But when his lips parted and his tongue probed my lips for an opening, I squeezed my lips together even tighter.*

He pulled back. "What's the matter?"

"I . . . I've never done this," I admitted.

"What—French kiss?"

"Yeah."

"It's easy," he said. "Just close your eyes and open your mouth a little." I was so relieved by the fact that he didn't bust out laughing. I did as he said—closed my eyes and opened my mouth a little. And Reginald Devereaux gave me my first real kiss. It tasted like Doritos and Hawaiian Punch, but it felt like fire.

My cell phone rang, and Peaches' number flashed across the blue screen. "Hey, girl, what's up?"

"Do you want to go on a double date with me and Quinn tonight? He's got a cousin in from out of town."

"Who's Quinn?"

"Alias Brother Robertson."

"Oh, it's *Quinn* now?"

"Don't start."

"Do you know anything about this cousin?" I asked.

"Not much. I know he's from Oklahoma. Just down here on a little vacation."

"Oh, brother." I rolled my eyes. "You know what that means."

"What?" she tried to act like she didn't know.

"Either he *just* broke up with somebody or he *just* lost

his job. Somethin' ain't right. He's too old to be going to visit a cousin."

"Well, do you have something better to do tonight?"

"I was just on my way to Chili's to get me a salad—which might be preferable to whatever mess you and Quinn's cousin have in store for me."

"Whatever, girl. At least this way you don't have to pay for your own food. Be at my place at eight so we can ride to Quinn's apartment together."

I made a U-turn and went back home. I threw on a striped sweater with frayed denim jeans and a pair of brown leather boots with heels perfect for sitting. Unlike Peaches, I had to be comfortable in whatever I wore. She, on the other hand, was a slave to fashion. I know for a fact that her rhinestone belt buckle *had* to hurt when she bent down to pick up her purse. But she straightened herself up, pushed it back into place, and took it in stride.

We talked about Quinn the whole way over. Or shall I say, *she* talked about Quinn. I just listened. It reminded me of old times, when she'd lost her mind over Raphael. The sun rose and set on Raphael back in the day. Yet I knew that Peaches wasn't the same person she had been nine years ago. She had grown, blossomed, gotten wiser in the Word of God right alongside me. I loved her, and I was happy for her.

"I'm sorry," she said after some time. "I'm just going on and on about Quinn. What's up with you, girl?"

"Oh, nothing." I smiled. I wanted to tell her about Stelson—about how we'd gone to Abuelita's and talked a few times on the phone since then. About how he and I had gotten off to a rough start but were actually getting to know each other now. But I wasn't ready to talk about his being white.

Quinn's cousin, Mark, was surprisingly handsome. Peaches and I did a double-take when he walked from what appeared to be the main hallway into Quinn's living area. *Dang!* Mark was tall and had deep ebony skin and a head that was perfect for shaving bald—no dents, no cuts. Just smooth, black man. Old boy was looking good, dressed in FUBU from top to bottom except for the matching red Nikes that completed his outfit. A little more hip-hop than I was used to, but he was definitely workable.

Quinn introduced us. "Mark, this is LaShondra, Peaches' best friend. LaShondra, this is my cousin, Mark." We shook hands, and I sat down again on the couch. Mark sat down next to me, still smiling.

"No time for that now," Quinn said, "the movie starts in twenty minutes."

I hated to see Mark put on the coordinating knit cap before we left, but it was quite chilly outside. Christmas was just around the corner, and the weather was flowing with the season.

"Are you enjoying Dallas?" I asked Mark during the short walk to Quinn's Lincoln LS.

"I'm enjoying it a whole lot more now," he said.

Well, we all know how this double-date thing works. Especially when one of the dates is a blind one. The primary couple sits in the front, making goo-goo eyes. The secondary couple sits in the back restlessly, trying to make small talk and not ruin the evening for the primaries. I took my rightful place at the back door on the passenger's side and waited for the doors to be unlocked. Mark took his place on the other side of the car. Quinn came to my side as well, to unlock and open the door for Peaches. He gave Mark the eye, like "come around here and open the door for this lady," and Mark gave him the eye like "man, please get a life." Peaches slid into the front seat, probably unaware of the silent exchange that I'd been forced to witness. Mark got in the car and shut the door, so Quinn went ahead and opened the door for me.

Now, I have to admit: wrong or right, I've never been one of those women who expect a man to open the door for them. It was nice when it happened, but I wasn't going to hold my breath about it. But the way Mark looked at Quinn was uncalled for. *I'm not gonna trip.*

"You look very nice," he complimented me in the backseat of Quinn's car.

"Thank you," I said.

"I don't usually go out on blind dates—I mean, I'm pretty sure that the woman is going to be pleased with me, but sometimes I end up with an African booty-scratcher." He laughed at his own joke.

"So, how are you enjoying the city?" I asked him again, since he never really answered the first time.

"Oh, it's cool. Cuz is showing me around the new city hot spots. Well, actually, he ain't down like he used to be—all sanctified now. He had me in church the other night. But it was cool—lots of people to see. Probably the same people I'd see up in the club. Maybe the two of us could get out and see the city," he suggested.

"I don't know if you want to paint the town with me—I'm not really with the club scene," I informed him.

"Oh, all right then. Well, maybe we could do some one-on-one touring," he hinted, looking me up and down.

"Hmm . . ." I dismissed the idea.

We sat through the movie with very little conversation. Mark took it upon himself to put his arm on the back of my chair. It gradually eased down—first a finger, then a hand, until finally his whole arm draped my shoulders. *Is he crazy?* I kindly removed his arm from its newfound resting place and crossed my arms on my chest. He got the message.

After the movie, we went to dinner at a trendy grill. We waited outside for nearly half an hour before our table was ready. Peaches and Quinn were all snuggled up while Mark and I were still trying to make small talk.

"So, what do you do?" he asked me.

"I'm a vice principal at a middle school."

He nodded, the corners of his lips turned down in a condescending expression. I knew that common courtesy called for me to reciprocate his question, but I wouldn't give him the satisfaction of going on and on about whatever it was that he did. When it was clear that I wasn't going to ask him, he spoke up for himself.

"I'm a computer programmer."

"Oh, that's nice," I congratulated him.

"Yeah, it pays good. *Damn* good," he announced like somebody from one of those career advertisements on television in the middle of the day. "I make, what, probably two or three times what the average man makes."

"Oh. So what dragged you away from your computer?"

"Just took some time off—you know, vacation. Could have gone anywhere in the world, but I haven't seen my cuz in a while. Got some other family here, too." He sniffed and swiped at the bridge of his nose with his thumb.

I excused myself to go to the restroom, and Peaches followed. We met at the center mirror. "So, what do you think?"

"*You* owe *me* one after tonight."

"Whatever! You haven't seen anything *that* chocolate, *that* fine in a long time. Girl, Mark would give Morris Chestnut a run for his money." Peaches smiled.

"Mark is real throwed-off, okay."

"Throwed-off like what? Crazy? Nerdy?"

"Throwed-off like I'm surprised his neck has the strength to hold up his overblown head. He's one of those brothers that has a good job and looks half decent. He knows he's at a premium, so he thinks I should be throwing myself at him. Girl, please," I smacked, "if he was all that, he wouldn't be vacationing two hundred miles from home and staying with a family member. Just up here lyin'."

"Shondra," she said, applying a fresh coat of lipstick, "get off it. Mark is a decent brother. Give him a chance."

"He already had his chance. It's over." I squashed her hopes.

"Do you think he might be a Boaz in disguise?" she asked.

"He's a Boaz without the 'Bo'," I hinted. "Now, don't make me get ugly."

"All right, Shondra," Peaches laughed.

"But don't let that worry you. You and Quinn go right on having a good date. I'm having fun just watching how well he treats you—I think you snagged a good one this time."

"Yeah, I did, didn't I?" she agreed, pausing to smile at herself in the mirror.

"You go, girl."

We rejoined the brothers at the table to dine in peace for the rest of the evening. I stayed my distance from Mark, and he stayed his distance from me. As I sat there pushing my green beans back and forth across the plate to ease my boredom, I thought about how different this dinner was from the dinner I had with Stelson. We'd talked. We'd laughed and shared a few things.

"What you over there grinning about?" Mark poked me on the shoulder.

"Oh, nothing."

"Humph." He looked at me out of the corner of his eye and placed the cherry from his margarita on the tip of his tongue. He swirled his tongue around the base of the cherry before plucking it from its stem and taking a sloppy bite into it. "That was for you."

"Okay, I'm ready to go," I announced, but Quinn and

Peaches were too far into each other's conversation to hear me.

"Don't be scared." Mark moved in closer to me and whispered, "Sex is the most natural thing in the world. I know you're a church girl, but I can show you some things that will have you climbing the walls."

"First of all," I whispered back to Mark while pushing him off me, "you don't know me from the man in the moon. How dare you suggest that we have sex? I find that very disrespectful—church girl or not."

"Might as well cut out all the games," he said. "That way we can both get what we want. I'm only in town for a few more days anyway."

"Second of all," I continued, "your technique needs a little work."

"What technique?"

"With the cherry." I slowed my speech and lowered my voice to sexy bedroom whisper. "See, the way you chewed it up like a piece of bubble gum tells me that you don't know how to savor a good moment. You don't know how to turn a fleeting moment into a night of pleasure—you know, make it last? You'd be done before I got finished with you. Even if I had the notion to give you a chance—which I *do not*—it wouldn't have worked out, Mark. I know a selfish lover when I see one."

Mark looked at me as if he didn't know if I was a nut or a she-devil. "Oh, I guess you think you all that, huh?" He sucked his teeth.

"You'll never know."

"That's what's wrong with black women today," he said as he moved back to his rightful spot two feet away from me. He chewed his food so hard I thought his teeth would fall out.

I gave Peaches "the look." She in turn gave Quinn a nudge in the ribs, and we were out of there. Mark asked

Quinn to drop him off at one of their other relatives' homes to play dominoes and said that he probably wouldn't be back at Quinn's apartment until the next day. When Mark stepped out of the car, he purposely waved at Peaches and Quinn—but not me. In a way, I was glad he didn't. He was so mad, he might not have been holding up all five fingers.

"Well, what did you think?" Quinn asked as we drove back to his apartment.

"Don't ask, Quinn." I shook my head and looked out my window, trying not to laugh. "I don't want to say something that I'll have to repent for later."

"Yeah," Quinn laughed for me. "That Mark is something else. He begged me to set him up with somebody tonight."

"I can't tell," I said. "No offense, Quinn, but Mark thinks he's God's gift to women."

"Yeah." Quinn looked at me in the rearview mirror. "I believe Mark rode the short bus to school."

"You are so wrong!" I yelled.

"Baby, don't talk about him like that." Peaches caught her breath. "He is your cousin."

Baby?

"Yeah, that's my cuz. But I haven't seen him in a while. Let me take it upon myself to apologize. I was hoping things had changed for him—you know, that maybe he'd stopped all that lying and perpetrating he used to do when we were young and immature."

"I can assure you," I said, "nothing has changed. Keep him on the prayer list."

Taking the shortcut back to Quinn's apartment, we passed directly in front of Abuelita's Mexican restaurant. The parking lot was filled to capacity, and there was still a line out the door. I called Peaches' attention to the restaurant by tapping on her window. "That place right there has the best Mexican food in the world. It is absolutely delicious."

"Oh, really?" Peaches asked. "Looks packed. When did you go there?"

"Last weekend."

"How come you didn't tell me, girl? You know I'm down with Mexican food."

"Um . . ." I hesitated, "I went with . . . It was kind of like a business-casual thing with . . . um, one of the presenters from the career fair."

"Oh," Peaches said softly.

The final Wednesday-night tutoring session of the semester started on time, with ten students in need of some serious help before semester exams. Within the first fifteen minutes, I was swamped again. Brother Jenkins had already called to say that he wouldn't be able to make it in. The kids were coming two at a time, and the only thing I could think to do was to send some back into the sanctuary until I got finished helping the first round of kids.

Hands were going up faster than I could help anyone. "Yes, you must have the same denominator before you can add or subtract fractions.

"Reread that last section—the Fugitive Slave Act of 1850 did a lot to hasten the Civil War.

"Every complete sentence has a subject and a predicate. Here, I'll circle the ones that you need to look at again." I was here, I was there, and my brain was everywhere.

And then, suddenly, the voices in the classroom quieted down to silence. My back was to the door, but I felt the tap on my shoulder. "LaShondra."

I turned to greet a familiar voice. "Hi." My heart raced and stopped, all at once. *What is Stelson doing here?*

"I'm here to help with the tutoring. I don't know how

good I am with English, but I'm really good at math and science." He smiled and set his briefcase in a corner.

"Okay." I was dumbfounded. "Okay."

I faced the students and nervously introduced Stelson. "Everyone, this is Brother Brown. He's here tonight to help with tutoring. Let's see, now, everyone who's here for help with math or science, please move to these tables on the right. You'll be working with Brother Brown. Everyone else move over to the left with me."

The students were eager to divide up into smaller groups and get more individualized attention. I felt a sense of relief and wariness all at once. *What does he want from me?* My burden had been cut in half, but at what cost?

I watched Stelson with a suspicious eye, kept an ear open for what he was saying and how he said it. He was right in there, elbow deep, with the kids. He was explaining things to them, showing them how to work out the solutions. He gave them encouragement to keep trying, praised them when they got the correct answers, and led them to figure out their own mistakes when they'd gotten an incorrect answer. He was a natural teacher.

Stelson moved around the table with sure, confident steps. His deep voice soothed the students' anxieties and softened when he wanted their complete attention, so they had to give their all to listen. I watched his arms reach across the table. I suddenly wondered what they would feel like around my waist. *Help, Lord.*

"Sister Smith!" one of the students called my name.

"Yes?" It occurred to me that I'd heard her, but I wasn't listening.

"I ain't mad at you, 'cause he *is* tha bomb," DeAundra giggled. "But right now I need a little help here with this comprehension question."

"Okay, DeAundra, I'm here." I tried not to smile, but she *was* right about Stelson.

Together, Stelson and I served every student who came that evening. When the music started playing in the sanctuary, the students gathered their books and thanked us for the help. One of the students led us in prayer before, thanking God for the work that I had been doing for them and also thanking God for Brother Brown's help. Then the students headed back into the sanctuary. Stelson stayed behind to help me straighten up the classroom.

"Wow!" He took a deep breath. "That is nonstop action."

"I know," I said, putting the last chair back in place. "And thank you so much for coming to help. How did you know?"

"I heard you talking about the need for help the other day, and I decided to come lend a hand." He shrugged.

"Thank you, Stelson. I really appreciate the help, and I'm sure the kids did, too."

We picked up our things and walked down the corridors leading to the main entrance of the sanctuary. I stopped just shy of the main doors. "Well, thanks again for coming. You truly blessed me tonight."

"Oh." He caught on to my farewell motions. "I was planning on staying for church."

"Oh, okay."

He raised an arm toward the sanctuary doors. "After you."

For a moment, I'd forgotten what color Stelson was. In the classroom, he'd looked like an angel to me. But when I opened that main door and walked down the center aisle with Stelson Brown by my side, there was no mistaking his color. Heads turned; necks craned and almost broke trying to get a good look at him and figure out if the lack of space between us indicated that we had actually walked into church together. Their notions were confirmed when we sat down together and passed a smile.

I wanted to stand up and defend him—or myself—to the congregation. To explain that we knew each other only casually, that he had come to help with the tutoring program and that was it. I wanted to tell them that he was raised in the Assemblies of God and already knew what we believed. He wasn't some white guy off the streets who was doing some research project on African-American religion. Furthermore, I certainly had enough sense not to fool around with some white man who might only be trying to use me the way they'd always used black women. *But why do I need to tell them all that?*

Deacon Brower gave the benediction, and I followed Stelson out of the sanctuary. He pushed the swinging door open and allowed me to pass before him.

"Hi, Sister Smith!"

I felt a hand on my shoulder and spun around. It was Shannon—Emily's mom. I hadn't noticed her during the service. "Hello."

"Hey, who's your guest?" She put her hand on Stelson's arm, too.

"This is Stelson Brown. Stelson, this is Shannon."

"Stelson Brown of Brown-Cooper! We did business with you all a few years ago. I know your name from the contracts." She grabbed his hand with both of hers and shook so hard that her bangs fell from behind her ears. "It's a pleasure to finally be able to put a face with the name."

"It's nice to meet you, too, Shannon."

"Sister Smith"—Shannon looked at me eagerly—"why don't we all get together some time? Me, you, Stelson, and Paul."

I don't think so. "Hmmm . . ." I smiled like I didn't understand English.

"Here . . ." She reached into her purse, pulled out a business card, and pressed it into my palm. "Call me. I think we'd have a great time."

"Thanks," I said.

And then she winked at me. *What's that supposed to mean? Like we're in some secret interracial dating sorority?* "Bye. Don't you let her forget to call me, Stelson!"

Stelson had that same I-speak-no-English look on his face. Outside in the parking lot, he asked me if I knew Shannon well.

"No, not at all."

"She's certainly very friendly."

"Too friendly," I said under my breath.

CHAPTER 11

Testing time was always especially difficult on me when I was teaching. It was always an all-week affair: getting the kids pumped up and mellowed out at the same time, making sure I'd signed all the oaths and had enough pencils, fretting about what to do when the test was over. My principal that year, Mr. Wright, had a campus-wide movie planned for the afternoon so that the kids would have a chance to wind down and relax following the state assessment test.

The film was a boring piece of historical fiction set in the early nineteenth century, about a boy and dog—a wannabe Old Yeller, *if you ask me. We'd instructed the kids to remain quiet while we collected the testing materials and awaited dismissal instructions. Ms. Logan, one of my team teachers from down the hall, called to check on me. "Hey, Miss Smith, how's it going in your room?"*

"Okay, I guess. I think I'm more restless than the kids are."

"Aren't you watching the movie?"

"No, not really."

"Oh, I think this movie is so awesome. I would have loved *to live back then. I mean, you didn't have all the modern conveniences that we have today, but I can just imagine that things were so much simpler and less stressful, don't you?"*

"Miss Logan, if I *was alive back then, I would have been a*

slave." I put a bit of humor in my tone, but only because I had to work with her again next year.

"Oh, I'm so sorry," she sincerely apologized. "I guess I just wasn't thinking. I am so *sorry."*

It must be nice to be able to forget.

▣ ▣ ▣

My foot dangled over the edge of the bed as I scoured the newspaper for interesting articles and worthwhile stories. With cereal bowl in hand, I carefully leaned over the headlines and read the usual: somebody done somebody wrong; somebody was on the loose; somebody was suing for whatever. Nonetheless, my joy was intact. I went to my prayer closet for peace and direction. After praying and meditating, I revisited the Scriptures that pertained to prejudice. The passages kept calling me, as though they needed my care. "Lord, whatever You want me to know from these Scriptures, I pray that Your Spirit will reveal it to me so that I can do Your will. Thank You for speaking to me so clearly and for chastising those You love. I love You, Father."

Just as I prepared to leave the room, my phone rang, and I wondered who in their right mind would be calling me before noon on a Saturday. I rushed to answer it before whoever-this-is could get off the line.

"Hi, LaShondra. It's Stelson."

"Well, good morning, Mr. Brown."

He laughed. "Good morning to you, too, Miss Smith. How are you?"

"Fine." I flirted right along with him. "And how are you?"

"Fine as well. I was calling to invite you to church and dinner tonight. We have what we call Saturday Night Live at our church every other weekend. The youth department puts it on for kids to keep them off the streets. I go whenever I can to help out."

"Yeah, you told me a little about it the other night," I recalled.

"I've signed up to serve hot dogs tonight, but we could go somewhere else afterward. Are you free?"

"Yes, I think I can do that."

"And may I pick you up?" he asked hopefully.

"Sure . . ." I let the word out slowly.

My lazy morning came to an abrupt end with the formation of evening plans. I had to stop by the cleaner's, do some grocery shopping, get my nails filled, get my oil changed, and get myself ready to go before six. I hopped out of bed and threw on a pair of sweats with sneakers. My curls had completely fallen, but the wave left in my hair was enough to make it through the night. Besides, walk-in at my beauty shop was synonymous with live-in—you could expect to live an entire day in the beauty shop without an appointment. No, the present state of my hair would have to do. *Unless I wash it and blow-dry it out, then flip it up with the blow brush . . . Why am I even worrying about this?* After all, it was only Stelson.

Momma called and asked if I was going to come by for dinner Sunday. "Yes, Momma. You know I am."

"Why don't you come on over here tonight. We can make the sweet potatoes for tomorrow."

"I can't tonight." I let the words glide casually across my tongue. "I've made some plans."

"Oh, really? Where you going?"

Do I really have to answer this? "Momma, I'm going out to a church program." She waited for further explanation, but I was in no hurry to give her one.

"All right," she sighed. "All I'm tryin' to do is look out for you. I'm your momma and that's my job." It must be nice to be able to pull rank like that at a moment's notice.

"His name is Stelson Brown, okay?" I answered. "The people at my job can give you a good description of him, and I will leave his business card on my refrigerator—so if I'm not at the house by three tomorrow, you come look on my refrigerator, okay?"

"That's much better," she said. "You're a single woman in the new century. I don't care how tough or how smart you think you are, you need to let somebody know where you are. You ain't got to be afraid of the devil, but you do need to know how to beat him at his own games."

"Yes, ma'am."

"Shondra," she said, "have a nice time tonight."

"Thank you, Momma. I will."

Stelson's church was probably thirty miles on the other side of Dallas. The long ride over in his champagne Toyota Sequoia was pleasant. The lights from the dashboard cast a cozy glow across our faces as we talked and listened to smooth jazz on the radio. We skipped the small talk and landed right in the middle of an authentic conversation about college life. I told him about my experiences pledging Delta Sigma Theta. He told me about his experiences as a tutor, which had obviously prepared him for the challenge of tutoring the students at True Way.

We took seats on the third row. The church was spacious, with towering ceilings and wide aisles. Individual chairs instead of pews. It reminded me of a gymnasium more than anything else. And the Spirit within was definitely one of a pep rally. Energy. Livelihood. Smiles everywhere.

Stelson and I received warm greetings from the members who were seated near us. They seemed to know Brother Brown well, embracing him and asking him how things were going with the business.

"We're blessed," Stelson replied. Then he introduced me: "This is my friend LaShondra Smith."

I watched them, waiting for the moment their faces said, *she's black*. But before I could see it in a half smile or a subtle hesitation, they were already shaking my hand and welcoming me into our Father's house.

Taking in the breadth of the building, I realized that the congregation was a rainbow of colors, from the darkest ebony to the fairest ivory and everything in between. There were a few interracial couples with sandy-haired children, worshipping just like everybody else.

"Our God is a wonderful God; he lives . . ." I closed my eyes, forgot about the colors, and lifted my hands in worship, basking in the presence of the Lord, which poured out on each of us with no respect to color. "Come, let us worship the Lord in His great holiness." The beat was a little different, but the words were the same. The Spirit was the same.

Well, I thought I knew what Saturday Night Live would be like, but I wasn't prepared for what I saw that night at Stelson's church. Those kids were on the verge of hip-hop dancing, and I thought for sure lightning was going to strike us all down. But between songs, teenagers of all shades took the stage and testified to what God had done for them and how they were gaining victories in their young lives; how they were standing up for Christ at school, with their athletic teams, and on their jobs; how they had won souls for Christ. It was inspiring, and I was so proud of my little brothers and sisters in Christ.

The church kitchen was buzzing with children after the service. Stelson and other workers busied themselves squirting ketchup and mustard on hot dogs and passing out Dixie cups of juice. As handsome as Stelson already was, he looked even more attractive in an apron. I asked if I could help, but he assured me that they had it under control.

I watched and waited at the back table, smiling as parents walked by to pick up their children. The skeptical part of me started up again, looking, searching for what had to be wrong with Stelson. There had to be something, no matter how tiny it might be.

I did a little self-talk. *I can accept him just as he is, as good as he is, white as he is; he might not be black, but he is my brother in Christ.*

After all the kids had been served, Stelson courteously asked if he should stay to clean up, but the other helpers gave him the green light to go ahead and leave. "I see you've got a guest." One of the older black ladies smiled at him. Her silvery gray hair was the only testament to her age.

"Are you sure, Sister Milford?"

"Oh, we've got it. You go on 'head with your lady friend."

"Yes, ma'am," he agreed. "I'll see you all next time."

It was dark when we left the building, but the night was still young. Stelson took me to a posh restaurant that I'd only read about in the society section of the newspaper. For a ritzy place, it seemed to have a pretty casual atmosphere—jeans, boots, and sweaters. No blacks, but it wasn't the first time I'd been somewhere and been the only African-American in the house. We approached the podium together, and Stelson did all the talking, telling the waiter that we needed a table for two in the nonsmoking section. "Brown," he said.

The waiter, a white man in his mid-twenties, looked at us both as if we were there to steal something. I knew that look, but I guess Stelson didn't, because he smiled on back to the waiting area. "This place is great. You're gonna love it. The owner is one of my clients."

"Mmm."

A cute elderly couple got on the waiting list after us, followed by a young pair. Stelson and I laughed that their parents had probably dropped them off. We watched them, amused at their obvious nervousness.

"Did you enjoy yourself at church tonight?" Stelson asked.

"Oh, I had a great time in the Lord. Thanks for inviting me."

"Thanks for coming. It was nice having someone by my side for once."

"You never bring women to church?" I was a little puzzled.

"Usually after I bless the food that first time, I scare them off." He laughed softly.

I laughed, probably too loudly for that restaurant. "So is that your screening device?"

"Pretty much," he said. "I mean, don't get me wrong. I don't do it to scare women off. But I really don't feel led to start at spiritual square one with anybody, you know? I know my weaknesses, and I know I'm liable to get off course at any given time. I need somebody who can run with me. Somebody who can stand with me. I like a down-to-earth woman. But I *need* a Christian woman."

"Harris, your table is ready," the waiter called. The teenagers across from us rose and were met by a waitress who then led them to their seats.

"Didn't they come in after us?" Stelson asked me.

"Yeah."

"Hmm . . ." Stelson shrugged. "Maybe they're sitting in the smoking section."

The elderly couple had long been seated. And when two more couples came in after us and were seated within the twenty-five minutes that we'd been waiting, I told Stelson that I was going to ask the waiter what was going on.

"Excuse me." I placed my hand firmly on the edge of the podium. "We've been waiting for a table for nearly thirty minutes, and several couples who came after us have already been seated. How much longer before you have a table ready for Brown?"

"Hmm." The man ran his finger along the list of names. I looked down at the list and saw for myself that *Brown* was visible, while the names above it and the three names after it had been crossed off. "We do have a seat for Mr. Brown, but I'm having a hard time finding one for you."

"What?" I raised my voice. "Let me speak to your manager."

"I'm sorry. He's not available." The waiter took off his badge, but not before I read his name.

"Look, Aaron, get somebody else over here. Now!"

He seemed a bit flustered, now that I knew his name. "That won't be necessary. I can get you a seat—"

"What's going on?" Stelson walked up behind me.

"Aaron here won't seat us because I'm black," I almost screamed.

"Mr. Brown, th-that's not true," Aaron stammered. "I told her that—"

"Is Mr. Maxwell here tonight?" Stelson asked.

"Mr. Maxwell?"

"Yes. Victor Maxwell—the man who owns this restaurant. I know him very well."

"No, no." Out pops the sweat above Aaron's lip. "Mr. Maxwell isn't here tonight. Look, I'm sure this was just a misunderstanding."

"No, I understood you very well." I nodded my head. Then I turned to Stelson and said, "I don't want to eat here."

"Okay," he said, "we don't have to." Then he said to Aaron, "Mr. Maxwell will be in touch with you."

Stelson matched my pace, and we reached the car in record time. My heart was pounding, my face hot with anger. I wished that I could have known this was going to happen—I would have had a barrage of defensive terminology waiting on the tip of my tongue. But just like that night when I froze at the movie theater with Judith's boyfriend, I left. I felt small, like a child among adults. I was mad at the waiter, but I was also mad at myself for leaving. *Isn't that what he wanted me to do?*

Stelson opened the passenger's door for me, and I climbed inside, grabbing the door handle and closing it before he had a chance to. I watched him walk to his side, brow creased in thought. He got in and started the engine. "You still hungry?"

"Of course I'm still hungry." I rolled my eyes, ready to release my anger in Stelson's direction. "You think discrimination stops black folks from eatin'?"

"That's not what I meant, LaShondra." Stelson's eyes apologized. "I just—"

"Yes, I'm hungry. I'd like some fast food to go, and then I'd like to go home."

"Okay. Where to?"

"There's a Boston Market near my house. That will do." I put my elbow on the door panel and let my chin rest in my hand, keeping my head turned away from Stelson. I couldn't help but think of how things would have been different if I'd seen it coming. But I hadn't, and there was no way I could take it back now. Yes, Stelson would call his client and let him know what an awful experience we had. But his complaint would do little to eradicate the painful experience that so many of my African-American brothers and sisters live every day.

There were several cars ahead of us in the drive-through, making the wait so long that I wished I'd gone inside. Then again, I'd had more than enough of people staring at us.

"LaShondra, I'm really sorry about what happened at the restaurant."

"It's not your fault," I said, still looking away.

"I know it's not, but I still feel bad about the experience you had there."

"It was just as much your experience as it was mine." I turned my nose down and looked at him.

"What's that supposed to mean?"

"It means that when you're with a black woman, your social status is greatly diminished," I said.

"That's ridiculous." He shook his head.

"Is it?" I blinked my eyes very deliberately.

"LaShondra, Aaron is one prejudiced person who happens to be in charge of when and where people get seated in one restaurant. And actually, Aaron won't be in charge of that much longer."

"No, but he'll get a job somewhere else and do the same thing. Maybe he'll grow up to be a loan officer and deny mortgages to black people. Or he might be a doctor and treat disease in his black patients with a little less tenacity. There are any number of ways that he'll be able to keep right on being Aaron. Matter of fact, now that he's lost his job because of a black person, he'll probably be worse."

"Do you really think it works that way?" Stelson asked me, finally pulling up to the window. He paid for the food and handed it to me.

"How else does it work, Stelson?"

"Individuals making individual choices. I mean, I know that African-Americans—"

"See, that's where you're wrong." I held up my index finger and pressed my back into the door's panel so that I could face him. "You don't know *anything* about being African-American. If you did, you wouldn't have been sitting there like, 'Oh, maybe they're just sitting in the smoking section.' Everybody ain't sittin' in the smoking section, Stelson." I tried hard to keep from yelling at him. "You're out of your mind if you don't believe that there's a network of people out there like Aaron."

"I just don't like to jump to conclusions," he defended himself, entering traffic and heading back to my house.

"It's not about jumping to conclusions. It's about the black experience in America, Stelson."

"Look, I understand what it means to have someone look at you and assume that you're a *serial killer* or a *stalker*," he said with obvious reference to the questions I'd asked before agreeing to a date. "I know that's not fair."

I blew out a hard breath of air. "Stelson, you and I are talking about two different things. At worst, the general public probably assumes that because you're a good-looking white man, you must be arrogant and pushy. My first thoughts about you weren't that you were dangerous. I didn't give that a thought until you asked me out. But blackness has its own negative connotations from the start, and until you've worn black, you can't begin to empathize with me."

"I don't think that's true," he countered. "You're not giving me enough credit as a human being, let alone as your brother in Christ."

"I give you some credit, Stelson—you do try. And a lot of well-meaning white people like you have always tried to understand. It's just . . . I don't know how to explain it, Stelson. It's something you have to live."

Stelson didn't have a response for that one. *I don't even know why I let this little friendship get this far.* When he pulled up in my driveway, I flicked the switch to unlock the door and let myself out of his SUV. With my hand on the handle, I turned to him and said, "Good night, Stelson."

"That sounds final." He peered into me with his deep blue eyes.

"I think it is, Stelson."

He walked me to my porch but, respectfully, didn't approach the door. I reached into my mailbox and pulled out

Saturday's mail, thumbing through it as though Stelson weren't standing right behind me.

"Can I tell you something I've been wanting to tell you since I met you?" he asked.

"Go ahead." I stopped and looked at him.

"You're a beautiful person, LaShondra—inside and out. If I never see you again, I just want you to know that."

"Thanks, Stelson. So are you. Good-bye."

Through the peephole I watched him walk back to his car, one hand in his pocket, the other cupping the back of his neck. Part of me wanted to say something else to him, though I didn't know what there was to say. Stelson was white. I was black. And as much as I enjoyed our conversations the few times we spent together, we couldn't expect to live our lives in a bubble. We had to face reality.

He stopped, still thinking. I stopped breathing, wondering what his next move would be. Then he moved toward his car again. The engine revved up, and he backed out of my driveway.

Most of the mail was junk, but there was one from the Plainview Independent School District that caught my eye. I opened it, read it, and learned that I was scheduled for an informal conference on the first day of the spring semester. I was to meet Dr. Marion Hunt, the executive director of personnel, regarding allegations of unprofessional conduct and practices.

Lord, I don't have time for all this mess!

CHAPTER 12

What happened?" I called Peaches as soon as I got home from school. "I heard you got suspended!"

"I did," she blared.

"What happened?"

"I told Mr. Hopewell that he needed to get out of my purse and he could kiss me where the sun don't shine." She smacked her lips and popped her gum.

"What! Peaches, why did you do that?"

"Because he put his hand inside my purse, trying to see if I had some mace."

"What made him think you had mace?"

" 'Cause a white girl told him she saw me with some mace in the bathroom. Then he gone just come up and put his hands in my purse like some kind of crazy man, so I told him to get out my purse and kiss my behind. He better be glad I didn't slap him!"

"Oh, man," I sighed. "How many days are you suspended for?"

"Three days!"

"What about prom?"

"I can't go." She tried to hide her pain by increasing her volume, but it wasn't working. "When I got to the principal's office, I told Mr. Lathan everything. And I even told him that I was a senior and that I was already ready for prom. He said that

if I show up, I could get arrested for trespassing. I can't go anywhere near school property or attend any school functions while I'm on suspension."

"Did you tell him that Mr. Hopewell went through your personal belongings? Did you show Mr. Lathan that you didn't really have any mace?"

"Yes, I showed him everything in my purse when I got in the office. They saw that I didn't have any mace, and then they just started making up stuff. Saying that it didn't matter if I had mace or not, because I had been disrespectful to my teacher, but I don't give a care about Mr. Hopewell! I didn't have any mace, and he didn't have no business trying to go through my purse."

"You told your momma yet?"

"No. You know how my momma is—any phone call from the office means that somewhere down the line I did something wrong. I'm waiting until the last possible moment to tell her."

She had a point. "Dang, Peaches."

"Mr. Hopewell is so prejudiced!"

"All of them are," I griped with her.

"Now I can't go to the prom." Her cry broke through. "I swear, I cannot stand *white people."*

⧈ ⧈ ⧈

Quinn and Peaches rode together to singles Bible study, but she promised she'd save me a seat next to her. "Hey, girl." We hugged.

"Hey, Quinn," I said to him.

"Hello. Mark has been asking about you," he joked.

Peaches elbowed him. "Please. Don't even go there. Your boy needs prayer."

"I know, I know," he laughed.

I felt like the third wheel, with Quinn and me sitting on either side of Peaches. Next time I wouldn't take her up on the offer to save me a seat. They whispered and giggled and slipped in a touch or two, Peaches letting her hand fall on his arm in laughter, Quinn checking her wristwatch for the time—I just knew Brother Johnson was gonna kick them out of class. Still, I liked knowing that my best friend was in love.

Brother Johnson followed up on the previous week's session topic: the prenegotiations. "There are some things that you need to let others know up front. Can anyone give me an example of those things?"

"Kids from previous relationships," a sister called out.

"Marital status," another sister yelled. A few of us laughed. She added, "As silly as it sounds, you'd be surprised how many people will get involved without saying that they're married. They're like, 'but you didn't ask me.'"

"I agree," Brother Johnson said. "What else?"

"Other obligations that you might have," a newcomer commented. He was short and a little chubby, but otherwise handsome.

"Such as?"

"Elderly parents, siblings that you care for—ongoing obligations that affect the level of attention you can give to the relationship," he clarified.

"I understand completely. Anything else?"

"Where you stand spiritually," I said.

"That's imperative," Brother Johnson said. "Let's read Second Corinthians, six and fourteen. It says, 'Be ye not unequally yoked together with unbelievers: for what fellowship hath righteousness and unrighteousness? And what communion hath light with darkness?' I think we've all heard this quoted at one time or another. What does that mean to you?"

"It means don't marry someone who isn't a believer," Quinn said.

"In its simplest, most basic form, yes. Don't get married

to someone who hasn't accepted Christ. But let's take it further. A lot of people consider themselves 'saved' or forgiven. The issue isn't whether or not a person who has accepted Christ is forgiven. But what do you look for in terms of their spiritual maturity?"

"Someone who willingly serves the Lord, without grumbling about it. They don't see church as a chore but as a place to worship and receive power for living," Peaches said.

"A person who reaches out and wants to help others come to higher ground spiritually," the newcomer added.

A brother who had come in late added, "Someone who exemplifies the spirit of Christ by showing their love—helping you out, treating you well. Someone who's always ready to take your hand and go seek God for answers to life's problems."

Someone like Stelson.

All the way home, I knew what I had to do. But it took me another day to follow through. Stelson called on Wednesday and left a message asking if there would be a tutoring session. I purposely returned his call at his home during business hours and left the message that there would be no tutoring until mid-January because we were out on Christmas break.

I went on to church, glad to have the opportunity to contribute to corporate worship—something that I always missed when I had to tutor. I stopped off to use the restroom before entering the sanctuary. Shannon was there, with her wide, transparent smile. "Will Mr. Brown be here tonight?" she asked.

"Oh, I doubt that Stelson will be here," I said casually.

"Mmm. Well, I hope you guys give me a call so we can all do something some time." She shook the excess water from her hands and grabbed a paper towel from the dispenser. I had to give it to her, she was good. "You know, I was gonna say the other night—it looks like we've somehow got our checkers mixed up, huh?" She crossed her arms and waited breathlessly, as though she was prepared either to laugh or offer a defense, depending on my response.

"I don't know about *you*, but *my* checkers are fine," I said with a calmness that I could only attribute to the fact that I was in a church restroom.

She rushed to deny offense, her hands held out like a traffic officer. "Oh, I didn't mean anything by it. I was just saying, it's a shock, seeing a black woman with a white man like Mr. Brown."

The audacity! I put my hand on my hip and let my backbone slip. "Shannon, you've got a lot of nerve. Do you think white women have some kind of monopoly on interracial dating? That you have a privilege to be with *any* man because you're white, but I don't? That I can't be with a white man 'like Mr. Brown' because a white man 'like Mr. Brown' should be with a white woman like you?"

"LaShondra, I don't know what to say." She threw her paper towel into the wastebasket.

"Well, I am not trading any so-called checkers with you, and you can stop with the whole let's-get-together-sometime act. It's not gonna happen." I left her standing there with her mouth wide open.

I called Stelson later that night, when I knew he'd be home, to really talk to him. I wasn't sure exactly what to say, but I needed his conversation. To hear his voice, feel him laugh. "Hi, Stelson, it's me—LaShondra. Hey, I want to apologize for the other night. I took my anger out on you and I really didn't mean to. There's just so much to this whole black-white thing. I think we need to talk. When can we get together again?"

I heard pages flipping. "Um, it looks like . . . Thursday

morning and afternoon—but I'm flying home to Louisiana late Thursday night, so any time after six is out. Are you free?"

"Well, I do have some shopping to do."

"Do you mind if I tag along?" he asked.

"No, not at all," I said. "Actually, I might need your advice. I've got to buy something for my father. His birthday is on the thirtieth, and I'd like to go ahead and kill two birds on Christmas day."

"Okay."

Later Peaches called me to ask if I wanted to hang with her on Thursday and wade through the slush pile to snatch up the last-minute holiday deals.

"Oh, I can't. I've already made plans for tomorrow morning."

"What you got going on, girl?" she asked innocently.

"I'm just gonna, um, I'm gonna go get my dad's birthday gift and then get something quick to eat. Nothing much, but I know the traffic tomorrow is gonna be crazy out your way. The Galleria is always a mess." I laughed nervously, hoping that she wouldn't pick up on my tension.

"Okay," she said slowly, suspiciously. "I guess I'll see you Friday at my parents' house."

"Okay."

"All right, girl, keep it real. Bye."

My stomach churned. *Real?* I wasn't being real with her. I wasn't ready to be real with her. I wasn't even sure if I was ready to be real with myself at this point. In prayer I brought the situation before God and searched the Word for His answers, though I already knew. I mean, I didn't have to be Solomon to realize that I had to be true to myself. Problem was, *myself* happened to be changing. I liked Stelson despite the fact that he was white. I liked him more than Mark. I liked him more than a lot of other black men I'd known. He was kind and considerate at the same time that he was challenging and interesting. He was right there in the middle of being a gentleman and a leader: gentle enough to put others' interests above his; confident enough to stand for his beliefs. Yes, I liked him—a lot.

I studied him as he walked to meet me in the foyer of Dillard's. One hand in his pocket, the other swaying gently at his side. He was dressed in a cotton plaid button-down shirt tucked neatly into his jeans, and a brown suede jacket. As he looked down and zipped his keys up in his coat pocket, I noticed how his dark hair shined in the sunlight, catching the rays and dispersing them throughout.

"Wow!" I looked over my shoulder and saw two women leaving Dillard's. One was tall and seemed cheerful, full of the Christmas spirit. The other one, short and maternal-looking, was an odd match for her much younger shopping partner.

They were clearly gawking at Stelson. I really didn't mind that they were making remarks about his looks. But it did occur to me that those women didn't care one bit about whether Stelson was a good person or knew God or had a good attitude. This was my second time witnessing the frenzy that went on in his presence—women preparing themselves for his scrutiny, hoping that he might acknowledge them. And yet, he walked into that foyer without the least bit of arrogance trailing him.

"Hey, Shondra. You look great. You ready?" He hugged me casually.

"Thanks. Yeah, I'm ready."

He put his right hand at my back and opened the door for me with his left. I didn't look back to see the expressions on their faces. I'd seen it before, and I saw it plenty of times that morning in the mall. Honestly, it was enough to make you want to go check yourself in the mirror. The staring, staring, staring was irritating. Everywhere I turned, somebody else was looking at us, trying to figure out if we were actually together. I made a mental tally—we were an equal-opportunity spectacle. For once I was glad to see other interracial couples—like the relief I'd always felt when I walked into a meeting or a workshop and saw another face of color in the room.

"You okay?" he asked me.

"Yeah, I'm fine." I rolled up the corners of my lips. *I am fine. I'm not gonna let these people's attitudes stop me from doing what I have to do.* And it was then, for the first time, that I realized: people do what they want to do whether others like it or not. Why should I be any different?

After Stelson helped me pick out the perfect pair of boots for my father, we decided to ride together in his car to the Marble Creamery. The Marble Creamery wasn't actually one of those "black" places (I wasn't ready to go black-place yet with Stelson), but its ownership regularly employed people of color. It was located in one of those upwardly bound neighborhoods with its fair share of educated African-Americans who, like myself, wanted to "buy black" whenever we could. We placed our orders, got our ice cream, and headed toward a booth.

"I am eternally grateful," Stelson said, taking a huge spoonful of caramel-flavored ice cream with crushed Heath bar into his mouth. "I'm gonna take a pint of this home with me."

"I told you it was good."

"By the way, I got you something." He reached into the inner pocket of his jacket and pulled out a red envelope. "Merry Christmas."

"Stelson, you didn't have to do that," I said.

"I know. I wanted to."

"This is so nice of you." I took the card from him. He'd written my name across the front of the envelope and sealed it with a gold sticker. I opened the card and read it aloud:

"Christmas is when all God's children celebrate
The greatest gift of all.
I count it a blessing
To share it with you.
MERRY CHRISTMAS!
—Stelson"

"Thank you, Stelson."

"You're welcome." He nodded. "Okay." He ignored the spoonful of ice cream quickly melting on his tongue. "You wanted to talk."

"Okay, can we just let the card moment pass first?" I laughed. My pulse quickened at the thought of actually pouring my heart out to this white man sitting across from me. I felt my soul's veil lift, exposing LaShondra in a way that I dared not bare her in front of a white person. I was bifacial, I knew: one face for white people and one for blacks. But after this veil-lifting, what would I be—an Oreo? A sell-out?

"I'm anxious to know what you have to say," Stelson said.

"Well, in case you haven't noticed, I am somewhat uncomfortable with this race issue," I began. I shifted a little in my chair, searching for the right words. The tangles in my mind pushed and pulled, attempting to loosen themselves.

"I gathered that." He nodded. "What's the problem, as you see it?"

I paused.

"Look, LaShondra, you don't have to be politically correct here," he said. "I'm not gonna get up and walk out. I can take it. Go ahead and say what's on your mind."

I let it rip. "Okay, here it goes. I don't trust white people. I don't like white people. I think that for the most part, white people are a bunch of crooks who have never done anything but steal, cheat, and kill. And anybody who comes from that lineage has a little bit of it in 'em—I don't care how good they try to be. White men are arrogant and manipulative, and white women are simple, whiny, and lazy."

I expected him to flinch, sit back, draw in some air and cross his arms. But he didn't; he just sat there with his hands flat on the table, eyes focused on mine. "And how did you arrive at those conclusions?" he asked.

"Life. Experiences."

"Your personal experiences?"

"Some were mine; some are secondhand. But they're true for the most part." I shrugged. "A lot of it came from my dad."

"What about white Christians?"

"I . . . I really didn't think much about white Christians. I mean, there might be a few, but deep down inside, I've always thought that if white people were *really* Christians, they wouldn't have let slavery go on for three hundred years and they wouldn't keep hiding behind the cross and systematically discriminating against other human beings. The fact that black people are still behind in this country is no accident.

"But then . . ." I shoved in a mouthful of ice cream.

"Then what?"

The ice cream on my tongue transformed from solid to liquid and slipped down my throat. "Then I met you."

He waited patiently for me to continue. "And you were kind and helpful, and I just never got that white vibe, you know? I've never felt that you, Stelson Brown, had anything but my best interest at heart. I mean, I suspected that you were prejudiced and deranged, but you're passing every test. You're doing better than the brothers." I laughed. "And now I'm thinking, if Stelson isn't everything I thought he was, maybe I've been . . . wrong . . . about a lot of things. Then I met the people at your church, and I felt so . . . accepted. I was ready to pigeonhole them, but I couldn't, because they treated me with such kindness. I really wasn't expecting that. I've been studying love, and for the first time, I think I understand what it means for people to know that you are Christian by your love."

That's *what He's been trying to tell me.* I spoke the words to Stelson, but they hit home with me. It was never about black or white—it was about my relationship with Christ. Could I relinquish my definition of myself—first black, then Christian? Was my attitude toward white people reflective of the Holy Spirit, which I claimed to have dwelling within me?

"Okay, you still haven't told me what the problem is. You had low expectations, but I'm turning out to be a decent person. So what's the problem?"

"I don't know." I looked down. "It's just that—you will never, ever find yourself in my position. It's like if you said, 'yeah, I feel sorry for women when they're in labor.' I'm sure you do—but you will never give birth. That pain is something you yourself will never know personally. And sometimes, like when we were at your client's restaurant, I feel as though our lack of common reference puts us worlds apart."

He nodded. "Okay. I can agree with the fact that I can't know your pain as intensely as you do. But there's a lot that I won't ever be able to do: I won't ever be a woman, I won't ever be Japanese, I won't ever be a plant, I won't ever be African-American, and I can't change the past. Does that mean that I can't have a relationship with you here and now?"

"What about you, Stelson?" I stepped from under the microscope. "What do you really think about black people—in the recesses of your mind?"

"I grew up in Louisiana around a lot of different cultures, races, and languages. Everybody is mixed up in

Louisiana—I'm one of the few people I know who doesn't have a living black relative, though I'm sure I've got some in my family tree. But Louisiana isn't a bubble, you know? I picked up on some biased views just like every other American does."

"And you've never acted on those biases?" I asked.

"Before I finished college and started working, I was pretty reticent to interact with people of other races. I had the generic white American fears—that black people would rob me or beat me up or steal my car.

"But then a couple of things happened. One of them was experience in the business world. The more I dealt with people, the more I found out that the only color that matters to ninety-nine percent of the population is green, no matter what race or nationality they are. I've dated white women, black women, French women, Creole women, an Asian woman. I've worked with clients from several different countries and backgrounds, and I can tell you: money makes chameleons. Especially when you're dealing with people who aren't rooted in Christ."

"Well." I pooched my lips out. "I can't argue with that."

"The second thing is something that I wouldn't have known if I hadn't experienced membership in an integrated church. I will always be grateful for my roots in the Assemblies of God. But when I joined Living Word and saw God pouring out his spirit on every nationality, I knew it was the right place for me. I've learned through my church experience that love doesn't have a color. Maybe it does for people who haven't experienced the love of God, but not for those of us who know better."

"And it was just that easy for you?" I asked.

"I don't know if 'easy' is the word for it—I guess the word is 'simple.' If you can be talked into something, you can be talked out of it. But when you experience something for yourself, you can't deny that. It becomes your undisputed truth, and no one can convince you otherwise. That's why it's so important for us all to come out of our little shells and live. Get to know one another beyond what we see in the media and what we've heard through the generations. Sometimes the truth isn't in the facts, and the facts don't always tell the truth. The truth is in the experience."

I played around with my ice cream, pondering Stelson's words while he went to the restroom. It was as though he wanted to leave me there alone to weigh his words, let them settle into my fabric. I had a decision to make. The only thing that kept me from opening up to Stelson was ignorance and fear. I hadn't had any significant relationships with white people, and I was afraid that I might forget who I was if I did. *But am I going to throw away this gift because it came wrapped in different wrapping paper?*

When Stelson returned, I was ready to give him the green light. "This is new for me, Stelson. I've never had any kind of relationship with a Christian man, black or white. You have to give me some credit here, for my lack of experience. I'm gonna give this a shot."

"So, this is a relationship, then?" he asked.

"Are you asking me to categorize this?"

"Yes."

I thought about the question. "It might be," I answered.

"Well, just in case it is, I want you to know that I hope we're in agreement to pray about the direction that it goes—whether it's a friendship, a fellowship, whatever."

"I agree."

"Well, it's done, then." He held up his ice-cream cup and we toasted. *Okay, that was goofy.* But it felt good.

Just to our left, two women laughed and got their dates' attention. One of the sisters rolled her eyes at me and went back to the low whisper that she'd been using before. Now, I had seen enough eyes rolled to know that she was not pleased with what she saw.

I willed myself to focus on Stelson, and we talked a little about our Christmas plans. He planned to be in Louisiana for the weekend, but he'd be back on Monday to prepare for yet another business trip to Florida the following week.

"Busy man," I remarked.

"Unusually busy," he said. "We rarely do this much business so late in the year."

The couples next to us got up from their seats and walked toward the door. I was glad to see them go. They'd been talking about us since we toasted, and I didn't know how much more of it I could handle. I had had it up to my neck with people staring at us everywhere we went. As they reached the doorway, one of the men yelled to the other, "Yeah, man. You better be careful out there tonight. Bundle up! They say there's a whole lotta jungle fever going around." I looked up and caught the brother's glance at me.

I felt myself standing, my feet preparing to carry me straight up to this brother's face. "Hey! Hey!" I called to him.

"LaShondra." Stelson grabbed my arm.

The brother yanked his coat tighter, smiled at me, and continued on out the door.

"LaShondra." I felt Stelson's hand gripping me tightly.

"Let go of me."

"LaShondra, honey, that's not gonna help anything," he said, coaxing me back to my seat.

It took me a moment to pull myself together. It had been a long day, and I'd been a spectacle the whole time. "Maybe that's what's really bothering me more than anything," I said. "Maybe it's this constant pressure, with everyone staring us, talking about us. It's ridiculous. Don't you feel it, too?"

"Yeah, but it's not new to me. I told you, I've been out with the entire rainbow. You learn to ignore ignorance. It's not your fault or our problem."

We did our best to finish our ice cream in peace. And just when I thought all the pieces were back in place, I felt a tap on my shoulder and heard my best friend's voice say my name.

I jumped like I used to when my momma came through the door as I was doing something I knew I shouldn't be doing. "Oh, hey, Peaches."

She looked at Stelson, then back at me. "I thought you were . . . um . . ."

"Peaches, this is my friend, Stelson. Stelson, this is my best friend, Peaches." To say that it was an awkward moment would be an understatement. Peaches was looking at me like, *what in the world?* And here was Stelson, just cheesin' away, oblivious to the situation at hand.

Stelson got up to shake her hand. "Hello, it's nice to meet you, Peaches."

"My name is Patricia." She barely let him touch her fingertips. Peaches clutched her purse and looked at me again, still not sure what to make of things.

"Um, Stelson, would you excuse us for a moment?" I asked him.

"Sure," he said, grabbing my empty ice-cream bowl so that he could dispose of it for me. "I'll go ahead and get the car warmed up."

Peaches took his place across from me. "Get the car warmed up!"

"Peaches, it's not . . . well . . ." *How do I unravel this mess?*

"Go ahead—say it's not what I think it is, so I can tell you that you are flat out lying." She slapped her hand on the table. "Go ahead—tell me that you were not at this parlor having ice cream with whoever that was just now."

"Let me start at the beginning. His name is Stelson Brown."

Her nostrils flared, and she breathed heavier as she bit her lip, smearing lipstick onto her teeth.

"Okay." I came from a different angle. "We met at my job—he's the engineer that I invited to the career fair last month at—"

"He's *white,* Shondra."

"I know." I nodded calmly, hoping that she would see the humor in her observation.

"You didn't tell me that you were gonna be hanging out with a white man today. Come to think of it, you lied to me. You said you couldn't go shopping!"

"I told you that I had plans already." I lowered my voice, hoping that she would follow suit.

"You did not say anything about plans with somebody else—let alone a white man! See, you're already actin' like 'em. Evasive! Coverin' up stuff; lyin' through omission!"

"Peaches, I did *not* lie to you. I have never lied to you. You know me better than that."

"*Know* you? Pulleaze!" She raised her hands as if to say "stop" and stood up. "You might as well have lied to me—matter of fact, I would prefer a lie right now. I don't know what's worse—the fact that he's white or the fact that you kept it from me."

"And is there any wonder why?" I asked her, drawing my back to the bench.

She cut her eyes at me and waved her hand as though she were warding off a dog. "Go on with your little white man." She got up and took her place behind the last person in line.

She was beyond reason; I knew that. And yet, I hurt for her and with her. We'd shared everything, but I had let the fact that Stelson was white come between us. I didn't say another word to her. I just left her there and walked back to the car, wondering if this Boaz was worth all the trouble.

CHAPTER 13

I begged Sister Lewis to substitute for me in children's church and promised that all the materials she'd need were in the plastic tubs. "There are crayons, scissors, and glue to complete the activities. The kids can look at the charts and tell you whose turn it is to pray, pass out the materials, and distribute the snacks. Again, thanks so much for sitting in for me today. I just . . . I really need to be in service."

She looked at me, perhaps noting the swelling in my eyes. "Sure, Sister Smith. I understand."

I let my mind drift out of the church from time to time—back to the night before. After another disappointing breakup, this time with one who said he just wasn't happy with the relationship anymore, I plopped myself down on the third pew and had a big, fat pity party, crying through everything—even the offering. I knew that my heart couldn't take much more of this slashing and patching.

I paid attention long enough to hear Pastor mention that the tape library had acquired a set of tapes for singles by Missionary Preston of the New Hope Church of God in Christ. She wasn't much older than I was—probably in her early thirties—and I'd listened to her teach a few times when I was in the Purity Class at Gethsemane. I was the first one at the table picking up a set after service. I listened to it all the way home.

"I think that the crux of a happy marriage lies with God, as does everything else in the life of a Christian," she preached. "When two people who are already committed to Christ come together, they complement each other. Those two whole people don't have to beat around the bush when it comes to what they will or will not accept in a relationship." There was a break as the congregation cheered her on.

"You see, the world has made this courtship and marriage process way too hard. If people would stop actin' *married before they* get *married, we'd probably cut the chase time in half." There was a hum of laughter. "I mean, think about it. People who weren't looking to be married would stop tying up those of you who are seriously seeking a mate. But that's not how the world operates, and that is precisely why relationships between men and women of the world will continue to decline. But that should not and does not have any bearing on what* you *can expect as a couple united in Christ. I believe that God arranges marriages between His people."*

That was all I needed to hear. That's what I want, Lord: a marriage that *You* arrange. *It was then—with that one request—that I stopped long enough to get back to square one. And it was there, at square one, that God met me and began to teach me to honor Him, to honor myself, and to be ready for my man of God.*

⧈ ⧈ ⧈

I spent Christmas morning at my parents' house, opening gifts and eating everything in sight. They loved their watches that Jonathan and I chipped in to buy, but Daddy said he wasn't gonna wear his to the bank. "They'll think I've got too much for a black man. They might report me to the social security administration or something—put me under audit."

"Daddy, please. Can we have one day without reference to racial prejudice?" I begged him.

"Humph." He let the sound jerk him backward and then settled back into his slump.

"I'll wear mine to church this coming Sunday." Momma admired it in the sunlight that streamed through the kitchen window. The watch fit snugly just above her plump wrist. "Yeah, this is perfect. Won't be slippin' and slidin' all down my arm."

"Nothin' slips and slides up and down your arm anymore," Daddy joked.

"Mmm-hmm," she moaned, and rolled her eyes at him.

"It looks pretty on you, Momma." I hugged her. "Merry Christmas."

"Merry Christmas, baby," she sighed, with her eyebrows drawn in tightly.

"What?" I asked her.

"I just hate to see you all alone at Christmas. Don't you have any men friends? I know you get tired of hanging around here every year with just me and your daddy."

"Momma, please—not today, okay?"

"All right." She pulled me in tightly for another hug. "I'll leave it alone. You goin' by the Millers' house today to see Peaches and Eric?"

"I might," I said. "I don't know. I do have a gift for Eric, but Peaches . . . she and Eric might not be there."

"Well, if you do, tell 'em I said hello and to have a merry Christmas."

Aunt Emma, my father's oldest sister, came by to chat a while and show us her new Cadillac. As always, the volume increased with Daddy's side of the family around. It didn't matter if you were in the next room or two feet away, they always yelled at you. A second cousin stopped by to show off his new girlfriend for a few minutes. A couple of members from Gethsemane brought greetings and more food—pies and cakes from the saints' ovens were always mouthwatering.

"This 7Up cake looks delicious." My mother complimented Mother Jamerson on her way out the door to deliver the rest of her baked goods. "It'll be gone by Friday, with my sweet tooth."

"Shondra," Momma asked as she helped Aunt Emma pack a bag of food to take to Grandmomma Smith, "how did things go with your man friend the other night at church?"

"It was fine." I took a bite of 7Up cake and prayed that she would leave it alone. But I knew better.

"Hmm. You gonna be seeing him today?" She sat down across from me at the kitchen table.

"No, ma'am. He went to Louisiana with his family."

"What's his name?" Aunt Emma asked. "You know we got family in Louisiana."

"I'm pretty sure we don't have any relation close enough to speak of," I said.

"Well," Daddy said, "we're kin to the Mohares. What part of Louisiana is he from?" As if I might possibly be able to tell him whether Stelson knew the Mohares personally.

"I'm not quite sure. I didn't ask him all that, Daddy."

"Well, you just make sure you know who his people are. A lot of folks from Louisiana *look* black, but they're not *near* as black as you think they are."

"What difference does it make what color they are?" I asked him. He looked at me as if I'd lost my mind. In an instant I lost my nerve and abandoned the assault. "I mean, everybody's got a little bit of everything in 'em by now."

"She's right, Jon," Aunt Emma jumped in, "our great-great-grandmother was a full-blooded Indian."

"That's *Indian*, not white." He beat an open hand on the table.

Aunt Emma laughed and slapped my father on the back.

"I betcha if you go back far enough into anybody's roots, you'll find a bunch of stuff, Jon. You probably got white in you, too."

"Well, if it's in me, I can guarantee you it wasn't by choice. It's not like the slaves had a choice in the matter." He mumbled, "Damned white men are sick in the head! I guess it doesn't really matter to me what shade of black you are—so long as you're not white, you got a chance of being all right in my book."

"That doesn't make any sense, Daddy. People are people."

"Get on out of here with that nonsense. The problem with people *is* people. Now, how about that?" He stuck his neck out like a belligerent child.

"You sure can show out in front of company," Momma said.

"This ain't company; this is Emma. Besides, a man ought to be able to say whatever he good and well pleases in his own home." Daddy went to the living room to take a nap in his recliner. Momma and I stayed in the kitchen straightening up while Aunt Emma told us all about how she got a low-interest rate on her new Cadillac. Momma was never too crazy about Daddy's family, and the feelings were mutual. So when Aunt Emma finished bragging, she left.

"Well, I think I'm gonna go take a nap, too," Momma said, removing her apron and hanging it on the oven's handle.

"Okay, Momma. I guess I'll go on home. I'm kind of tired, too."

"Why don't you go lay down in your old bedroom?"

"No, that's all right. I think I'm gonna go on by the Millers'."

"Shondra . . ." She touched my shoulder and held it until I turned around to face her. "You all right?"

"Yes, ma'am." I tried to drum up a smile, but I knew she wasn't buying it.

"Hmm." She made a clicking sound with her cheek and back teeth. "I know you don't want to tell me all your business. But whatever it is, I'll be praying for you, baby." She rubbed her hand across my forehead, and I knew that she'd already begun praying. I leaned down and hugged her. If she only knew . . . "Yes, Father, in the name of Jesus, watch over her, Lord. Give her peace in the midst of the storm, Lord. Give her the wisdom to make it through, Jesus." I stood still and closed my eyes, letting her pray over my life. "In the name of Jesus, Amen."

"Amen."

I thought I noticed Quinn's car in the Millers' driveway. I really didn't want to stop, but I did have Eric's gift with me.

"Hi, Shondra!" Mrs. Miller hugged me. "Merry Christmas!"

"Merry Christmas to you, too, Momma Miller."

Peaches had a large family—two sisters and three brothers. All except Peaches were married, and they all had at least one child. The house was alive and festive—loud talking, laughter, the smell of good food, and bits of wrapping paper on the floor. I longed to go inside and be welcomed by their familiar voices and company, but I didn't think Peaches would appreciate my presence. Besides, I didn't want to impose on her first Christmas with Quinn.

"Peaches is up in the back playing pool, I think." Mrs. Miller stepped back and held the door open for me.

"Oh, I just came by to drop off Eric's gift," I said, handing her the gift-wrapped package across the threshold.

"You sure, baby? We got plenty food."

"No, thank you." I shook my head reluctantly and tried my best not to look at her. "I'm gonna go . . . I've been at my momma's house all morning. I'm gonna go home and get some rest. Y'all have a merry Christmas."

"Shondra, is everything okay?"

"Yes, ma'am," I said. "I'll see you, Momma Miller."

I should have gone inside. I thought about how stupid it was for me to stand outside on the porch at my best friend's parents' house on Christmas day. I didn't even get to watch Eric's face when he opened the gift, or hear Peaches fussing that I'd gotten him another "loud" gift. "He can play with this at *your* house," she'd say. Then Eric and I would beg her to let him keep it at their house, and she'd give in.

The wreath on my door had lost a few mistletoe leaves. I brought it inside to glue them back on. After repairing and rehanging the wreath, I pulled out furniture polish and dusted around the house. I ran across the letter from central office again and decided that the best place to put it was back in my Bible. Still, alone and with nothing but time on my hands, that situation grated on me. *What are they gonna say? What will this lead to?* I kept cleaning. The dusting led to sweeping and then to mopping. I got so bored, I pulled out all my bras and pantyhose and soaked them in Woolite.

"Hello," I answered the phone while I waited for the Woolite to work its magic.

"Hi, it's Stelson."

"Hi!" I was enthused to speak to someone—especially Stelson.

"I just called to wish you a merry Christmas."

"Oh, thank you. Same to you. How's your family?"

"Everyone's fine. My sisters and their families came late last night, and we stayed up till midnight so the kids could open their gifts. It was a lot of fun. What about you?"

"I went to my parents' house and ate; then I dropped off my godson's gift, and now I'm just relaxing," I tried to make it sound as if I were enjoying my boredom. "Stelson, when did you say that you'd be back again?"

"I thought I was going to stay until Monday, but I might leave tomorrow. I mean, I'm enjoying my family, but I didn't know that *everyone* was going to be staying here with my mother. If I'd known that, I would have rented a hotel room. But now that I'm here, my mother would be insulted."

"Yeah," I said. "Well, if you do come back . . . early . . . would you like to get together or something?"

"Are you asking me for a date, Miss Smith?"

I smiled, feeling a rush of warmth across my face. "Yes, I am, Mr. Brown."

"I'll be back tomorrow."

Stelson and I spent quite a bit of time together that weekend. We went to church twice (once at his and once at mine), we shopped, we ate, we went to a movie, and we talked about everything under the sun. Things above the sun, too. I listened to him talk about the changes God made in his life and how a deeper commitment to Christ had benefited him in so many ways.

"I can't really remember a time when I didn't know about God or know that Jesus loved me. Growing up in a Pentecostal church was definitely a blessing. But when I got out on my own, I rebelled a bit, I guess you could say," he admitted over coffee Saturday night at a 1920s-style North Dallas bookstore. The place crackled softly with ragtime tunes.

I made a whirlpool with coffee stirrers in my hot chocolate as I waited for him to go on. For once, I felt that the man I was seeing had worthwhile things to say. I eased forward into his presence. Our legs met and touched slightly under the table, just enough to say *I'm glad to be here with you.*

He continued with his testimony: "I guess you could say I did the prodigal-son thing. Making bad choices about women and money and priorities. It's almost unbelievable the amount of money I blew chasing what I knew had no eternal value."

"Like what?"

"I got into gambling—running to Vegas, betting on horses in Louisiana, whatever I could bet on. Then it was women—the more the merrier. It wasn't so much about sex as it was power and image, though. Then there was just the love of money itself. I made more as an engineer than anyone I knew, so I busied myself with the pursuit of things. You know, the whole yuppie cause. That went on for a good five or six years."

"Mmm." I swallowed. "When did you finally decide to make the return?"

"I just got tired of it all, you know? I looked at some of the older guys I worked with who were still obsessed with money and what it could do for them, and I started thinking, what's the point in all this? I mean, you can only buy so many cars before the thrill is gone. Once you've had the experience of being able to afford pretty much everything you want, that gets old."

"I'll be the judge of that," I interrupted him.

"No, really. It's true. I mean, when you're poor, you think all your problems would be solved if you just had more money. And when you get money, you go crazy for a while. But after that, it's like—what's next? Kind of like when you turned eighteen. You thought it was gonna be this big shebang, and it was for a while. But then you woke up one day and thought, okay, I'm eighteen. So what? That's how it happened for me. And it took me a while to realize that the 'so what' was God. I'm just glad that I had those roots, you know? That I knew where to turn when I was searching for the meaning of life."

"You're right. That's priceless." I nodded.

"What about you?" he asked. "Did you have your rebellion, or did you stick with the straight and narrow?"

I almost choked on my hot chocolate. "Stelson, don't make me laugh. I was on the crooked and wide for a while there. Actually, it's kind of embarrassing to talk about."

He set his mug on the table and gave me a comforting smile.

"I grew up in church and loved Jesus from the moment I first heard of Him. I learned the commonly quoted Scriptures and songs just the same as I think every child who grows up in the church does. Then I met a guy that I thought I really liked, and started living promiscuously—in and out of relationships, in and out of beds, you know? I won't say that I was addicted, but I certainly had no desire to stop satisfying my flesh. I knew it was wrong, and I felt bad about doing wrong. . . . I don't know. I really can't explain it. I guess I just figured fornication was the sin that I was gonna keep on doing until I got married—then it wouldn't be a sin anymore.

"And I might have kept right on doing it if I hadn't received a call from a former lover who was HIV-positive. I felt like I had been thrown up against a brick wall when I found out that I might have been exposed. Not knowing whether or not I was dying of a totally preventable yet incurable disease was the most horrific experience in my life, Stelson. I felt stupid and ashamed and guilty and afraid all at the same time. What's worse, I could almost hear Satan laughing at me because the whole time I had been such a willing participant in my own demise.

"But God . . ." I felt myself trembling at the mention of His name. "But God. All I could do was to ask for forgiveness and pray for the best. While I was waiting for the results of the HIV test, I laid out before Him and committed my life to him completely. I didn't care if I had one year or fifty years left, whether I would be sick or well, whatever. The tests came back negative, and I haven't looked back."

"That is a wonderful testimony, LaShondra." Stelson shook his head in astonishment. "Thank you for sharing it with me."

We met for breakfast before he caught his flight to Florida Monday afternoon. Even at Yhani's, an eccentric bakery boasting worldwide flair, people were staring and shushing others from talking about us too loudly. "It's like we're always on display," I said to Stelson.

He nodded while taking a bite of his steak. "You'll get immune to it after a while. I had the same experience when I went to Africa as a teenager on a missions trip."

"I just don't like feeling like some kind of a freak show." I looked around the room. Heads turned sharply away from me, people pretending that they hadn't been looking at us.

Stelson seized my attention. "Shondra, I haven't connected with anybody as well as I've connected with you in a long . . ." He looked up toward the ceiling and then looked back at me again. "No, never."

"Connected?" I asked.

"Yeah, connected," he repeated. "I gotta tell you, when I went back to my office the day of the career fair, everyone was like, 'Where did *that* smile come from?' And I told them I'd just had lunch with an exceptional, beautiful woman."

"And you knew I was exceptional after one lunch?"

"I knew when you walked into the foyer with your head held back and your shoulders squared that you were an extraordinary woman. There is nothing more attractive to me than a confident, secure woman. And when I found out that we shared the same source, I thought, 'I have got to see this woman again.'

"By the way, what's that fragrance you're wearing?"

"What? I'm not wearing any perfume."

"It smells flowery and light, like maybe some kind of body spray."

Flowery and light? "Stelson, it's called oil sheen." I couldn't stop myself from laughing. And Stelson looked so pathetically cute across from me, attempting to grin and bear his own ignorance.

"It's okay, Stelson. You're gonna be all right. Come here," I said, leaning over our table as though I'd thoroughly considered what I was about to do. He met me halfway, and we kissed. *I just kissed a white man.*

CHAPTER 14

Solomon McHenry was the one boy from the church that Momma always said she hoped I would marry. He was quiet, serious, and never would help pass a note during a sermon. My mother knew the McHenrys well and swore up and down that she'd almost seen Solomon as a son-in-law in her dream. I, on the other hand, loathed Solomon. He was extra greasy in the places that he wasn't ashy. Where Momma saw tall, I saw lanky. Dark: crusty. Handsome: nine times out of ten, the boy had something hanging off one of his nose hairs. Yes, he could quote the Scriptures, and he played a mean tambourine. But that was about all Solomon could do for me.

Momma had it bad about volunteering folks for stuff. Didn't matter what it was, if somebody at the church said they needed a child to do something, Momma would hastily offer me or Jonathan to fit the bill. So it should have come as no surprise to me when Momma informed me that she'd told Sister McHenry to bring Solomon over on Thursdays for help with his math.

"Momma, can't Jonathan help him? Jonathan's better at math than I am!" I complained.

"Hush your mouth, Shondra. Jonathan ain't even in high school yet. You'll be just fine." She didn't even look up from her Bible. Just turned another page, as though it were written: thou

shalt make thy children suffer unnecessary trials and tribulations.

"Momma, I just . . ." I racked my brain for an excuse good enough to cancel the check she'd already written for me. It was no use.

"You never know—you might like working with Solomon," she hinted.

"I will never *like working with him."*

Sister McHenry dropped Solomon off every Thursday at 6:30 for weeks, and I worked with him begrudgingly. Until he started getting it. I taught him, I questioned him, and I quizzed him until he knew how to solve for X a million different ways. Slowly I began to see Solomon for what he was: a hard-working boy who was in the same boat as me, with parents who pushed harder than we could pull sometimes.

One Thursday I had all the flash cards and triangle cutouts ready on the table, but Sister McHenry's gray Thunderbird failed to groan up to the driveway. "Momma, will you call them to make sure they're on their way?"

"Oh, I forgot to tell you . . ." She sipped her tea quietly, holding out her pinky finger. "Solomon won't be coming anymore. Sister McHenry said that he's doing well enough on his own now. She said to thank you for all your help."

"But we hadn't even finished!" I protested.

"Be careful, now, LaShondra. If I didn't know any better, I'd think you were looking forward to tutoring that handsome Solomon."

I nodded. "I mean, there was a lot more we needed to cover, that's all."

She took another sip. "I hope you *learned a lesson in all this. You never say never."*

Deniessa called me to confirm our next girls-only night. "So, you and Peaches should be here by six?"

"*I'll* be there by six. I can't speak for Peaches."

"You two aren't riding together?"

"I don't know, Deniessa. I haven't talked to Peaches since Christmas Eve—and it was not pleasant."

"What happened?"

"Well, I'm . . . seeing a white man." I heard myself say the words for the first time. "And I didn't tell her. She happened to see us out together and . . . I don't know. It's just crazy."

"Wait a minute. Go back to the white man."

Deniessa and I didn't know each other well, but I figured that since she'd let me peek at the skeletons in her closet, telling her about Stelson wouldn't hurt anything. "His name is Stelson Brown. I met him at my school. We went out a few times; we went to church a few times; we have a good time when we're together. It's just . . . I didn't tell Peaches anything about it because . . . well, you know why. I didn't know how she would react."

"So you haven't talked to her in, what, over a week now? And this is all over a white man?"

"Not over a white man. Over other things—over a misunderstanding mostly. She thinks that I lied to her so that I could go out with Stelson, but that's not true—well, not totally," I said.

"Okay, I'm still on the white man," she admitted. "Okay, how did you end up going out with a white man? I thought you couldn't bring yourself to do such a thing."

"I know—and this crow I'm chewing is hard to swallow. I really can't explain it, Deniessa," I admitted. "It just happened. I went out with him; we have a lot in common—"

"Like what?"

"Our church backgrounds, our beliefs as Christians; we like the same foods and some of the same music. He likes working with kids—a lot of stuff. Now, let me ask you, Deniessa, would you be asking me all this if Stelson wasn't white?"

"Eventually, yes," Deniessa said. "But you gotta do a reality check, LaShondra. After all the things you said the last time we were together, the fact that *you* are with a *white* man is breaking news. I need details here. Let me ask you a nondiscriminatory question—is he fine?"

"For the record, yes, but that's irrelevant."

"No, that makes a lot of difference. I mean, if you're gonna be with a white man, he can at least be one of the good-looking ones," she laughed. "Is he rich, too?"

"He's an engineer, a partner in his firm. And, just in case you're wondering, he is also very kind and smart, and he treats me very well. Those are the kind of things you're *supposed* to be asking me, you know?"

"Whatever, girl. I ain't mad at you. Just so long as he treats you right—that's the most important thing." She gave me her stamp of approval. "So are we still on for Saturday?"

"Yeah. I'm in."

Deniessa called me back within the hour. "Peaches will be by to pick you up at three o'clock Saturday."

"What?"

"You two can talk this problem out on the way over. Bye!"

Three o'clock doesn't mean three o'clock to Peaches. I've always known that. But as I sat in front of my television waiting for her, I grew annoyed at her lack of respect for my time. Maybe that was part of why I knew she wouldn't respect my decision to see Stelson.

At 3:15 she blew the horn. I threw my bag over my shoulder and marched toward the door. On the way out I glanced at my reflection in the mirror. I didn't like what I saw—a frown brought my whole face down. But even worse was the attitude behind it. I was ready to give Peaches a piece of my mind about a lot of things. A little piece of my mind, a little piece of her mind, and we could both be out of our minds by the time we got to Deniessa's place. I sent up a prayer before I left my house. *Lord, forgive me for having a bad attitude. Replace it with Your love and understanding. Help me to help Peaches and let me be open to hearing her out as well. Thank You for the friendship that we share, and bless it to continue to grow. In Jesus' name I pray, amen.*

"Hello," I addressed her cheerfully as I buckled myself into the front seat.

"Mmm," she mumbled, throwing the car into reverse.

She popped in a gospel CD and started driving. We rode all the way to the interstate without a word. And then it started.

"Why?" she asked. "Why a white man? Why the lies, Shondra? Why?"

"Okay, first of all, I did not lie to you, Peaches. I told you that I had plans."

"But you didn't tell me that those plans involved a man, let alone a white man! I feel like I got kicked to the curb!"

"I didn't kick you to the curb for a white man." I turned to her, raising my knee up onto the seat and shifting my weight. "I just didn't want to tell you anything about him until . . . until it was either over or until I thought it might actually go somewhere."

"Well, is it over?" she asked.

"No. I think it's far from over."

She looked at me for a second, then back at the road. A dimple punched itself into the side of her face as she clenched her teeth. "How could you go there? I just . . . I just can't understand it. It's beyond me. It's like I don't even know you anymore."

"How can you say that? I'm still Shondra."

She sped up to pass a station wagon. "The Shondra *I* know wouldn't give a white man the time of day. The Shondra *I* know takes pride in her race. And the Shondra *I* know wouldn't sell out, because she knows that *our* people have come too far for her to turn her back on the brothers. *That's* the Shondra *I* know." Her deep crimson lips quivered in anger. "Ooh, this is crazy, Shondra. Crazy."

"Why does everything have to be black and white?" I asked.

"Because it *is* black and white. What planet are you living on, Shondra? Do we need a history lesson here?"

"I'm not talking about history. I'm talking about now. And I'm not talking about America, either." She smacked on her gum, shaking her head back and forth defiantly.

"Peaches, don't you ever just get tired of it all—this race stuff?"

"Yeah, I'm tired of it. But that doesn't mean it doesn't exist." She voiced all the objections I had within myself. "You are still an African-American woman, and you will never be held in the same light as a white woman for as long as you are black. It's not gonna change in our lifetime, Shondra."

"My point is—" I slowed down. Thoughts and words were coming faster than I could give them voice. "I think that if you went up to any person on the planet and said, 'Are you tired of racism?' they'd say yes, yet they don't have a clue where to start. It's not a matter of some hate-crime law being passed or an equal opportunity statement in a company's employee handbook. It comes down to people who can see other people as individuals and embrace all of humanity through the love of God. And even if they can't embrace humanity with God's love, if we could just judge everyone on the basis of their character, that would cut out seventy-five percent of the problem right there."

She scratched her head and looked past me to her blind spot before changing lanes. "I know all that—I've heard Dr. King's speech probably a million times. But it's hard to see them as people when they don't see us as people. I don't see how you can get past that, Shondra. You're acting as though you haven't been black all your life."

"Well, you know I told you, God has been working with me on love. And I really think that this racial thing is a big chunk of it. We've got to stop judging people by their skin," I explained, but I felt as though I were talking to a brick wall.

"Well, when they stop, I'll stop." She raised her right hand and swore like we used to do when we were kids. "Cross my heart and hope to die; stick a needle in my eye if I'm lyin'."

"So there's no hope for white people with you?"

"What about the *slaves*, Shondra—the *slaves*?" Peaches made a fist and pounded it on her chest three times. "How can you just dismiss hundreds of years of injustice? What about all the blood they shed? What about all they went through? How can you look in his face and not think about what his people did to ours? That ought to just make you want to pop him dead in the eye. Pop!" She swung at the air.

"What about the blood Jesus shed?"

"That ain't got nothin' to do with it! We're talking about slavery and salvation. Those are two different things." She opened her fist and beat her palm on the steering wheel.

"No, we're talking about forgiveness and reconciliation, and that's what Jesus came for. We have to forgive them, they have to forgive themselves, and we also have to forgive ourselves."

"We didn't do nothin' wrong!" Peaches screamed. "Ooh! It's worse than I thought, girl. You've been brainwashed."

"No, Peaches. You remember that class we took with Dr. Fielder at Jarvis? Man, Culture and Society?" I reminded her.

"Yeah. I made a C. Brought my whole GPA down."

"Do you remember how angry we felt when we walked out of there that day that he told us the *truth* about the slave trade—that it was a trade? Something for something. It wasn't all about white people going over on ships and snatchin' black folks up out of the rugged jungle. White people could not have penetrated the country without the help of natives any more than a white man can come into the hood without some kind of black connection. Africans—black folks—were very active in capturing other Africans, and earned money by trading Africans from other tribes as well as their own. You remember that lesson?"

"Mmm-hmm." Her eyelashes made one slow beat.

"As quiet as it's kept. The slave trade was about the love of money. And you know who's behind that, don't you?"

"Yes," she relented. "I know the love of money is the root of all evil."

"Then call it like it T-I-Z: humanity has fallen for the enemy's tricks since Adam and Eve. But we don't have to keep falling for them, no matter how many thousands of years they've worked. The brainwashing doesn't come from mere men; it comes from the enemy.

"Now, I agree that a lot of white people are prejudiced—but so are a lot of black people. You know you don't feel sorry when you watch the news and learn that a Mexican got killed working at a construction site, do you?" I quizzed her.

"It's not that I don't care," she squirmed. "I just didn't know him."

"Oh, but let somebody black get killed in a car wreck—you're the first one sending money to the family's memorial fund, aren't you?"

"I like to help my own," she defended herself.

"And there's nothing wrong with that. But when we see others as less than ourselves because of their citizenship status, we're no better than the worst white racist.

"Let me ask you, Peaches," I said softly, "what would it take for you to feel like you could see past a white person's skin color? What would have to happen before you could actually be, let's say, friends with a white person?"

"I don't know if that's possible," Peaches said frankly. Then her eyebrows jumped, and she exclaimed, "I know what we could do!"

I was afraid to ask. "Okay, Peaches, give me the answer to the million-dollar question."

"Line up all the white folks, have 'em bend over, and let all the black people kick them square on their behinds one good time. Then I might call it even."

"I'm gonna pray for you, Peaches—hard, serious prayers."

"Please do," she yelled, "'cause I just can't see it happening with a white man! Girl, I saw you sittin' there with him and almost fell out on the floor!"

I looked at her to see what kind of yelling this was—angry yelling or hilarious yelling. Peaches finally met my gaze, wiping tears of laughter from the corners of her eyes. "Whoo!" She held on to her stomach.

"You are too crazy." My heart settled back into my chest, and I waited for her to unload her first impressions.

"Shondra, girl, I came through that door, and I saw him—what's his name?"

"Stelson."

"Okay, we're gonna have to do something about that name later. But anyway, I saw Stelson and I was saying to myself, 'Oh, he's a cute white man.' And I saw the back of your head and I was like, 'She reminds me of Shondra.' And then I got to that profile and I was like, 'Aw, naw! Not my girl! Not *my* girl!' Whoo!"

"So you think he's attractive?" I asked her.

"Yeah, I mean, he's got a cute thing going, for a white man. I just . . . he's still white, Shondra. And he's that kind of white that doesn't even show a hint of diversity anywhere down the line—except for maybe that dark hair. Other than that, he's just a regular old white man with a tan."

"He treats me well. A whole lot better than Quinn's cousin, Mark!"

"Mark is not a good comparison. Pick somebody else."

I thought, *Let's see. Who in my past treated me the way Stelson treats me?*

"Gerald?" she asked.

"Please—he only treated me well 'cause he wanted some."

"Dandre?"

"He was all right, but we didn't have a good time together. We didn't click. The more I think about it, I don't think I've ever clicked with anyone the way I click with Stelson. To be honest, up until now I never was able to think clearly about any man, because once we started having sex, it was like I was overly invested and I didn't have any kind of perspective on who he was. But Stelson . . . he's so solid, you know?"

"No, I wouldn't know." She regained her normal composure, attitude slipping away. "I can't see it, girl. I just can't see it."

"And that's exactly why I didn't tell you. I *know* you."

"Me! What about you, Miss 'I can't stand white folks' and 'I'm on white folks overload'? Now here you are eatin' ice cream with a white man up in a black establishment!"

"I know, I know." I rocked my head on the headrest. "But Stelson . . . he's changing my mind. Not just about him—about people, period. I mean, all this stuff that I've always believed about white men and white people . . . Stelson's not like that."

"So, how long you have been seeing him?"

"About a month, I guess."

"Give it some time." She rolled her eyes. "My momma always says you gotta be with somebody at least four seasons before you can say you know 'em."

"Hey, I'm sorry I didn't say anything," I apologized.

"I can't say I blame you. Ooh! You told your parents yet?"

"Not yet."

"Ooh, I want to be there. I *got* to be there! Pop me some popcorn and get ringside seats."

"Whatever!"

"You know your daddy's gonna knock you out," she said.

"It's not going to be like that, Peaches." I shoved her shoulder. "I'm already praying."

"Well, Stelson must be doin' something right for you to be going through all these changes."

"Yeah. He's really somethin'."

She leaned up toward the steering wheel and looked at me from a different angle as we approached a traffic light.

"What?" I asked.

"You really like this white man, don't you?" Her eyes slits, she peered into me as though looking through distorted glass.

"Yes. I really like *Stelson*." I tucked in my lips to hide the smile.

She sat back and gave her attention to the road again. "Well, I'm sorry for actin' up at the Marble Creamery.

You're still my girl, even if you are with a cute little ol' white man."

Deniessa was waiting on us with a batch of fresh homemade chocolate-chip cookies. I felt my buttons getting tighter before she even opened the door. "Hey! Did y'all make up?" she initiated a group hug at the door.

"Yeah, we're okay," I said.

"Girl, please," Peaches added, "you know it's gonna take more than a white man—"

I cleared my throat.

"*Any* man to break us apart."

"So what, we can't talk about your man?" Deniessa looked me up and down. "Bad as you all talked about my man last time—uh-uh. We will not discriminate."

We followed Deniessa past the formal living room to the kitchen. The place was full of AKA paraphernalia: plaques, pictures, and ivy plants lined her walls.

"Girl, you've got this looking like an AKA shrine up in here. No wonder Jamal didn't want to stay," Peaches teased her.

"Anyway!"

We gathered in the kitchen to prepare dinner: baked chicken, mashed potatoes with gravy, and corn. Peaches huddled into her corner to make her secret Caesar salad to go along with the meal. While the food baked and simmered, we propped ourselves up on the bar counter and watched Tyler Perry's play *Diary of a Mad Black Woman*. Peaches turned the volume sky high, which caused us to talk even louder.

Peaches filled us in on the latest between her and Quinn. She said that she would soon let him meet Eric. "So I guess this means things are serious," I suggested.

"I think it's about that time," she confirmed. Obviously, I had been missing out on her life.

"Speaking of serious, let me take my turn." Deniessa

reached into the basket of fake fruit on top of the counter and pulled out a box. She opened it and announced, "Jamal asked me to marry him."

"Pa-dow!" Peaches screamed. We towered over the velvet box to examine the ring. The band was combed platinum, with a clear, sparkling solitaire in the center. "This ring ain't playin'. Why you keepin' it in a box?"

"I've decided that I'm going to pray about this." She slid the ring on and wiggled her fingers. "Maybe he just asked me to marry him because his fresh supply of sex and housekeeping was suddenly cut off. I mean, how come he couldn't pop the question beforehand?"

"'Cause he was gettin' the milk for free, hello?" I said.

"I understand that." She nodded and pushed a loose braid behind her ear. "But is that all I'm good for? He knew that I wanted to get married three years ago. Why couldn't he see that I was a good woman while we were living together? I'm still the same person I was before."

"No, you're not," Peaches corrected her. "You're a different woman altogether. He now understands that you are not 'free.' The problem was, you sold yourself cheap, girlfriend. If you wanted Jamal to take you seriously, you shouldn't have ever let that joker move in."

"Well, your decision to pray and seek God for guidance is the best thing. You will definitely get the right answer if you go to Him," I told her.

"I have you two to thank for that," she said. "The last time we met, I really started thinking about how far I've gotten from God and church and everything that I know is right. You two reminded me that I needed to get back to the Word of God. And that's exactly what I've been doing."

"Well, praise God," Peaches smiled.

"As for this ring, I think I'll let him sweat it out a little longer." She removed the ring from her finger and put it back in the box.

Peaches put her hand over my mouth and said to Deniessa, "In the meanwhile, Quinn has a cousin named Mark—"

"No!" I struggled between screaming and laughter.

I asked Deniessa and Peaches to pray for me as I returned to school. "I have a meeting with the personnel director."

"What does that mean, exactly?" Deniessa asked.

"It means that they're probably going to conduct an investigation." I rolled my eyes. "Just more mayhem for me."

"Did you call the attorney like I told you to?" Peaches asked.

"Yeah."

"You got all your *I*s dotted and *T*s crossed?"

"Yep. My documentation is tight," I was glad to say.

"Then hold on tight and stay on your knees, girlfriend. God's gonna bring you out of this." Peaches put her hand on my right shoulder, and Deniessa placed hers on my left. We touched and agreed that God would see me through.

CHAPTER 15

My first year of teaching, I taught in one of the more affluent white neighborhoods of Plainview. I didn't make nearly as much as my students' parents, but I wasn't about to go down as the broke black teacher on staff. I did everything I could to acclimate to my surroundings while staying true to my heritage. I was determined that those little white kids in my class would leave knowing that black people were human beings.

One of our lessons that year involved career investigation. I planned an interesting unit, with research activities and an actual lesson in budgeting that fascinated those little seventh-graders. I should have known that we were playing on two different levels when several students raised their hands and asked what "layaway" was during our conversation about making purchases. As I began to explain the concept of layaway and how it was available at major chains like Walmart, one student blurted out, "What do you mean, not have enough money *to buy something?" The concept was foreign to her. She explained that she had been told she couldn't have things because she hadn't earned them or because she was too young, but she'd never been told that she couldn't have something because her family couldn't afford it. Things came to screeching halt when I overheard a conversation between two boys in the computer lab.*

"You've got to be pretty stupid not to be able to afford the stuff at Walmart," one of them said.

"Yeah—like a moron," the other agreed.

Okay, little Richie Riches, not everybody lives in a half-million-dollar house with a three-car garage and a pool out back. I vowed then and there that Jason and Bryan might have it made at home, but they would not *have it easy in my classroom. They would get a taste of the real world, if I had any say in it. They would learn what it meant to work hard—maybe even harder than the rest of the kids—to earn their A's. Little white snobs.*

◘ ◘ ◘

Dr. Hunt's office boasted of her achievements, both educational and social. I learned, during my wait in her office, that she did her undergraduate work at Baylor University and her graduate work at Texas A&M University. She was the recipient of several civic awards, as well as an honorary board member for an adoption agency. There were several pictures of what appeared to be her family—husband, three adult children, and one huge picture of an infant draped in a soft white blanket. Behind her desk, on one of the bookshelves, there was a plaque that read:

> *This is your pilot, God speaking. I will be handling all of your problems today. I do not need your advice on exactly how to do my job. There may be turbulence along the way, but do not worry. I control the wind. So sit back, relax, and enjoy the life.*

"Hello."

Startled by Dr. Hunt's silent entrance, I jumped a little. This prospect of investigation had my nerves on end. I knew I hadn't done anything wrong, but just the thought . . . the process . . . the accusation . . .

"Hello." I stood to greet her. She was a short, gray-haired white woman with piercing black eyes. Her round face gave mention of her Native American heritage somewhere down the line. I'd seen her only a few times in my career with Plainview. I'd heard that Dr. Hunt was retiring at the end of the school term—the contenders were already making their interests known in the district. Though her name was well known in our school system, I'd also heard that Dr. Hunt was not a people person, that she was brusque and impersonal. Still, I'd always wondered, how do you get to be the executive director of personnel if you don't know how to deal with people? If she was anything like Peaches, she came in, did her job, and left. She obviously led a life outside school. Maybe she was just one of those types who didn't mix business with pleasure.

I watched her walk around her desk and sit down, hoping to pick up on her body language and get a feel for her attitude. To my dismay, she was also hard to read.

"Miss Smith, as you know, we are planning to conduct an investigation into your administrative practices with the district." She read from a paper as though she hadn't given it much thought already.

"What are the allegations?" I asked.

"Let's see here. One is that you routinely give lenient consequences to black students but enforce firm consequences with white students referred to your office. The second allegation is that you have shown favoritism in dealing with parents and students by prompting teachers to change grades for black students who fail, yet neglect to provide reasonable options for white students in the same predicament.

"Miss Smith, is there anything you want to say before we begin the investigation?" She gave me that judge look, as though she was asking me to state my plea.

The union adviser, Beth Lang, had instructed me to

keep my mouth shut when I didn't have an attorney present, because I might talk too much. My best bet, according to Beth, was to wait until they produced specific evidence (assuming that they could) and then dispute the findings and evidence piece by piece if necessary. I followed her directions—to the best of my ability. "All I can tell you, Dr. Hunt, is that I am not racially biased toward my students."

She looked at me like, *that's it?* I hoped that she wasn't getting the wrong impression. I cared about my job and my career and, of course, my livelihood. I'd worked long and hard to earn the bachelor's and master's degree. But if all that could be taken away by a couple of good ol' boys, it wasn't worth much.

"I mean, is there anything that you want to explain?" She restated the question.

I wanted to blurt out everything—that Mr. Donovan and Mr. Butler were in cahoots to ruin my career. But I knew that once I started, there would be no stopping until I'd spilled every last bean. "No."

Dr. Hunt took off her glasses and looked at me for a while and then said, "I take it that you've been advised by counsel to remain silent."

"That's correct," I admitted.

Then she got that friendly, woman-to-woman smirk on her face. "Wise decision, Miss Smith."

I wiped my palms on my slacks, eased a bit by her implicit support.

Dr. Hunt put her glasses back on, wrote some notes, and flipped through her files for a few documents. Then she delivered the blow. "It is standard procedure to place principals on paid administrative leave while we investigate. During this time of suspension, you are to have no contact with school district personnel in regard to the allegations. You may not return to the campus except to collect personal belongings. Should you have a need to collect such personal belongings, you must contact your building principal so that he can arrange for district security officers to escort you on and off the premises as well as observe your actions while on campus. All district properties, including your laptop and the data contained on your laptop, must remain on the premises. If you need to retrieve personal data from your computer, please make arrangements with personnel in the computer technology department.

"Upon the completion of our investigation, you will be contacted for a summative conference. At that time, we will inform you of our findings and take necessary actions to resolve the case. Do you have any questions?"

I was prepared to hear that I would be placed on administrative leave. But to know that there was a place that I couldn't go because I was suspect was ridiculous. Yes, Beth had prepared me for the words "administrative leave." But she hadn't prepared me for the humiliation. My lips tightened, and I forced myself to hold back the tears. "How long do you think it will take to conduct the investigation?"

"It will probably take two to three weeks." She sighed sympathetically and took her glasses off again. "Miss Smith, please be assured that we will conduct a full and thorough investigation. I'll contact you as soon as we have completed our inquiry."

I pushed myself up from the seat and forced my hand to swing forward and meet hers. "I look forward to hearing from you soon, Dr. Hunt."

I walked out of the building and to the little Honda that I still owed nineteen payments on. *What if I lose my job?* As I buckled the seat belt, I allowed myself the release of emotions I'd suppressed in Dr. Hunt's office. *Administrative leave. Suspension.* I knew in my head that the battle had already been won, but I still *felt* defeated. Mr. Butler and Mr.

Donovan were probably somewhere laughing it up while I sat alone, slumped over my steering wheel, crying my eyes out.

Despite all the sermons I'd heard about hating the enemy and not the person, I came as close to hating Mr. Butler and Mr. Donovan as I could fathom. When the enemy has a face, it's harder to put a tag on him directly. But I had to, or there was no telling what I might do when I went back onto that campus to get my things. Better yet, I decided to go on home. I'd completely backed up my computer on zip disks that were already in my possession. And I couldn't bear the thought of seeing Mr. Butler's sinister smile.

Father, You said that You would never leave me or forsake me. Right now, all I have to stand on is Your Word. Thank You for those promises, and give me the strength to make it through this. In Jesus' name, amen.

I called Peaches and gave her the news. She was a tower of steel. "Okay, Shondra, this is not the end of the world. People go out on administrative leave every day."

"No, they don't!" I fussed, convinced that she was simply pacifying my anger.

"How would you know?" she asked.

"I . . . I—"

"That's my point," she said forcefully. "You don't work in HR. You have no idea how often this kind of thing happens. Believe me, it's not the first time and it won't be the last. You have to keep your head up and keep your knees bent in prayer, Shondra. Let those people conduct their little investigation; they'll come up with nothing, and you'll be back to work in no time."

"But what about my professional reputation, Peaches? Once I'm accused, I might as well be guilty. I don't want to live behind a shroud of suspicion." It was nice to have someone to whine to, even if she wasn't going to join in on my pity party.

"First of all, neither your colleagues nor your superiors are at liberty to discuss this investigation with anyone, other than to gather evidence. If they do, they're liable for everything from obstructing an investigation to slander—and you will sue the pants off of them. Secondly, you are not responsible for other people's misconceptions. If there's one thing God has done to prepare you for this, it has been this relationship you have with Stelson. You're not allowing other people's thoughts to dictate what you will do or how you feel about yourself. Girlfriend, you are growing up! What are you now—thirty-five?"

"Thirty-one," I corrected her. I wasn't in a joking mood.

"Whatever. Look, people are falsely accused all the time. Anybody with half a brain knows that just because some-one points the finger your way doesn't mean you're doing anything wrong. You cannot let these white people—I mean, these people at your job—have your mind."

"I know better." I sniffled and wiped my nose.

"All right, then, act like it," she commanded.

"You want to do lunch?"

"Well . . ." She hesitated. "I'm meeting Quinn. But I could cancel it—"

"No, no. Don't do that." I knew Peaches. If she'd really wanted to cancel it, she wouldn't have mentioned it. Be-sides, what I desperately needed was some quiet time alone with my Father.

"Are you sure?"

"Yeah. I'll catch up with you later. Remember, I'm on administrative leave. I've got two to three weeks off now." I gave her a laugh to ease her conscience.

"Don't worry, Shondra. It's going to be all right."

"Thank you, girl. You sure know how to give a sister a swift kick on the backside."

"Hey, that's my job. Always ready to kick butt!"

My house seemed different in the middle of a weekday—when every able-bodied adult was out working. The sun's light streamed through every window, and except for the gardeners performing their morning rituals, it was unusually silent. I rarely took off a day from work. When I did, it was to keep an appointment or attend some event that carried me away from the house for most of the day. During my two-week summer vacation, there was always the sound of children at play up and down the streets. But not now. This weekday silence was unnatural.

There were three voices vying for my attention: one saying that I needed to go on to my prayer room, stay positive, and keep focused on God; another telling me that I needed to get busy thinking of a master plan to get even with Mr. Butler, with his old funky self; and the third one telling me to go curl up on my bed and have a good cry while eating an entire package of Mrs. Baird's cinnamon rolls. I had a tough choice to make, since each idea did have a certain charm about it.

I kicked my shoes off at the sofa, took my jacket off and hung it on the coatrack, dropped my purse on the kitchen counter, and headed to the prayer room, consciously choosing to obey the voice that I knew was right. With every step in the right direction, I felt stronger. I felt the power of submission to His will, the surety of His sovereignty. He gave me that, even as I fell to my knees in brokenness.

Stelson called me later that afternoon. "I tried to get you at work today, but they said you were out. Are you not feeling well?"

"Yes, I'm fine. I'm out on administrative leave." I explained the situation to him.

"Don't worry. If you stay in any business long enough, this kind of thing comes up." He brushed it off.

"So, you've been falsely accused?"

"They say the first lawsuit is the worst," he laughed. "It's always intimidating when someone accuses you of something you didn't do. The first time it happened to us, a former employee threatened to take Brown-Cooper to patent court."

"What did you do?"

"Well, the first step was to conduct an internal investigation. I can tell you the rest over dinner, but it'll have to be Wednesday night after church. I'm all tied up for the next few days," he said.

"That's a long time from now, Stelson." I needed to see him.

"Not really." He kept me at bay. "You'll probably need some time to conduct the internal investigation."

"You think I did it, don't you?" I bristled.

"No. I never said that."

"But you think that I *could* be wrong?" I quizzed him.

"Anybody could be wrong, LaShondra."

I'd never been confronted so gently. I smacked my lips one good time. "Okay. Wednesday night. Your church or mine?"

"I'd like to do mine. I probably won't leave this place until late, as it is. By the time I pick you up at your house—"

"You don't have to do that. I can pick you up. Just e-mail me the directions to your house," I offered.

Peaches invited me to a play at the local junior college Tuesday night. Quinn was directing a jazzy production of *Hamlet*. Eric sat next to me, yawning a few times and impatiently asking when the play would be over. He liked the lights and the scenery but grew bored with the plot. "Ooh, Momma! Here's Mr. Quinn's name!" Eric announced during the intermission.

"Yes, baby. He's the director—he makes sure that the actors are doing what they're supposed to," she explained. Eric's eyes never moved past Quinn's name on the program. Obviously, my godson had come to adore Quinn. He was quickly taking up space in their lives. Perhaps the space I occupied, once upon a time. I had to step aside, I guessed, to let them become a family, if that was God's will.

"Since when did Quinn get to be so artistic?" I whispered to Peaches as the cast and crew bowed at the end of the play.

"This is his dream," Peaches informed me as we clapped. "He wants to get into the entertainment industry."

"Well, at least he's keeping his day job in the meanwhile." I eyed her and held out my hand.

"Amen." She gave me five.

After the last curtain, we waited for Quinn backstage. Eric was so excited to be on the wooden platform, I told Peaches that she had a star on her hands. "He is too happy to be on this stage," I said, pulling him behind the curtain.

Quinn grabbed Peaches by the waist and lifted her a few inches from the floor. "What did you think?"

"It was great, baby." She gave him a smack on the lips, and Quinn lowered her. They pulled Eric in and made a circle, sharing in Quinn's successful debut. I waited for Peaches to call me into their little love world. She made the motion after Quinn released her.

"I really enjoyed this production, Quinn," I congratulated him, shaking his hand. "I can't wait to see you on Broadway."

He lowered his head and smiled. "I've got a long way to go."

"Well, you have to start somewhere," I encouraged him. "You just have to stick with your heart."

"Thanks." He seemed reticent.

Does he know I'm on administrative leave, or am I just paranoid? Later, as Quinn, Peaches, and Eric walked me to my car, Quinn apologized for the lateness of the hour. "I know we've all got to get up early tomorrow."

I went along with him. "Oh, don't worry. I'll be all right."

I stayed up late Tuesday night, watching television and reading. It wasn't until almost one o'clock that I remembered what I was supposed to do before I saw Stelson Wednesday evening. *Conduct an internal investigation.* I wanted to get started, but I desperately needed sleep. *I'll do it tomorrow.*

I brought the investigation before God in prayer on Wednesday morning. The more I thought about it, the more sense it made. I fired up my computer and printed out my notes, searching through my documentation for any errors in procedure or policy I could find. Statistically, they were right to think that I took harsher disciplinary action against white students. *But that isn't really true.* I spent hours going through those files, pulling up records from my past two years as an administrator. Over and over again, the statistics showed a pattern on my part. Okay, they had a leg to stand on. But I had my reasons, too. *Lord, what are you trying to teach me?*

By the time Stelson called for me to meet him, I was still stuck. I couldn't wait to rack his brain with the evidence. And I couldn't wait to see him again. I'd missed his company, his charisma. The smell of his cologne. Then, there was that certain quality about us that I couldn't quite explain. *Chemistry.*

I grabbed the printout of the map to Stelson's house and

proceeded to a well-hidden sector of eastern Dallas County. I'd heard of the outlet malls in Rockwell, but it always seemed too far out for me to use my gas getting there. Beyond the shopping center, which boasted of clearance prices on the hottest designer brands, the main street into Rockwell resumed its country charm. When I first saw Stelson, I thought he was a Lexus, vegetarian, party-all-night kind of guy. But now that I knew him and his testimony, I knew he'd already had his fling with the high-maintenance lifestyle.

It was so dark out, I really couldn't see much of his neighborhood. The houses were spaced a good half acre apart, with huge yards that probably required a drive to the mailbox. Stelson's house was preceded by a wrought-iron gate, which he'd already opened for me.

I pulled up into the circular driveway and took in Stelson's home. It was a two-story, contemporary home with gorgeous landscaping. There was a grand column on the porch and a little bay window that I guessed was perfect for a kitchen nook. Off-white trim accented the deep-red brick exterior, giving the home a touch of classic charm. The house didn't have a big country porch with a swing on it, but it certainly looked as though it belonged to Stelson—cozy and well kept.

He was out the door before I had the chance to honk. "Hey," he said, hopping into the front seat.

"Hey," I said.

"Did you have any problems getting here?" he asked.

"No. The map was perfect." I backed out of the driveway.

His church wasn't far from his home. We rushed into the sanctuary and joined in praise and worship. I knew enough of the members now to catch a few waves and winks across the pews. My feet started hurting, so I kicked off my shoes and let my feet press flat against the floor, yet worshiping God. *Lord, I lift Your name above all others. For there is none like You.*

After the songs, one of the younger ministers read an Old Testament and a New Testament Scripture. The sermon followed immediately thereafter. Stelson and I shared a highlighter, placing emphasis on the message scriptures that spoke most clearly to us. For me it was Ecclesiastes 7:21–22: *Do not pay attention to every word people say, or you may hear your servant cursing—for you know in your heart that many times you yourself have cursed others.* At first glance, I so identified with verse 21. But I quickly became fixated with verse 22. I knew that I'd cursed others in thought and occasionally with my mouth. *But in my heart?*

I wasn't ready to brief Stelson on the internal investigation when he asked me about it at dinner. In a way, I was hoping he had forgotten about it. We ordered a trio of finger foods for an appetizer and muddled through the preliminaries without incident.

"So, what have you come up with?"

He remembered.

"Well, I looked through all the files and, statistically, my practices are questionable," I admitted. I went on, still searching for the words to convey my confusion. "I was prepared to justify my actions on the cases in question, but then I thought about some things tonight during the sermon."

"About the heart?" he asked.

I jumped. "Yes—the heart. How did you know?"

"When I spoke to you on Monday, I forgot to tell you that you always start with your key players in an internal investigation. You examine their motives, their strengths and weaknesses, and so on. All of those factors should be taken into consideration. People have their own agendas.

"In our case, we were sued by a former employee for revenues earned by an invention that he crafted while working at Brown-Cooper. Through the experience, we learned to express the distinction between company-owned inventions and the intellectual property of our employees. He had his agenda, and we had ours. So," he pushed me, "what is it about the heart that struck you tonight?"

"Look, I know what you're getting at. Actually, the Holy Spirit and I already talked about this. I know that the bottom line with me is and always has been race." I took a long sip of tea. "The hard part is knowing where to draw the line, Stelson. How do I keep my old self and gain this new self? Which one is better? Should I have to choose between being black and being like Jesus?"

"You were His before you were black, LaShondra."

He's right. I closed my eyes and tried to imagine myself before I was black—when God was ordering the steps of my life. Maybe back when He was piecing together my genealogy. He made me black for a reason, I was sure. But that blackness was never meant to override the calling that He'd placed on my life. Still, there were issues.

"The fact remains, Stelson, I don't like the way the white teachers treat black students at our school."

"What have you done about it so far?" he asked.

I sighed and plopped my arms down on the table. "I guess I've been subconsciously playing the role of the great equalizer, you know?" He gave an understanding nod. "It's not so much the specifics of any one student's case as it is the attitude that I take in handling discipline procedures. I always come at it like it's a race thing—and maybe it is, in some cases. I don't know, Stelson. I am not going to enforce harsh punishments for stupid, silly stuff. Problem is, white teachers and I rarely agree on what's stupid and what's serious."

"Why do you think that's so?"

"Number one, I think they're scared of black kids. Maybe because of what they read or see on television—

who knows? Number two, they don't understand our culture. They think that every time a black child gets loud, it's disrespectful, but that's not necessarily the case. And number three, I think that some of the stuff white kids do is just as bad but goes unreported because it's not a big culture shock to them when a white kid cheats on a test. To me, cheating on a test is worse than carrying a pick in your back pocket. And to me, constantly bullying someone is worse than having a fight."

"Which brings us to the heart of the matter—that sometimes truth is relative," he said.

"Relative to what?" I asked.

"Relative to perspective. Intentions. Interpretations."

"Therein lies the problem."

"What do you think can be done about the difference in perspective?" he asked.

"I don't know, Stelson. I guess we all have to learn to negotiate differences instead of making judgments about them." I smiled. "I think I got it."

The look in Stelson's eyes had gone from professional to personal. He smiled, now, nodding as though I were still talking.

"What?" I asked him.

"You are so wonderful," he said.

"Stelson, I am not trying to hear that right now." I sat back in my chair and folded my arms.

"No, really." He shook his head. "It takes a lot of courage to look at yourself in the mirror and evaluate your beliefs against God's criteria. That's challenging for anybody, no matter what their race or sex. It's hard work, LaShondra. But you've submitted yourself to it."

"You are so positive, you know that?" I pursed my lips. "I bet you pop out of bed every morning like a Pop-Tart, don't you?"

I gave his hands a little squeeze, and to my surprise, he

squeezed mine back. My heart rate went up a notch with his unexpected gesture. Suddenly, my focus switched from my problems to the man in front of me. My eyes zeroed in on his lips as they came closer to me. I met him halfway, closed my eyes, and we kissed. The buzz was exhilarating.

I'm gonna have to tell my parents about Stelson.

I spent the next two and a half weeks in a crash course on love. Aside from tutoring on Wednesday nights with Stelson, and children's church on Sunday, I pretty much stayed home undergoing this metamorphosis. I bought several books on humanity, prejudice, and God's love. I also prayed and fasted a few days as I felt the Holy Spirit birthing me into this new level of love and consciousness. Stelson remained prayerful but gave me the space I needed to go through. We talked every day, even when he went to Michigan for a convention. Sometimes he'd call me in the middle of the day just to check on me. "I'm fine," I'd say. It was nice to have somebody looking out for me.

Dr. Hunt called me exactly three weeks after our initial meeting to schedule our second conference. In the meanwhile, I had a chance to talk with Beth Lang again. She told me that I needed to be ready to discuss the findings, and be willing to undergo some type of diversity or sensitivity training. Because the Holy Spirit had prepared me for their findings, the second conference was actually anticlimactic. I conceded that the statistical data was troubling, and that I needed to be more aware of how I handled discipline, including having conferences with teachers when there was a difference in interpretation of a student's actions.

"Dr. Hunt, do you think that maybe our campus could use some additional training in diversity?" I suggested.

Dr. Hunt seemed pleased with my approach to solving the problems. "In speaking with your colleagues and reviewing your files, it became clear to me that this was simply a matter of miscommunication, perhaps deeply rooted in cultural differences." Without placing blame, we settled on an amicable solution: I agreed to enroll in a sensitivity class at the local university, and she would get with the staff development coordinators to ensure that our entire campus staff received adequate training as well.

It had been a tough but productive hiatus. *Thank You, Lord, for bringing me out on top.* I went back to work with a renewed sense of commitment to my students and staff. Miss Jan hugged me when I got into the office. I hadn't been expecting it, but I welcomed it. "Oh, my goodness," she said, "we are so glad to have you back. I know it must have been hard—it was certainly hard on me. But I did what I know you would have told me to do. I prayed for you, Miss Smith."

"Thank you, Miss Jan. I certainly needed it."

I did my best to steer clear of Mr. Butler, but he found me in the main foyer during the lunch hour. I smiled at him, intent on keeping our conversation civil. "Good afternoon, Mr. Butler."

He shot me a sly grin. "Did you enjoy your little vacation?"

Vacation? How do I tell this man off and still stay in the Spirit? "It was a very blessed three weeks," I answered truthfully.

When I got back from cafeteria duty, I found a huge gift basket of chocolates attached to balloons on my desk. "Oh, when did this get here?" I asked Miss Jan.

"A few minutes ago." She rushed into my office. "Open the card! Open it! It's from Stelson, isn't it?

The card read, *Happy Work-Day.* Miss Jan was right. It was from Stelson.

CHAPTER 16

The paternal side of my family was religious on holidays. They were C.M.E. members—Christmas, Mother's Day, and Easter. They believed in God and Jesus but, for the most part, they were not spiritually active until necessary. Aside from the holidays, thunderstorms were the only other occasion that Grandmomma Smith would pull out a Bible.

"Y'all cut off those TVs! Open some windows! Git off that phone! Everybody sit your butts down and shut up!" Her three-hundred-pound frame shook the floor as she walked the perimeter, settling the whole house down.

We scrambled to the main room, obeying her orders with fear and trembling. Jonathan and I sat Indian-style on the oval rope carpet.

"Wh . . . why we got to stop playin'?" Jonathan stuttered.

"'Cause God is doin' His work right now, chile, that's why. Now, you shut your mouth and don't ask you grandmomma Smith no more questions. Children ain't supposed to ask no questions. Just do as you're told," she grumbled while gently cracking her Bible open to a place she had marked with a red ribbon. I thought for sure she was gonna get struck down for talking to us so mean while holding the Holy Bible. We sat quietly as the storm passed over. She rocked back and forth, humming a generic gospel hymn.

The good thing about Grandmomma Smith (which I didn't come to appreciate until I was an adult) was her ability to teach me things—things that you could not learn by reading a book. I never asked her to teach anything; she'd just see that I didn't know how to do something and then insist that I learn it before I left her house.

"Shondra, you mean to tell me you can't blow a bubble with bubble gum?" she asked me one day while we were outside sharing the candy we'd gotten from the ice-cream man.

"No, ma'am." Was I in trouble?

"That's a shame. Seven-year-old girl don't know how to blow a bubble. Your daddy says you got straight A's, but let me tell you somethin'—white folks can teach you a lot of stuff in them books, but they can't teach you common sense, they can't teach you how to survive, and they can't make people like you. Come here, gal. I'mo teach you how to blow a bubble. That's somethin' every little girl oughta know." Somewhere in the lesson, she'd cuss and command me to pay closer attention, to watch her every move and catch on. That's how it always was. When she taught me to tie my shoes, she pushed me until I could do it in ten seconds flat. "One of these days you're gonna have to do it fast and do it right the first time. Now, untie 'em and do it again! And don't start that cryin', 'fore I give you somethin' to cry about for real!" She stayed on me until I learned how to perform these life skills right—quickly, the first time. These things, she said, I would take and use for the rest of my life: on my job, in my marriage, with my children.

I was afraid to go to Grandmomma Smith's house, because she was quick to cuss anybody out—man, woman, or child. She wasn't your everyday grinnin', bakin', let-you-get-away-with-murder kind of grandmother. Grandmomma Smith was raw. She was intense and curt, but she never whipped us. She didn't have to.

Stelson had been right about the fact that I would, at some point, become immune to the staring. It still bugged me. But spending time with him, being in his company, was worth the buzz in public. When I was with Peaches, I was somewhat guarded. She told me that I was being too sensitive. I told her that she was being insensitive. We agreed to disagree and moved on. It was nice to have her reality checks every once in a while. Fortunately or unfortunately, Peaches was too busy with Quinn to pay much attention to what went on between Stelson and me. Apart from our singles Bible study class, I rarely saw her.

When I was with my parents, it was as though Stelson didn't exist. Momma made known her suspicions about my dating someone, but she didn't press me much. She'd heard through the COGIC grapevine that I had brought a white man to church. I wasn't sure if she'd put two and two together yet—or maybe she had, but was hoping that the relationship would play out with little incident. Daddy said the "joker" must be ugly since I wouldn't bring him around the family.

Truth was, Stelson wanted to meet my family, but I wasn't ready for all that. No need in getting the family all riled up for what might turn out to be nothing. Yet, I could no longer deny that this thing with Stelson was working its way up to something substantial. I'd put off telling my parents by convincing myself that I was still praying about it. But I already knew what I had to do. Sooner or later, I would have to get real.

Deniessa was dying to meet Stelson, so I agreed to bring him to the spring Greek Show at Paul Quinn College. The workweek had worn us both down, but we agreed to put a little pep in our step and get out on a Friday night. I was way too old for the Greek Show scene, but since Deniessa was the sponsor of an undergraduate AKA chapter, I gave myself permission to hang out with a bunch of youngsters at the competition. I was all Delta'd out—T-shirt, shoes, and hat. Stelson arrived on my doorstep wearing khakis, a T-shirt bearing the American flag, and a pair of loafers. Despite the fact that the name Stelson brought about a feeling rather than a visual image, it was nice to get a good look at the handsome man standing before me.

"You look nice, babe." I winked at him.

"So do you."

We arrived well after dark, which meant that we had to walk halfway across the campus to get to the gymnasium. We heard the Greek calls long before we even got to the door.

"Why are they screaming?" Stelson asked.

"They're not screaming; they're cheering," I explained. "Think of it as Mardi Gras. It's gonna be wild, loud, and a lot of fun."

"I trust you." He pushed the hair off his forehead. We found seats on the non-Greek side, squeezing in behind what was obviously a group of male pledges. The gym was packed with young, promising black students, and their elation was contagious. Being there took me way back, back to a time when being black meant everything to me. The sanctity, the safety, and the oneness of being black always seemed tangible at Greek Shows. Sitting there in the gym, cheering the Deltas on as I had years earlier, I didn't feel any less black because Stelson was with me. Even though people were giving us that somebody-*would*-have-to-bring-a-white-person-to-a-Greek-Show look, I was still Shondra. That much would not change.

It occurred to me that while I was well versed in what to expect at events where the crowds were predominantly Caucasian, Stelson was sorely unprepared for the Greek Show. He sat there with his eyes wide open, taking it all in as though he was seeing a side of America that he never even knew existed.

Deniessa's chapter was the last to perform. She squatted down near the edge of the platform and paid close attention. When it was time, she brought out the canes they needed for the dance portion of their routine. I think I clapped louder than the AKA's when they were finished. Their show was good, but I knew that their routine wouldn't beat the Deltas from Paul Quinn.

After the winners were announced, the DJ cranked up the music, and the Greeks did their struts on the floor. Social clubs and other non-Greeks were not to be outdone in their strutting and dancing. I called out with the Deltas a few times before Stelson and I descended from our places in the stands. Deniessa fought the traffic and met us midway down.

"Stelson, I'd like for you to meet Deniessa," I said. "Deniessa, this is Stelson."

"Hello, Deniessa."

"Hi, Stelson. It's nice to meet you. Shondra talks about you all the time," she said, with every intent to embarrass me.

"Oh?" He seemed surprised. "That's nice to know."

I looked down and noticed that she was wearing the engagement ring. "And what's this?" The ring was breathtaking, even with gymnasium lighting.

"I said yes." She bobbed her head and looked toward the sky, beaming with pride.

"I knew you would!" I hugged her. "You go, girl!"

Stelson congratulated her as well.

"Well, I've got to go check on my girls and make sure everybody's got a ride back," she said. "Thanks for coming. It was nice meeting you, Stelson."

"Same here."

As we walked back to the car, Stelson remarked, "That was interesting."

"Did you like it?"

"Yes, I did. Thanks for inviting me," he said, looking past my shoulder. "Move over. This car is coming pretty close." He tugged my arm and then let his hand slide down my arm and into my hand.

I grabbed his warm hands. Strong. I felt the hair on the back of his hand. Definitely masculine. Almost automatically, he laced his fingers between mine.

We stopped for dinner at what was fast becoming our restaurant of choice—Abuelita's. Afterward, Stelson ordered dessert. "I think I'm gonna try something sweet this time."

"I'm stuffed," I said, turning down the waiter's request for my order. When Stelson's glazed flan arrived, my stomach suddenly made a little more room for dessert, and I wished that I had ordered after all. My eyes must have told the story.

"You want some?" Stelson asked.

"Oh, no, thank you," I politely refused his offer.

He shifted forward. "You know you want some." Then he started licking the back of his spoon as if he had no manners on earth, giving me the go-ahead to grab my spoon and dive in, poor manners and all.

"You gonna save some for me?" he asked as I took my third bite.

"Look, I don't play with dessert."

"I guess I'll know next time, won't I?" he teased. He put both elbows on the table, exposing that hideous lion tattoo.

"Stelson," I ventured to ask, "what on earth possessed you to get a tattoo?"

He let out a full, smooth laugh. "Oh, man. I knew it was coming." He blushed with embarrassment.

I thought it interesting to actually be able to see how he felt through the change in his skin color. I tilted my head to the side, smiling, and waited for his response.

"Don't laugh, but my mother asked me what I wanted for graduation, and I told her I wanted a tattoo."

That was the most ridiculous thing I'd ever heard. "Why not a class ring or a . . . anything but a tattoo!"

"Well, she wasn't too happy about it, but she'd given me her word, so she gave my uncle permission to take me to the tattoo parlor. I had planned to get this huge tattoo of an eagle—I mean, it was going be spectacular. But the minute that needle hit my arm, I had second thoughts. So, the guy did the best he could to turn it into something recognizable. When I got home, my uncle told my mom the whole story. She never let me live it down."

"Man . . ." I shook my head. "The things we did back in the day."

"Hey, I've been wanting to ask you something." He squinted at me, as though he had been examining my face. "May I see you without your glasses?"

I removed them slowly. I couldn't see a thing without them, but I felt like a gawky nerd miraculously converted to a princess.

"LaShondra, you are absolutely beautiful." He nodded. "Everything about you—the shape of your eyes, your skin, everything. I was looking at you tonight and thinking, how did I get so blessed? How did I earn her companionship, and how do I keep it?"

I melted. The butterflies in my stomach found their wings and began to flutter. They'd been working overtime since the walk after the Greek Show. "Thank you, Stelson." I leaned over and kissed him softly. "Just keep on being the wonderful man that you are."

"So, you think I'm wonderful?" He stuck out his chest.

"Yes." I stroked his ego with a soft tone. "I happen to think that you are very understanding and kind, and that you have patiently and prayerfully jumped through all my hoops."

We were almost finished with the flan when my cell phone rang. "Hello."

"LaShondra," my father's frantic voice called, "it's your grandmother."

"What's wrong, Daddy? What happened?"

"Uncle Fred found her. She died in her sleep. Just come on over here. We're all at her house."

I turned my phone off, laid it on the table, and then stared at it, as if it were a foreign object.

"What's the matter?" Stelson asked.

I looked up at him, my heart racing. "It's my grandmother. My uncle found her dead. I've got to get to her house."

"Oh, LaShondra, I'm so sorry." Stelson took my hands in his. He quickly paid the check and we walked back to his SUV.

"I've got to hurry and get over to my grandmother's house," I said to myself again as we hurried across the parking lot. My thoughts scattered and then gathered again as my shoes scraped and scurried the loose gravel on the ground.

"I'll take you," Stelson offered.

"Oh, I couldn't ask you to do that." I shook my head, holding my hand up.

"You didn't ask. I'm offering."

"Okay," I accepted. "She lives on the south side, near Wellesley and Oak Park."

I had known that my grandmother was not in the greatest health. But we had all been expecting at least to have some warning—a progressive illness or a short hospital stay prior to her dying. You know, the usual things that signal "time is running out." Not that I would have wished pain and suffering on her. Just that I would have had a chance to say good-bye to the woman who scared me into doing things right. Selfish, when I thought about it.

It was hard to believe that someone I'd known my entire life was suddenly gone—no matter how old she was. Grandmomma Smith had loved me in her own way, and I don't think I ever told her "thank you."

The more I thought about my grandmother, the more frenzied I became. I tried to lay my hand on the center rest, but the trembling wouldn't stop. I clasped my hands together in a last-ditch effort, but that didn't work, either. Stelson reached over and took my hand. "May I do something for you that I always do in a situation like this?"

"Okay," I said, not giving a second thought to whatever it was that Stelson was about to do. He started saying the Twenty-third Psalm aloud, and we laced our fingers for the second time that evening. His words were smooth, sincere, calming. I joined in, saying the words with him, getting into the rhythm of the familiar beats and pauses of the psalm. My heart knew this place, these words, this comfort. My breath was coming back to me.

"Surely goodness and mercy shall follow me all the days of my life. And I will dwell in the house of the Lord forever. Amen."

The prayer was over, but Stelson kept holding my hand. I don't know how he got from that restaurant to Grandmomma Smith's house in fifteen minutes flat, driving with one hand, but he did.

"Right there." I pointed as we approached Grandmomma Smith's frame house. There were already several cars parked along the curb near her house. The porch light was on, and her rocking chair sat empty. Any other night, her wheelchair would have been right next to the rickety rocker, and she would have been rocking in it. She did that sometimes until late in the evening, despite everybody's warnings.

"LaShondra." Daddy met me on the walkway, with Momma following behind him. He looked so small, so fragile. He'd been running his hands through his salt-and-pepper hair and wiping his reddened eyes. The lines in his face seemed deeper, sunken.

"Oh, Daddy." For the first time in my life, I felt myself holding my father up, keeping him from collapsing or losing himself. It was strange. I'd never seen my father "weak" in any form or fashion. Grandmomma Smith was everything to my father. We all knew he was her favorite, and Momma had always known that Daddy was nothing but a big momma's boy. Daddy bore down on me, and Stelson stood behind me, holding us both up.

Momma stood behind Daddy, patting him gently on the back. She looked at me, then at Stelson, then back again at me. I closed my eyes and hugged Daddy tighter.

Daddy was careful to steady his breathing before he rose up. In doing so, he finally noticed Stelson's presence. His lip quivered as he asked, "Who's he?"

"Daddy, Momma, this is Stelson Brown," I said in a professional, automated tone. "He's . . . we . . . we've worked together." The warmth of Stelson's palm left the small of my back, suddenly replaced by a cool breeze.

"Mr. Smith and Mrs. Smith, I'm so sorry for your loss. My condolences to you and your family." Stelson shook both of their hands. Momma shot me a glance that could have killed.

"Thank you." Daddy turned his lips up and looked Stelson over. He was not pleased.

"Stelson . . ." I turned to him. Nothing could have prepared me for the expression of disappointment in his eyes. I could not even look at him. "Um, I . . . thanks for bringing me."

Stelson took a deep breath and summoned his booming professional tone. "It was nice meeting you both. And again, my condolences. Good-bye, Miss Smith."

Stelson turned and walked away, and my heart shattered

into a million pieces. The sight, the thought of him walking out of my life was unbearable. *Did he really mean goodbye?*

Daddy walked toward the house. I stood at the center of the walkway for a moment, contemplating my next step—whether it would be toward the house or toward Stelson. I wanted—no, I *needed*—to talk to Stelson. Momma watched me for a second and then tagged behind Daddy.

The wind brushed my face as I nearly broke my ankle trying to catch up with Stelson before he got to his car. "Stelson, wait."

"LaShondra, I'm tired of waiting," he said without turning around. "What ever happened to 'you're so wonderful' and 'you've jumped through all my hoops'?"

"I meant what I said, Stelson. But you can't expect me to tell my father about us *tonight.* That would be a little too much for him," I reasoned.

"The problem is not tonight. The problem is *every* night. You know, if you'd told him about us earlier, we wouldn't be in this predicament. We've been dating exclusively for months now, LaShondra. Months. I'm beginning to think that this is a little too much for *you.* You can't admit our relationship to *yourself,* let alone your father." He talked to me over his shoulder, striding toward his SUV.

"Stelson, you're right, okay? I'm sorry. I should have told him before now. But I cannot do it tonight. Not under the circumstances."

"I understand why you can't do it tonight." He stopped at his door, pulled his hair back, and held it at the crown. "What I don't understand is why you couldn't have done it *before* tonight."

"I'm under a lot of pressure here, Stelson." My defenses jumped to the rescue, my mouth working overtime. "Not just from our relationship—from my job, my friends, myself, even God. And now my grandmother is dead. Everything is happening at once."

He let his hair fall and slowly turned to talk to me as I drew near him. "LaShondra, I know this is a lot to handle. And so does God. Have you ever stopped to think maybe that's why He placed me in your life?"

I thought for a moment about what he'd said. *Ding! Ding!* Then I threw my head back in a soft laugh, feeling the tendons in my neck stretch upward toward the starlit sky. "No, Stelson. I never thought of it like that."

"Well, it wouldn't be the first time He sent help in the form of a problem." Stelson kissed my chin. "Pray about that tonight. Good night, LaShondra."

"Good night. I'll call you tomorrow," I told him.

"No," he said. "Call me when you're ready to see past the color of my skin."

He waited until I was safely in the house before he left.

Grandmomma Smith's house was just the way I remembered it. The hard wood floors creaked with every step. A portrait of her parents and of the legendary Uncle Eddie George hung in the short hallway that led to the family room. There, on the glass coffee table that none of us dared to touch, were pictures of decades gone by. She and Grandpa Smith along with their five children in front of the old house in Ellerson. A picture of Jonathan and me. Pictures of my cousins and other relatives, some that I didn't even know. Grandmomma Smith had a curio cabinet filled with antique dolls, most of which she'd made herself. (We couldn't play with those, either.) Despite all the children, grandchildren, and great-grandchildren that had come through her house, everything was still intact. Still exactly where she'd put it. Exactly where she'd left it in the forbidden living room. I guess every grandmother has one of those rooms—the one where you can't sit down unless you're an ordained minister or a licensed insurance salesman.

"Where's Momma?" I asked Daddy upon entering the second living room.

"She's in there with your aunt Debra Jean and everybody." He pointed toward the kitchen.

"Daddy, it's going to be all right."

"I know." He forced a smile. "She's with Jesus now." And he turned, leading me on into the family room. *Did my daddy just say that?*

It was a little after midnight when my parents dropped me off at my house. They were oddly silent all the way, careful not to pinch each other's emotions. "Hey," Daddy said to me as I left the car, "I already called Jonathan. He'll probably be in by Wednesday."

It was late, but I needed a hot shower and a good prayer to get to sleep. It had been a long, stressful Friday. On nights like this, I simply broke down at my Father's feet and meditated on Him. His love, His patience. The lessons He taught me in life. I laughed again at Stelson's revelation, and how I'd almost missed the lesson completely. The epitome of my perceived natural-born enemy had come to love me, to support me in my time of need. In the process, I'd gained a new perspective on life and humanity. And love.

CHAPTER 17

I remember my parents' earlier years as husband and wife. They were both in their thirties when they got married, and had me two years later. I witnessed much of the turmoil of their newlywed years. They claim that their first real fight was over what to name me. They were in agreement that a boy would be named Jonathan Jr. But if I was a girl, Momma wanted to name me LaShondra and Daddy wanted to name me Shannon. "I told your momma, it was bad enough you were gonna be *black," my daddy replayed the argument for me. "You didn't need a black name, too. If you had a white name, you could at least get a foot in the door for the interview before the white man sees your face. See, I know how the game is played. The further you get without being detected, the better off you'll be. I told her, the only reason I got this job now is 'cause my name is Jonathan Smith. But your momma had to be like everybody else and give you one of those soulful names!" (Back then the popular name for African-American baby girls was LaAnything.)*

"Your momma threatened to put my tires on flat if I named you before she woke up. I told her if she put my tires on flat I would put her eye on flat!"

Momma hollered in from the kitchen, "Yeah, and I told him that if he ever laid a hand on me, it would be the last hand he laid anywhere!"

"Yeah, leave it to your momma and her Ebonics to name my firstborn," Daddy shook his head.

"Excuse me. I have an excellent command of the English language, which I employ at will," she bragged with perfect diction. "But I choose the mode of expression that I feel most comfortable with during informal conversation, you hear? Now, take that to the bank." Momma did have a totally different tone and set of vocabulary for talking to white people out in public or on the phone.

"Oh, give me a break," Daddy said. "That's just like illegals coming over here and trying to make Spanish more than what it is. When you go somewhere, you ought to learn the language and use it correctly—and don't go naming your kids all kinds of mixed-up names if you expect them to make it in the main society. Simple as that."

And they both told the story so affectionately.

⊡ ⊡ ⊡

I was exhausted on Saturday morning, but I knew that I had a ton of work to do. My family would be expecting several relatives and old acquaintances to drop by, and I looked forward to fellowship and food with everyone. Maybe a game of spades and a slice of sweet potato pie.

Momma called me a little before ten. "You goin' over to your grandmomma Smith's house today, ain't you?"

"Later on," I said.

"What you gonna do today?" She was snooping.

"Relax."

"Humph. Well, I do expect to see you at your grandmomma's house some time today, spending time with your family during our time of bereavement." Translation: get your jigglin' butt over to Grandmomma Smith's house so they won't be saying that Jonathan's kids think they're too good for the family.

"I will be there, Momma."

Stelson was next on my list. I'd thought long and hard about what to say to him, and I was expecting a good day or two of the silent treatment—which is exactly what I would have given him if the shoe had been on the other foot. But he welcomed my call with his usual upbeat attitude.

"How are you?" he asked.

"Not so great," I said. "I owe you a huge apology, Stelson. I know I've been—"

"I accepted your apology last night," he cut me off. "What I want to know now is if you're ready to jump through *your* last hoops. At this point, it's up to you to let the people in your life know that you're seeing a white man. I just pray that you do it in love, and soon."

"Okay, Stelson. I know this is my issue. And I am going to tell them as soon as I get the chance." I meant that with all my heart.

"And how do you define 'soon'?" he asked.

I didn't mind the pressure, but I didn't want an ultimatum. "I can handle my family, Stelson. Just let us get through the funeral, okay?"

"Fair enough. Are you up for karaoke tonight?"

"Karaoke?" *I know he didn't just say karaoke.*

I agreed to the outing, partly because Stelson had been open to attending the Greek Show. Well, that and the fact that I really wanted to see him.

Momma didn't say much to me at Grandmomma Smith's house. But she watched me. I wanted to pull her aside and talk about Stelson, but there was too much going on: people coming in and out of the house, food to keep warm, and children underfoot. It was nice reuniting with my more animated relatives. They had plenty to laugh about from the days in Ellerson. I learned that I had a cousin who used to play with Ray Charles. Somebody else had fallen asleep drunk in the bathtub and almost drowned. The Smiths could keep any party going with their storytelling skills.

For a while Daddy was his old self again—loud, boisterous, obviously the favorite of his brothers and sisters. Their family dynamics often puzzled me. There was something about Daddy that they all liked. He'd had a good job, he was the first to get a house, and I think he raised the bar for economic achievement with the Smiths. Not that we were rich, just that we never wanted for much. But then, there was something about him that they didn't like. I couldn't put my finger on it—whether it was jealousy or resentment, I couldn't tell. Whatever it was certainly got filtered on down to Jonathan, Momma, and me. I got the feeling that they were proud of me, too, but they would never say it to my face.

Bringing Stelson into the picture wasn't going to help anything. Still, I missed him. I looked forward to the day when I could share my family with him and vice versa. Maybe, someday, they would accept him. But even if they didn't, I still wanted him right next to me at times like these.

I left Grandmomma Smith's at six in order to be ready for Stelson's karaoke by seven. I tried not to pass judgment on this little hole-in-the-wall that Stelson took me to, but it was hard. The room was abuzz with neon beer signs and flashing stage lights. There was the faint odor of cigarette smoke, and a fencelike wooden railing that ran throughout the building, giving it a Western feel. There were only three black faces in the crowd, and those were obviously in the company of white friends or lovers.

I ordered a steak, and Stelson had barbecue ribs. The food was scrumptious, and I had no qualms about licking my fingers in that restaurant. I saw enough butt cracks and cleavage to last me a lifetime at Tiny Tim's; I figured all was fair in here. Between songs, Stelson and I applauded the singers, decent and horrible. Two little girls sang one of Britney Spears's songs and got a standing ovation. They sounded a mess, but the crowd encouraged them nonetheless. I was starting to like old Tiny Tim's place.

Out of the blue, Stelson dared me to sing.

"What?"

"I'd love to hear your singing voice." He motioned toward the stage.

"You are asking for a slow and painful death if you want to hear me sing," I laughed.

It all happened so quickly. Stelson grabbed my hand, pulled me toward the stage, and got the crowd chanting my name, "LaShondra! LaShondra! LaShondra!" I'd learned from my brief experience in the crowd that once you were out of your seat, they didn't relent until you sang at least a few bars. Even I had heckled a noticeably shy woman into singing Aretha Franklin's "Respect" only moments before.

When Stelson finally got me to the stage, I whispered in his ear, "I can't believe you did this."

"Hey, I'll sing with you if you want me to," he laughed.

"No." I shooed him away. "You asked for it." He stepped back, and I threw my jacket to him. The crowd cheered as though I had *really* taken something off. They just didn't know—I was about to cause them permanent auditory damage.

"First I was afraid . . ." From that point on, everybody sang along with me, including Stelson, as I closed my eyes and belted out the words to Gloria Gaynor's "I Will Survive" as if I had been down that road a million times. I cracked on all the high notes and was off tune, I'm sure, for most of the song. But that didn't matter, the crowd's cheers made me forget, if only for a while, that I was a grown black woman with problems and issues. For those

few minutes, I was the crazy me that I used to be when I was a kid, out on the playground chanting with my little friends—back when all I had to worry about was doing my homework and making my bed. I did a Diana Ross diva move and pulled Stelson up on stage with me. He and I shared the microphone for the last few chorus lines. I felt as goofy as all outdoors, but it was unadulterated fun. Lost in the music and the moment, I screamed/sang the words to the triumphant song of overcoming love's pain. "*I will survive. Hey, hey!*" We screamed with the crowd when the song was over, and rushed back to our seats doubled over in laughter.

"Oh, Stelson," I said, holding my sides, "I haven't done anything that crazy in a long time."

"You were great, sweetheart." He kissed me on my cheek—and a little too close to my ear. I do believe my ear-lobes picked up a signal and transmitted a message to my entire body: we are back in business—be on alert.

"You weren't too bad." I raised an eyebrow and then gave him a smile.

We left Tiny Tim's much later than I had predicted, but the night had been worth the few hours of sleep it cost me. "Thanks for everything," I said as Stelson pulled into my driveway.

"You're sincerely welcome." He parked and came around to open my door.

We walked up to my porch, and I motioned for him to join me on the swing. I smiled, remembering Peaches' reaction to my choice of model 2104 when I'd had the house built.

"Why you want that big, country porch?" she'd asked. "People don't have porches anymore."

That night I was glad I hadn't listened to her. Stelson sat next to me and gently pushed us off. The swing creaked slightly as we swayed in the crisp spring evening air. I pulled my legs up onto the seat and rested my head on his solid chest. His skin lay flat on his muscles. I wondered if he had an inch to pinch anywhere. We rocked there for a while, enjoying what was left of Saturday.

"My grandmother used to have a swing like this, only it was in the backyard. There was a big old cover on top of it. She'd make us stay outside all day, playing in the hot sun until we were just about to drop. If we told her we were thirsty, she'd say, 'Go get some water from the hose,' and we had to drink that hot, nasty water." I laughed. "We got about two shades darker every time we went to Grandmomma Smith's house in the summer. We *had* to play over there. All that watching television and playing video games was out when we went to Grandmomma Smith's house. In the summertime you played until you were funky, and the only way you got in the house was when she felt sure that you would fall fast asleep after a hot bath and dinner."

"Sounds like your grandmother was pretty tough," Stelson snickered. "She reminds me of my uncle Rellis. That man would whip any child with or without a moment's notice. He didn't care whose child you were, and he didn't care anything about child protective services. He told me one time that if I called them, he'd whip me right in front of them and then he'd turn around and whip them, too, just for comin' on his property."

"Your uncle Rellis must have been black."

Stelson laughed.

"I can't imagine you gettin' a whipping," I thought out loud. "When I was little, I used to think that only black kids got whippings."

"You didn't get out much when you were little, huh?" he laughed.

"It's not that. I used to watch *The Brady Bunch* and all those shows with white families, and I never saw those kids get a whippin'. Contrast that with *What's Happening!!* and *Good Times.* The black kids got whippin's, but the white kids never did."

"Well, that certainly wasn't the case in my house. I used to think we were the only white kids that got whippin's."

"What was the worst whippin' you ever got?" I asked.

"Let me think." It took him quite a while to come up with one. "Hmm. I guess it would have to be the time that I stole ten dollars out of my momma's purse." The Louisiana drawl came out with his memories, taking him back in time. "It was so stupid. I must have been about ten years old. There was no one else in the house except my mom and me. I heard the ice cream truck coming and I asked her if I could have some money. She said no without offering any kind of explanation. I guess I just got so mad, I decided I was going to get the money on my own. So I sneaked into her room and took ten dollars out of her purse—ran around the corner because by that time the truck was already coming up the next block over. I bought myself a Bomb Pop and a Chick-O-Stick. And I walked right back into that house with the Bomb Pop and that Chick-O-Stick like she wasn't going to notice."

"You came back in the house with the evidence?"

He nodded. "LaShondra, I can't even tell the story now without thinking about that whippin'. I promise you, that beating she put on me kept me out of the Louisiana state penitentiary. I thought I was gonna die that day. I really did."

"I just can't see that. You're too good, you know?"

"So are you," he said.

"How do you figure I'm too good?" I asked, raising my head to look at him for a moment, then slowly lowering it as he spoke again. I wanted to feel his chest vibrate with every word.

"Your faith, your confidence. The way you give yourself

to kids that no one else wants to spend time working with. And the way you handled me with a long-handled spoon. It's like you bring out the best in me. I really, really like that."

Stelson pushed us off again. I glanced at my watch. "Ooh, I've got to get to bed. We're just all out here swingin' on the porch like we don't have church in the morning."

"Yep." Stelson stole a peek at his watch, too. "Doesn't look like I'm going to make the eight o'clock service."

He stood by me as I searched for my keys. "Thanks again for everything tonight."

"It was my pleasure. By the way, I've got another business trip scheduled for Tuesday. I haven't looked at the itinerary yet, but I'm pretty sure I won't be back until Thursday afternoon at the earliest."

"How can you not be sure of when you're going to be back?" I asked him—it sounded like an old line. I hadn't asked him that the last time he left for business, but for some reason I wanted to know.

"Well, my secretary arranges all these things for me. And to answer the real question that I think you're asking, it has never mattered to me how soon I could get back home—not until now."

I felt a little ashamed. "I'm sorry, Stelson. I wasn't trying to insinuate anything. It's just that I've played the game before and I am *not* the one."

"Neither am I. And that's precisely why I'm here with you right now." Moonlight wedged between us and illuminated Stelson's face. I felt his touch on my arm, and the hairs on my arm stood at attention. Then he leaned in and hugged me for only an instant. My heart felt like it was gonna thump right out of my chest. In that moment the sleeping giant within me woke, and girlfriend was hungry. I wanted to jump up and wrap my arms around his neck, hook my legs on his hips. *Good Lawd, it's been a long time.* But Stelson pulled away.

"Good night, LaShondra."

"Good night, Stelson."

Call me special, but I watched him through the peephole as he walked back to his car. Was he walking, or was he gliding? He was smooth, but it was a different kind of smooth. The kind of smooth that's inherent. Stelson wasn't trying to be masculine or divine. It just oozed out of him. It was an inside-out thing. He was a man who had been perfected in God's love, and he couldn't have stopped it from flowing out of him if he wanted to.

CHAPTER 18

Daddy came in from work and hung his jacket on the coat-rack. I ran from the living room to greet him, but stopped when I noticed his hand all bandaged up. "What happened, Daddy?"

"What's the matter, Jon?" Mother rushed in behind me, wiping her hands on her apron. "Oh, my goodness!" she exclaimed, gently examining the white gauze wrapped around the wound.

Daddy grimaced and pulled his hand back, walking past us and taking a chair in the kitchen. "Got bit by a dog. Little mutt snuck up on me and took a chunk out of my hand."

"Daddy, why don't you just quit working there?" I asked innocently.

"A grown man's supposed to work. How do you think we got all this food? How do you think we pay for your clothes and this house?" he fussed.

I shrugged my shoulders. "That's why you go to work?"

"Let me see it again, Jon," Momma said, stepping between Daddy and me. She held his hand in hers and turned it over.

Momma grabbed Daddy by the arm and led him into the bathroom, where she tended to his hand. I eavesdropped on their conversation and learned that my father had fourteen stitches and would be off work the next day, with pay. When she'd finished changing the bandages, they both went back into the kitchen and Momma made Daddy something to eat.

"Daddy"—I approached him casually—"are you gonna have a scar on your hand like the one behind your ear?" It was my roundabout way of inquiring about the long, interesting flaw that always showed itself to me with my father's profile. It looked puffy, like there was a big worm or something under it. He'd never talked about it, but I couldn't understand how something so obvious went without mention in our home. "Huh, Daddy?"

Daddy's eyes narrowed, his glance piercing through me. "You stay out of grown folks' business. You hear me?"

He said it with such ferocity that I never asked him about the scar again.

▣ ▣ ▣

I called Peaches to let her know that Grandmomma Smith had passed. I gave her all the details, and she let me know that she'd be at the funeral.

I wanted to call Stelson, just to say good morning and see if he was up. I wanted to hear his voice and listen to him tell me something good. Stelson, Stelson, Stelson. I wondered if he had dreams, if he dreamed in color or black and white. I wondered if he drank coffee first thing in the morning. I wondered when he worked out and when he prayed. I wondered how he cleaned his feet. Then I started wondering if he wore boxers or pajamas or anything at all to bed. *Mmm, mmm, mmm.* It was way past time for me to get to my prayer closet.

I thanked God for everything that had recently happened: Grandmomma Smith's peaceful passing, seeing my family members again, and the wonderful thing that was happening with Stelson. I went straight to the Word and pulled out my notes on the lesson I was planning to teach to my class that morning. In the last few minutes, I prayed for my family. I also prayed for strength to make it through the day so I could come back home and take a nap. I knew

I had a long week ahead of me with the funeral, hosting my brother when he got in, and whatever mess the devil might bring me at work. And the fact that Stelson would be gone wasn't making it any better. *Lord, I need Your strength and wisdom to make it through this week.*

Just before I left for church, Jonathan called to let me know that he'd be flying in for the services on Wednesday.

I got in the sanctuary just in time to praise with the saints. It felt so good to be thanking and praising God for what I knew he was about to do with my family and in my life.

Pastor, with the help of the musicians, got us settled in our seats. This Sunday it was all us. No need to recognize visitors. Shannon had been noticeably absent since our crossing in the restroom, and brother Paul sat alone every week on the third pew from the drum set. I just hoped that his next visitor truly loved him for who he was.

After church, I turned my cell phone on to check my messages. My mother had called. "LaShondra, everybody is over at your Grandmomma Smith's house, but I'm at the house, getting ready to make a few calls and get to the grocery store so I can start getting food ready for the wake Wednesday night and the meal Thursday. Why don't you come on over, and we can get busy working on this together, hear?"

I felt funny going over there, like a schoolchild wondering if the teacher had called home. I wasn't in the house a full minute before Momma started pouncing all over me. She zeroed in on me like state-of-the-art radar. "What's the matter, LaShondra? You sure actin' funny."

"Momma, I just got in the house." I set my purse and keys down on the kitchen table and poured myself a glass of orange juice. "Yes, love, it's so nice to see you again."

"Is it about that white man that brought you to Grandmomma Smith's? Isn't he the one on the refrigerator door?" she asked, still not convinced.

I nodded. "He's a man that I met on my job." I had to be creative in how I told my mother the part of the truth that I wanted her to know at that moment.

"He works with you?" She followed me to the table.

"Not really. He's an engineer."

"Uh-huh." She walked back to the counter. "LaShondra Monique Smith, is there something you need to tell me?" She'd read me, and I knew there was no turning back.

Give me the words, Lord. "Momma, Stelson and I are dating."

She stopped chopping onions and turned abruptly to look at me. Her face filled with confusion, and I immediately regretted the blunt way that I'd told her. Then again, there really isn't any other way to say things like that. Momma walked away from the counter and fell into a chair at the table. Her fleshy arm plopped down on the kitchen table, causing the pepper shaker to topple over and sprinkle a square inch of seasoning.

"So, you're dating a white man, huh? After all we did for you." Then she squinted her eyes, trying to make sure that there was no trace of humor in my face. I started praying in my Spirit. *Lord, please send love. Please send it now.*

"But I really like him. He's a good man."

She was still looking at me upside my head.

"Momma, it's about more than Stelson, though. I . . . I'm learning so much. It's time for us to stop spreading all this hate in the name of black pride and for the sake of preserving our history—or whatever it is that we think we're doing by not accepting other people."

"That's easy for you to say, missy. It is so easy for this generation to forget its roots." Her neck and index finger worked hard to stress her message. "You never had those books that said *used* in big black capital letters when you were in elementary school. You never went in through the back door of a restaurant and paid with the same green money as the white customers, but you couldn't eat inside. You never drank from a nasty old water fountain that said *colored*. You never had little white boys throwing rocks at you 'cause you went into a whites-only store. You didn't go through that, LaShondra! Maybe that's why it's so easy for you to come in here and tell me what's got to change. You don't know nothin' 'bout what it felt like to be treated so badly. That *hurt* like nothin' you could ever imagine. That hurt to the bone." She rose and stood over me with her hand on her heart, breathing heavily, wanting me to understand the pain she'd lived with. Her face was contorted with anger, anguish. She waited for me to say something. And when I couldn't, she walked away and stood by the window, looking for an answer, I supposed. "That's what I thought. You *don't* understand."

"You're right. I don't know what it means to have been treated the way you were treated forty years ago," I told her. "But—"

"It ain't just about forty years ago, missy. Oh, no, don't fool yourself. It's still going on." She laughed bleakly.

"I know that. But, Momma, you're not just a person. You're a child of God. We have to see this for what it is."

"And what is it? What is the world according to LaShondra Monique Smith?" She sat down again quaintly and folded her arms across her chest.

I thought about Stelson and how much I liked him. I wished that Momma could have known that Stelson was good people. "I just know that it's not right to judge people by the color of their skin—no matter what it is."

"You still haven't said nothin' about white folks. Slavery. Ku Klux Klan. Lynchin', beatin', stabbin', lyin', cheatin', stole everything from us and never give us a dime for it!"

She was angry now, as if she were arguing against the whole world.

I didn't have time to go all into a history lesson, so I asked her one question, slowly, one word at a time. "Who came here to steal, kill, and destroy?"

"The enemy, of course. So are you saying white folks are the enemy, 'cause if you are, I might agree with you on that one. That's what Malcolm X used to say."

"The enemy is a master at deception. Momma, I know we can't change the past. History is history. What happened happened, and people are hurt because of it. But that is the way of the world. We don't follow that way. You taught me so yourself."

She looked at me out of the corner of her eyes and let out a long Lord-where-did-I-go-wrong? breath.

"All I'm asking you to do is get to know Stelson. You know me; you know what kind of person I am. You know you raised me right and you taught me all about love. Do you think I would be dating Stelson if he wasn't all that? This is new for all of us, but God's love is stronger than anything. Please give him a chance. That's all I'm asking."

Still no response.

"You know that W-W-J-D bracelet you bought me last year for Christmas?"

She nodded.

"Well, we are going to have to think in those terms. Jesus was conscious of people's backgrounds, but he never let those stereotypes interfere with the love and kindness and respect that he showed everyone. We've got a lot of good black leaders, good black organizations, good black this and good black that. And there is nothing wrong with helping those that need it most. But if your heart is fixed on hate and fear and prejudice, there is a problem, and we're not doing what Jesus would do."

I gave my whole platform as she looked at me in amazement. I felt as though I was telling my mother that she had been wrong, in so many words, but I knew that I had to tell her. The same as I had told myself.

"You know, Momma, if this family hadn't been harboring so much hate and prejudice to begin with, I wouldn't have been so afraid to introduce him to everyone."

"Well," she sighed again, "it's gonna take God almighty to help your father get over this one."

"What about you, Momma?"

She looked away, the ornery smirk ebbing from her face. "God's already been dealin' with me about this. I knew something was comin' down the line—just didn't know what. I can get through it. But I don't know about your father. You're puttin' us all in a bad position."

"I think he'll be all right, Momma." I was optimistic.

She looked at me again, as though she was contemplating some weighty matter. She tapped her fingers: rhythmic, methodical—sounded like a horse galloping in the distance. Now it was I who knew that there was something unsaid. "LaShondra, this thing is much deeper with your father than it is with me. There's a lot that happened. A lot more that you don't know about." She wrung her fingers now.

"What? What happened?"

"Well . . ." She hesitated again. "Your father never talks about it. He only told me the story once, right when we started courtin', so I'd know if anybody ever said somethin' about it. And I think he told Jonathan once, right before he went into the service. I really shouldn't be talking about it to you now." She looked away from me. "But I will, 'cause I think you need to understand where your father is coming from." Her eyes dashed between me and the window. "You know, your daddy is a very smart man, LaShondra. He was the valedictorian of his high school class."

My eyes widened. "I never knew that."

"Yes. Your father had dreams. He had things he wanted to do with his life. He used to read all kinds of books, learning everything he could to get ready for his life. You know he still reads the entire newspaper every morning. And you know your daddy is good with math, too—'specially money. Ooh, your daddy can take a nickel and by the time he's done with it, it'll be a dime. That man is something else." She laughed as she talked of a father I knew little about.

"Well, his last year in high school, 1958, he was getting set and ready to go to Harley College on a work detail. He wanted to be a banker."

"Daddy was going to Harley?"

"Yep. Finest black college in all of Texas." A proud smile came across her face.

"What's a work detail?"

"That's when you agree to work to pay for college—mow the grass, tend the hogs, work in the kitchen, whatever you got to do.

"Well, I wasn't dating him back then, but I'd heard about Jonathan Smith. All the girls said he was the smoothest black thing in Ellerson. He was at all the dances and all the get-togethers, and he was always surrounded by a bunch of girls, like he was some kind of movie star. He was the smartest, best thing going as far as we all knew. By then they had put your daddy in the papers and everything, and black people were starting to get a little afraid 'cause we knew every time a black person start doin' good, white folks start gettin' mad. When they see black kids doin' better than their kids, they can't take it. Grandmomma Smith told your daddy to keep his nose clean and just get off to college without trouble. But trouble came lookin' for him.

"It all happened one afternoon when your daddy was out with a few of his buddies, riding around in a '57 pickup that Frederick Evans's daddy had bought used. It wasn't much, but it was more than a lot of white folks in Ellerson had. Your daddy and his friends were out just having fun, doing their last things before getting ready to go off to college. They drove all through downtown Ellerson, and into some of the parts of town that they didn't have no business. Well, your daddy had to use the restroom, and his buddy Fredrick Evans told him they couldn't stop, 'cause they was in the wrong part of town. Your daddy couldn't hold it no longer, so they pulled over between two quiet-looking buildings and he did his business and hurried up and hopped back on the back of the truck. And soon as he sat back down, he looked up into one of those buildings and saw a white woman looking down at him. She'd seen what he'd done.

"Well, it wasn't hard for the police to find them, 'cause Ellerson was so small at that time. They arrested Frederick, your daddy, and the rest of 'em 'cause that white woman said your daddy, a black man, had showed her his privates. Your daddy already knowed they was gonna beat him, but when Sheriff Lipscomb got wind that Jonathan was the uppity black boy that had been in the papers and was goin' off to college, they almost beat your daddy to death in that jail cell. Tried to beat him till he couldn't think straight. You know that scar your daddy has right behind his ear?"

I nodded.

"That's just one of 'em. He's got a lot more scars, but most of 'em you can't see, 'cause they're in his mind. The beatin' the family took in the papers was almost worse than what your daddy took behind bars. Everybody had heard that Bessie Jean and Clyde's son was in jail for showing hisself to a white woman. Even though most of the black folks knew better than to believe what they read in the papers, the white peoples around town started treating the blacks worse off than before; it got so 'til the black people wanted the Smiths out of there 'cause it made such a ruckus in the community. When your daddy got out, Grandmomma Smith and your grandfather moved the family to Dallas. Wasn't far, but it was far enough to at least get out of town. But by that time your daddy had stayed in jail so long, they went ahead and filled his work detail slot at Harley College with somebody else."

Stunned, I searched for something to say. "But couldn't he go back the next year?" I asked finally.

"He was so sick and disgusted with everything, he just decided not to try anymore. He gave up. And that anger, that disappointment, that injustice has been with him ever since. That's the way it was back then, LaShondra. You could lose *everything* over something as simple as peeing on the side of the road. *Everything*, just like that." She snapped her fingers.

"But he didn't lose everything. He still has you; he still has us and his family. Don't we mean something to him?" I asked. "I mean, so he didn't go to college. A lot of people didn't go to college, especially back then."

"It's not so much about college as it is about his life being stolen from him, all on the word of a white woman.

"Now, I married your father 'cause I could see that underneath all that rough-and-tough stuff, he's still got a heart. He acted all mean around everybody, but I'd catch him stopping to smell a flower or making a car halt so that a child could fetch a ball that had rolled out in the middle of the street. But sometimes I hear him over in the night, grinding his teeth in his sleep. Just mad. Just angry."

I shrugged my shoulders and asked, "Why didn't he tell me this before?" I couldn't help but feel betrayed. My father had a dream that died, almost literally, on the side of a country road—and I knew nothing about it?

"He doesn't talk about it." Her face was blank, as was her point.

"That's it? He just doesn't talk about it? What's it supposed to do—go away?"

"No, it's here. It's in the way he talks, the way he thinks, the way he feels about white folks. You know, a lot of us don't fool with white people 'cause we never have and don't have a desire to. But people like your father, the ones with the stories they do or don't tell . . . it's different for them. Everything's different when it happens to you."

I couldn't deny that, but I couldn't conceive of being at odds with my father about Stelson—for however long or short we might be together. My father and I wouldn't have won any father-daughter awards for our relationship, but it worked for me. I had a father I could depend on, and I valued that. "Momma, I've already lost Grandmomma Smith. I don't want to lose Daddy, too."

"Well, there ain't but One that can fix this mess," she said. Momma lifted herself up from the table.

"I know. Will you agree with me and Stelson and pray that God will come in and change this whole thing around?"

"We ain't got no choice but to pray."

"You're right. We don't," I agreed with her. "We cannot let the enemy come in here and tear this family apart."

"You got that right, baby." She gave me that old-folks wise smile. "I taught you well. Let's get in here and pray."

We prayed until the power of the Holy Spirit fell upon us. Momma began praying in her heavenly language, and I suddenly felt relieved, knowing that the Spirit was uttering the right words, communicating precisely what needed to be said—more than either of us knew to pray.

We decided that I'd tell my father myself.

After cleaning up the kitchen, we got our purses and carried on with the rest of the day, stopping first at the grocery store. You would have thought we were getting ready for Thanksgiving, the way that list looked. Greens, sweet potatoes, cornmeal. Down one aisle and up the next, tossing things into the cart.

It felt good to be at her side and to have someone else, for once, be in charge of things. For as much as I loathed Momma's pestering and nosiness, I took comfort in her authority, the sureness of her role in my life. They say that a girl isn't a woman until she loses her mother. I believed it that day.

We ran all over the store for about an hour. When we got back in the car, Momma picked me for more information about Stelson. "What kind of church does he belong to?"

"I guess you could say," I said, still trying to keep the tone light, "that he goes to a nondenominational church." I knew how Momma felt about nondenominational churches. She said they were all a bunch of renegades and cults. "But he was raised in the Assemblies of God," I quickly added what I hoped would be redeeming information.

She was silent for a moment. I briefly glanced at her to read her expression. She looked at me real crazy, then turned her head away from me. "Humph. I heard our church and theirs used to be tied up a long time ago."

"That's right, Momma. We were."

"And I hear you've been taking him to True Way with you," she said.

My mouth dropped. "Who told you that?"

"Word gets around. 'Specially when it's got church folk to spread it. I heard about your friend already. They say he's respectful. Gives a good offerin', too." She held her purse tightly to her stomach.

"Somebody is talkin' way too much," I said.

"Aw, girl, please. They don't mean no harm by it. Just lookin' out for you."

"I doubt they would have done that if Stelson were black."

"Well, he ain't. And you're wrong—they would do it if he was black. Saints always look out for each other's kids. You'd be surprised what I know." She patted her purse and looked away from me.

It was almost ten o'clock by the time Daddy got back from Grandmomma Smith's house. They'd been working on the funeral arrangements all day long. Momma and I were almost finished with the evening's cooking. When he walked through the door, Momma grabbed his light jacket and kissed him on the cheek. "Let me hang up your coat."

Daddy came and sat in the kitchen. He looked drained. Empty. Not himself. "Hi, Daddy."

"Hey, Shondra. What you doin' over here?" He took off his shoes and placed them together beside the refrigerator.

"Just helpin' Momma out. How is everybody?"

"Fine." He tried to give me a little grin but failed pathetically. He took off his shirt and placed it on the back of his chair before sitting to join me at the table. Any other time, Momma would have fussed at him for leaving his stuff all over the kitchen. But not this time.

"The family needs to meet at Grandmomma Smith's house at ten so we can go over to the church."

"Which church?" I asked.

"My mother's church," he barked at me. Momma looked at me like, *go along with it.* "My mother was a member of New Zion Baptist Church. She'd been a member there since we moved here in 1959." He folded his hands and began with a sketchy outline of how Grandmomma Smith had been involved in the church, obviously intermittently. Still, he'd said that the church was sorry to hear of her passing and was more than happy to host services for one of its own.

"That's great to know, Daddy."

"Did you get in touch with Jonathan? I tried calling him, but I couldn't get through."

"Yes, Daddy. I called him. He'll be here Wednesday afternoon."

"Yeah, Jonathan loved Grandmomma Smith. And she sure loved him. My momma was so proud of him going off into the service. She was proud of all y'all, you know." He looked up and gave a real beam this time. "I mean, your cousins are okay and all, but she always said that you and Jonathan would grow up and make something of yourselves, no matter what the world brings. People like you and Jonathan make black folks proud." Daddy smiled to himself.

CHAPTER 19

We, the jury in the above-entitled action, find the defendant, Orenja—Orenthal James Simpson, not guilty in . . ."

My heart almost stopped.

"Yeah! Yeah!" Daddy took off running with his hands in the air. He ran through the house like a mad man, screaming, "Yeah! Yeah! Not guilty! Not guilty!"

"Jonathan Smith Senior, if you don't stop all this clownin' and sit down somewhere," Momma called to him after several minutes of his rampage. "The doctor told you to take it easy these next few days—don't, you gonna end up having a heart attack!"

"Yeah!" He ignored her and ran another circle through the living room, kitchen, and dining room.

"Daddy!" I caught him by the arm. "I'm not taking off another day of work to come see about you again."

He acquiesced and sat down, panting, at the kitchen table. "Aw, girl, hush. You didn't want to go to work today anyway. Whoo! Good God almighty. I don't believe you understand what just happened. This is one small step for black mankind."

"Jon, you know good and well O. J. killed that girl and her man friend," Momma said. "Two people are dead. Even if he didn't kill them, he certainly had something to do with it."

Daddy shook his head and motioned for me to get him some

water. I pulled a glass from the top shelf of the cabinet, rinsed it out, and filled it with ice and water from the refrigerator door.

"Whoo!" He wiped perspiration from his forehead. "It doesn't matter whether he did it or not. The courts never have cared whether or not a black man was truly guilty. We've been saying that since we got off the boat. Now they *finally get to see what it feels like to have a jury overlook all the evidence and find somebody not guilty. I believe Malcolm X called it 'Chickens coming home to roost.' Whoo! I can die now. I've seen it all."*

"You will *be dead, you keep up this whoopin' and hollerin'," Momma said. She took the empty glass from his hands and refilled it. "It really don't matter what color the people are, Jon. If he did it, he should have been found guilty."*

"Well, the law says he didn't do it, so as far as I'm concerned, O. J. Simpson is innocent." Daddy put his feet up on the chair in front of him and raised his pinky while he sipped the water. "Not guilty. Boy, I can't wait *to go to work tomorrow with a big smile on my face."*

Daddy skipped into the living room and picked up the remote control. He turned up the volume. He switched channels three or four times, laughing at the astonished looks on the faces of the white people as they heard the verdict time and time again. Not guilty. "Ha!" he screamed. "Look at 'em! Serves 'em right, after they let them cops who beat Rodney King go. Whoo! You wait till I get to work tomorrow!"

"So, do you think O. J. did it?" I asked Daddy.

"It doesn't matter what I think." He shook his head. "The book says he's innocent. But that's beside the point."

"Well, what is *the point, as you see it, Daddy?"*

Daddy sat up straight, set his glass down on the cloth place mat, and looked me squarely in the face. "The point is, a black man killed a white woman in America and got away with it. Score one for all the innocent black men who died or are still serving time for crimes they didn't commit."

⧈ ⧈ ⧈

God blessed me with a very peaceful workday on Monday. I needed it after such a hectic weekend. Mr. Butler was out, the kids were taking another standardized test, and all was pretty quiet. Stelson called me at ten to see if I wanted to eat lunch. I agreed, but right at eleven-thirty it started pouring down, so he called me back to say that he'd just drop off lunch for me if I didn't feel like getting out.

Later I led him into my office and asked Miss Jan to hold any calls for the next thirty minutes unless it was someone from my family. She nodded.

"So, how's the family?" he asked, carefully passing me my food.

"We're gonna be fine. Thanks for asking. The funeral is gonna be at eleven on Thursday. I think if we can just get past that, we'll be okay." I was eager to change the subject.

He motioned for me to give him my hands. I did so, and he blessed the food. He took a bite of his tortilla and continued talking about his upcoming trip. As he talked, I noticed how easily we broke rules with no consequence. Talking while eating was something that I reserved for those that I felt completely comfortable with. During our first lunch, we'd both been careful to position our silverware and our napkins in just the right places. But here, only four months later, we were letting it all hang out, so to speak.

"Cooper and I will be presenting a new design to a mid-sized cosmetic manufacturing company. They already have machines that do much of the work in manufacturing and packaging their cosmetics, but there is still an unacceptable margin of error in their system because they rely heavily on humans to put on labels, combine certain colorants and chemicals, and a whole lot of other things. My firm has designed a more efficient machine. It'll help them with their production, eliminate the need for so much overhead, and ultimately lead to higher customer satisfaction and increased revenues."

"And if you do get the contract?"

"It's a multi million-dollar deal, I can tell you that much." He smiled. "It would certainly look nice on our records, and the employees could all look forward to a pretty good quarterly bonus."

"You go, Stelson," I was impressed with his passion both for his business and for the people who worked hard to make it a success. "And all of this starts tomorrow? Shouldn't you be somewhere rehearsing or something?"

"I needed to see you," he said, inspiring a welcome spark in me. "I missed you yesterday."

"I missed you, too."

He just sat there, sipping his soda. That little dent came up, the one just above his jawbone. I took a moment to peruse him, sitting there in his heavily starched white polo shirt. Everything about Stelson was undeniably sexy. His chin, the curve of his lips, the way his fingers held on to that jalepeño.

I didn't want to go off the deep end with this, but perhaps it was time we had this discussion about sex. I cared deeply about Stelson, and I felt certain that we were on the same page spiritually. But spending so much time with him was beginning to take a toll on my flesh. We needed to talk. Stelson was straight up sexy, and my libido saw *way* past his color.

"Stelson, let me ask you a question. Have you slept with any women since you sincerely dedicated your life to Christ?"

"I've made my fair share of mistakes by listening to my flesh." He nodded his head in confession. "But I learned from them."

I smiled and waited for him to take his turn.

"And you?"

"After my brush with HIV, I quit cold turkey. God has really worked on me in isolation since then. I really haven't had a steady man in my life since then—until you. And, to lay all my cards on the table, Stelson, I have to let you know that I am very attracted to you. I also need to let you know that this is truly different for me. I have never been in a serious relationship with a man without having sex, so this is a first. But I'm very happy to have found someone who is in the same boat I'm in spiritually."

He swallowed and cleared his throat. "The other night, when we were on the porch, I wanted you. And I still do, but my spirit knows that that would only compromise both of us. When God gives me something beautiful, I try not to destroy it."

"So you had a serious relationship with a Christian woman without having sex?" I asked him.

"Yeah, as a matter of fact I did. We dated for about four weeks. It went very well, but there were other issues."

"That does not *even* count. Four weeks! I went that long without, even when I *wasn't* celibate!"

"That does count!" he argued his case. "Four weeks is a long time."

I laughed. *Men.*

"But you know what?"

"What?" I asked.

"With God's help, we can do this, LaShondra.

"Well, I've gotta get going." He took one last gulp of soda.

"Oh, okay." We gathered up the empty wrappers and cartons and stuffed them into one big sack, then put them in the trash. I knew my room would smell like salsa and candles with that trash in there, but it was okay. It would remind me of our lunch.

"Hey, let's pray before you go."

We held hands and bowed our heads. I spoke first. "Father, we come to You now giving You glory, honor, and praises for who You are. We thank You for Your many blessings and for Your love and kindness and mercy. Now, Lord, we pray that You would watch over us and keep us from all hurt, harm, and dangers seen and unseen. Lord, give us the strength and wisdom to fulfill Your plan in our lives.

"Father, be with Stelson as he travels throughout the land, and let Your will be done in every aspect of his life, Lord. In the name of Jesus I pray, amen."

Then Stelson prayed, "Father, I thank You for another day that wasn't promised to me. I thank You for saving me in the midst of my sins and for giving me a new life in You. I also want to thank You for this wonderful woman that You have introduced me to. I thank You for her openness, her kindness, and her loving spirit. Lord, be with LaShondra and her family on this week. Give them the strength they need to make it through this difficult time. All these blessings I ask in Your son Jesus' name. Amen."

We opened our eyes simultaneously and stood there for a second. Then Stelson bent down to kiss me. "Until Thursday," he said.

"Call me when you get in," I think I said.

"I will. Bye."

As I watched Stelson return to his car, I glanced over at the track field. There was Katelyn Donovan, working out with the off-season team. Out of curiosity, I pulled up her grade report on the computer when I got inside. I wanted to know if she had been doing better with her math grades. A message popped up on my screen: *Changes have been made at the administrative level.* I pushed *OK* and viewed her grades. She had a passing grade for the fall semester—a 91, to be exact. Mathematically, that was impossible to achieve with a 59 for a six-weeks grade. I scrolled over to her second six-weeks average: *Math 88.* I sat for a minute with my thumbs beneath my chin, my index fingers resting on my nose and the rest laced.

Okay, this is just wrong. I knew it. Mr. Butler knew it. I thought about all the kids who'd come through my office, and how Mr. Butler and I had sat down with sobbing parents and explained to them why little Johnny couldn't play football or was going to have to come to summer school or repeat an entire school year. And he had put on a little smirk when the parents left, saying that they should have been thinking about their child's grades sooner. I had agreed with him because, even though he did have a smart-aleck attitude about it, he had been right. Now all of a sudden, politics came into play and the rules didn't apply to everyone. But was this my battle? Did I need to stand up, say something, rock the boat over this one girl? I printed her grades, put them in my old "Katelyn" file, and decided to pray about it.

Maybe the file would come in handy. Maybe not. I got the feeling that this would be handled divinely, though the particulars of this incident might not be the straw to break the camel's back. I felt confident that Katelyn knew her math facts and strategies well enough. She was just being lazy that six weeks. I did feel sorry for her, though. What if she grew up thinking that money was the most powerful thing in the world? What if she got the message that people are for sale? Would she also be for sale?

As if he had some type of tap on my computer, I saw Mr. Butler approaching my office. Ever since I returned from administrative leave, he had been watching me like a hawk. I couldn't prove it, but I knew that he was so busy watching me that he wasn't handling business. Come to think of it, maybe he'd been doing that long before I was suspended. Who knows? I was up to my neck with Mr. Butler, and I couldn't wait for him to retire. I put Katelyn's file away and cleared space on my desk for whatever Mr. Butler might bring with him for the two of us to look over.

"Ms. Smith"—Mr. Butler came into my office quickly—"I know you're fairly new at this. But I think you should understand something—something that I hoped you would figure out during your suspension, but you obviously didn't. The school system is just like any other business. We cater to our customers. Especially to those who support us the most. Lots of stores have programs for their most valuable shoppers—gold cards, special coupons, early shopping hours. It's no different here." He explained it as if it were actually okay.

"Mr. Butler, I don't know where all this is coming from, but this school is not a store. We don't have platinum VIP programs. What we have are students coming from every level of the economic spectrum, who deserve to be treated fairly."

"This isn't a fairy tale, Ms. Smith. Money makes the world go 'round. The sooner you learn that, the better." He walked out without looking back.

I watched him go up the stairs. His whitened hair swayed slightly with his steps. The girth of his arms challenged the seams of his jacket sleeves. He'd worked for the school district for as long as I'd been alive, I figured. He'd be retiring soon. Not soon enough, that was for sure. Maybe he was just tired of fighting the education battle. It can be disheartening at times.

Maybe, long ago, he'd decided to become a teacher so that he could make a difference, as all of us in the field once did. I imagined that on the first day of school, he had put his name on the chalkboard in big, bold letters. He'd introduced himself to the students, later met their parents, and taught with a zeal that had actually benefited students. He'd stood for something then. But that was a long time ago. Maybe he was just ready to give it up, not rocking the boat in his last years on board. I was usually more respectful to Mr. Butler than I was that morning, but he had a lot of nerve coming into my office trippin'. I knew that he was just harassing me, coming to feel me out, maybe even to intimidate me. *But why?* I'd run everything past the handbook and brought my daily challenges before the Lord in prayer, asking Him to purge my thoughts and allow me to administer in love and respect. *So why is this man still riding me?*

Mr. Butler was elderly and in need of prayer. I watched him turn the corner at the top of the steps. He limped a little from the strain of fighting the incline. Then he was out of view. *Lord, help him. He has no idea how the enemy is using him.*

Wednesday morning brought light spring showers. Since I'd taken off the rest of the week, I slept in a little. When I got up, I prayed, then had cereal for breakfast and got dressed for the day. I ran to the grocery store to get a few things before Jonathan arrived, and before I knew it, it was time to go to the airport. I hated going to the airport. One wrong turn and you could be lost in the maze indefinitely. It wasn't as if you could just turn around and get back on. Oh, no. By the time you even realize that you're lost, you're on your way out and you'll need to pay another dollar and fifty cents to get back into the mix. I was careful to slow down and read the signs, despite the fact that somebody behind me gave me the finger once. I didn't care. The last place I wanted to be lost was at DFW Airport. *Help me, Lord. Gate Six. American Airlines. Flight #128. Okay, okay.* I pulled up to the curb as Jonathan had instructed me. He said he'd be waiting so I wouldn't have to park.

And there he was, waving at me with his free hand. His light brown skin matched Momma's exactly, but his strong bone structure was Daddy all over. Dressed in his uniform, Jonathan was the perfect clean-cut brother. I could only hope that God's plan would lead him to the classroom. I pulled to the curb and popped my trunk so he could put his bags in the car. The curb attendant was impatient, ready for me to pull out. I quickly unlocked the doors, and Jonathan hopped in. We hugged for an instant, just long enough for the airport worker to blow his whistle and hurry us out.

"Hey!" Jonathan looked me over. "You're looking thirty-one now."

"Whatever!"

"That's a compliment," he said. "Weren't you tired of looking like one of your students?"

"It's a funny thing," I laughed. "When you're young you want to look old. But now that I'm older, I'm trying to hold on to every bit of youth I can."

"Well, you're looking good," he reiterated.

"Look at you—all suave. What's up with the bald head?"

"Just something to do." He shook his head and smiled.

"I like, I like." I ran my hand along his head. "I'm glad you're staying with Momma and Daddy, 'cause I don't have time for all these little women friends of yours calling my house for you."

"What women friends?" He grinned.

"The ones that are gonna be all over you when you hit the streets with this bald head. It looks really good, Jonathan. Makes you look distinctive." I poked out my lower lip and nodded, giving him my seal of approval. Jonathan's six-foot-three frame barely fit into my car; his long legs were cramped beneath the dashboard.

My cell phone rang. "Hello?"

"You picked up Jonathan yet?"

"Yes, ma'am. We're on our way there."

"Well, you need to hurry, LaShondra. Your father wants to speak with you."

"About what?"

"Well, evidently, one of your nosy cousins saw you and Stelson together the other night. Your Daddy got wind of it, and he's been carryin' on about it, tellin' them they ain't nothin' but a bunch of liars and gossips," she whispered.

Oh, great. This is not how I wanted my father to find out. If only I had told him sooner. "We'll be there in half an hour." I hung up the phone and banged my palm against the steering wheel. It was one of those moments when I knew that I knew better and should have acted sooner, but because I didn't, things weren't working out the way I wanted them to. Rather, I was at the mercy of my snooping family. All because I didn't act on my leading to tell my father earlier. *Lord, there's got to be a million things I could have accomplished by now if only I would act when you speak. Forgive me, and make me more faithful to Your prompting.*

"What's wrong?" Jonathan asked.

"It's a long story, Jonathan, but here it goes. I'm seeing a wonderful man named Stelson Brown. He's nice, he's decent, and he loves the Lord. He's also white."

Jonathan's eyebrows went up an inch. "You serious?"

"Yes, I'm serious. The problem is, I haven't told Daddy about him. Stelson took me to Grandmomma Smith's house the night she died, and somebody must have seen us together when we walked back to his car. Anyway, Daddy heard something and now he's accusing them of lying about what they obviously saw. Bottom line, I should have told Daddy sooner, but I didn't. Now I have to tell him in the middle of all this stress."

"You're dating a white man?" Jonathan seemed amused.

"What's so funny?"

"I just never thought . . . I didn't think you would give a white man the time of day."

"Neither did I, Jonathan, but God worked this thing in the most mysterious of ways. It just kind of happened, you know?"

"Hmm." He put his chin in his hand and looked out the window.

"So, are you okay with this?" I asked him.

"I'm okay; I guess I'm just shocked, that's all. But if you really like him, Shondra, don't let his color stand in the way. One thing I've learned in my travels is that people are the same everywhere you go. Everybody wants better education and safer streets. But more than anything, people want the freedom to choose."

Jonathan prayed with me before we went into the house. "Lord, give Shondra the strength to stick with her convictions and the wisdom to express them respectfully to our father. Send Your love to temper the anger that has welled up inside our father for many, many years. And teach us all to be loving, caring, and godly in our dealings with every human of every race. Renew our minds in dealing with people that we have been taught to hate. Father, I thank You for my sister's example of courage. Now, Lord, help her to stand. In the name of Jesus we pray, amen."

Momma met us at the door and squeezed Jonathan tightly. Her eyes glistened as she kissed his cheeks. In the house, everything was quiet. Too quiet. The carpet snuffed out the sound of our steps, so that we almost sneaked up on Daddy in his chair. He jumped a little at the sight of us hovering above him. "Hey!" he yelled, and got up to hug Jonathan. "Ha! Ha! You lookin' good, boy! Lookin' good!"

"It's good to be home, old man," Jonathan teased him.

"Who you callin' 'old man'?" Daddy punched Jonathan's arm. "I'll show you an old man!"

Daddy looked past Jonathan and saw me. He sucked his teeth a bit and pushed Jonathan aside. "Shondra, your cousin Jessica's goin' around saying that she saw you all hugged up with that white man from your job. I told her she ain't nothin' but a lyin' heifer and—"

I shoved my hands in my pockets. "Daddy, it's true."

His eyes grew so wide they could have popped out. His knuckles plunged into his waist. He looked at Jonathan, Momma, and then back at me, as if to ask if this was a sick joke. I held my breath, trying to freeze that second in time, stop it just long enough to step out of it—maybe even run away from this confrontation, as I had done with so many others. But there would be no running this time. I liked Stelson. And even though this wasn't exactly how I'd pictured myself telling Daddy, it was all out there now. I would have to endure the hell that I knew was about to break loose.

Daddy asked the question softly at first, in the sarcastic whisper that he reserved for those he believed to be "hard at understanding." "Are you out of your mind?"

"No," I responded. *Stand, LaShondra. Stand in love.* "His name is Stelson, and we've been seeing each other for a while now." I put my hands behind my back because I didn't know what else to do with them. My nails pressed into my palms. I knew that Jonathan and Momma were standing right next to me, probably praying for me, but I felt as if my father and I were the only two people in the room. Here was the man who had taught me to stay strong in the race, to keep my nose clean so "they" wouldn't have anything on me, to put forth 110 percent so that I could keep up with "them."

"Let me repeat the question: ARE YOU OUT OF YOUR MIND?" He pounded his fist on his palm and sank lower, eye to eye.

I took a deep breath. "Daddy, I know how you feel about white people. And I'm not asking you to change.

Right now, I am only asking you to respect my decision to be with someone who is not black."

"And the answer is hell, no!" Daddy screamed in my face. I took a step back, and he took one toward me. "Did you hear me? The answer is no! All this damned time, I've been thinking that if anybody would have a problem, it would be Jonathan, 'cause he's in the service. But you—come to my momma's house with a white man! Do you know how . . . how stupid that is?"

My father had never called me or anything I did stupid—ever. *How could Daddy say that to me?* The stinging behind my eyes produced tears that I willed to keep in place, while the hurt inside me quickly converted itself to anger. I followed his outburst with my own. "Do you know what's stupid, Daddy?" Momma reached for my arm, but I pulled away from her grasp. "The way you're always going around here talking about how white people keep black people down, but I don't see you doing anything to help the situation! You don't vote! You haven't mentored any of these young boys in the neighborhood who need role models, and you see them every day! You ain't even a member of a black organization! All you do is sit around this house complaining and ruining everybody's hopes and dreams! Well, I'm sorry yours got ruined, but *you* made the choice to stay angry all these years."

"I didn't have a damn choice!" Daddy yelled, coming within an inch of my face.

"Yes, you did! And you made it. You decided to be prejudiced and racist and to pass it on to Jonathan and me. But I will not let your racist issues dictate what happens in my life, Daddy!"

"Is that what you think I am? A racist?" He stepped back.

"That's exactly what you are! A closed-minded racist who goes around trying to make everybody think the same way you do! That's what you are!" I yelled. Breaths came faster than I could pull them in and push them out, and I couldn't stop myself from shaking.

"Well, I'm the racist who put clothes on your back and food on your plate and a roof over your head all these years! If I'm a racist, so be it! I know what I know—white people never mean you any good. And I'll be damned if my own daughter hasn't sat up here and broke bread with the enemy."

I lowered my trembling voice to gain control of it. "Stelson treats me better than any man I've ever dated. Isn't that what any loving father wants for his daughter?"

Daddy looked at me and shook his head. His face, like melting wax, had slipped a few inches. Then, as he walked out of the living room, he said, "I used to be so proud of you." He walked to the bedroom and closed the door.

My insides turned to mush, and my protective shield of anger dissolved. I was nothing but a mass of hurt and pain. Until now, I had never realized how much it meant to me that my father was proud of me. His adoration, his esteem, and his high regard for me had always pushed me to succeed. As a child I had always brought my report card to him first, seeking Daddy's coveted nod of approval. I'd always run things past him to get his stamp. But now, as an adult, I was devastated by the rejection that only a father can give.

"Shondra, he didn't mean that." I felt Jonathan's hand on my shoulder. "He's just upset right now."

"You know how your Daddy is," Momma added. "He's just spoutin' off right now. He'll calm down in a minute."

"But he did say it," I cried.

The door to my parents' bedroom swung open, and Daddy shouted, "And another thing—that white man is not welcome in this house!"

Oh, shut up!

It was almost comical, the way he added insult to injury by slamming the bedroom door shut after screaming. *Purposeful. Crafty. Destructive. Sounds like the work of the enemy.* I decided to practice one of the things my Sunday school teacher taught me years before. She'd said that when someone is going out of their way to make you miserable, recognize that it's the enemy using that person to discourage you. Just like Daddy, I had a choice to make. I could be angry and bitter. Or I could pray for my father and forgive him—even if he never apologized or accepted Stelson. Holding a grudge against my father would only mean making his mistake all over again. *Father, I forgive him. I don't care if he ever grows to like Stelson. I just don't want this rift between the two of us.*

I went home and bawled.

CHAPTER 20

I hid my new navy blue sailor jumpsuit in the suitcase I'd packed to spend the night at Aunt Emma Smith's apartment while Momma and Daddy went out of town. Jonathan and I rarely spent time with the Smiths, so I figured that whatever our parents were doing, it must have been important, because Momma didn't bother to check my suitcase. She had specifically forbidden me to take that jumpsuit, but I had *to. There were three more weeks until the start of second grade, and I was itching to wear that outfit. It had big gold buttons down the front of the heavy polyester blend, and the red stars on the sailor's flap had a glittery shine to them.*

As soon as we got to Aunt Emma's apartment, I pulled that jumpsuit out of the suitcase and put it on. Aunt Emma asked me why I'd changed, and I told her that I was practicing to be a model. She got herself another beer out of the refrigerator and disappeared behind her curtain of beads.

I called to her from the living room, "Can I go outside and play? I see some kids out there, Aunt Emma."

"Yeah. Be back before the sun goes down!"

Jonathan, then almost four, begged me to take him with me, but I shut the door in his face. I didn't have time to fool with Jonathan—not when I was stylin' in my sailor jumpsuit. I walked right on over to that bunch of kids near the generator and introduced myself. "Hi, I'm LaShondra." I looked over their shoulders for a second and noticed that they were busy painting pictures. "Can I play?"

There must have been at least five of them, but only one of them looked up at me. She was white with dirty blond hair and green eyes. "We're not playing; we're painting—can't you see that?"

"Well, can I paint, then?"

One of the boys moved aside to let me in. He was older than me—probably almost a teenager, I guessed. I sensed that they didn't like me, for whatever reason. I knew that they were all white, and I knew that I was infringing upon their painting, but I had no doubt that they would soon recognize my worth. Especially since I was wearing that outstanding jumpsuit. I set my knees down on the cement and began to paint carefully, so as not to get a drop of it on my clothes.

They talked over me, never really including me in anything. I didn't really care, though. It was worth it to be able to listen and make new friends. I just painted and hoped for the best. The kids moved around me, a few at a time, switching places and taking turns passing the paint around. In front of me, behind me.

Within minutes, it started getting dark. I cursed Aunt Emma in my head. She knew I was only gonna be out here for a few minutes. Nonetheless, I had made new friends. "Are y'all gonna paint again tomorrow?" I asked the only little girl who actually addressed me.

"No," she laughed, shaking her hair out of her face. "Probably not." Come to think of it, they were all giggling as they quickly gathered their painting materials and sped off in different directions.

I went back to Aunt Emma's apartment, bursting in to show her the painting I'd done. "Put that back out on the porch till it dries!" she fussed.

"Yes, ma'am." I turned to obey her orders.

"Shondra, what's that stuff on the back of your clothes?"

I froze. "What stuff?"

"Looks like paint. Come here."

Oh, no. I was so careful. I passed through the curtain again. "What is it?" I whimpered.

"Chile, they done painted a whole bunch of stuff on your back. You didn't feel them paintin' on your back?"

"No, ma'am," I cried. "I was just paintin', myself. What kind of stuff? Can you get it off, Aunt Emma? Can you please *get it off?" I was shaking like a leaf at the thought of what Momma would do if she found out that I'd taken that jumpsuit out of the house and then let a bunch of white kids paint all over the back of it. Aunt Emma was ready to whip somebody's tail. "Did you see which building they went into?"*

"I don't know which way they went. There was a lot of 'em."

"What color were they?"

"White."

"Mmm-hmm. See, I thought you was going out there to play with some of the black kids. I wouldn't have never let you go out there if I'd known you was tryin' to play with that other bunch. They're always up to no good." She unzipped my jumper from behind and told me to go into the bedroom and take it off. "I bet you'll know better than to fool with those little bad-ass white kids next time."

I went into the bedroom, took off the jumpsuit, and laid it across the bed. There were yellow smiley faces, orange triangles, and a multitude of other simple drawings on the backside of it. Someone had also written ha-ha.

The only thing worse than the good ol'-fashioned, countrified Holy-Ghost-with-fire whippin' I got from Momma was the fact that she couldn't get the paint out. And I never got the chance to wear my outstanding navy blue sailor jumpsuit again.

Everybody and their momma was at the funeral. All the Smiths came out to pay their last respects to Grandmomma. I saw cousins, aunts, and uncles that I hadn't seen in decades. The ceremony went very well for an African-American funeral, partially due to the fact that it was a closed-casket ceremony. Daddy and the rest of my aunts and uncles agreed that it would be too heart-wrenching to have the casket open. I, for one, was happy about that because once one person loses their composure, it's *on* at a soulful funeral.

The family was dressed in white to celebrate her full life. A few of my younger cousins pinned red corsages on the children, grandchildren, and great-grands. I was proud to be a Smith that day, for all it was worth. Despite the ugly things that happened in my family's history, we were still standing. I only wished that Stelson could have been there.

Daddy didn't say a word to me all morning. He would not even look my way.

I sat on the third pew, between Jonathan and Peaches. Quinn accompanied her and ended up helping the ushers pass out programs. I never did figure out how that happened. Peaches' mother came to the funeral, too. We had a few words in the church parking lot after the ceremony.

"Shondra, I'll tell you, I've never seen Peaches so happy," said Mrs. Miller. Her deep brown skin showed tear traces along her cheeks, but she was smiling now. "Since she's been with Quinn, you'd think she's found a pot of gold. I told her, it probably won't be long before they jump the broom."

"You think so, Momma Miller?"

"A mother knows these things." She winked at me. "He's really good for her, and I think Peaches finally knows how to appreciate a good man. I told her from the very beginning that that Raphael wasn't no good. But sometimes it takes a few heartbreaks before you know how to spot a good one. Speaking of good ones, where's Stalton?"

"Peaches told you about Stelson?" I crossed my arms and rested my weight on one leg, wondering what else Peaches had told her.

"Told me he was white, too." She smiled, no hint of an attitude. "Where is he?"

"Stelson is in Chicago."

"Well, the both of y'all need to quit playin' hard to get. Me and Joe got married the minute we knew we couldn't live another day without each other, and we've enjoyed every minute of it. You put God in your marriage and you ain't got to worry 'bout too much else. You're gonna have your ups and downs, but the ups are higher and the downs don't go so low or last so long when you got Jesus right in the middle of it."

After burial, we all went back to Grandmomma Smith's house to eat. The house smelled of food and incense that was intended to cover up my uncle Fred's cigarettes. Daddy and the rest of his brothers and sisters ate in the front dining room. Momma and a few others squeezed in, but there wasn't much room for the rest of us. The children ate out in the backyard, and most of the young men plopped themselves in front of the television in the den.

I ate in the kitchen and listened to the women talk about things that I wouldn't otherwise have found out. My cousin April was pregnant again by that married man. Cousin Beatrice would soon be finishing law school. Uncle Willie's ex-wife won a trip to Hawaii, and she was taking a twenty-five-year-old man with her.

My cousin Jessica was in the kitchen, as usual, sopping up every bit of gossip she could. I started to tell her how much I *did not* appreciate her blabbing to the whole family about Stelson, but I knew it wouldn't do any good. She'd been blabbing for as long as I could remember. Besides, it wasn't her fault that I hadn't had the courage to stand up to my father before then.

When the kitchen cleared a bit, Aunt Ruth asked me, "Your daddy approve of this thing between you and the white man?"

"You'll have to ask my father that question."

"I ain't askin' him; I'm asking you," Aunt Ruth fussed. "Me and your uncle Fred always told our kids about marryin' outside the race."

Jessica sat down to grill me as well. She was well into her forties but always thought she was my age. Leave it to Jessica to put on a spaghetti-strapped halter top over an industrial-strength full-support bra. Like that was okay. One glance at her feet told the rest of the story. Looked like she'd been out on the highway bustin' rocks with her heels. She pushed her braids from her forehead and asked, "What did he say, girl?"

I just smiled and shook my head. "There's not much to say. I'm a grown woman. I can date who I please."

"But what does he *think* about it?" Jessica gave me that sister-girl smile, fully expecting me to go off about my daddy so that she could in turn bring tidings of our family's turmoil to the rest of the house.

"Aw, hell . . ." Aunt Ruth got up from the table and talked like I wasn't even in the room. "Jonathan's kids always did think they was better than the rest of the Smiths."

"You know, it really doesn't matter what color a person is," I said, glad to get that off my chest. "If you like someone, their race is not important."

"Not in la-la land." Jessica joined her stepmother at the counter and made herself a second plate of chicken and baked beans.

Finally, my great-aunt Catherine spoke up. She held her beer bottle up in the air as though toasting. "I, for one, am glad to see a white person. I'm tired of looking at y'all bul-lack asses all the time." She laughed out loud and winked at me. I felt like toasting with her.

"Really, Aunt Catherine." Aunt Ruth shook her head. "Do you always have to cuss like a drunken sailor? We can't even have a decent funeral. You and Bessie—always cussin'!"

"Well, my cussin' partner is dead and gone now." Aunt Catherine wiped the sweat off her nose. "I sholy am gonna miss Bessie." She took another drink of her beer.

Jonathan and I got back to my house just after seven. In my bedroom, I kicked off my shoes and listened to my messages. I guess I didn't realize how loud my answering machine was, because Stelson's message was heard all through the living room. "Hey, LaShondra, it's Stelson. We got the deal! I thought about you the whole time I was there. Well, it's a little after five-thirty now. I'm gonna work out for a little while, but I should be finished by seven. Call me at home." I felt the corners of my lips turn up as I listened to his message.

"So, that's Stelson, huh?" Jonathan asked, standing in the doorway of my bedroom.

I tried to sound nonchalant, but my face gave it away. "Yes, that's Stelson."

"Ol' Shondra," Jonathan teased me, "I never thought I'd see the day."

"What day?"

"The day you stood up to Daddy about racism and prejudice." He folded his arms and leaned against the frame of my bedroom door. "It's been a long time since anybody challenged him about it."

"I didn't know anybody had ever done so," I said.

"I did. It was a while back, right after I got into the service." Jonathan came and sat next to me on the bed. "We had a long, drawn-out talk about one of my comrades. His name was Blake Uretsky. I called Daddy once to tell him that I had leave for a weekend and that I was going home with Blake to check out San Diego. Daddy pitched a fit—told me that I was selling out. All kinds of stuff."

"Did he tell you that he wasn't proud of you?" Those words still pinched me.

"No. He told me that I was letting him down. And that hurt. It really did. But I prayed about it, and you know what I asked myself?" He waited for my blank stare. "I asked myself, who am I, if I'm not black?"

"I don't understand." I shook my head, shaking up some of the last remaining doubts in my head. "We're always gonna be black, Jonathan."

"Who are you, aside from being a black woman? What is your character? In your life, in your identity, what takes precedence over the color of your skin?" he asked me, looking sincerely into my eyes.

"My relationship with God," I said quickly.

"Exactly. And if your duty, as a child of God on this planet, is to love everyone, then you must do so regardless of what color you are. Your first allegiance is to God. You can be black and be proud of your heritage all day. But you can't love God and hold these grudges against white people at the same time. That's contrary to His Word."

"It's not so much a grudge as it is a . . . a resentment. I can't help feeling that they have an obligation to us, you know? They mistreated us; they snuffed out nearly every ounce of our identities and then promised us things that never came to pass. Deep down inside, it still hurts to be black in America."

"I feel you, Shondra, but everything that I am is because He lives in me. I am proud of my natural heritage. Our ancestors did a lot with a little, and the strength of their character inspires me, makes me want to celebrate what we as African-Americans have overcome. But I cherish my spiritual heritage even more because *that's* where I'm free."

My heart received that. "And you told Daddy all of this?"

"No, he wasn't trying to hear all that. But I realized then that Daddy hadn't been right about everything. I know he loves me and that he's only acting out of fear. But if the hate he has for white people is strong enough to surpass the love he has for his children, something is way out of line. I've been praying for Daddy ever since, and I think that this relationship between you and Stelson might be the answer to those prayers."

"Okay, do you think that maybe you could let me know the next time before you start praying for a change in our family?" I slapped him on the back of his neck. "You've prayed up a big mess for me."

"But it's a good mess, right?"

I stopped trying to hide the smile. "Yeah, it's a good mess, when I think about it." He left me alone to call Stelson.

"Hey, LaShondra. I'm so glad you called."

"Congratulations on the deal! I'm so happy for you."

"Oh, it was great. God was so good to us in Chicago. It was uncanny. Cooper and I sold it, no problem . . . Can I see you tonight?" His voice was filled with anticipation.

"Well, I guess so. But I'm not up to doing too much. I've had a pretty draining day," I told him, kicking off my shoes. Truth was, I would have gone anywhere with Stelson if he'd asked.

"Pizza? A movie maybe?" he suggested.

"Well, actually, my brother is here. We could do pizza and a movie here if that's okay with you. I'm sure Jonathan won't mind hanging out with us, and I'd love for you two to meet."

We watched *Cooley High* and *Stir Crazy,* rewinding the funny parts and saying every line that we knew out loud. Stelson sat at the foot of the chaise, and I propped myself up on the pillows at the head. Jonathan sat on the sofa, and we all took turns lifting pizza and drinks from the end tables.

Between movies, we got into a conversation about ages, and Jonathan exposed that I had recently turned thirty-one. "You're not supposed to tell a woman's age." I pinched his arm.

"Oh . . ." Jonathan winked at me. "Sorry, sis. Don't worry, you're still young."

"When was your birthday?" Stelson asked.

"*Several* months ago."

"Oh." Stelson smiled. "Happy belated birthday."

"Thank you."

At around midnight, Jonathan said that he was ready to hit the sack. Stelson and I took him back to my parents' house. Jonathan hugged Stelson and told him that he liked knowing that his sister was in good company. "Take care of her, now," Jonathan charged Stelson.

"Will do," Stelson agreed in all sincerity.

Like I'm some kind of child. When Stelson got back into the car, I asked him, "What was all that 'take care of her' stuff about?"

"It's a man-of-God thing," he assured me.

"Mmm."

Stelson and I returned to my house and claimed our places on the big country porch's swing. After such an emotional day, it was nice to come out and take in fresh air. In good company.

"Thanks for the pizza and the movies. I didn't think I'd ever find somebody who loved those old school movies like I do," I shared with him.

"I didn't, either." He looked into my eyes. Then he leaned toward me, cupping my chin in his hand. Gently. His soft lips pressed against mine once . . . twice . . . and again. My eyes were closed, and I didn't want to open them. I just wanted Stelson to keep on kissing me over and over again.

The heat of that moment hit me like two tons of bricks, and I wanted to go back in my house and get it *on*. We'd kissed before, but never like this. Every nerve in my body stood at attention. His hand slipped down my face to my neck. I knew where he wanted it to go. For that matter, I knew where I wanted it to go. I wanted more of him. More of his touch and his kisses. Stelson was absolutely, completely intoxicating.

I pulled back from him just a bit. Our eyelashes tickled each other. His breathing was faster than mine. I opened my eyes and backed up a little more. Stelson looked at me, still holding my chin. We looked at each other for a moment more. Then a smile appeared on his face. I didn't see anything funny, but I reciprocated.

"You've got to stop doing that to me, you know."

"Me! You started it!"

"Let me finish it, then." He kissed me again, less intensely this time. We laughed through it, stealing our last pecks at each other before leaning back into the swing.

"You're somethin' else, Stelson." I laid my arm across his chest.

"You, too, LaShondra."

He kissed me again. "Good night."

"You're leaving already?"

"I'm leaving while I still can." He smiled wearily. "I'll see you later, love."

Awww. He called me "love." "Good night." I hugged him and sent him on his way.

I raced back into the house to call Peaches, feeling like a teenager in love.

"Peaches!" I yelled to her.

"What?" she answered in a groggy voice. "What time is it?"

"It's after midnight, but I need to talk to you."

"Girl, we ain't on college time! We are grown. We need to start these heart-to-hearts before the news comes on," she fussed.

"Stelson called me 'love' tonight."

"Girl, you are in there," she yawned.

"You think so?"

"People don't just call people 'love,' LaShondra. A man can have about fifty girlfriends, but he's only got one 'love' in his heart. I believe it was Houdini that said it best: 'One love, one love, you're lucky just to have . . .' "

"Peaches! I am serious."

She laughed. "I hear you, girl. But seriously, 'love' is right up there with 'baby.' He's one step away from telling you he loves you, girl. I'm tellin' you."

"Oh, Peaches, I love him. I really do." It popped out of me. "Not because he's perfect or fine or any of that. Stelson is . . . he's just got the love of God in him, and it overflows. It spills over into everything he does and everything he touches."

"Touches? Okay, have we left out a few details here?"

"Naw, I ain't left out no details."

"Just wanted to make sure."

"It's just that he's so perfect," I told her.

"And the problem is . . . ?"

"I'm just saying, he's the type of man that every woman says she wants but runs away from when he actually comes into her life. I almost pushed him out, you know? I almost thought he was too good for me."

"The devil *is* a lie. There's nobody who's too good for you, LaShondra. Period."

"Hmm. So I guess you're not still trippin' about Stelson being white, huh?"

"I'm coming around," she said. "It's not what I'd choose for myself, but your life is your life. As long as he treats you right, you go, girl. You've got my blessing. It might take me a while, but I will get over it. Besides, you've never listened to me before. Why start now? Just keep praying for me, Shon. You know I can be a little throwed-off sometimes."

"Right, right," I agreed with her.

"Whatever! And don't call me no more after midnight 'less you got a ring on your finger or you're about to deliver," she laughed. "I'm talking about some carats or some contractions five minutes apart, okay? Girl, I am too sleepy!"

"Thanks, Peaches."

"Anything for you, 'love'!" she shouted.

"I'm getting off this phone with you."

"You go, girl. Bye."

"Bye."

As I lay in bed that night thinking about life, my mind drifted to Grandmomma Smith. I know that as a child I feared her. But as an adult, and knowing what I knew then about what happened with my father, I respected her more. She had loved my father through all that, as only a mother could. Maybe that's why Daddy held her so near to his heart. Maybe that's why she was so tough on all of us. She wanted us to do what Daddy hadn't done. I flipped my pillow over to escape the cool wetness of my pools of tears.

CHAPTER 21

I'd curled, modeled, and primped in front of the mirror for two hours. I needed the perfect outfit, the perfect hairstyle, and perfect makeup to create the perfect ambience for my debut on the campus of Jarvis Christian College. But after the two-hour ride and several sweltering treks up and down two flights of stairs to my dorm room, I looked like broke-down Shondra, minus one penciled-in eyebrow.

Daddy sat down on the slab of hardened cotton that I would soon call my bed. He wiped his forehead and announced, "Whew, Shondra, you need to hurry up and put that egg crate on this bed."

"I will, Daddy. As soon as you all leave," I hinted. I loved my family, but I was ready for them to leave so that I could be freeeeee! I'd waited eighteen years and trudged through twelve years of school in anticipation of this great day.

"Well, I see we've worn out our welcome," Momma said, looking at Jonathan and Daddy. She sat at the desk where I would spend countless hours in years to come, writing, reading, thinking, growing. "You got all your paperwork?"

"Yes, ma'am."

"You got the calling card I gave you?"

"Yes, sir." I stood leaning against my door, the tip of one tennis shoe resting on the other. "Well, I guess that's everything."

We were all waiting for Momma to break down, but she didn't. She wiped her chest with one of my newly purchased towels and said, "Well, I guess that's it, then. Come give us a hug."

My family formed a receiving line. Jonathan hugged me first and expressed how happy he was to be getting the television all to himself at home. Momma wrestled with the flood that raged behind her eyelids. "You remember your upbringing, hear? Don't get down here actin' like you ain't got no home training. You keep your head in the books and your eyes on the Lord, you hear?"

"Yes, Momma. I will."

She and Jonathan left the room. Daddy put his arm across my shoulder and stood at my side. I wanted to see his face, but he'd arranged us otherwise. "Well." He kicked at the nothing on the ground, and I witnessed a single drop fall onto the floor. I would never know if it was sweat or tears. "This is it, LaShondra."

"Sure is, Daddy."

"You just remember, a lot of black folks bled and died so you could have this chance. You're here on the shoulders of your peoples."

I stalled the tears as long as I could, but lost the battle. I seized my father's neck and felt him hug me back. Then he reached into his pocket and handed me a fifty-dollar bill. Without looking up, he said, "For emergencies."

◘ ◘ ◘

My phone rang as I was getting dressed for work Friday morning. It was Jonathan. "You're lucky I'm already up," I told him.

"Hey, I've got an idea. Why don't we have Sunday dinner at your house? I think it would be a good idea for Daddy and Stelson to meet."

"Daddy's not even talking to me right now, Jonathan. I don't know."

"Well, he's talking to me, and I'm talking to God. So get

this thing all ready to go, okay? Just order something and serve it in some crock pots."

"You're wrong for that!" I pouted.

"Seriously, Shondra, call Stelson and invite him over for the Sunday meal at your house. I'll work on Daddy. Don't worry, he'll be there with bells on. What time?"

"I don't know. I guess if I go to church at Gethsemane with you and Momma, we could all be out by the same time. Stelson's church lets out by one o'clock."

"Okay, so we'll play it by ear and have the meal at your house."

"All right," I blew it out, "I'll tell Stelson."

We had to cancel our plans for miniature golf Saturday night due to rain. Peaches and Quinn followed me to Stelson's house instead for another night of movies. This time we brought Chinese food. "Hey," Stelson greeted us at the door. "Glad you could make it." He squeezed me tightly and dusted my lips with his. He gave Quinn that "brother" hug and kissed Peaches on her cheek. "Come on inside."

Okay, where is all the furniture?

"Sorry I don't have much for us to sit on in here," he apologized, leading us past a bare dining room with nice, shiny hardwood floors. High ceilings added another dimension to the spaciousness to his home, which was perhaps even more pronounced without any furniture. "I'm not much for decorating."

"Needs a woman's touch," Peaches said, talking to Stelson but glancing at me.

"You're right about that," Stelson agreed. He took one of the sacks of food from Quinn and led us to a living room. It did have furniture: a large, pillowy sofa, love seat, and chair ensemble.

We took turns making our plates and then assembled around the television to watch *Total Recall*. As the credits rolled and Quinn prepared to put another DVD into the player, Stelson asked Peaches and Quinn to excuse us while we went out to the covered patio to talk privately. The rain had stopped, but the recently showered earth shimmered beneath the moon's glow.

Stelson led me out to the veranda. He had a spectacular view of Lake Jones, lit by strategically placed lamps near the shore. It was beautiful, but I was not the one for a lake and all the little critters that come along with water. I cuddled up next to him on a wicker love seat and tucked my feet under my behind.

"This is nice," I said.

"It is, isn't it? Sometimes I just come out here and marvel at God's handiwork. It's very humbling."

"Mmm.

"Stelson," I asked, "what are you feeling?"

"I'm feeling . . . I don't know. What do you mean?"

"I mean, when you are with me, what do you feel?"

"I feel blessed."

"I have a confession to make," I said, facing him. "When I went out to lunch with you that first time, it was only to make the white women at my job jealous." He laughed and pulled his hair back. "What are you thinking? Do you ever think about the fact that I'm a black woman?" I needed to know.

"Not *nearly* as much as you do."

"What's that supposed to mean?" I raised my head.

"The fact that you are black is always on your mind."

"That's because I'm always black."

"I'm always white, but it's not always on my mind." He shrugged.

"That's because neither your race nor your sex has ever been a disadvantage to you. If it were, you'd understand." I relaxed a little and settled back into the tiny space between his neck and shoulder blades. "This relationship has been harder on me than it is on you. It's difficult sometimes for me to see past color. But I'm learning."

"Close your eyes," he said. Stelson reached over and gently lowered my eyelids with his fingertips. I felt his lips near my ear, the warmth of his presence. He whispered, "I love you, LaShondra Smith."

He said he loved me. He said he loved me. Then he kissed me, and my heart melted right outside on the patio. *Just love him.* This kiss wasn't one of those get-physically-turned-on kisses. It wasn't like any other kiss I'd ever experienced in my life. Our souls were connecting, as if our very spirits became one. I felt so peaceful when his lips left mine. Stelson had kissed me with everything he had in him. And I received it. I made up in my mind that if I had to walk around for the rest of my life with a blindfold on, I was gonna love that man. Period.

When I got home, I knew I needed to pray. I felt myself coming to a point within, where I knew I needed guidance. This whole thing had come in a series of powerful, convicting truths and awakenings, building from subtle observations to this very substantial relationship with Stelson, with twists and turns along the way. The final destination, however, was at a place that I'd never known before. Neither had anyone I knew of. True to Himself, God had given me my very own Boaz. But I needed Him now more than ever.

I prayed for the answer, but I didn't get it. Instead, I felt the urge to call Peaches, of all people. I explained the situation to her the best way I could, sparing few details about what happened out on the veranda.

"So, what did you say when he told you he loved you?"

"I couldn't say anything. He kissed me."

"Then?"

"Then what?"

"Then what did you say?" she pushed me.

"I didn't say anything. I just . . . I just sat there. I don't think he was expecting me to say anything. He just wanted me to know that he loved me."

"Look, I've seen how Stelson treats you. He adores you, LaShondra. Your problem isn't loving him, your problem is letting *him* love *you*. I know you, and that always happens with you no matter what color the man is. You need to sit back and let the man woo *you*, for once in your life. I mean, get your big behind right up there on that pedestal and become his queen, 'cause if you won't, somebody else will. You done went all this far with a white man, and now you wanna bring up one of the issues you've always had with brothers. Girl, please! You are in a godly relationship. Everything is different. Everything is better."

I didn't say anything. I just let her talk. As she expounded on the message that I needed to allow myself to be loved, unexpected tears began to flow down my cheeks. She was speaking the gospel—I really didn't know how to be loved.

"You still there?" she asked after a while. She heard me sniffle and slowed down a bit. "LaShondra, Stelson is not perfect, but God's love is. So the next time Stelson puts his arms around you, you accept that embrace like it was God Himself, 'cause, girl, I'm telling you, all that's good and perfect comes from Him. Accept it."

I wiped my tears and thanked Peaches for speaking to me. "Girl, you broke it down for me."

"Somebody had to," she laughed. "Daddy *is* good to us, isn't He?"

"All the time," I agreed, then asked, "How did you learn all of this, Miss Thang?"

"Girl, I didn't know. The Holy Spirit is teaching me right along with you. I'm just telling you what I learned about a week ago, when Quinn asked me to marry him."

"What!"

"Yeah. He proposed in a roundabout kind of way. He was all asking me what I thought about the name Patricia Robertson."

"And what did you say?"

"Girl, he ain't gettin' no answer till I get a ring, okay?"

"Peaches, you are wrong!"

"No, I ain't! We are not tryin' to do a Harper from *The Best Man* here. This is real life—a sister needs a carat!"

"I'm gonna keep praying for you."

"Please do."

It had been a while since I'd been to the old church—probably a good two years or so. The church was just as I remembered it: run down but somehow dignified by its towering steeple. Jonathan, Momma, and I walked up to the front steps and through the wide white doors into the vestibule. Gethsemane smelled the same. I closed my eyes and breathed in deep. A flood of fond memories came crashing down on me with an intensity that I was not prepared for. I stopped for a moment and let my heart feel whatever it was that overtook me. I could almost see Mother Dear sitting in her usual spot on the front row next to the Sunshine Band. And there I was, sitting next to my friends, passing notes and discussing the contents of my almost-empty purse. Then Mother Dear popped me on the leg and told me to pay attention to the preacher and spit out my gum. It was all there. It had never left.

I opened my eyes and used my hands quickly to fan the tears away. I checked myself in the mirror before entering the sanctuary. The ushers led us to the fifth pew, and we sat quietly as the announcer read off the list of announcements and asked the saints to govern themselves accordingly. My eyes roamed the edifice and came to a standstill at the altar. How many times had I been there with the saints praying all around me, praying for me, tarrying for my soul's sake?

Their heavy, worn hands rubbing my back and coaching me on what to say to the Lord. And there, on that altar so long ago, I'd cried out to Him for everything. I'd been to that altar and back out into the world so many times I couldn't keep count. And every time I'd come back, God had forgiven me. He never did keep count. It seemed that through the years, in His own way and in His own time, God had given me everything I'd ever asked for, even though I didn't deserve it. *Thank you, Lord.*

I enjoyed the foot-stomping, hand-clapping service and sermon delivered by one of the newer assistant ministers at Gethsemane. He spoke on faithfulness and the importance of staying on the course through tough times. Following the benediction, we hung around talking to old church friends for another half hour. Jonathan had on his navy garb, and Momma made him take pictures with almost every saint in the building.

After church, Jonathan and Momma went back to my parents' house to pick up Daddy while I went back home to get prepared. I called Stelson and told him to come on over. In the meanwhile, I took the steaks and other side dishes from a local steak house out of the foil packaging and placed them in nice serving dishes. I pushed the sacks and containers deep into the trash can.

"Shondra," Jonathan called in the midst of my preparations, "Daddy made chicken!"

"Does he know that Stelson is going to be here?"

"Not exactly. But he does know that we were having dinner at your place. Maybe it's the sign of a truce between the two of you," he cheered.

"You guys hurry up. I want to tell Daddy before Stelson comes waltzing through the door."

"We're on our way."

Jonathan must have driven like a bat out of hell. They pulled up in record time, and I estimated that I had roughly ten minutes to tell Daddy that Stelson would be at dinner. Daddy walked past me at the door and went straight to the kitchen to put his chicken in the oven. I followed him, with an intentionally cheerful attitude. *I will not let the enemy tear my family apart.* "Hey, Daddy."

"Mmm," he grumbled, searching through my utensil drawer.

"I'm glad you came."

"Where are your forks?" he asked.

"Daddy, stop. Listen to me," I commanded him. He finally put one hand on the counter and stopped. Daddy looked into my eyes. He probed me, searched me, and examined me. We were deadlocked, each looking for the soul of the other, like two alien creatures, each searching for that familiar place inside the other. Daddy stood back and waited for me to blink or cower. But I didn't. One of us was going to have to back down, and it wasn't going to be me. I wasn't going to take any less than his full respect and love—the kind he had always given me. The kind I deserved.

"Stelson is coming over for dinner." Daddy took a seat at my kitchen table and crossed his arms defiantly. I sat across from him, hoping that his decision to sit down was a good thing. I spoke softly, "Daddy, listen. I want you to meet the man in my life. I know you don't approve of interracial anything, but this is my choice. If you can't respect that, then you never really respected me."

He raised his head sharply. "Who taught you to talk to your father like that? This white friend of yours?"

"No, you did. I was so afraid to tell you about Stelson because I knew you'd react this way. But with all due respect, Daddy, I have to live a life that is pleasing unto God. If that means going against your beliefs about white people, then so be it. You're the one who taught me to stick with my beliefs no matter what anyone else says. I'm still your daughter. But I don't apologize for the fact that I owe more allegiance to Christ than to the black race."

"So that's the way it is, huh?" He bobbed his head. "Just gonna forget about your people?"

"I don't have to forget where I came from to move on with my life. That's where you've been stuck, Daddy. You think that if you let go of that pain and anger and hurt, you'll be left with nothing. But that's not true. When you forgive and move on, you free yourself up for joy, Daddy. Joy. Do you even know what joy is? Have you experienced it, day in and day out?"

"I'm leaving." Daddy stood up, his chair screeching like a car slamming on its brakes.

Momma tried to calm him as he walked toward the door. "Jonathan Smith, listen to somebody for once. You said just the other day that you wished you could live to see the day that blacks and whites could get along."

"I also said that would be when hell freezes over," he added.

"Well, your daughter just threw down some ice. Now, you just sit down and enjoy this dinner. You never know, Jon, you might actually like Stillman."

"Stelson," I said.

"Stelson." Momma stood next to him at the door now.

Daddy stopped, facing the door, with his feet flat on the center of my welcome mat. *What if he walks out that door?* He put both hands in his pockets . . . jiggled the loose change. He tilted his head back, letting the overhead lights cast a glow on the center of his head. He just stood there, thinking. Weighing his past against his relationship with me, I guessed. I prayed with everything in me, and I felt Momma and Jonathan doing the same. *But what if he walks out that door?*

Then Daddy took a deep breath, cleared his throat, and asked in a shaky voice, "What kind of bread did you get?"

Thank you, Lord.

Daddy was civil, and that was enough to be thankful for. He shook Stelson's hand, for the second time, in my living room. They were both apprehensive and silent throughout most of the dinner. Jonathan, Momma, and I did everything we could to keep conversation going. I'm sure we sounded like a sitcom with all that gibberish. But Daddy knew now. And we'd survived.

I came face to face with an undeniable truth about myself that day. Of all the people who I thought would have a problem with my dating Stelson—my parents, Jonathan, Peaches, my coworkers, the general public—the person with the biggest issue was me. I gave it all up to the Lord that evening in the comfort of my prayer room. As I knelt beside the bed, letting my knees settle on the floor, I laid it all before God.

Lord, I am tired of fighting this battle within myself. I am tired of running back and forth between what I feel, what I've heard, and what You have revealed to me as the truth of Your love. Help me to stand up to my fears and fight against the enemy in this battle for my mind one last time. I claim victory right now in the name of Jesus. Amen.

I jumped through my last hoop, deciding then and there not to let the past overrun my future anymore, to stop reaching back, feeling for what had been comfortable in order to determine what should be acceptable for me in the days ahead with Stelson. After all, I already knew in my heart that Stelson was the one. He'd loved me, actively, even before I was ready to love him, without expecting anything in return. He did right just because.

CHAPTER 22

Momma and I sat glued to the television, watching the royal wedding ceremony of the Prince of Wales and Lady Diana. She looked like Cinderella as she walked down the aisle wearing the train that seemed to go on forever. I wished, for the entire ceremony, that I were Lady Diana. That I could ride through the city as royalty, with millions of people watching and wishing me well. Waving at the commoners, in love.

"Momma, where are they at?"

"They're in England."

"Are there any black people in England?"

"Yeah, a few," she speculated.

"Can a black girl be a princess?" I asked.

"Not in England. Maybe in Africa—but you don't want to marry no African man," she warned me. "They can have as many wives as they want. You just get you a good man who goes to church, baby. You'll be just fine."

▣ ▣ ▣

Jonathan was ready to go by five Monday morning. I dragged through the house, trying to convince myself that it *is* humanly possible to get out of bed two hours before the sun gets up.

I was a little late getting to work that morning after dropping Jonathan off at the airport. I was sad to see him go. It might be years before I'd see Jonathan again. We took a few pictures at the airport, gave hugs, and prayed for his safe journey. I thanked him for his role in helping me with Daddy. "Hey, maybe that's why I was here after all." I watched him until he was out of view, and then made my way out of DFW traffic and onto the city's main highways.

Traffic was heavier than I'd anticipated coming out of the airport and heading into the mid-city. I called ahead to tell Miss Jan that I'd be later than I thought. "I'll do my best to hold down the fort. Just get here as soon as you can," she said, sounding more cheerful than usual.

"Okay."

When I finally made it to school, I rushed past Miss Jan to catch up on all the work that I was sure had been piling up on my desk since Wednesday. But there was something else on my desk, to my surprise: a dozen yellow roses in full bloom, baby's breath sprinkled throughout the bouquet, and a fluffy, brown teddy bear centered at the base of the vase. I stood there looking at it for a second.

"Isn't it beautiful?" Miss Jan was standing right behind me, smiling, with stars in her eyes.

"Oh, this is so beautiful!" I exclaimed.

"It's romantic." She sighed and laid a hand on her chest.

I walked to my desk and plucked the card from the holder in the center of the roses. I read the card out loud.

To LaShondra—Happy Belated Birthday—Stelson.

I breathed in the scent of the roses, letting the aroma settle deep in my lungs.

"Stelson again?"

"Yes."

Miss Jan complimented me. "He seems like a good catch."

"He is," I told her. "He really is."

Miss Jan left the room, closing the door behind her. I sat down at my desk, still marveling at the beauty of the bouquet. I picked up the phone and called Stelson's office.

"Brown-Cooper, this is Jolynn Abernathy. How may I help you?"

"Miss Abernathy, this is LaShondra Smith."

"Oh, Miss Smith! How are you?" she asked in a friendly tone.

"I'm fine, thank you."

"Shall I put you through to Mr. Brown?"

"Well, actually, I wanted to know if he would be staying in the office for lunch today. I'd like to surprise him, if you think that's a good idea." My heart pounded.

"Certainly. I'm sure he'd love that. He was going to have me order Subway for lunch today. Would you like for me to include your order as well?"

"That would be perfect. I'll take a six-inch turkey and cheese on wheat. What time should I be there?"

"Eleven-thirty," she squeaked.

The Brown-Cooper receptionist was as pretty as she was cheerful. Her bright green eyes and auburn hair stood out like major attractions, but her attitude was even more fluorescent. "Hi! How can I help you?"

"I'm here to see Mr. Brown."

"I'm sorry, he's at lunch." She gave me a sincerely overdramatized frown and slumped over. Then she bolted up straight in her chair and pushed her fake breasts forward. "But I'd be glad to tell him you came by."

"I'm having lunch with Mr. Brown," I informed her.

"Oh," she blinked a few times, "Okay. I'll call his secretary."

I took a seat in the waiting area and scoped out Stelson's office. The motif was contemporary: mauve and hunter green with oak trimmings. There were photographs of Stelson and Mr. Cooper hanging on opposite walls in the waiting room. Stelson looked considerably younger in his picture. He'd obviously put on a few pounds since then, but those pounds had fallen in all the right places. *That's my man.*

"LaShondra?" Stelson stepped out of the side door.

"Hey!" I smiled.

"Come on in." He hugged me and led me down a short hallway. "Miss Abernathy, this is LaShondra Smith."

"Hi!" She shook with her right and enclosed mine with her left. Her hands felt soft, but the skin sagged a little. She looked much younger than she was. "I am so glad Mr. Brown has found someone to help keep his mind off work. I have a life now, thanks to you."

"You're welcome," I said.

"Hold my calls," he asked her. She nodded.

"What a pleasant surprise." He closed the door behind me.

"Oh, Stelson, the roses are beautiful." I hugged him, my voice giving way to emotion.

"Hey, hey, it's okay," he tried to calm me.

"They are so beautiful," I tried again.

"I'm glad you like them. Love, are you okay?"

"Yeah." I let the air escape from my lungs and released him. "It's just that . . . Stelson, I've been so afraid to love you because I've never really loved anybody before and I don't know exactly how to do it and I don't know exactly how to let you love me but you are so good to me . . . I just don't know what to do. I mean, I know what to do, I guess, but this is all new for me."

"Hey"—he tried not to laugh—"it's okay. It's new for me, too. I've never felt this way about anyone, either. But I know that it not only feels right, it is right. If you want me to slow things down, that's okay. Just let me know, LaShondra. I want to be everything God wants me to be for you."

"Well, you're doing a pretty good job of it by being Stelson," I assured him.

"Even with the tattoo?"

"Even with the tattoo."

Ask any teacher—time flies after spring break. That goes double for administrators. Between March and May I had about a million and one things to do: get notices to parents about missing textbooks, library fines, and school property lost throughout the year; have conferences with the parents of students who might be retained; interview new teachers; look at staffing for the following school year; reestablish end-of-year procedures; make sure that the students' cumulative files were ready to go on to the high school; and deal with the never-ending referrals from students who had caught spring fever and were acting as if they didn't have good sense.

There was also the added pressure from Mr. Butler, which had become more concentrated than before. I prayed every morning, as usual, but he made me add a little extra for strength at work.

The only good thing on my desk that semester was a wacky picture of Stelson and me taken at Six Flags over Texas. We were standing on either side of Bugs Bunny, with Bugs Bunny holding up bunny ears behind our heads. Just thinking about that day and all the time we spent together eased the pressures of work.

Outside school, I couldn't have asked for a better spring. Stelson and I were becoming an item—attending church services together, eating a few Sunday dinners at my parents' house, planning our weekends together, and calling each other every night.

He remained a faithful tutor at my church on Wednesday nights and often stayed for service afterward. Slowly the church members were beginning to know and accept

"Brother Brown." I fell in love with Saturday Night Live at his church. We both attended and volunteered to serve the youth regularly.

Stelson made a few more business trips that spring, and he always brought me something back. I never asked him to—he just did it. In His own time, God opened my heart fully to the idea of having a serene, peaceful, minimal-drama relationship. Not perfect, not without its idiosyncrasies, but victorious nonetheless.

The news of Mr. Butler's official notice of retirement was music to my ears. I personally helped his secretary stuff the teachers' boxes with invitations to his retirement party at the administration building. I mean, I was counting the days till he packed up his boxes and drove off the lot. Sure, there would be other Mr. Butlers and Mr. Donovans in my life, but it was a relief to get *these* antagonists out of my life and to know that, hopefully, I'd have Stelson with me to face the challenges ahead.

I was able to get things organized in my office and close out the year smoothly. Stelson took a vacation during the second week in June. His family had a reunion, and I finally got the chance to meet his "peoples," as Daddy would say. Most of Stelson's immediate family still lived in Louisiana, but the reunion was in Dallas because his mother's eldest sister lived there and she had nine children; thus, her offspring accounted for half the living family tree. Stelson's mother and brother got in town Friday evening and stayed with Stelson the whole weekend. One of his sisters, her husband, and their two kids didn't get in until late Saturday afternoon, but they stayed with Stelson as well. I was a little apprehensive about hanging out with them because I didn't want to infringe upon their family reunion.

"Nonsense, baby," Mrs. Brown told me in that sweet, airy voice that I hoped I'd have in my golden years. "You go far back enough down anybody's family tree, and you'll find that we're all family anyways."

Stelson treated his mother with the utmost respect. He waited on her hand and foot and went out of his way to make sure she felt comfortable. He bought a special comforter and pillows. He tried to cook for her, but she fussed so much that he finally gave up and let her have full charge of the kitchen. She made a pot of gumbo that converted me forever to Cajun food. I ended up taking a bowl of it home.

"Didn't I tell you?" Stelson laughed.

"Yes, baby, but I didn't think it would be like *this.*"

After the weekend of the reunion, Stelson hung around my office some during the day, helping me rearrange things and take care of business. It was nice having him there. He was pretty good at getting things organized and prioritizing our list of things to do. He installed some programs on my computer and did something to my files to get them organized in my computer's filing system. He even put a shortcut to a gospel radio station on my desktop screen. I was impressed.

The morning of my interview for the newly vacant principal's position at my school, he brought me fresh fruit and a carton of grape juice. "What's all this healthy stuff?" I asked him.

"Nothing wrong with eating healthy every now and then." He shrugged. "Besides, you need a good breakfast before you go off to an interview."

I took a deep breath. "Don't get me all nervous."

"You're gonna be great, sweetheart." He pulled me close and gave me a power hug.

"Thanks," I said. And then it plopped out of me. "I love you, Stelson." *Who said that? Did I just say that?*

He just looked at me and smiled. "I love you, too, LaShondra."

I reached up and kissed my Boaz. His face touched mine slightly in our embrace. I loved him. I loved him as I'd never loved anyone before. My whole heart was exposed. For once, all my defenses were down. There was something completely serene about it, but at the same time I felt vulnerable. I felt as though I was giving myself to him. Letting him go to a place in my heart that I didn't think any person was capable of inhabiting. It was a fresh corner of my soul that had long wished to be filled—until this morning, and Stelson was in it. He was in that place that I didn't really know existed, at the level that I couldn't even have imagined before that moment.

It wasn't just the kiss, the embrace, or his touch that let my spirit go there. It was the fact that I knew Stelson loved me with the love of God and I loved him with the same perfectness that had already linked us eternally through Jesus Christ. I don't know how long we kissed, but when we stopped, my face was wet with tears.

Stelson looked down. "Why are you crying?" His hands quickly went to my cheeks and wiped the tears away.

"I've said that I don't know how many times," I laughed at myself. "But I never had an inkling of what it meant until now."

He laughed, too. "That's the same way I felt when I told you that night on the veranda. I just felt like laughing and crying and screaming and praying and shouting all at the same time."

"I know," I agreed. "It's like you've finally arrived. Like you've found the person that God has . . . has given you to make this life on earth more bearable until it's time to go home."

"Like you've found the one your heart loves." He quoted the Song of Solomon.

"I love you," I told him again.

"I love you, too."

We said it over and over again until we both began laughing. I started getting that bubbly feeling—like I was too old to be acting so silly, but too young at heart to care. I loved and was undeniably in love with Stelson Brown.

"Okay," I wiped the last tears away, "I guess I'll see you later at the church tonight?"

"Yes, I'll see you later, Principal Smith."

The interview went well, and I was not one bit surprised when they called me back for a second interview three days later. I finally learned that I'd gotten the appointment just before we took the three-week break. I was elated to finally be in a position to allow God's hand to rule in that school through me. Now I could do some things that I'd wanted to do but never could because the school had been running on the good-ol'-boy system. It was truly a blessing that I could foresee affecting generations—not to mention that I'd gotten a considerable raise. I knew just what I was going to do with the first chunk of extra money: buy a much-needed TV-VCR combination for my children's church class. My kids were always sitting around straining to see what was on that little thirteen-inch screen we had. I'd requisitioned another one, but the budget was too tight to get one out of the youth department's funds. It was *on* now!

Stelson treated my parents and me to dinner the night after I got the good news. We went back to Abuelita's.

"My baby!" Momma sat up tall and rocked on her behind. "A principal."

"Kick those kids into shape," Daddy said, smiling. I couldn't recall a time that I'd seen him smile like that. Ever. My Daddy, smiling, laughing, enjoying himself. He folded his lips in, them poked them out. "I'm proud of you, Shondra. Always have been."

Thank You, Lord.

Stelson asked us if we didn't mind him ordering a family-size plate of chicken fajitas. We agreed to the order.

Stelson excused himself to go to the restroom, and Momma cornered me about him. “Shondra, you better hold on to him,” she said, giving me that same eye she used to give me when I was talking in church.

“Momma, I know Stelson is great. And we both love each other very much.”

“You ain’t got to tell me that.” She smiled. “I can feel it just sittin’ here.”

I was surprised that Daddy hadn’t put his two cents in yet. “Okay, Daddy, what do you have to say about all this?”

“Nothin’.” He looked away.

“That’s not like you,” I said.

“Shows how much you know about me.” He respectfully tipped his head to me.

Momma gave me a look that said *leave it alone,* so I did.

Stelson came back, and we carried on as though we hadn’t been talking about him the whole time he was gone. The fajitas came, sizzling and spreading a mouthwatering cloud around our whole table. Stelson asked Daddy to bless the food. Momma and I looked at each other, and I was just about to nudge Stelson when Daddy agreed to pray. *Miracles never cease!*

The fajitas were delicious. We sat around for a few minutes after we’d finished, talking about Jonathan and about Stelson’s family. Daddy asked Stelson if he knew any of the Mohares from Louisiana.

“I graduated from high school with a girl named Beatrice Mohare,” Stelson offered.

“What was her father’s name?”

“I’m sorry. I don’t know, Mr. Smith.”

“Did she have any brothers or sisters?”

“I’m not sure.”

“Yeah, that was probably them,” Daddy surmised. Let Daddy tell it, he knew everybody’s peoples.

The band had gone around to a few tables to sing

happy birthday, so when a few members came down from the stage again, I didn't think twice about it. But when they stopped at our table, I wondered what was going on.

"Señorita Smith?" the leader asked me.

"Yes."

"This song is for you," the leader said, signaling for the band to play. Then he started singing something in Spanish. I didn't know what he was saying, but it was a beautiful song. I winked at Stelson and then turned back to give my full attention to the leader. As they sang to the chorus, I began to recognize the song—the slow, rhythmic beat, the sound of the guitar.

"Cásame, por favor, mi amor. Cásame, por favor, mi amor."

It was the same song they sang to the woman in red the first time we'd eaten there! My mouth opened so wide, I know I looked crazy. I turned to face Stelson, but he wasn't in his seat. He was kneeling down before me, holding the most beautiful solitaire I'd ever laid eyes on. *Taa-dow!*

The band finished its song, and the whole restaurant hushed.

"LaShondra Smith, will you do me the honor of becoming my wife?" he asked, holding my hand. The diamond seemed to catch every ray of light, sparkling brilliantly atop a thick gold band with dainty wisplike engravings covering the band.

"Yes!"

The whole restaurant cheered and hollered and screamed for a good minute as Stelson and I embraced. My hand trembled as he slid the ring on. It fit perfectly. We kissed tenderly as the noise died down to its normal rumble.

"I love you," I told my future husband.

"I love you, too," he whispered as he kissed me again.

My parents congratulated us, and Momma asked to see the ring. It fit me perfectly. “I knew it,” she sighed.

“I knew it, too,” Daddy agreed. He looked half happy, half not.

I took the happy.

Reading Group Guide Discussion Questions

Chapter 1
Turning thirty-one felt like a watershed in LaShondra's life. "It was time to reevaluate some things; carefully consider how to expend my time and energy," she thought. What age(s) served as that kind of mile-marker for you? From where you sit now, how does your present measure up to the goals or assumptions you formulated in the past? Read **Jeremiah 29:11–13**, **Matthew 6:25–34**, and **1 Corinthians 13:9–12**. What do these scriptures suggest to you about the future?

Chapter 2
From her first "crush" through a tangle of ill-fated relationships, Shondra had developed a pretty clear idea of what she wanted in a life partner, her Boaz. Do you? What have your past relationships taught you about Mr. *Wrong*? What vision of Mr. Right has emerged from those experiences? Read **Genesis 2:18–25** to refresh your memory of God's vision for the "perfect match"!

Chapter 3
Driving through the neighborhood in which she had grown up, LaShondra mused, "I had roots there, even if

the ground was less than desirable." Where are your roots and how do you feel about them now? Are you still planted there—or have you been repotted, transplanted, or uprooted? What insights do Jesus' parables about the sowers and seeds in **Matthew 13** (**especially verses 18–23** and **24–30**) have in relation to the soil of your past?

Shondra and her father have different ideas about how blacks should become part of America's so-called melting pot. What ideas do you have on the subject? Read **Isaiah 56, especially verses 6–8**, and **Revelation 21–22**, and consider the vision that God has for the nations and races of the world.

Chapter 4

God was dealing with LaShondra about love—and then led her to **Galatians 3:16–19**, a text that says nothing explicitly about love. Read that scripture again in your favorite Bible version, and reflect on what love, prejudice, and **Galatians 3:16–19** have to do with one another.

It felt incredibly unfair to Shondra that God was convicting *her*, a black woman so often the *victim* of prejudice, on that subject. How does that conviction feel to you? How do you wrestle with the kinds of racial or ethnic prejudices Shondra described? Read **Numbers 12** and consider how Miriam and Aaron, newly freed slaves themselves, must have felt when God convicted them of their prejudice toward Moses' Cushite (black) wife.

Chapter 5

Shondra mentions several times the dynamic of acting or being different in the presence of whites (or non-blacks)—her dialect, her smile, her comfort level. "The less I saw of white people, the more I could be myself," she admitted honestly. How do you alter yourself in "mixed" company? Are such alterations based solely on race—or also on gender, age, or other factors? Is there integrity in such changeability? Why or why not? Consider two contrasting scriptures for insights into the question—especially as they relate to motives (see **Romans 12:1–2** and **1 Corinthians 9:19–24**).

Chapter 6

LaShondra sincerely wrestled with the question of how to look beyond race/skin color in her relationships with others—and yet still retain her own racial identity. How do you resolve that tension for yourself? What does **Romans 5:14–20** teach us about dealing with the question of an identity (racial or otherwise) that loves as Christ does, beyond worldly considerations?

Chapter 7

LaShondra corrected her own estimation of Stelson: "Anybody can be nice. Stelson was kind. Kindness is something that comes from the inside." What did she mean by that? How would you distinguish between niceness and kindness? In Scripture, the word often translated as "kindness" in the King James Version is usually rendered "love" or "loyalty" in more modern translations (e.g., **Genesis 20:13**). Do a biblical study of the concept of kindness by reading one or more of the following passages: the **Book of Ruth**; **1 Samuel 20:13–17** and **2 Samuel 9:1–7**; **Isaiah 54:1–8**; and **2 Peter 1:5–8**.

Chapter 8

In the singles' ministry, Brother Johnson applied **Acts 10:34–35** to the search for a life partner. One of the women responded, "But, we're talking about *my* man." There seem to be two truths here: first, that we are called to love and accept all people, as God does; and second, that we will choose one person for a spouse. How should the first truth influence the second? What role should one's personal preferences play as we prayerfully seek God's life for our future? (Because, let's keep it real: Personal preferences *will* play a role!)

Chapter 9

Shondra was shocked to learn that her "historically black denomination" actually had its earliest roots in a racially integrated revival, way back in the early 1900s. Did that fact shock you, too? Why or why not? Such early strides toward racial reconciliation and equality can both encourage and frustrate us today. Read **Acts 2, especially verses 1–21**, for a reminder of the Spirit's early movement toward unity in the body of Christ. What can we learn from the story of Pentecost to encourage our churches today?

Chapter 10

During the tutoring session, LaShondra had "forgotten what color Stelson was." But, in the sanctuary, she became highly aware of his race once again. Why? What made the difference? Interracial relationships—whether friendship or courtship—may be relatively easy to negotiate one on one. The challenges arise when society gets involved. How can you handle that? Consider **Acts 10:1–11:18** as a case study in how God deals with us, individually, in small groups, and then before the "critics"!

Chapter 11

After the incident in the restaurant, Shondra told Stelson, "Until you've worn black, you can't begin to empathize"—even though she also pointed out that the discriminatory experience was his as well as hers. Her point seems to be that they experienced it differently—even though it was a shared experience. How can "well-meaning white people" participate with integrity in such an experience? How can black folks allow white friends to be *with* them during such an experience? What wisdom does Scripture have to offer us on the question of standing together in the face of trials, injustice, and pain? (See **Isaiah 58:1–12**; **Galatians 6:1–5**.)

Chapter 12

"It was never about black or white—it was about my relationship with Christ," Shondra realized, and asked herself the tough question, "Could I relinquish my definition of myself—first black, then Christian?" Ask yourself the same question: Can you? Read **Philippians 3:4–11** and consider Paul's decision around the same issue of ethnic identity versus his identity in Christ.

Chapter 13

Shondra discovered that, even as she explored a deeper relationship with Stelson and a stronger connection with him than she had ever before experienced, she was also feeling more and more disconnected from her family and friends. How did she handle that? How would you? She wanted to be true to herself and to her roots—but who she *was* was changing, while her roots were very much the same. How do we bring our loved ones alongside as we move on in our spiritual journey? How can we cope if our family or friends refuse to grow with us? **Psalm 55:12–14** captures the pain and **Proverbs 16:7** offers a foundation to build our hope on!

Chapter 14

When Peaches and LaShondra finally had it out over Stelson, Peaches didn't pull any punches. She threw out every argument that Shondra had been having with herself for months. As a group, discuss the issues and questions Peaches raised—and keep it real. Are you persuaded by

Shondra's responses? Why or why not? She quotes some deep scriptural and spiritual principles—but how do *you* feel about dating a white man? Then, break it all the way down: How do you feel about a white *woman* dating a brother? Has reading about Shondra's experience influenced your feelings at all? Why or why not?

Chapter 15

Stelson urged LaShondra to conduct her own "internal investigation," and she realized that the real issue was the heart—her own and the hearts of the teachers on her staff. Scripture tells us that the heart—and judging it—is God's territory (**1 Samuel 16:7**). The Bible also makes it clear that God and God alone is judge of such matters (**Psalm 7:8–11**; **Psalm 50**; **James 2:1–13**). Shondra recognized her need to do less judging—and more negotiating of the heartfelt differences in perspective concerning the behavioral issues with black and white students alike. If you applied that insight to your own life, what would it look like?

Chapter 16

"It wouldn't be the first time [God] sent help in the form of a problem," Stelson reminded Shondra. She marveled as she acknowledged the truth—that in a season of trouble and trial, one she counted as an "enemy" had become a friend closer than a brother. Doesn't that sound like a story Jesus would tell? (Indeed, he did, in the parable of the Good Samaritan! See **Luke 10:30–37**.) What has that parable/principle looked like in your life? If you haven't seen it yet, look again for God's help in the least likely of people or places.

Chapter 17

LaShondra's surprising experience at the karaoke bar took her out of herself for awhile. She could forget her race, her gender, her grief, her family, her job—and just revel in the pure, childlike fun of the evening. When was the last time you had an evening (or afternoon or morning) like that? The healing power of laughter, of joy, is well documented—in medical science and in Scripture (see **Proverbs 15:13** and **17:22**). How can you create more space in your life for the re-creation that recreation brings?

Chapter 18

When Shondra braced herself to tell her mother about Stelson, what she prayed for was love. Not peace or patience or grace or wisdom or understanding—not anything but love. Why? What could love bring into that emotionally charged confrontation that nothing else could? (See **1 Corinthians 13** and **Colossians 3:12–17**.)

Chapter 19

LaShondra had to acknowledge—to herself and to Stelson—that the more intimate their friendship became emotionally and spiritually, the more she wrestled with her sexual desires for Stelson. What a blessing that they could talk candidly about their mutual attraction—as both a challenge and a cause for celebration. Scripture recognizes that passion is both of those things as well. Read **Song of Songs** to understand a biblical celebration of sex and physical intimacy; then read Paul's cautions about lust in **1 Corinthians 6:12–20**. How do you balance the challenge and celebration of your sexuality? What commitments have you made, individually or in a significant relationship, concerning your sexuality?

Chapter 20

Ask yourself Jonathan's question: "Who am I, if I'm not black?" Take time to answer that question honestly, from the gut—and then look at some of the following passages to learn what Scripture has to say on the subject: **Genesis 1:26–31**; **Romans 8:14–17**; **Ephesians 5:8–10**.

Chapter 21

LaShondra's father thought blacks and whites would get along "when hell freezes over." Momma snapped back, "Well, your daughter just threw down some ice." What kind of ice are you throwing down in your relationships with folks from other races—ice that will cool the enemy's fires of hatred, bigotry, racism, and prejudice? Read **Philippians 2:1–8**; **Colossians 3:1–17**; and **1 John 4:7–5:5** for some wise counsel in building community, even (and especially) across cultural differences.

Chapter 22

After Stelson's proposal and Shondra's acceptance, Mr. Smith looked half happy and half not about the engagement. Shondra "took the happy." Was she in denial? Why or why not? Read **Romans 5:1–5** and consider how that progression in Shondra's life might have produced in her the hope that enabled her to "take the happy" from her dad.

Another sensational novel
by Michelle Stimpson!

Please turn this page
for a preview of
Divas of Damascus Road
available in July 2006.

■ ■ ■

*D*ianne woke from ten minutes of sleep and touched her sister's forehead. Still felt as hot as the surface of Momma's heating pad set on high. Dianne dangled her feet from the edge of the bed and steadied herself for the drop. She studied her toes for a moment—there were only splotches of red paint left at the center of each nail. She smiled at these ten tiny remnants of last weekend's sleepover at Aunt Gloria's house. The sooner she got through the week, the sooner she could get back to Aunt Gloria's house.

Dianne's feet hit the wooden floor, a cool awakening. She made yet another trip past the empty living room, kicking empty plastic bags and carefully sidestepping discarded syringes. Smelled like the "funny" smoke that always made everyone laugh. Dianne took a deep breath as she passed the living room. Try as she might, the smoke never made her laugh. Certainly didn't make her laugh at the moment, not with her little sister in the other room sleeping like a doll and burning like fire.

She couldn't have known.

She turned on the bathroom light, stepped up on the stool, and then placed one knee on the countertop. She wobbled a bit, but caught herself by grabbing hold of the faucet. This was no time to be falling. She had to get the red medicine from the cabinet and give Shannon some more. Dianne was a big girl. Her momma had said so. She could take care of Shannon while her momma was gone.

"Sugarbee," Momma had authorized her, "you take care of things while me and Otis go out, okay?"

"When will you be back, Momma?" Dianne had asked. It wasn't the first time they'd left her to fend for herself and her little sister, Shannon. But each time they left, it seemed they were gone longer than before and Dianne had to do things that she wasn't quite sure about. The last time they were left alone, Dianne went to the restroom to run bath water and when she pulled the shower curtain back, a black, shiny rat looked up at her and bared his two front teeth in a high-pitched gnarl. Dianne and Shannon stayed in the fortress of their bedroom forever, it seemed. Shannnon's diaper stank, but she was the lucky one. Dianne had to relieve herself in the purple pail—her Easter basket.

"We won't be gone long this time," Joyce Ann lied. Dianne was used to the lies now. They came with the territory, but Dianne didn't care. Children really don't judge. They'll accept you just as you are.

"Okay, Momma. But what if a rat comes out?"

"Otis killed that rat, I told you," Joyce Ann assured Dianne with all the frenzy of an addict craving a hit.

"But if *another* one comes out, do you want me to call Aunt Gloria?" Dianne asked, hoping that she could secure this one lifeline.

"No!" Joyce Ann stopped tying her shoes, grabbed Dianne's shoulders, and pulled her nose-to-nose. "You listen to me, Sugarbee. Don't call your Aunt Gloria for nothin'! *Nothin'*! You hear? And if she calls here, you tell her I'm asleep. Don't you dare tell her that I left you here with Shannon. You do and I'll get Otis to tear you up! You hear?"

Otis pulled his head up from the pillow just long enough to give Dianne a glance. All he needed was the go-ahead from Joyce Ann and he would finally get the chance to beat that little whiny, skinny thing to a pulp. Every once in a while, he got the chance to pop her, but for some reason Joyce Ann never would let him whip her like she needed. Between Joyce Ann and her sister, Gloria, Otis never had enough time to have his way with the girl. "And you better take good care of Shannon, too," he warned. "Don't let nothing happen to *my* baby." Not that he cared about his daughter. Just that he needed to lay claim on something. Truth be told, he wasn't even sure that Shannon was his.

Dianne didn't need that warning. She'd never let anything happen to Shannon. Shannon was all Dianne had in life. Well, Shannon and Aunt Gloria—but for now she was down to Shannon.

That was two days ago.

The phone startled Dianne and she fell to the floor despite herself. It had to be Aunt Gloria. Nobody else would call. Her momma's friends never called; they just came by.

Dianne left the bathroom and ran down the remainder of the hallway to the kitchen where she jumped up and grabbed the phone from the receiver, all in one motion. She put on her best smile and answered. "Hello?"

"Hey, Sugarbee, this is your aunt Gloria. How are you?"

"I'm fine, Aunt Gloria. How are you?" Dianne used her most proper words.

"Well, things aren't so hot over here. Your cousin Rhonda got a real bad virus, the doctor says, so I've got to keep an eye on her. Otherwise, you know I would have been over to see my Sugarbee!"

A giggle escaped from somewhere deep down within. Dianne always did like the way Aunt Gloria sang her nickname. She wished that she could go to Aunt Gloria's house. Aunt Gloria would know what to do about Shannon sleeping all day and the fever that wouldn't go away. She would know how much of the red medicine to give

Shannon. She could even go and get more, because the bottle that was full yesterday was now almost empty.

"Is Joyce Ann there?"

Dianne crossed her fingers behind the nightgown she had been wearing since her mother left. "Yes, but she's sleeping right now."

"How long she been asleep?"

"Not long."

"Hmm. Is Otis there?" Aunt Gloria clicked her cheek like his name had left a bad taste in her mouth.

Dianne uncrossed her fingers. "No, he's gone."

"Well . . ." Dianne could tell that her Aunt Gloria was thinking. Dianne held her breath and hoped that Aunt Gloria would *keep* thinking, come on over, and discover them there alone. It wouldn't be her fault if Aunt Gloria used her key to come in and check on them. But that didn't happen. Probably because she had just told a lie, the child figured. "I've got a good mind to come over there . . . let me see . . . Tell your momma that if Rhonda gets to feeling better, I'll be over first thing in the morning. If I have to take Rhonda in to the doctor, I'll be by later on in tomorrow afternoon. Either way, I will be there tomorrow. Okay, Sugarbee?"

Dianne exhaled. "Okay. I'll tell her."

After a few attempts, Dianne finally managed to get the phone back on the hook. Though saddened by the fact that Aunt Gloria wouldn't be by on that day, Dianne took heart in knowing that tomorrow held promise. Tomorrow, somebody would come by and save her. Save Shannon. So if they ran out of medicine tonight, that would be okay.

Dianne knew how to open the childproof bottle. She had watched her mother closely, in the way that children who are left to look after themselves often observe their part-time caregivers, knowing that sooner than later they'll have to perform those same actions alone. With her palm,

Dianne applied pressure and turned the cap to the left. It came off easily, now that she had done it so many times in the last two days. She tried to make sense of the letters on the bottle, sounding out the few words she could. If she were in the other reading group, she probably could have read those words. But Mrs. Coleman, her kindergarten teacher, had put Dianne with the rainbows instead of the butterflies. Everybody knew that the butterflies were smarter than the rainbows. "Sweetie, if you can make it to school a little more often, maybe you can move up to the butterflies." How many times had Dianne gotten herself up, gotten dressed, and walked into her mother's room only to find Joyce Ann sprawled out on the bed, looking like the capital letter *X*?

And then she'd look over and see Shannon right next to her mother. Who would care for Shannon when she crawled out of bed looking for something to eat? What if she stuck her finger in an outlet? What if she was wearing that same diaper when Dianne got home from school? What if she cried until her eyes were red and puffy? Dianne couldn't go to school on those *X*-days. She just couldn't. Maybe next year, in first grade, she would get to go to school more often.

Dianne rushed back to Shannon's side now, propped Shannon's head up in the crook of her elbow and poured the last of the medicine down her sister's throat. "Swallow it, Shannon," Dianne whispered softly. "It will make you all better."

Shannon's eyes fluttered. Instinctively, Dianne lifted one of her sister's eyelids, expecting Shannon to fight the movement and awaken with a cry. Instead, Dianne saw Shannon's eyeball slowly roll backwards. Dianne dropped the empty bottle of cold medicine and shook her sister. "Shannon! Shannon! Wake up! Stop doing your *eyes* like that! Wake up!"

But Shannon wouldn't wake up. The color in Shannon's

face was all gone except for a pinkish rash on her cheeks and arms. Dianne rushed to her counter and squeezed lotion into her hands to soothe the rash. That's what her mother would have done.

Dianne convinced herself to sleep that night, clutching to the hope that everything would be all right tomorrow when Aunt Gloria came by. She prayed for her cousin Rhonda to be better.

The next morning, without even opening her eyes, Dianne placed her hand on Shannon's forehead. Cold. Clammy. Felt like plastic. Dianne, in her innocence, was relieved to know that her sister didn't have a fever any more. And then she heard the front door open. Finally, relief.

Dianne jumped out of bed and ran to the front door, only it wasn't Aunt Gloria. It was her mother and Otis. It was an odd homecoming, with everyone wearing exactly what they'd been wearing the last time they saw each other.

"Momma, Shannon is sick," Dianne spoke first.

"Did you give her medicine?" Joyce Ann asked.

"Yeah, I gave her the red medicine in the cabinet."

"That ain't for kids!" Otis shouted as he pushed Dianne aside and rushed toward the girls' bedroom.

Dianne's stomach churned as she waited for a word from Otis. He would tell her what an awful job she'd done, how Shannon needed to get a shot or how they needed to run out and get more medicine right away. But instead, Otis cried out, "She's dead! Joyce Ann, she's dead! Come here!"

Joyce Ann screamed a horrid, long shriek as she ran past Dianne. Sounded like someone had stabbed her in the heart. Dianne's own heart tore, right down the center. The pain was almost tangible; a throbbing, drowning feeling. Dianne knew what death was. The next thing Dianne knew, she was latched onto Shannon's body—her arms and legs wrapped around the stiffening corpse—screaming unintelligible words, writhing in emotional anguish. She wanted to say, "I'm sorry! Come back!" but the words got all twisted on the way up the path from her heart to her mouth.

To Otis, having grown up near a slaughterhouse, Dianne's jumbled words sounded like the torrents of wild squeals from pigs. That cry, forever etched in his mind, was the realization of final pain; of knowing that this was the end, that the end would be painful, and that there was not one single thing you could do to stop it.

The end was nearing for Otis, too. His grief was tempered only by the fact that this whole thing looked like a crime scene to him. He would have to suspend his pain—assuming that Shannon was his child—while he figured out what to do. "Get her off!" he screamed to Joyce Ann, who was really in no better position than Dianne. Her baby was dead.

"Get off! Crazy! You're gonna put bruises on her! Help me pull her off, Joyce Ann! Do you want to go to jail?" His train of thought registered with Joyce Ann immediately. As much as it pained her, she would have to stop and think. Think.

"Sugarbee, baby, let her go," Joyce Ann wailed. "Let her go, baby." Joyce Ann put her hand on Dianne's arm and, like an animal, Dianne bit into her mother's rough, ashen skin.

"Ow!" Joyce Ann recovered her hand.

"Aaaah!" Dianne screamed and kicked when both adults, working in unison, managed to pry her from Shannon's body.

"You let go of her!" Otis wrestled Dianne away from the bed altogether, pinned her onto the floor, and screamed into her wet face, "This is all your fault anyway! If it weren't for you, she wouldn't be dead!" Those words went straight from Otis's mouth to Dianne's, where she inhaled them deeply. The language began to ricochet in her tiny spirit. *My fault?* Still, Dianne held the air, those words, in her lungs. In an instant, Dianne looked over Otis's shoulder to Joyce Ann. Dianne's eyes pleaded for exoneration, permission to release the words Otis had spoken into her soul. A simple, "No, it ain't her fault" or "Don't say that" would have done. But Joyce Ann simply lowered her eyes.

It must be true then. It *is* my fault, Dianne thought. Then she gulped down Otis's words. That is how the guilt came to live in her.

When Otis let her go, Dianne did what any guilty child would do: she found a hiding place while the chaos around her escalated. There was quick, frantic talk amidst wailing. "Hush up, Joyce Ann!" she heard. "Wait! Let me pull up the covers first," someone whispered.

Then she heard her mother on the phone. "We need an ambulance! My baby's . . . she's not breathing!"

Dianne knew that she was in trouble when the ambulance came roaring down the street. Its flashing lights in the middle of a summer morning brought about misplaced memories of Christmas.

"Dianne, open up!" Joyce Ann bammed on the bathroom door. "Open this door now!"

Slowly, Dianne unfurled from her foxhole between the toilet seat and the dirty-clothes hamper. With the slightest turn of the lock, Joyce Ann whished through the door and kneeled down to Dianne's level, grabbed her shoulders, and shook the child with every word. "Dianne, you keep your mouth shut, you hear? If they ask, you tell them that you got up in the middle of the night and gave your sister some medicine. You slept in the bed with her while me and Otis slept in our bed, and when we all got up, she was dead. You hear, Dianne? You hear me?"

The child's reply sounded more like a surrender. "Yes, ma'am, okay, okay, Momma."

When the police came, Dianne told them exactly what Joyce Ann told her to say. And she didn't even try to cross her fingers or her legs or her tongue this time. What's the harm in telling a lie after you've already killed someone?

▣ ▣ ▣

The invitation to Aunt Gloria's wedding had come in the mail just three weeks ago and since that time, Dianne's emotions had traveled up and down like a never-ending roller coaster. Her first thought was to do what she always did: send a gift and a note with a skittish explanation for why she couldn't be there. A big deadline at work; she was just getting over the flu; she had to work double shifts because someone at work was sick.

But this time, Aunt Gloria had followed the invitation with a call. "Hey, Sugarbee! How you doing?"

"Oh, I'm fine, Aunt Gloria. I got your invitation, but I won't be able to make it," Dianne's voice descended. "I'll be sure and send you a gift."

"I'd rather have *you* than a gift." Gloria stood her ground, looping her index finger through the phone cord. Her wedding day wouldn't be complete without Dianne.

"Well, it's just that . . . I have a huge project I'm working on at my job and—"

"Dianne, have I ever asked you for anything?" Gloria interrupted Dianne with a question she hoped she'd never have to ask.

Dianne's jaw dropped, her stomach tightened, and her mind went blank. She didn't have an answer prepared for *that* one.

"Have I?" Gloria repeated.

"No, ma'am."

"I'm asking you to do this one thing for me, Sugarbee. *Please* come to my wedding. It means the world to me."

Dianne squeezed her eyes shut. She was a vacuum, taking in all the fear that constantly surrounded her. Fear, concentrated fear. In all the years she's been living in Carson, no one had ever questioned her about the decision to move from Dentonville. Everyone understood that she needed to put space between herself and the past. "You don't know what you're asking."

"I *do* know what I'm asking. I'm asking you to come and be a part of this family again."

"I can't *be* a part of this family again."

"You can't stop being what you *are*, Dianne."

But Aunt Gloria didn't have to tell Dianne that. Dianne lived with who she was all day every day. She was the little girl whose story unraveled in the Dentonville papers for weeks: "Parents Say Little Girl Was Dead When They Woke Up"; "Autopsy Reveals Child Died from Acute Meningitis"; "Investigation Results: Parents Charged for Leaving Children Home Alone"; "Charges Reduced to Child Endangerment—Nurse's License Expired, Testimony Inadmissible"; "Child Left with Sister's Corpse Will Be Taken In by Family Members." That was the public side of the case. The private headlines, however, read much differently in Dianne's mind: "Child Could Have Saved Sister If She'd Gotten Help Sooner"; "Girls' Mother Left and Never Looked Back."

"So," Aunt Gloria snapped Dianne back to the present, "are you coming?"

Now, a different set of headlines danced through Dianne's heart: "Aunt Provides Loving Home for Abandoned Child"; "Cousins Become like Sisters to Girl Left with Corpse"; "Aunt Asks Child (Now Grown Up) to Come to Wedding as Token of Gratitude."

"I'll be there."

Something within them both knew that it was time to stop running.

About the Author

MICHELLE STIMPSON is an educational consultant who graduated from Jarvis Christian College and has a master's degree from the University of Texas at Arlington. She is a member of Delta Sigma Theta sorority and lives outside Dallas with her husband and two children. Visit her online at www.michellestimpson.com.